The Penny Tree

HOLLY KENNEDY

The Penny Tree

HOLLY KENNEDY

NAL
ACCENT

NAL Accent
Published by New American Library, a division of
Penguin Group (USA) Inc., 375 Hudson Street,
New York, New York 10014, USA
Penguin Group (Canada), 90 Eglinton Avenue East, Suite 700, Toronto,
Ontario M4P 2Y3, Canada (a division of Pearson Penguin Canada Inc.)
Penguin Books Ltd., 80 Strand, London WC2R 0RL, England
Penguin Ireland, 25 St. Stephen's Green, Dublin 2,
Ireland (a division of Penguin Books Ltd.)
Penguin Group (Australia), 250 Camberwell Road, Camberwell, Victoria 3124,
Australia (a division of Pearson Australia Group Pty. Ltd.)
Penguin Books India Pvt. Ltd., 11 Community Centre, Panchsheel Park,
New Delhi - 110 017, India
Penguin Group (NZ), 67 Apollo Drive, Mairangi Bay,
Auckland 1310, New Zealand (a division of Pearson New Zealand Ltd.)
Penguin Books (South Africa) (Pty.) Ltd., 24 Sturdee Avenue,
Rosebank, Johannesburg 2196, South Africa

Penguin Books Ltd., Registered Offices:
80 Strand, London WC2R 0RL, England

First published by NAL Accent, an imprint of New American Library,
a division of Penguin Group (USA) Inc.

Copyright © Holly Kennedy, 2007
Conversation Guide copyright © Penguin Group (USA) Inc., 2007
All rights reserved

REGISTERED TRADEMARK—MARCA REGISTRADA

ISBN-13: 978-0-7394-8242-1

Set in Bembo
Designed by Spring Hoteling

Printed in the United States of America

For my mom, one of the strongest women I know.

Acknowledgments

First and foremost, I would like to thank my agent, Liza Dawson, for reminding me that this is a career, not a race. Without her support, guidance, and infinite patience (something I sadly lack), this book would be a pile of ashes in my fireplace.

Beyond that, there are a few others I would like to mention: My nephew, Chaunce, because watching you fight hystiocytosis as a little boy broke my heart and seeing how you've survived it as a young man inspires me always.

My husband, Rick, who developed my Web site, reads and rereads anything I throw at him, makes countless copies of each manuscript, couriers them wherever I need them couriered, and puts up with me waking him at three in the morning whenever I have one of those "eureka moments" only other writers fully appreciate.

My editor, Ellen Edwards, who fell in love with *The Penny Tree* and has been a delight to work with. Thank you for your enthusiasm. Chandler Crawford, my foreign rights agent. It's an honor having you represent my work.

Jacquelyn Mitchard, for her gracious support and friendship; Susan Wiggs, who has encouraged me from the beginning; and Linda Holeman, because it's always fun sharing this journey with you. I can't imagine three better role models.

Dr. Reeni Soni, for explaining the medical realities of meningitis; Dale Kapitaniuk, for his kind assistance with questions relating to the operation of a funeral home; and Sally Weingartner, who patiently read every version of this story as it evolved, offering comments and suggestions.

My heartfelt thanks also goes out to these individuals, who gave up their time to read for me and offer input: Charlie Newton (my toughest critic), Marilyn Edwards, Sydney Holt, Karen Veloso, Denise Miller, Julie Block, Andrea Kennedy, Jacquie Gabriel, Gail Kennedy, and Michele Thompson.

I'd also like to mention an alarmingly funny book used for research called *The Hypochondriac's Guide to Life. And Death* by Gene Weingarten. Special thanks to the Manitoba Arts Council for their assistance with a grant during the writing of this novel; the Maui Writers Retreat and Conference; as well as my family, friends, and supporters in Athabasca, Alberta.

Last of all, a big hug for Thomas, Marcus, Andrea, and Russ, because much of what I write about, I learned from each of you.

There will come a time when you
believe everything is finished and
that will be the beginning.

— ANONYMOUS

ONE

Seventy paces into the forest, from the tip of an outcrop rock overlooking the Pacific Ocean, there is a penny nailed to a Douglas fir tree. If you found it, you would see *In God We Trust* curved around the top, and the year, 1969, on the bottom-right-hand side, but the nail used to pound it into the tree isn't centered in the middle the way you might think. Instead, it's as far over on the left as possible. Why this came to mind when Annie Hillman woke that morning, she would never know. All she knew, when she opened her eyes, was that even though twenty-five years had passed, she could still remember standing next to her dad, staring up at that huge tree when she was twelve, agreeing that it just didn't seem right to put a nail through the neck of a good man like Abraham Lincoln.

Sliding out of bed, she pinched the bridge of her nose, willing back the hangover she knew she deserved. She finger-combed her tangled blond hair, pulled on an old T-shirt with a pair of jeans, and then tiptoed past her boys' bedroom door, reassured by the silence that they were still asleep. In the kitchen, she scribbled a note: *Gone for a paddle. Back in half an hour. Love, Mom.* Then she opened the fridge, saw four brown paper lunch bags, and remembered that her seventeen-year-old niece, Sawyer, who'd babysat for the boys, had stayed over the night before. Poking her head into the living room, Annie saw that Sawyer was awake, copper red hair pulled back and both arms stretched over her head in midyawn.

"Thanks for making lunches," Annie whispered.

Sawyer stood and pulled one foot up behind her like a flamingo. "No problem."

"I'm going for a paddle. Back in a while."

"Okay. See ya then."

Annie stepped out the front door, thinking about her dad again. His old balsam-wood kayak was now hers, and as she went down the steps, she wondered what he'd think of her life if he were still alive today. It wasn't exactly rosy. She and Jack had been married for fourteen years but now their divorce was almost final, and at last count she had less than three hundred dollars in the bank. Beyond that, she'd been fired six months ago, another first she could now add to her list of personal failures and humiliations for the decade.

It happened early on a Friday morning. She had just arrived at the physical therapy clinic in Seattle where she'd been working for a year when her boss called her into his office to tell her he was letting her go.

Annie squinted at him. "Why?"

"Because we keep getting complaints."

She frowned. "Is this about that Myrna Phillips?"

"She's been a client for years," he pointed out.

"Fair enough," Annie said. "But I'm her physical therapist, not her bartender."

"Maybe," he conceded. "But when you think about it, Annie, physical therapists and bartenders aren't that different, are they? Of course, bartenders aren't expected to *fix* anything. All they have to do is *listen* to customers. You, on the other hand, are expected to be courteous enough to *listen* to our customers *while* you're fixing them!" His voice went up at the end and red spots of exasperation arrived on both cheeks.

Take a deep breath, Annie wanted to say. Count to ten.

Instead, against her better judgment, she narrowed her eyes. "Let me ask you something. If you were dealing with a few bill collectors who don't stop phoning, mixed in an eleven-year-old coming off a week of chemotherapy, and added a thirteen-year-old who keeps sneaking out at night to go see his dad, would you feel like listening to a sixty-year-old multimillionaire who keeps putting her back out because she's having sex with her twenty-five-year-old gardener *and can't stop talking about it?*"

He cringed, lifting both hands in the air. "Annie! This isn't something I want to know."

"Me, either," she replied.

He hooked his fingers together as though thinking about this, then reached for a file folder on his desk. "There are others," he said, flipping it open. "Last month, when Rod Talmage complained about the pain in his lower back, you rolled your eyes and told him he should try giving birth. . . ." Annie's mouth opened but nothing came out. "Two weeks ago, Karen Veloso asked if you'd massage her neck when you finished with her feet, and you said, 'Only if you'll do mine.' Last Monday, when Marilyn Edwards told you she was exhausted, you scoffed and said, 'Welcome to my world.' Then Gail Kennedy complained about her bad knee and you told her to 'Buck up, things could be worse.' And when Sydney Holt griped about her tennis elbow, you said she should try scrubbing floors. . . ."

As he continued, Annie clasped her hands together between her knees, staring at the carpet. A wave of despair hit her when she realized that he wasn't going to let her explain, that before she'd even come into his office he had already made up his mind. And as she stood to leave, she also realized that the truth was she couldn't explain it herself, how she'd let it come to this. She needed her job, but all she knew was how she felt—like a pressure cooker building up steam, like a juggler with way too many balls in the air.

"Annie?" he said, interrupting her thoughts. "Know what I think you need?"

"To work on my bartending skills?" she ventured.

"No." His voice was suddenly tinged with concern. "You need a break."

She closed her eyes for patience. *You think?*

"I mean it," he said. "You need to take some time for yourself."

"Good thought," she said, trying for a smile. "I'll keep that in mind."

Days later, a sinking depression that she hadn't seen coming took root. It went everywhere she went, a constant weight that tugged at her and pulled her down, killing any optimism for the future she had left and leaving her overwhelmed by even the basics required to make it through each day. She spent huge swaths of time sleeping, blissfully ignoring all the realities that wouldn't leave her alone, like making meals, refereeing the boys, obsessing over how she was going to pay the rent. Then, in the middle of a downpour one afternoon, as rain drummed on the roof and coursed through the gutters, her roof started leaking.

She was asleep on the couch, still in her pajamas, when she woke to the sound of water gushing. By the time she made it to the kitchen, the ceiling had warped inward like a blister and then burst open, spraying water everywhere. Frantic, she'd grabbed a mop and pail and tried to clean it up, but the water was relentless and the hole too big, so she finally settled for plucking overdue bills off her wet kitchen floor—bills she couldn't pay any more than the one she knew her landlord would try sticking her with after this mess.

It was still raining when her boys got home from school an

hour later. They found her sitting on the front lawn in her pajamas, the back of one hand pressed against her mouth as she cried
and the other holding a staple gun. Frustrated by all the water,
she'd finally taken a ladder from the garage and climbed up onto
the roof, dragging an orange tarp along behind her. Then, after
stretching it out over the hole, she'd stapled it to the roof, bare feet
braced against the gritty surface of the wet shingles as she'd duck-
walked her way around it in the rain, slamming the gun down
over and over until it finally ran out of staples.

Her younger son, Eric, made a small sound at the back of his
throat and she looked up and wiped her forehead with the back of
one wrist, startled to see them standing there. Eric looked scared,
but it was the blank look on Luke's face when she told them
everything would be okay—the way he turned and went inside,
pretending he hadn't heard her—that made her realize she needed
to get some help.

Her doctor was on vacation, so she went to a walk-in clinic
the next morning and saw a doctor who didn't look old enough
to have a driver's license, let alone a medical degree. And yet,
when he asked how she was doing, she started talking and she
couldn't stop. She talked about things she'd only thought about
before. Things about her and Jack that made him flush, things
about Eric getting sick that made him lean forward sympatheti-
cally, things about Luke that made him frown. She started six years
ago, certain this was where the problem had begun to take shape
in the first place; trying to justify why she had come, ashamed and
embarrassed that it seemed necessary at all. Twice she brushed
away tears, hands trembling as she dug in her purse for Kleenex he
didn't seem to have. Then, half an hour after she had sat down, she
stopped talking and folded her hands together, exhausted.

Tapping his pencil against the desk, the doctor asked a few
questions about Jack: whether she had any family who could help

living nearby; if she'd had any suicidal thoughts she wanted to share. Annie tilted her head, a tiny frown between her brows. No, no suicidal thoughts, she conceded, although this probably wasn't the best time to ask something like that.

Looking uneasy, he explained that asking was standard procedure.

"Oh, right." She laid her head on his desk, wondering what the protocol was for a situation like this, when patients took up more than their allowable slot of time because they were in the middle of personal crises. Running a finger up and over his almost empty in-basket, she silently counted the medical textbooks on the back of his credenza, wondering if he actually used them or if they were just for show, a way to put patients at ease because he was so young. She closed her eyes. Suddenly, she was exhausted and the steady drone of road construction outside had somehow morphed from being annoying into a soothing hum.

The doctor cleared his throat. "Ms. Hillman?"

Startled, she sat up and smoothed down her hair. "Uh-huh."

He handed her a prescription with a flourish, smiling at her like it was a gift. "You're going to be *fine*," he assured her.

She raised an eyebrow. "Really?"

"Really."

Annie stared at the prescription for Zoloft. "How do you know that?" she asked. "Especially when *fine* is so far away from where I am now?"

He shifted in his chair, looking uncomfortable.

Dropping her gaze, she folded the prescription in half, then in half again. "Did I mention my son Eric had a chemotherapy leak last week? That as it backed up one of his veins, burning his skin like acid, it took two nurses to hold him down as he screamed and there wasn't a damned thing I could do to help? Or how my oldest, Luke, hasn't said more than a dozen words to me in months?"

She stood and shouldered her purse. "I told you I got fired, right? And didn't I just explain how I'm now on a first-name basis with the *owners* of two collection agencies who won't stop calling me? That I can't even *remember* what being happy feels like? That I have *never* felt more alone in all my life?"

"Would you like the name of a therapist?" he asked, inserting his pencil into the breast pocket of his white lab coat.

Annie waited until he looked at her. "I can't afford one," she reminded him.

Flushing, he dropped his gaze. "There are support groups that would cost less."

"It's okay," she said, on her way out the door. "I'll be *fine*."

By then, she was shaking all over, and although she didn't realize she was doing it, as she left, she hurried through the standing-room-only reception area of the clinic muttering *idiot* under her breath like a bag lady who'd lost her marbles, like someone who clearly wasn't on her way to being fine.

When she got home, her sister, Marina, was waiting on the front steps. "I had a feeling things weren't great when we talked the other night," she explained, linking an arm through Annie's. "So I took the day off to come see you."

Marina was big on feelings, something Annie had never fully understood but always admired, like the way she somehow knew Annie had felt lost after their parents bought them single beds when they were nine and ten to replace the queen-size bed they'd shared for years. How, for weeks after that, Marina got up each night and tugged her bed over next to Annie's, even on days when they'd been fighting. Then, the next morning, she'd push it back onto her side of their bedroom, never saying a word. Thinking about this now, Annie realized how deeply she loved her sister, and how much she was loved in return.

"Why don't you move home?" Marina suggested, pulling her

inside to make coffee. "That way, Mom would stop bugging you about seeing the boys more often, Sawyer could watch them whenever you need a break, Harrison would take them fishing on weekends, and I could help you find a job."

Annie swallowed her first Zoloft and shuffled over to the couch, wondering if they really did take a few weeks to kick in or if she would be a unique case and start feeling happier within hours. Suddenly being a unique case appealed to her. At least that way she'd have something to set her apart from all of the other divorced, depressed single mothers out there. Lying down, she flung one arm across her face.

Marina cleared a spot on the coffee table and sat facing her. "Come on, Annie," she said. "Why not move back to Eagan's Point? At least for a while."

Until then, Annie hadn't actually considered moving home, probably because she'd been too busy bailing water out of the leaky boat her life had become. Sighing, she rolled onto her side and came up on an elbow. "Maybe you're right. Maybe it wouldn't be such a bad idea, especially now that I'm a Zoloft junkie with no job and only half a roof to put over the boys' heads."

Marina's shoulders fell. "That's not what I meant."

"I know, but it's a good suggestion anyhow."

Within days, Annie had given her landlord notice, and a month later (after begging Jack not to argue with her about it), she and the boys had packed up a U-Haul and moved from Seattle to Eagan's Point, where she took an administrative job at the town funeral home until she could find work as a physical therapist. And now, almost five months later, she was still there, with no physical therapist job in sight. Things were better, although *fine* was still a long way off. Lately, Luke skipped more school than he attended, Eric had just announced he was trying out for the basketball team (even though he hadn't been given a clean bill of health yet), and she was still taking Zoloft, although at least now she was on the lowest-possible dose.

If her dad were still alive, Annie knew he would be quick to point out all the good things, like how Luke was such a bright kid that he brought home top marks even though he was skipping, or how Eric had survived the almost unsurvivable. But here's the thing, she thought. All that aside, this isn't where I thought I'd be at thirty-seven. Broke, depressed, almost divorced, parentally challenged, and with a paper-pushing job where I'm surrounded by dead bodies instead of live ones.

"No," she murmured. "This isn't how I pictured it."

Reassuring herself that things could only get better, she grabbed the newspaper off the grass and pulled it out of its wet plastic bag. She was eager to get out on the water. This was her favorite time of day and half an hour in her kayak would lift her spirits the way nothing else could. She frowned as she looked up into the trees surrounding her, trying to determine what it was that felt different about this morning. After raining all night—the kind of steady, drizzling rain that often settles in on the West Coast and refuses to leave—it had finally stopped, but there was something else, something she couldn't quite put her finger on. Impatient, she shook it off, knowing she'd feel better when she was paddling, that as soon as she put some distance between herself and the shore she'd feel more optimistic about everything. Retracing her steps, she opened the door and tossed the paper inside, turning away before it landed faceup on the floor, revealing a picture on the front page that would have made her skip her morning paddle if she had seen it.

Two

Annie hurried down the alley thinking about what had happened months before she and her dad stood in front of that Douglas fir tree twenty-five years ago. Today, the suddenness of it all was what she remembered most. Until then, her life had been good, the way it should be for a twelve-year-old, and she was happiest bouncing around the neighborhood on her pogo stick or kayaking with friends. She didn't want or need anything else, content to spend her days immersed in the secure and predictable rhythm of her life. Then, one morning, her sister came into their bedroom and closed the door behind her with an air of secrecy, and nothing was ever the same after that.

Normally they each defended their space with an unshakable vigilance meant to offend the other, but that day Marina looked pale and distracted as she stepped over the strip of masking tape that separated their room in two perfect halves.

"I found something you aren't gonna believe," Marina whispered.

"Try me," Annie said.

"We were store-bought."

"What?"

"Store-bought. You know, *adopted*."

Annie squinted at her. "You need to have your head read."

"I'm not joking," Marina said, waving a fistful of paper. "It's all here. Both of us. Adopted from St. Joseph's Orphanage in Chicago."

Annie considered grabbing a shoe and beaning her with it, but instead she smiled and nodded and played along, telling herself Marina was watching too many soap operas again, like when she had sent a sympathy card to an actor on *As the World Turns* after his wife died from choking on a fish bone and then he found out that his dentist was really his father. Sighing, she leaned forward, speaking slowly and clearly, as if Marina were a very small child.

"This . . . isn't . . . funny."

"Who said it was?" Marina shot back.

Frowning, Annie grabbed the papers to see for herself, slowly flipping through them as she read the signatures, the dates, and everything else that looked much too official for Marina to have concocted on her own. Annie went through them twice, and when she was finished, her hands were trembling and her mouth was dry.

"Where'd you get these?"

Marina flopped onto her bed. "In that old tin box on the top shelf of Mom's closet. You know, the one Uncle Max gave her at his fire pit when we went to Alberta last year? The one we found when we were snooping around for Christmas presents? It was locked, so I picked it open with a bobby pin. . . ."

Tuning her out, Annie rose from the bed and smoothed down her jeans. It was Saturday and her mom was out getting groceries, but her dad was home. They'd gone kayaking before breakfast, as they did every Saturday, and then he'd promised to oil her pogo stick after he was done reading the paper. She pinched her mouth shut and headed for the door.

Marina pushed up onto her elbows. "Don't you *dare* say a word."

But Annie was unstoppable, and as she ran downstairs, she knew just where to get the answers she needed. Whenever she was upset, her dad always made things better. He was older than a lot of other dads, but that didn't bother her. He was a great storyteller and a laugher, and nothing she did ever seemed to faze him. He ran a small accounting firm in Eagan's Point, and for as long as she could remember, he would finish breakfast, slide on his glasses, and leave for work at exactly seven each morning. Then, after dinner, they would walk to the corner store, and as they passed houses with porches and attics and big backyards, he would mesmerize her and Marina with stories about growing up in Germany as a boy. If anyone could clear up this misunderstanding, Annie knew he could. By the time she rounded the corner into the living room, Marina had almost caught up to her, and then there he was, sitting in his favorite armchair ten feet away—the same chair she curled up in each night when he traveled around northern Washington during tax season.

"Is it true?" she blurted, waving the papers at him.

He lowered the newspaper, frowning. "Is what true?"

"That we were *adopted*."

Pushing forward on his chair, he folded the paper in half. "You mean *hand-selected*."

Annie stiffened like she'd been given an electric shock. "Then . . . we were?"

"Yes," he said softly. "You were."

For the few seconds in which no one spoke, his face filled with a look of such shame and misery that Annie was rattled. Her knees went weak and she started to shiver, not wanting to believe what she'd just heard. Then Marina stepped past her, sounding as upset as she was.

"Why didn't you tell us?"

He slumped like the weight of the world had just come down on him. "Your mom and I felt it would be best to wait."

"Until when?" Marina asked, incredulous.

"We were planning to tell you . . . soon," he managed, spreading his hands.

"W-what about our real parents?" Marina asked. "What happened to them?"

His hands flexed against the arms of the chair and he looked around as if he were trying to think of some way to explain. Then, after what seemed like an interminable silence, he shook his head. "Ahhh, where do I start?"

He leaned forward, resting his elbows on his knees. "You had different parents. Marina, yours died in a house fire when you were a year old, but your only relatives were a grandfather in his seventies and your mom's parents, who were also older and in poor health. They did their best for as long as they could, but they couldn't take care of a baby, and even though giving you up wasn't easy, in the end they all agreed it was the only way they could offer you the kind of life your parents would've wanted for you."

Annie watched Marina's face crumple from the gravity of this news, and then her dad turned to face her. "And, Annie? Your mom was only seventeen and barely able to take care of herself. There was no way she could raise a baby on her own. We were told that she'd traveled from Russia to the U.S. with a group of young women who were hired as seamstresses. She gave birth to you at Mercy Hospital in Chicago."

Tears welled in Annie's eyes and she crossed her arms over her chest as something hardened inside, a small piece of herself that had taken in every word, every tiny detail, but was still having trouble comprehending it as truth.

"Marina was a year older, but you shared the same crib, and whenever they separated you, it was chaos. Marina, you howled like someone was choking you, and Annie, your eyes would glaze over and you'd refuse to eat until they brought Marina back. You made it impossible to choose," he said, giving them a shaky smile. "So we took both of you."

Annie inhaled a slow breath to steady herself, thinking about what he'd just said. She glanced at Marina's soft red curls and flawless skin. As sisters, they had always been polar opposites—where she was small boned with thick blond hair, Marina towered over Annie with curly red hair that fell to her waist—and yet whenever they'd brought it up, their mom would simply explain it away, saying, "Well, life would be pretty boring if everyone looked and acted the same, now wouldn't it?"

"You picked throwaways then," Annie finally said.

"No, we chose two kids to love as our own."

She stared over his shoulder. "And what if you hadn't?"

"Hadn't what?"

"Loved us."

His face softened. He reached out, circled their waists, and pulled them in close. "We were in love with you long before we ever brought you home, and once you decide something like that, there is no turning back. That's how real love works. You take the good with the bad and only when you accept that there will always be both can the love you have for someone take on heights you never dreamed possible."

Annie hadn't moved, standing stiff as a board as he tried to hold her. Glancing down at the papers she was still clutching, she loosened her fingers and watched them fall to the floor, wishing that she'd never seen them, that this whole day could somehow be erased.

"So I was a mistake," she whispered.

Without missing a beat, he said, "No, a dream come true."

But she wasn't listening. Instead, she was thinking how everything in her life was a lie. How someone else had given birth to her and then rejected her. How her mom wasn't really her mom and how her dad would never be her true dad.

Hours later, in the middle of that first night when she couldn't sleep, a dull ache worked its way into her chest and settled down like it planned to stay, and it was then that she first knew grief. At twelve she'd experienced many emotions, but never before had she known true sadness or the deep feeling of loss that came packaged with it. And as it descended on her, it did its job well—robbing her of an innocence she would never have again and a piece of herself that until then she had given away easily to those she loved.

Within days, her appetite slipped; she just pushed food around on her plate. She withdrew from everyone, even at school, where she dropped out of the tetherball play-offs and stopped handing in assignments. Then one day in class, her friend Julie Coyne threw her head back and laughed, the same laugh Annie had often heard from Julie's mom, and a pang of envy crawled up Annie's back. Days later it hit her again during gym class; she slid down the outside wall of the school and cried as she watched Chris Carby's slightly bowed legs, which were just like his father's bowed legs, pushing him around the running track.

Annie's parents spent weeks blaming each other for what could have been avoided by telling their girls the truth years earlier. The air was thick with tension and their late-night conversations escalated enough that Annie would hunker down in her closet and listen against the wall, sick to her stomach, but unable to pull away. She would hear her dad pacing, then his voice low and raspy with barely contained anger.

"I never should've let you talk me into hiding it from them."

"Tim, I didn't talk you into anything!"

"No, Erna, you didn't talk me into it. You simply pushed until I gave in."

"We agreed not to let them grow up feeling inadequate," her mom reminded him.

"But keeping it from them for so long was a mistake. Now look where we are!"

And so it would go. Back and forth as they dodged each other's accusations, unwilling to recognize that no matter who was right or wrong, their anger with each other stemmed from a fear that their girls wouldn't be able to forgive them and get past this—a fear they might lose them because of some sad lapse of judgment from over a decade before when adoptions weren't as socially acceptable and secrecy about it far more commonplace.

After the initial shock that she was adopted wore off, Annie realized nothing would ever be the same. Then she started to worry. On Saturday mornings, when her dad tapped on her bedroom door, poked his head inside, and whispered that their kayaks were ready to go, would she break into a smile the way she always did? Or when her mom rag-curled her hair on Sunday nights, as she had for years, using an efficient tug, pull, and twist as she wrapped strands of Annie's hair around strips of cloth, would Annie complain if her mom yanked too hard? Or would she sit there stoically until she was done, afraid that if she talked back her mom might throw up her hands and leave? After all, if she wasn't good enough for her real mom, and had been given away once, it could happen again, couldn't it?

In the beginning, her mind danced around pockets of private thoughts like these, and as it did, she drew even further into herself. She started locking herself in the bathroom to stare in the mirror, studying her twelve-year-old face as she never had before—at unruly blond hair so thick she had trouble putting it in a ponytail, at the mole just above her top lip, then at her lips themselves, which to her had always seemed too big. She would rub a finger over the bridge of her nose, squint at her stubborn widow's peak, and finish off wondering if her real mom's eyes were anything like hers.

Born with one blue eye and one green, she'd been told by her dad that she was sun-kissed and destined for a life of adventure. "How rare is that?" he'd say, punching his fist into the air with pride. "One in a million? Not even one in five million, I'm sure." Always ready with a solution to every problem, he'd armed her with the facts she needed in case anyone teased her about it. "It's called Heterochromia Iridium," he explained. "Alexander the Great had it and so did Aristotle, not to mention David Bowie."

Annie had always been particularly proud of her eyes, but now when she looked in the mirror, they mocked her, slamming home the fact that she was different, a reject whose own mother hadn't wanted her.

The truth that she and Marina were adopted opened the door to questions neither of them had the courage to ask, although for weeks afterward, Marina wouldn't stop talking about it after they went to bed.

"Doesn't it feel weird that we're not *real* sisters?" she whispered one night.

"Uh-huh," Annie replied.

"No offense, but I used to wonder. I mean, we don't look anything alike."

"Right," Annie said, wishing she'd go to sleep.

Half talking to herself, Marina said, "Do you think my grandparents might still be alive?"

"I don't know," she replied. "Ask Mom and Dad."

A few nights later, Marina finally worked up enough nerve to ask their parents a whole list of questions, and although Annie was silent through it all, she did get answers to some she didn't have the guts to ask herself.

"Weren't you able to have your own kids?" Marina asked at one point.

"Uh . . . no," their mom said, lifting her back against her chair. "We weren't. So we had to decide if we were going to live without kids or else adopt."

Marina frowned. "Why'd you adopt girls instead of boys?"

"It wasn't like that. We decided to adopt a child who needed us as much as we needed him—boy or girl. Then we went to St. Joseph's. They were short staffed that day, and when we walked in, you were crying. They'd just moved you to your own crib, although you'd been sharing one with Annie, and that's where you wanted to be. Before long, Annie was pulling herself up against the bars of her crib, crying as loud as you were. You were both inconsolable, so the woman showing us around excused herself to go get help, and your dad picked Annie up and sang her some awful German lullaby." Erna shook her head. "Within seconds, she stopped crying, and then so did you. You stuck your thumb in your mouth and watched them from across the room, and when I walked over, you looked at me and held out your arms."

"And that's when you knew?" Marina asked, eyes hopeful.

"Yes," her dad said, watching Annie. "That's when we knew."

"We came home to think about it for a week," their mom said. "We hadn't considered two kids until then, but when we flew back, any smidgen of doubt was gone the moment we came through the door and saw you both asleep in the same crib again."

"Have you ever regretted getting us?" Marina asked in a small voice.

"Never" came their dad's adamant reply.

"Not once," their mom agreed.

You'd never tell us anyhow, Annie thought, pushing away from the table.

At first, she moved through her days feeling like a jigsaw puzzle that was missing a few pieces—incomplete and unremarkable. She ate when everyone else ate, and slept when they slept, but her thoughts were silently bubbling with resentment and anger. Why hadn't her real mom at least given her enough time to prove she was worth keeping? And why for all those years did her parents have to hide that she and Marina were adopted?

The first time Annie ran away, she left in the middle of the night with catlike composure: chin up, back straight, and determined to make it on her own. By morning she was huddled under a tarp in someone's boat, cold and hungry because she'd forgotten to bring any food. She finally gave herself up late that night after standing outside Julie Coyne's house, watching her and her mom through their kitchen window. As Annie stood there in the dark, what rooted her to the spot and turned her heart over was their laughter, the kind that rushes out of you in waves when you can't hold it in—only theirs was identical and it made her want to reach out, tap Julie on the arm, and ask if she could have her life.

Technically, the next time she ran away was when she refused to go home after a sleepover at Julie's two weeks later. They were playing Monopoly when Annie's dad came to pick her up, and she told him she was staying. No matter what he said or did, she wasn't going home. At first he laughed, but when he realized she was serious, he turned to Julie's mom, arms out in a gesture of helplessness, face flushed with embarrassment.

"Want me to drive her home later?" Mrs. Coyne suggested.

A flicker of hurt crossed his face, but he nodded in agreement.

After he left, Mrs. Coyne told Julie that she and Annie were going to have a chat. Then she took Annie by the hand, tugged her into the kitchen, and made a pot of tea. When it was ready, she gave Annie a cup and slid into the chair across from her.

"Anything you'd like to talk about?" she asked.

Annie nodded. There was. "I was wondering . . ." She hesitated, took a breath and started again. "I was wondering if you could give me asylum."

Her heart was pounding and she felt a deep flush slowly working its way up her neck. A dog barked outside, underscoring the silence between them. She glanced up at Mrs. Coyne, who looked genuinely confused.

"You want . . . asylum?"

"Yes." Annie took a sip of tea and set the cup down, feeling more grown-up than she could ever remember. "I read a story in the paper last week about this athlete from Russia who'd traveled to the U.S. to compete in a race, but then defected and asked for asylum."

Mrs. Coyne frowned.

"I looked asylum up in the dictionary," Annie explained. "And that's when I found the loophole I've been looking for. You see, it means '*To offer shelter and support to distressed or destitute individuals.*'"

"I know what it means," Mrs. Coyne said, gently taking her hand. "But why do you want to do this? Ask for asylum, I mean."

"I want a fresh start," Annie explained.

"At what?"

"At my life," she whispered.

Mrs. Coyne studied her for a moment and then said, "Me too," not sarcastically, but with something in her voice that told Annie it had crossed her mind, which wasn't that surprising if you considered the fact that she had four kids.

"You know, there are days when I'm this close to running

away," Mrs. Coyne said, holding up her thumb and forefinger. "Days when I'd love to walk straight through town and out the other side. It'd be nice to go where I could take a hot bath without someone pounding on the door, to get away from doing laundry, cooking, cleaning, and helping my kids with their homework . . . all of it."

Uncertain of what to say, Annie shifted in her seat.

Mrs. Coyne folded her hands together and sighed. "But you know what, Annie? Whenever I get like that, I try to imagine a world without my husband, a world without Julie or Brent or Dean or Nicole, and I end up feeling like someone has socked me in the stomach. And I think, my God! A world without my family? I can't imagine . . ."

Annie's shoulders slumped. "You aren't going to give me asylum, are you?"

"That depends," Mrs. Coyne hedged. "First, I need to make sure you understand the rules. Things like . . . do you realize once you've been given asylum, you can't go back?"

Annie blinked in surprise. "Never?"

"Never," Mrs. Coyne repeated solemnly. "When someone's granted asylum, all ties with their past are cut. You cross an invisible line that has to be honored and you can't go back to see family, friends, your old home . . . none of it."

"I didn't know that," Annie murmured.

"Most people who ask me don't," Mrs. Coyne assured her with a smile. "Why don't you take some time and think about it? Then if you decide you still want to go this route a few months from now, we can talk again."

Filled with an unfamiliar ache that caught her off guard, Annie tucked her hands under her legs, thinking. Until that moment, she hadn't considered *never* going back. She just knew she had a burning need to get away *now*. She finished drinking her tea, thanked Mrs. Coyne, and told her she'd think about it a little more before making a decision.

Days later, when Annie's mom went down to the basement to get pickles from the cold room, she pulled the door open and found Annie sitting on a burlap sack of potatoes, smoking. "And just what do you think you're doing?" she asked, hands on hips.

Annie took a drag off her cigarette and gave her a cocky smile, even though inside she was thinking, *I'm really in for it now.*

Her mom grabbed her by the wrist, pulled her to her feet, and marched her up the stairs into the kitchen. "Let me tell you, if you think you're going to get away with a stunt like this, young lady, you're kidding yourself."

Fair enough, but grounding her for a week had seemed extreme, although Annie didn't react when her mom told her this. Instead, she kept her face expressionless, certain her dad would either reduce her sentence or toss it out completely when he got home, especially based on all of the garbage she'd been going through the last few months.

She was on the tire swing when he pulled into the driveway after work.

"Hey, Annie girl, how was your day?" he asked, climbing out of the car.

Shrugging, she dropped her head and pushed off the ground with one foot, spinning the tire in lazy circles. Looking concerned, he'd set his briefcase down and headed across the grass toward her, but he only made it halfway before her mom called out to him from the back door and he turned around. Annie kept her head down, watching them from the corner of her eye, straining to hear what they were saying.

When her dad not only stood behind her mom's decision to ground her, but added another week, she was speechless. Not bothering to think it through, she ran away again that night, sneaking out the front door with the stealth of a seasoned burglar, since the screen on her bedroom window had been bolted on after her last escape and the back door squeaked in the worst possible way. When she got to the end of the driveway, she turned around and took one last look at the only place she'd ever called home, telling herself that she wasn't afraid (even though none of the streetlights were working) and that they probably wouldn't even notice she was missing until Marina told them.

That time she lasted four days before phoning to tell her parents she was at a gas station on the outskirts of Seattle. After hanging up, she went inside to use the bathroom, and while balancing on a cracked toilet seat, she took a black felt pen and wrote this message on the wall: *Everything in my life just fell apart. Where do I go from here?* When she climbed down, she snapped the cap back on and stared up at the wall. Her dad often stopped here to gas up on their way home from trips into Seattle as a family, so as she walked outside she told herself if anyone ever bothered to answer, she'd take their advice to heart.

An hour later, her parents pulled into the gas station, the car barely coming to a stop before both doors flew open and they ran to where she sat waiting on a bench. Her knees were drawn to her chest and she was tired and scared and nursing a black eye from an older girl she'd met the day before who'd punched her and stolen her knapsack.

For the next few days, she did whatever was expected of her at home and at school, but inside she was making plans to run away again. Only this time she would be prepared. This time she would buy a one-way bus ticket to Canada, where her uncle Max lived in the small town of Athabasca. She'd plan ahead so nothing could possibly go wrong. And when she got there, she'd spend hours sitting with him and his friends around his old fire pit, debating everything that was right and wrong in the world—trying to figure out where she belonged in the scheme of things.

She decided to go on Friday night, leaving for school later than usual that morning so she could write a note, knowing she wouldn't get any time alone after school. She'd already pried the screen off her bedroom window and had hidden under her bed a duffel bag filled with everything she needed: a box of matches (wrapped in plastic to keep them dry), a small tarp (in case it rained), a flashlight (including spare batteries), her sleeping bag, a change of clothes, a box of granola bars, a bag of beef jerky, her all-time favorite book (*The Pigman*), her journal, and the faux-fur wallet Marina had given her for her birthday, filled with eighty-four dollars she'd been saving to repaint her kayak.

Later that morning, when her dad knocked on her classroom door and stuck his head inside, panic bubbled up inside Annie's chest. He never came to the school. What was he doing here now? He and the teacher had a whispered conversation. Then he waved Annie up to the front of the class and told her to get her things; they were taking the rest of the day off. He had a knapsack and his walking stick, and when they got outside, she asked him where they were going, but he just smiled and said, "You'll see."

Minutes later, they were hiking along a trail that followed the shoreline outside of Eagan's Point, with massive trees towering up into the sky all around them and waist-deep ferns growing thick on both sides. They walked in silence for a while. Suddenly her dad took Annie by the hand and veered off the trail, weaving through the foliage and trees until they came out onto an outcrop rock that was twenty feet wide and just as long, overlooking the ocean. For a few seconds neither of them spoke. Then Annie said, "Wow," amazed by the view despite her determination not to be.

Her dad sat down, pulled two sandwiches out of his knapsack, and handed her one. Annie took a bite, watching him bring out nectarines and a thermos of coffee. "I found this place years ago," he explained. "And now I come here whenever I need to be alone. On a clear morning, you can see Vancouver Island from this spot better than any other within miles."

They ate in silence and Annie stared off into the distance over the water, still finding it hard to look him in the eye. When he was done, he stretched out on the rock and hoisted himself up onto one elbow, resting his head in his palm. Pointing down below, he told her they passed by here every Saturday on their morning paddle.

"Then why haven't you shown me before?" she asked.

"Because it didn't seem important until now" came his cryptic reply.

After Annie had drawn out eating her nectarine for as long as she could, she wrapped the pit in the plastic wrap her sandwich had come in and tossed it into her dad's knapsack. When he stood and brushed the dirt off his pants, she did too, feeling nervous all over again.

"Annie?"

She kept her eyes on the toe of one shoe as she traced a circle on the rock. "Uh-huh."

"I'm fifty-eight," he said solemnly, "and you're twelve. Add them together and we share seventy years on this earth."

If you wanna look at it that way, she thought, keeping her head down.

"So today, I'm asking you to take seventy paces into the forest with me from the edge of this rock so we can find what we're looking for."

She feigned disinterest. "What are we looking for?"

He didn't answer. Instead, he took her hand in his and slowly walked backward until both of their heels were within inches of the edge of the rock. Lifting his chin toward the bush, he said, "Start counting."

Together, they counted off seventy paces, which put them in front of a Douglas fir tree that was so massive Annie couldn't wrap her arms halfway around it. Her dad set his knapsack down and circled it, squinting up into the endless branches soaring above them. "This will do fine," he said with a smile, and Annie stared at him like he was losing his mind. Bending down with one hand on his knee for support, he unzipped the knapsack and took out a hammer, then stood, pulled a penny out of his pocket, and handed it to her.

"What's this for?" she asked, taking it from him.

"It's a 1969 penny. It took me two days to find one with the right year on it. Then I polished it until it looked like new, and now we're going to nail it to this tree."

This just didn't make any sense. "Why?" she asked.

He brushed the back of his hand against her cheek and his eyes went watery with emotion. "Because 1969 was an unforgettable year, a year like no other. It was the year the whole world watched as the U.S. put the first man on the moon, and it was the year the *Concorde* made its maiden flight. One of my favorite movies of all time is *Butch Cassidy and the Sundance Kid,* and it won an Oscar for best screenplay that year. I also remember that it was the winter of 1969 when your mom almost drove me crazy playing 'Sugar, Sugar' by the Archies until she finally wore the record out. But you know what was even more important than all that?" he said, touching the tip of her nose for emphasis.

"In 1969, there were three million, six hundred thousand, two hundred, and six people born in the United States, and you were one of them. And do you know that the first time I ever held you, I looked into your eyes and lost my heart? The same way I'm sure every father does when he holds his child for the first time. I knew right then and there—on that very spot—that you were meant to be my little girl, and adopted or not, that's just the way it is, Annie. You're my daughter, and nothing will ever change that. I love you, I'm proud of you, and your mom and I will always be there for you if you need us."

Tears filled Annie's eyes and everything that had been hardening inside her over the last few months slowly began to crumble.

Her dad ran a hand over the gnarled bark of the tree. "My father gave me a penny tree when I wasn't much older than you are, and when he did, he said he believed everyone needs a special place to lick their wounds and regroup, somewhere that feels safer than anywhere else in the world. So that's what we're doing here today. We're nailing that penny to this tree because I want you to have somewhere to go that grounds you, an axis for your world to spin around, and a place that's all yours and no one else's—for times when life throws things at you that you aren't sure how to handle. And it *will* throw things at you, Annie: things that test you and push you to your limits; things not unlike what you're going through right now. Only from now on, instead of running away from them, you'll have somewhere to think them through. Your own special spot where you can hurt in private when you need to be alone, and where you can weigh all of the pros and cons to make the decisions you need to make."

"So you're giving me a tree?" Annie said, looking up at it with her blond hair falling to the middle of her back.

"Yes," he said. "I am."

Her face trembled with emotion as she turned to look at him, suddenly so pleased with this that she forgot she was supposed to be mad at him, so touched she felt something shift inside, and instantly recognized it as forgiveness.

"Sound like a plan?" he asked.

Unable to trust her voice, Annie nodded as she held the penny up against the tree where she thought it should go, certain that she'd never loved him more than in that moment. It was also then that she realized that running away had had more to do with her desire to be chased and brought back than it did anything else. That she'd really been testing her parents to see if they'd come find her and bring her home, to give her solid, unwavering proof that they loved her. And even though she hadn't consciously been waiting for some grand gesture to make her feel extraordinary and overwhelm her with emotion, that was exactly what did happen when her dad nailed a 1969 penny to a Douglas fir tree the year she turned twelve.

Thinking about this, Annie lifted her kayak down from where she stored it on two hooks behind Carby's Bait & Tackle. Over the years, she'd returned to her penny tree often and her dad was right—it did ground her. It became her haven from the rest of the world, a place that never changed, no matter how much she did, and a spot she never outgrew, no matter how many years passed. In the beginning, until she'd learned it wasn't doing any good, she'd even dug holes in the ground around the base each spring, dropping in time-released fertilizer tablets she'd seen advertised on TV. It was her way of giving back—a small measure of thanks and protective nurturing on her part for this special gift she'd been given. As time went by, making trips to her penny tree had become a ritual, a habit as natural as going to church on Sunday. Even now, she found it soothing to know it was still there.

THREE

nnie carried her kayak to the water and climbed in. No matter how hard she kept trying to hide it from herself and everyone else, she wasn't happy, but if she focused on the daily rituals in her life, those small, reliable physical events that filled each day to the brim, it was manageable. As she pushed away from shore, a flock of seagulls called out to one another, wheeling in the air above her head. When she saw the unmistakable tip of her dad's outcrop rock in the distance, she smiled, remembering how optimistic he used to be about life, how certain that everything would work out in the end if you just gave it a little time.

Paddling through the mist that often skimmed the water this early in the morning, she heard sea lions barking somewhere nearby, and then a voice calling out her name. Chris Carby was waving from shore at the Docks. She waved back but kept going, relieved he was far enough away that he couldn't see her face, flushed red after what had happened between them the night before.

Chris was still the same guy she'd grown up with—patient, dependable, and more than willing to offer a helping hand—only now he had a shock of blue-black hair and a set of abs that were hard to miss. Years ago, he had left Eagan's Point to get a business degree, been briefly married to a woman from Houston, and finally moved home to run his dad's shop after his dad had died of a heart attack. Since then, Carby's Bait & Tackle had become one of the largest outfitters for sport fishermen in the area. Annie had had dinner with him at his house the night before. Chris had insisted, telling her he wanted to cook instead of going out, so they could "have some privacy" and "talk without half the town listening in," and she'd agreed, although she had felt a bit awkward about it. After all, it was no secret to anyone who knew either of them that Chris had had a thing for her years ago.

After she arrived, Chris poured wine and she helped him make a salad. A few times she caught him looking at her like he was on the verge of saying something, which made her even more nervous. Although they had grown up together, and had once been close, they hadn't stayed in touch or seen each other for years, so she felt unnaturally awkward with him now. In some ways, it was as though they were both starting from square one, getting to know each other all over again.

Half an hour after she arrived, Chris stepped outside to grill steaks and she quickly finished her third glass of wine, rehearsing lines to let him down easy, just in case. She tried, *I'm not ready to start dating yet,* but that sounded lame. After all, her divorce was almost final, and Jack had certainly moved on, so what was she waiting for? She mulled over, *I need to focus on my boys right now. I don't have room in my life for anyone else*, but she was certain that he'd know this wasn't true. Because, really, deep down inside, she wished she did have someone in her life and lately it saddened her beyond description that she didn't.

Suddenly Chris was back, empty plate poised in the air as he said something.

Annie shifted in her chair. "Pardon?"

"I asked if you plan on staying. Here, I mean. In Eagan's Point."

"I'm not sure," she said. "Depends on how well the boys adjust and if I can find work at the hospital or the clinic instead of the funeral home."

He opened the oven and pulled out two baked potatoes. "Right."

As he peeled off the tin foil facing away from her, Annie noticed his muscular back tugging against the fabric of his shirt and how strong his arms looked with his shirtsleeves rolled up to the elbow.

"You don't like your job then?" he asked, straightening.

She blinked, suddenly feeling dizzy, like the entire room was wrapped in gauze, which made sense since she rarely drank anymore. "Uh . . . no. Not really."

He grinned and motioned to her wineglass. "Want some more?"

She shook her head, trying not to stare at his shoulders. No, she didn't want more. What she wanted was to curl up on the couch and ask him to stretch out next to her. To skip dinner and have him hold her, to close her eyes and feel his breath on the back of her neck as he asked about her day, the way no one had in ages. That was what she wanted. And it was this, the realization that she'd gone from crafting ways to discourage him to wondering what it would feel like to have him hold her, that brought on a wave of unexpected tears—tears that embarrassed her and sent her pushing out of her chair and down the hallway into his bathroom.

Minutes later, after flicking sharp, cold drops of water on her face, she emerged to find him waiting for her in the kitchen. The table was set and he'd put out a basket of fresh rolls. He stood. "Everything okay?"

Annie thought about this longer than was necessary. Part of her wanted to tell him the truth. That she wasn't okay. That even though she might look content, like she was moving forward in life with a sense of purpose and direction, it was all a farce.

Because inside, she was living with an aching kind of lonely she'd never known before, and she was scared about the future, and worried about her boys, and no longer sure she was any better at being a mother than she had been a wife. Another part of her didn't want to dump all of these problems on Chris when she hadn't seen him in years.

"I'm fine," she finally said. "The wine's making me emotional, that's all."

Looking relieved, he pulled out her chair, and Annie caught herself going down a path that she never had before, wondering what it would be like if she and Chris really were more than old friends, telling herself that she'd be crazy not to consider a relationship with him. Then, he asked if she wanted another glass of wine, and she was stupid enough to say yes.

Now, paddling her kayak past the last house on the edge of town, she pushed harder than usual, trying to put last night out of her mind. If bursting into tears in front of Chris hadn't been bad enough, then what had followed certainly gave her good reason to avoid him for a few days, at least until she could figure out what to say.

She had just started out, but she could already feel her arms and shoulders loosening up. Thinking about the day ahead of her, she made a mental note to call Marina and ask if she wanted to meet for lunch. Interestingly enough, that they were both adopted (and not real sisters after all) was the common denominator that had brought them even closer together as teens and then women than they'd been as kids. Over the years, Annie had come to love what she'd once thought of as Marina's ditsy free spirit, although when Marina had named her daughter after Tom Sawyer because of his thirst for adventure, Annie couldn't help but ask Marina's not-quite husband if he was okay with it. Harrison had just shrugged and said, "It's better than naming her after Huck Finn, isn't it?"

Marina had met Harrison a year after she'd graduated from high school, when he arrested her at a demonstration to save a historical building in downtown Seattle. After Annie had bailed her out, he followed them outside, explaining to Marina that he hadn't really wanted to arrest her. Could he buy her a cup of coffee to make up for it? Without hesitating, Marina said yes, leaving Annie wrestling with an armful of picket signs that read: *Save Our History* and *Down with Mini-Mall Development.*

Harrison was six foot six, with almost no hair and an old-fashioned handlebar mustache. He was an imposing man, the kind people stepped back from, and yet underneath he was a marshmallow, showering Marina with flowers, slipping poems underneath her pillow, proposing on a snow-crusted mountain pass in the middle of the Canadian Rockies. Within months, they had moved in together; Sawyer was born a year later, although it took five more years before they finally got married. Today, Marina ran a pet rescue shelter in Eagan's Point and Harrison worked as a state trooper.

When Annie paddled past her dad's outcrop rock, she smiled. Although she and Marina had shared a lot of ups and downs in each other's lives over the years, she'd never told her about her penny tree. It was private and she was protective about it, the way she was about memories from that day. Like how, after her dad had nailed the penny to her tree, they had sat with their backs against it, talking. How he told her that Benjamin Franklin had designed the first U.S. penny (minted in 1787), how the Lincoln penny followed in 1909, and how it was the first U.S. coin ever to picture a president, replacing the old Indian Head penny. He showed her how, if she looked closely at the back of any penny, she would see a miniature Abraham Lincoln sitting inside the

Lincoln Memorial, and how above it (in tiny letters) it said *E Pluribus Unum*, which meant "Out of many, one."

Even now, Annie remembered how intent he'd been giving her that history lesson, how his dark eyes no longer looked as worried as they had before. After they'd made their way back down the walking path into town that day, they never talked about her penny tree again. She didn't bring it up and neither did he, although now and then he'd give her a knowing wink when she slipped in the back door after disappearing for a few hours.

It was a gift unlike any other. She'd stormed up there after Chris Carby said her new braces made her look like the front grille of a train, and she went when she got her first period and wanted to be alone. She paced around the base in frustration when her parents wouldn't let her pierce her ears, and she spent an hour there when she didn't make the volleyball team. The problems that took her to her penny tree grew in direct proportion to her maturity, and then something happened that made every other visit pale in importance—something that left her huddled at the base, shaking.

Just after she'd turned thirteen, a drunk driver ran a red light, swerved, lost control, and slammed sideways into the front of her dad's car. The hospital called while she and Marina were outside taking turns driving the go-kart he'd built for them. Annie saw her mom grab the phone from where she was sitting on the deck, then watched the color drain from her face. The other driver had died on impact and her dad had been thrown through the windshield.

She and Marina could usually be counted on to fight over who got to ride in the front seat, but that day Annie didn't say a word as she climbed into the back. She was trembling as she braced her palms against the vinyl seat and had to fight the urge to throw up.

"Damn that man anyhow!" her mom swore under her breath as she drove. "Why'd he have to go out tonight?"

"Because we were out of ice cream," Annie said.

"No, we weren't" came her clipped reply.

"We have ice cream?" Marina asked, sounding confused.

Her mom's eyes were on the road and her jaw was working, but she didn't answer.

Annie leaned forward to defend him. "We have chocolate, not vanilla, and you need *vanilla* to make ice cream floats."

There was a long silence.

"Mom?" Annie said.

"I don't care what flavor we have or don't have," she said, startling Annie with the anger in her voice. "This has *nothing* to do with ice cream."

Annie sat back and crossed her arms. For months now, her mom had seemed to spend half her time reading diagnostic medical textbooks and the other half hell-bent on finding something to be mad at her dad about. Minutes later they pulled into the hospital's emergency entrance. Her mom slammed the car into park and they all jumped out. But as Annie pushed through the doors behind Marina, her sweater snagged on one of the latches and she had to stop to unhook it. Glancing up, she saw the town's only tow truck drive by pulling what was left of her dad's car. The windshield was gone and the driver's door was crunched in like an accordion, but it was the blood that made her knees go weak. What looked like buckets of it covered the moon yellow hood. That image was burned into her memory, growing into a fear of driving from which she had yet to recover.

They were at the hospital until two that morning, Marina and Annie sitting on waiting room chairs as their mom paced, folding and unfolding her arms. By the time a doctor finally came to tell them Tim Fischer had been stabilized but was being moved to Seattle by ambulance, the girls had fallen asleep lying curled toe-to-toe, unable to fight their exhaustion any longer. They were allowed to visit their dad a week later when he was still in intensive care. He'd sustained severe head injuries, one of his lungs had collapsed, and he had a broken leg. He was sedated with a ventilator in his throat. His right leg was in a cast and half of his face had fallen. The left side of his mouth sagged and drool rolled onto his chin and down his chest. Seconds after Marina stepped into his room, she burst into tears and left, but Annie stayed, eyes brimming as she wiped his chin with a cloth, accepting the good with the bad.

Annie's dad was never able to return to work, so her mom went from a part-time job in medical records at the health clinic to a full-time job at the hospital. After school, Annie often watched him do physical therapy with Rosa, who came each week for the next five years. After a while, Rosa let Annie help, teaching her the benefit of one stretch versus another and how muscles and bones could work together to heal. On days when Rosa wasn't there, Annie massaged the muscles in her dad's legs; by the time she turned seventeen, she wanted to be a physical therapist.

One day in twelfth grade, a letter bearing the University of Illinois seal was waiting for her when she got home from school. She ripped it open with trembling hands and, grinning, read her acceptance out loud, squatting next to her dad's chair. He said, "I'm proud of you, Annie girl," and for a few minutes, getting that letter felt better than anything that had ever happened to her before. But being young, she hadn't yet developed the foresight to recognize that attending school in Chicago also meant saying good-bye. When the realization hit, her face fell.

"I'm going to miss you," she whispered.

"I know," her dad said, resting his chin on her head. "But I'll always be here, and even years from now, when I'm not, you'll know where to find me when you need me." And he was right, Annie thought. Because even though he died of a massive stroke a few months later, over the years, each time she'd made a trip to her penny tree, it felt as if her dad was right there with her.

FOUR

K nown for their community spirit, the people of Eagan's Point had a quiet pride, the kind you see in those deeply content with where they live. Located an hour north of Seattle, and built on a peninsula facing the Strait of Juan de Fuca and Vancouver Island, the town was home to two thousand people, most who had grown up there and never left, and some who had left and returned years later. The business section stretched out along one side of the peninsula on two streets that ran parallel to each other, separated by a green belt with a walking path. Two rows of trees made a perfect green tunnel down the middle and both streets dead-ended at what everyone called the Docks, where a handful of businesses supported the local fishermen.

The residential part of town was split in two. Half ran parallel to the business core on the opposite side of the peninsula and the rest spilled inland, into a wider area where you could also find the hospital, two schools, a community center, the firehouse, three churches, the vet's office, a recycling depot, and Kozak's Funeral Home. On the peninsula, a row of houses faced the ocean with a narrow back alley as their only access point. Parallel to those homes ran a string of three crescents, each lined with houses facing a central grassy area, each leading to a main road.

Annie and the boys lived in a rented house on Ranier Crescent, just down from the Docks. It was sixty years old, vine-

covered, falling down, but one of only a few that had been available to rent within walking distance of the ocean. At least, living
there, she could easily slip out the back door for a paddle every
morning, a wonderful treat after having lived in downtown Seattle and Chicago.

When she came through the door, Annie tripped over
Sawyer's knapsack. Steadying herself against the wall, she moved
the knapsack out of the way with her foot and it flopped over
onto the newspaper. Distracted, she hurried into the kitchen,
where Eric was seated at the table wearing the black knit cap
Sawyer had given him the day before.

"You're a liar," he said, glaring at Luke. "You said you'd do it
if I did."

"Did not," countered Luke from where he sat perched on the
counter.

"Yes . . . you . . . did!"

After work on Friday, Marina had dropped off a pair of hair
clippers, telling Annie it would save money if she cut the boys'
hair on her own. Instead of explaining how past attempts at cutting her boys' hair had been quasi-catastrophes, Annie thanked
her, put the clippers on top of the fridge, and forgot about them.
Later, after Marina went home, Annie came into the kitchen to
find Luke revving them at high speed as the last chunk of Eric's
hair floated to the floor, leaving him completely bald.

"What are you doing?"

Eric swiveled around and Annie felt the blood drain from her
face. The last time he'd looked like this was five years ago when
he'd lost all his hair for the second time from intensive chemotherapy treatments.

"Mom, it's okay," he said, giving her a lopsided grin. "We
wanted to shave our heads. Luke's doing his too."

"Really?"

"Uh . . . that's not exactly true," Luke said.

Now it was Eric's turn to glare.

Luke set the clippers on the table. "See . . . we were watching a basketball game on TV and I said I thought it'd be sweet to shave your head like the pros do. Then he reminded me about the clippers Aunt Marina got for us and—"

Annie lifted a finger to stop him from talking just as Eric lunged off the stool, and the scuffle that followed left Luke with a swollen lip, Eric with a torn T-shirt, and her with the start of what became a massive headache. The rest of the weekend had been like living in a war zone, and now that it was Monday, she was sick of it.

"Stop it! We're not rehashing this again. If you aren't ready for school when I get out of the shower, you're both grounded. Got it?"

The phone rang and Luke lunged for it.

Annie raised a hand to stop him. "Don't answer that."

"But what if it's Dad?"

"Yeah," Eric echoed.

She wanted to tell them it was probably a bill collector, but she didn't. "If it's your dad, he'll call back. Go get ready for school."

They grudgingly agreed and she left the kitchen to take a shower.

Although her boys shared a bedroom and the same parents, that was all they had in common. Eric was slight, with blond hair and blue eyes, where Luke was huskier, with chestnut hair, green eyes, and a dimple in his left cheek that only showed up when he smiled. Eric lived for basketball, with Steve Nash posters lining his side of the bedroom and a binder of collector cards at the foot of his bed. Luke spent most of his time listening to CDs on his Discman or else glued to the used Xbox Jack had given the boys for

Christmas. Neither boy had been happy about moving to Eagan's Point, but at least Eric was willing to give it a fair shot. When it came to Luke and the problems Annie had been having with him lately, she wasn't sure what to do. She turned on the shower and stepped in, yanking the curtain shut behind her. The phone rang again, but this time she didn't hear it as she raised her face to the hot spray of water and quickly shampooed her hair.

Seconds later, Eric knocked on the door. "Mom? There's a message for you." A slip of paper sailed under the door and came to rest next to the toilet. It said: *Auntie Marina called. Look at today's paper and call her back.*

Annie pulled back the curtain and fumbled for a towel. Was someone calling her? She listened for a few seconds, then tossed the towel on the toilet seat, where it slid off onto the floor, covering the note. Pulling the curtain shut again, she rinsed her hair and tried to think about something positive, like how the hospital had left a message on her machine saying they might have a job opening in six months, which meant that maybe she'd start the new year doing something she actually liked.

Her mom, Erna, had helped her get a job at the funeral home. One day Annie had returned home from dropping off résumés when her mom and Marina pulled up in her mom's fresh-off-the-lot Volkswagen Beetle. After they went inside, her mom held her face out to be kissed and handed Annie a piece of paper. "My neighbor said this guy's receptionist quit two days ago. Of course, it'd just be temporary until you find another job, but he's in a bind with no one to answer his phones and *you*," she said, nodding pointedly at Annie, "need to take care of your boys. His name's Rudy and he owns Kozak's Funeral Home. The number's right there."

Annie produced a tight smile. "So you think I should call this guy, tell him I'm unemployed, and ask for a job?"

"Why not?" Erna said, popping two vitamin C in her mouth. "It can't hurt to ask. That is, unless you're too proud to answer phones in a funeral home."

Annie felt the heat rise in her neck. How was it that her mom always knew exactly what to say to get under her skin? The phone rang and Marina snatched it from its cradle. "Hello?" Covering the receiver, she handed it to Annie. "It's Mr. Tucker, your landlord."

Blowing hair out of her eyes, Annie took it. "Hello? . . . Oh, sorry about that. It slipped my mind. Yes. I'll drop off a check tomorrow. Thanks for calling." She hung up, shot a quick look at her mom, and impulsively decided to prove her wrong. Taking the slip of paper she'd just given her, Annie punched in a few numbers and waited. "Hello? Is this . . . Rudy Kozak?" she asked, squinting to read his name. "Hello, Rudy. My name is Annie Hillman and I'm calling because I heard you might have a job opening. . . ."

Erna was squeezing drops of echinacea into a glass of water. "Tell him you'll work weekends," she whispered. "Lots of people die on weekends."

Annie put a finger to her lips, motioning for silence. "Yes . . . I guess I could."

Erna poured half the water into another glass and handed it to Marina. "Drink," she commanded. "Cold and flu season is right around the corner."

"Uh-huh," Annie said, frowning. "I see. . . . No, I don't think so. The salary I had at my last job would probably be out of reach for you, which I completely understand. . . ." Her voice drifted to a stop. "Really? Okay. That sounds . . . wonderful. I'll be there tomorrow."

Erna smiled and snapped her purse shut.

Annie slowly set the receiver back in its cradle and cleared her throat. "Well . . . that was interesting," she managed.

Marina leaned across the table. "You got the job?"

"Uh-huh. It seems a little odd, though, don't you think? That he'd hire me over the phone without asking for references *and* offer to pay me whatever I was paid at my last job."

"What's odd?" Erna said. "He has a need and you just filled it. Done."

"Who cares?" Marina agreed. "Take the job, set your salary, and keep looking for another one. Unless he's a mass murderer, how bad can it be?"

That was five months ago, and as Annie stepped out of the shower and toweled off, she had to admit it wasn't the worst job she'd ever had, just not what she wanted to do for the rest of her life. However, she now knew why Rudy had lost four receptionists in two years. He was fifty-nine, had never been married, was sadly overweight, and possibly the grouchiest man she'd ever met. She blow-dried her hair, slipped on a blouse and skirt, and glanced in the mirror.

Eric knocked on the door. "Mom? Where are my gym shorts?"

"In the dryer," she answered.

She finished putting on her mascara, opened the door, and almost collided with him.

"They're wet," he said. "And I've got tryouts today."

She frowned on her way down the hall to the laundry alcove. "Well, I put them in the dryer last night and turned it on." But when she yanked the door open, a jumble of wet clothes greeted her. Closing it, she reset the dial and pressed START. Nothing happened. "I don't believe this. Now the dryer's shot!"

Her stove had bitten the dust two weeks ago and it had taken her landlord two days to even return her calls. When he finally did, he apologized and said that he'd been away fishing and that it would take a week to get it fixed. She'd spent six days cooking meals in their toaster oven until the stove finally got repaired.

"It's okay," Eric said. "I'll borrow a pair of Luke's."

Annie watched him disappear into the bedroom with his freshly shaved head and a ferocious protectiveness came over her, a desire so strong to make things right for him that it scared her, the way it used to when he was so sick she knew if she couldn't manage the small things for him, the bigger ones would swallow them all whole. The way it still did now and then when she couldn't sleep at night and tiptoed in to check on him, hyperaware of his every breath. Eric had hystiocytosis, an unpronounceable disease that carried amazing clout, and whenever she had to explain it to someone, it left her exhausted before she began. How do you explain a disease that typically only affects children, has no known cause, and whose symptoms can range from mild pain to death from lung, liver, or brain failure?

Eric had just turned three when he started complaining that his legs hurt. That had quickly accelerated to middle-of-the-night crying sessions when Annie and Jack couldn't calm him. His pediatrician diagnosed growing pains, but days later Eric collapsed walking across the kitchen, his legs unable to carry the weight of his body. They'd rushed him to the hospital, where a biopsy was done.

Hystiocytosis is rare, but the diagnosis was clear. Eric had one large cell mass on his pelvis and another on his right leg. Simply put, it was eating his bone marrow, leaving his pelvic bones almost hollow and his leg in danger of breaking from even the slightest bump. Both masses were malignant and had to be treated with chemotherapy, radiation, and cortisone-like drugs, although Annie and Jack were warned that treatment wasn't often successful.

Eric spent a month in the hospital that first time, followed by CAT scans and chemo sessions. His hair fell out and he was put on a hormone-treatment program to regain the weight he'd lost. At first, Annie took a leave of absence from her job, staying by his side in the hospital and setting up a makeshift bed for him next to hers and Jack's when he came home. Eventually, she'd had to resign and was unable to work for years as Eric went through a succession of physical ups and downs that robbed him of much of his childhood and permanently altered the dynamics of their family.

"Ready to go?" Eric said, coming around the corner.

She nodded. "Basketball tryouts are today, huh?"

"At three thirty."

She tugged the wool cap down on his head and followed him into the kitchen. "And you're sure you want to try out?"

"Dr. Perrins said it was fine," he reminded her.

Sawyer was waiting for them at the door. "Call me when you make the team, Eric," she said, "and remember if your friends want a knit cap like that, they can get 'em at Target." She elbowed him playfully and he grinned. "I'm gonna get going," she said, turning to Annie. "I'm helping Mom at the shelter for an hour before my math exam. The vet's doing a checkup on a sphynx someone surrendered last week."

Annie was about to ask her what a sphynx was when Eric tugged on her sleeve. "Mom, something's wrong with the fish."

Distracted, she grabbed the newspaper off the floor and tucked it under her arm. She leaned down and tapped her finger against the glass tank, frowning. "Oh, they're fine. The tank needs cleaning, that's all."

The fish in question were two standard goldfish she'd bought five years ago. She was flipping through a magazine one day when she ran across an article explaining that children needed to *learn* how to grieve and that most parents don't prepare them. It suggested buying a goldfish, something your child could feed and take care of that typically only lived a few months anyhow, in turn allowing him or her to grieve when the fish had to be flushed down a toilet. Brimming with good intentions, she had raced out and bought the tank, the fish, and the food, but the boys' interest had lasted only a week. She was the one who had ended up feeding them and cleaning the tank. The whole exercise had become a source of amusement for Marina, her mom, and even her soon-to-be ex-husband, because the fish that were supposed to teach the boys how to grieve simply wouldn't die.

Stepping outside, Annie shut the door with three lunch bags clenched between her teeth and the paper tucked under her arm. She turned the lock, took the bags out of her mouth, and called out to Sawyer, who was climbing onto her scooter. "Thanks again for helping with the boys last night. If there's anything I can do to make it up, let me know."

Sawyer waved and rode off.

Annie slid into the car, tossed the newspaper on the seat next to her, and set her purse on top of it. "Seat belts, guys."

"Like we need reminding?" Luke muttered from the back.

Inside, the phone rang as she backed down the driveway, narrowly missing an already badly dented garbage can, but Annie didn't hear the ring, and when the answering machine kicked in, Marina left a message with an almost hysterical edge to her voice.

"Annie, where are you? Have you seen today's paper? If you don't call me back in two minutes, I'll call you at work, but if you're there . . . *pick up the phone*."

FIVE

*A*nnie was a nervous driver. She hated expressways, dreaded traffic circles, and in all the years that she'd lived in Chicago and Seattle, had preferred using mass transit to get around. Unfortunately, there were no buses in Eagan's Point. The boys' school was only a mile away, but because she never drove through town faster than twenty miles an hour, it took at least eight minutes to get there. Then, after she dropped them off, it took another three minutes to get to Kozak's Funeral Home five blocks away. Add two minutes if it was raining. And on those rare occasions when there was a winter snowstorm, she often refused completely and called Marina to arrange for a ride.

"This is unreal," Luke groaned from the backseat. "Can't you speed up a *little*?"

Annie ignored him, both hands clenched on the wheel.

"Why don't you leave her alone?" Eric said. "She's doing fine."

Luke hit him with a box of Kleenex, and by the time they pulled up to the school, the backseat was a jumble of flailing arms and legs.

Annie reeled around, glaring. "Stop it! You're brothers, for God sakes."

"Not by choice," Luke said, grabbing his knapsack.

"Same to you," Eric shot back.

Someone laid on a horn behind them, making Annie jump. The boys got out, slamming their doors, and before she pulled back into traffic, she watched them disappear into a throng of students.

Annie got to work ten minutes late, put the car in park, and leaned her forehead against the steering wheel. Her day had only begun and she was already exhausted. *My life's sliding backwards. I went from being married to not, from having a family to needing superglue to keep what's left of mine together, and from a job as a physical therapist to counting coffins and ordering embalming fluid.*

"Great fun," she muttered, getting out of the car.

The funeral home was an unremarkable gray stucco building with wrought-iron bars set into the windows and an impeccable golf course–like lawn that sloped down to the sidewalk. When Annie pushed through the front door, Rudy Kozak was leaning against the reception desk, waiting for her. He was wearing black chinos with a white cotton dress shirt and the look on his face was exactly the same as on every other day. His brow was furrowed, his mouth twisted into a frown, and a wisp of gray hair had been meticulously combed over his balding head in an attempt to hide what anyone else could see. His arms were crossed, resting on the hill of his belly, and he was quick to point out that she was late.

"Sorry," she said, handing him the paper as a peace offering. "It won't happen again."

When they first met, Annie had thought he was short-tempered because he didn't have a receptionist, but she'd quickly learned that this was just who Rudy was. As an only child, he'd inherited the funeral home when his dad died, and although his mom was still alive, she was in an assisted-living complex across town. Since Annie had started working for Rudy, she could count on one hand the number of times he had gone out for lunch with a friend. When he did, it was usually with Merv Singer, the owner of a casket manufacturer from Seattle.

Rudy disappeared into his office, calling back over his shoulder, "We have a shipment coming in later today, your sister called, and we're out of coffee."

Annie changed the radio station from the mind-numbing elevator music he always had on to something more upbeat. "Everyone else here might be dead," she often told him, "but we aren't." He never argued with her, but when she arrived at work the next morning, the radio was always tuned to his favorite station.

Grabbing the phone, she called Marina.

"McMillan's Pet Haven."

"It's me," Annie said, flipping through Rudy's schedule. "What's up?"

Marina's voice dropped three octaves. "Didn't Eric give you my message?"

"What message?"

"Never mind. Have you seen today's paper?"

Annie sat up a little straighter. "Why? What's going on?"

"Just go get the paper and call me back."

The phone went dead and Annie stared at it in amazement. She smoothed a crease in her blouse. She'd just given Rudy her paper and she was already late, so there was no way she could leave to buy another one. Snapping her fingers, she grabbed his phone messages from yesterday and hurried into the kitchen, opened the cupboard above the fridge and pulled down a box marked *emergencies*. Inside were six single packs of coffee, sugar cubes, and powdered creamer. While the coffee brewed, she paced, wondering why Marina was so wound up. After she poured Rudy a cup, she went into his office and found him with his elbows on the desk, squinting as he read the paper.

She set the steaming cup in front of him. "I keep extra tucked away, just in case."

He blinked at her in surprise. "Oh."

"Drew Williams called yesterday," she said, handing him a phone message. Drew was the president of the chamber of commerce, and Rudy had been waiting for Drew to invite him to the upcoming annual Eagan's Point Golf Tournament.

Rudy set the paper down. "When?"

"After you left yesterday."

"Did he mention the tournament?"

Frowning, Annie tidied the pens on his desk, grabbed the newspaper, and tucked it under her arm. "You know . . . I can't remember."

"Well, next time pay attention," he grumbled, reaching for the phone.

Closing the door on her way out, she hurried back to reception, where she slid into her chair and unfolded the paper. Smoothing it flat, she scanned the front page, quickly darting from one headline to the next until her eyes finally widened, freezing on a picture in the bottom-right-hand corner. She gave her head a shake, certain she was seeing things. There, on the front page of the *Peninsula Post*, was her University of Illinois graduation picture, taken fifteen years ago. She was wearing horn-rimmed glasses, with her hair in a stiff up-do, and her eyes were lit with that tender hopefulness you often see in people before they venture out into the world and get bit by reality. Her hands went clammy as she read.

DO YOU RECOGNIZE THIS WOMAN?

As the years go by, I often ask myself: How did I lose the only woman I ever loved? The answer isn't straight, or simple, but it occurred to me recently that I should do something about it, because if I don't, I'll regret it for the rest of my life. Do you recognize this woman? Her name is Annie Fischer. We knew each other years ago, but somehow we lost touch. She was the first woman I ever loved and I can't forget her. If you know where I can find her, please call (212) 555-1963.

Rudy's voice sounded like it was coming from far away. "*H-e-l-l-o?*" he said, snapping his fingers inches from her face. "Annie, didn't you hear the phone? Your sister's on line one."

Startled, she flipped the paper over. "Sorry."

He walked to the door, jangling his keys. "I'm going to the bank and then I have a meeting with my accountant, so I'll be gone a few hours, but I left a message for Drew, so if he calls, tell him I'll be at the tournament."

"Absolutely," she said, nodding her agreement.

After the door closed behind him, she pressed the HOLD button, where Marina was waiting with uncontained excitement. "So? Who do you think it is?"

"I . . . I don't know." Annie flipped the paper over and read the words again, trying to wrap her brain around the fact that they were there at all. "Maybe it's someone's idea of a joke?"

"Sounds sincere to me. Maybe it's someone you dumped

years ago who was so devastated that he buried himself in his career, spent years building a wildly successful company, is now rich, gorgeous, and determined to find you."

Annie sighed. "Where do you think this stuff up?"

"I live with a seventeen-year-old girl, remember?"

"Okay, if he's so gorgeous, why would I have dumped him in the first place?"

"Because he wasn't gorgeous *then*, but now that he's loaded, he can afford a personal trainer, a nose job, hair implants. . . ."

"This sounds like one of your soap operas," Annie said. "It's not even close to reality."

"Fine, then call the number so we can find out what it's really about."

The other line rang so Annie told Marina she'd phone her back later and took the call. "Kozak's Funeral Home."

"Ms. Hillman please."

"Speaking."

"This is Joan Marsh with Robertson Middle School. I wanted to make sure everything is all right with Luke."

Annie closed her eyes. "Why?"

"Luke isn't in school today, Ms. Hillman."

She took a long, deep breath.

"Are you there?"

"Yes," Annie said. "And thanks for calling. I'll get back to you, okay?"

"Of course. And Ms. Hillman?"

"Uh-huh?"

"This skipping? It's . . . well, it's unusual behavior for a boy his age."

Annie massaged the bridge of her nose. She wanted to tell her that this was nothing, that if she wanted to see unusual behavior, she should've been at their house Friday night when Luke shaved

Eric bald and started World War Three, but she didn't. "Thanks for your concern. Like I said, I'll get back to you." She hung up, bent forward, and rested her forehead on the desk for a few seconds before calling Marina back.

"McMillan's Pet Haven."

"I've gotta go track down Luke. The school just called and he's skipping."

"Again?"

"Yes, again. So while I'm gone, can you do me a favor and call the number in this ad to see who answers?"

"Sure," Marina said, brightening. "I love stuff like this."

"Really? And since when has 'stuff like this' happened to you?"

"It hasn't, but I've got my fantasies."

"Just call the number and phone me later," Annie said. "I'm sure it's a joke."

Initially, Annie had learned Luke was skipping when the school mailed her an attendance summary with a list of absences that didn't add up. She'd read him the riot act a few times since then, but what had begun as skipping the odd class had grown into a bigger problem. Now he was taking entire *days* off. She'd met with the principal last week, and they'd agreed to start monitoring the problem more aggressively, but this was the first time she'd had to deal with it at work and she wasn't impressed. Crossing her fingers, Annie phoned her mom, unable to think of another option that wouldn't put her job in jeopardy.

"Why don't I go look for him?" Erna suggested.

Annie was tempted, but having her mom handle the problem for her would do more damage than good when it came to her already battered relationship with Luke. "Thanks, but I need to do this myself. So will you come watch the phones for me? Just this once?"

Fifteen minutes later, Erna arrived, her stylish hair cut and expert coloring making her look years younger than her actual age.

Wandering around the reception area, she fingered the floor-length burgundy drapes covering the windows and said, "Schlepping through the city dump wouldn't be as bad as spending an hour here."

Annie wanted to remind her mom that getting this job had been her idea, but she knew there would be no point. A no-nonsense woman, Erna walked with her shoulders back and her head up. She never waffled or hesitated when it came to making a decision. It simply got made and she moved on. The only family she had left was her brother, Max, who lived in Canada and ran a small-town newspaper, so her life revolved around her girls and her grandchildren, and she was dedicated to all of them, although she often tested the limits of their patience. Whereas most families have at least one relative who can list every ailment he's ever had—believing this makes intriguing conversation—Erna's hypochondria wasn't limited to herself. She worried about everyone. Friends, family, even complete strangers—no one was exempt. And what made it awkward for those who knew her (and perplexing for those who didn't) was how earnest she was when she doled out advice.

As a teenager, Annie was once waiting in the hallway during a parent-teacher conference when she opened the door a few inches, peeked inside the classroom, and saw her mom holding a flashlight up against her teacher's eye.

"If they ache a lot, it could be simple eye strain," Erna was saying, "but it could also be something much worse. This is the Au-Henkind test and it's said to be one hundred percent reliable. Keep one eye closed and one open, and when I put the flashlight up against your open eye, if you feel pain in the closed eye, that's a positive sign for a condition called anterior uveitis, which is an inflammation of the iris and the surrounding tissues. . . ."

Another memorable incident happened a week before Annie

moved to Chicago to attend university. She came home late one night, hours after curfew, and was weaving down the hallway in the dark when she found her mom standing on a stepstool in the bathroom with a flashlight in one hand and her mouth wide open. Either unaware that Annie was drunk or else too self-absorbed with the task at hand to care, Erna grabbed her by the elbow.

"Good, you're home! Take the flashlight and look at my uvula."

Annie squinted at her. "Your what?"

"The pink thing that hangs down at the back of my throat. I want you to look at it and tell me if it's pulsing because I think it is, and it shouldn't be."

"Why not?" Annie asked, confused.

"Because if your uvula pulses in time with your heartbeat it's called Müller's sign and can be an early indication of heart disease."

Blinking double time, Annie took the flashlight and looked, but because she was drunk, everything in her mom's mouth looked like it was pulsing.

"Looks good," she declared, clearing her throat.

"Are you sure?" Erna pressed, motioning for her to look again.

This time, Annie held the flashlight with both hands to keep it steady. "Nope, no pulsing," she assured Erna after a few seconds. "You're good to go."

Days later, when Annie was packing to leave, her mom came into her room and gravely explained that she thought she had systematic sclerosis because she couldn't insert the tips of her three middle fingers into her mouth in a vertical stack without touching her lips or her teeth. Near tears, she'd sat on the edge of the bed shredding Kleenex. "Annie, maybe you should stay home for another year, because this is a progressive illness where your skin hardens and contracts, and it slowly kills you. . . ."

Annie looked up at the ceiling. "Mom, I'm sure you're fine."

At the rehearsal dinner the night before she got married, Annie watched helplessly as Erna leaned over to warn Jack's mother that her constant yawning could be an early sign of encephalitis or a tumor in the central part of her brain—both possibilities so serious that she really should see a doctor. At first, Jack's mom blinked at her in disbelief. Then she slung her purse over her shoulder and stormed out of the restaurant without a backward glance, telling Jack the next day that Annie's mom was the rudest woman she'd ever met.

As Erna's daughter, Annie didn't find her problem funny. Growing up, she and Marina had tried to ignore it whenever it surfaced at birthday parties, their dad's annual company picnic, school field trips with Erna as a chaperone or when the girls had friends sleep over. To alleviate their embarrassment, they'd laugh about it later once they were alone, using one-upmanship to see who could remember the most humiliating thing their mom had said or done. But that was years ago, and any shared camaraderie on this issue no longer existed. In fact, the few times Annie had brought it up since moving back to Eagan's Point, Marina had quickly changed the subject.

Now, as her mom pulled on a pair of white cotton dress gloves and ran a finger across the top of a filing cabinet, Annie wrote her cell phone number on a slip of paper and thanked her for her help. "Remember, answer the phone and take messages, but please don't touch anything else, okay, Mom?"

"Go," Erna said, flapping a hand in the air. "Everything'll be fine."

Six

*J*ack Hillman tented his fingers and pressed them to his lips, thinking about the ad on the front page of the *Peninsula Post*. He was a big man, six foot two and broad through the shoulders, with craggy good looks and quiet self-confidence. He wasn't a fighter, but he had a fighter's body, including a scar that cut his right eyebrow in two, which he'd had since his dad had backhanded him once for breaking a glass. His dad had been a cruel and intimidating man, and his rages were unpredictable, like standing in the path of an oncoming tornado, watching and waiting for it to touch down as it twisted in crazy circles, tearing up everything in its way.

By the time Jack was ten, he had convinced himself that if he were deaf, it wouldn't hurt so much when his dad beat him. At least then he wouldn't hear him coming, storming through the house as he yelled Jack's name, ripping the belt from his jeans. He would be blissfully unaware that a beating was coming until it hit him. Then, after that first sting of leather against his flesh, sloppy in its aim against his backside or arms or legs, he'd turn himself off and slip away to where the physical pain was separate from the rest, the way he'd taught himself when he realized that fighting back was pointless.

Of course, either way, there was a chance he'd pee himself—which would assure him a worse beating. Often, his dad would start with Jack's mom, yelling and throwing things, screaming at her for something she had or hadn't done. Then he would slam out the door and leave, returning hours later. Sometimes he acted like nothing had happened, but other times he came back madder than ever and resumed the beatings where he'd left off. Now and then Jack missed school until the bruises had faded enough that they wouldn't tell the story his dad didn't want told.

Growing up, Jack turned to music whenever he needed to escape. It didn't matter what kind of music, anything to take him away from where he was right then. CCR worked, but so had John Cougar, the Beatles, Kiss, Bryan Adams, AC/DC, or Rod Stewart. All he had was an old portable radio held together with a few strips of electrical tape, but in it he found refuge.

The year he turned fifteen, he came to breakfast one morning bearing a gift, hoping his dad wouldn't say no when he asked for permission to take the bus into Seattle after school that day. When the sun had filtered through his cracked bedroom window that morning, he'd wrapped up a clay ashtray he'd made in art class and tied it with string.

"What's this?" his dad asked when Jack set it down beside him at breakfast.

Jack slid into a chair, keeping his eyes lowered. "We had to do something in art class for our final grade, so I made this for you."

His dad opened it as Jack's mom put a pancake on his plate. "Now isn't that thoughtful?" she said, giving Jack an encouraging wink.

"Maybe if I hadn't quit smoking a month ago," his dad said. His eyes were two angry black points. Pushing his chair back from the table, he stood and tossed the ashtray in the garbage. "See you tonight," he muttered, and then he was gone, the screen door slapping against its frame.

Jack could still remember his mom, spatula in one hand as she rummaged through the garbage with the other. "Maybe ask your teacher if you can make something else," she tried. "Like a key holder, the kind you hang your keys on when you get home?"

"I've got a better idea," Jack said.

"What's that?"

"How about a new leather belt?"

Her face went pale, but Jack carried on, gathering steam now that his dad was gone. "Yeah, that's it. Maybe I'll make him a real thick one with a big belt buckle, the kind that'll cut into my skin when he beats me with it."

"You're out of line, Jack," his mom said, lowering her gaze.

"Really? That's funny 'cause I always feel like I'm first in line when it comes to him."

Later that day, he and his friend Howie took the bus into Seattle, where a local radio station was hosting a promotion for the Guess Who. The lead singer, Burton Cummings, would be drawing one winning ballot from a drum and the winner would announce songs with him on the radio for one hour. Howie's mom had mailed in a dozen ballots for Howie and Jack, and when Jack's name was called out over the roar of the crowd, he'd stood there, stunned.

"Who'd they say?" he yelled to Howie.

"It's you, Jack," Howie said, slapping him on the back. "Shit, he picked you!"

Tongue-tied, Jack made his way through the crowd up onto the stage, and for the next hour, for one blissful hour in his fifteen-year-old life, he sat next to Burton Cummings as they worked together to raise money for a local charity.

When it was over, Jack and Howie left wearing autographed Guess Who T-shirts, almost missing the last bus home. Fists buried in his armpits, Jack hunched down in his seat, telling himself whatever happened when he got home would be worth it. The crowd, the music, and sitting next to Burton Cummings, who had joked with him and shaken his hand to congratulate him—like he meant it, like Jack actually mattered in the scheme of things. *Worth it*, he thought, as his eyes brimmed with tears. *All of it, worth it.*

It was almost midnight when he said good-bye to Howie and ran down the alley to his house. When he got to the gate and saw lights on in the kitchen, his hands started to shake. He knew that his dad was waiting for him, that he'd probably get grabbed the second he walked through the door, and yet as he crossed the yard and made his way up the back steps, he felt something different in the air, a stillness that had never been part of where he lived, a quiet calm that was new to him. He slipped inside, but the kitchen was empty. Puzzled, he went into the living room. His mom was on the couch, her face swollen from crying.

"Your dad's gone," she said in a hoarse voice.

Hoping he'd left for good, Jack waited, not wanting to push her since it was after midnight and he was already skating on thin ice.

"We'll have the funeral Monday," she whispered.

Jack stared at her. His head started to buzz and his throat went dry.

"What do you mean?" he asked, feeling what he would later recognize as a burst of relief, the kind that shoots straight through you and up into the clouds before you have time to feel an ounce of shame or guilt.

"There was an accident at work. . . ." Wiping away tears, she explained what had happened and Jack lowered himself onto the couch next to her in stunned silence.

He didn't say anything when people offered their condolences at the funeral. He just stared at his feet. After all, they hadn't known his dad the way he had. They hadn't been privy to the crap that had gone on behind the walls of their house. As far as he was concerned, it wasn't such a bad thing that he was gone. His dad had been released from the world, taking all his anger with him, and on that same day, Jack had met Burton Cummings, an experience that ultimately helped him decide what to do with his life.

Now Jack was thirty-eight, and painful memories of growing up with his dad still followed him wherever he went, but they also made him unshakingly dedicated to his boys. He and Annie shared other wounds, past hurts and painful memories that would eventually fade but could never be completely erased. After Eric got sick, Jack had watched her spend years punishing herself for not having the answer to his problem, for not being able to fix it, and in the process, the life had gone out of her. Losing a child was the worst tragedy any parent could imagine, but the relentless, perpetual threat of losing a child also took its share of casualties.

Jack grabbed the *Peninsula Post* and looked at Annie's picture. Years ago, after he'd first met her, the logical part of his brain shut down when she was around. He was distracted and forgetful and constantly aware of her, and even though she never seemed to be looking at him, it always felt like she was staring. He'd heard once that men tended to marry women who were like their mothers, but with Annie that hadn't been the case. Where his mother had been quiet and emotionally closed, Annie's thoughts and emotions were completely uncloaked from the world. She was determined, whereas his mother had been tentative. She planned and took charge and never let anyone tell her what to do, while his mother had been lost after her husband died, with no idea where to turn.

Jack exhaled a long sigh. Before he and Annie had split up, he'd often thought of his life in terms of all that he'd survived and achieved: battling his father, landing on his feet with a solid career, meeting Annie, having the boys. But after they separated, he spent a lot of time thinking about everything he hadn't done and all that he had failed to be. Glancing at the clock, he turned the newspaper upside down on his desk, determined to put Annie and this ad out of his mind.

SEVEN

On her way home in search of Luke, Annie was careful to obey each stop sign, looking first one way and then the other (usually twice) before moving forward. She was a defensive driver and today was no exception. Driving was serious business to her, and she took pride in the fact that although she'd never quite mastered the art of parallel parking, and sometimes got disoriented when she had to back up, she'd never been in an accident. Not even a fender bender.

"That's 'cause people get out of the way when they see you coming," Luke said when she brought it up.

Annie drove a 1986 Yugo, a Yugoslavian import her dad had bought before he died, proudly giving his wife and daughters the only new vehicle he could afford. It was olive green and boxy and it stuck out like a sore thumb, but it was still in decent working condition. After Annie and the boys moved to Eagan's Point, her mom had given it to them. As far as Annie knew, it had only been on three long road trips—twice when her parents took them to Athabasca, Alberta, where her uncle Max lived, and two months after she'd moved back to Eagan's Point, when she took the boys to Portland for her mother-in-law's funeral.

In preparation for the trip, Annie had laid a map out on the kitchen table, using a yellow highlighter to outline their route, staying off the interstate wherever possible and building in hourly stops so they could stretch their legs. She marked where they'd stop for gas, where they'd eat lunch, and what hotel they'd stay in. The idea of driving all that distance had terrified her, but Jack's mom had been good to her and she felt it would have been disrespectful if she and the boys didn't go. Family was family, after all, and she was determined to instill its importance in her kids.

Early the next morning, she'd carefully placed a row of bicycle reflector stickers across the rear bumper and was installing deer whistles under both side mirrors when the boys, still half asleep, came outside with pillows under their arms.

"What's she doing?" Eric asked, muffling a yawn.

Luke stared at her, shaking his head. "Don't even ask."

The four-hour trip to Portland took almost seven and went as planned, other than Eric getting carsick and Annie having to pull over and breathe into a paper bag each time a semi passed them, rocking the car. By the time they arrived, she had a migraine. But when Jack's eyebrows shot up and he said, "You came," in a way that conveyed he was remembering all the occasions when fear had sidelined her, Annie knew her effort had been worth it. *Yes, I did*, she thought, leaning against the Yugo (hoping he wouldn't notice the stickers or deer whistles). *This is me, moving forward with my life. Doing just fine, thank you very much.*

When Annie got to the house, she turned the lock and stepped inside. "Luke?" she called out. There was no answer, but she took a quick tour anyhow, then checked the backyard, noticing that the dog was gone too. Climbing back into her car, she drove down to the Docks, and within minutes, she spotted Luke on the beach, sitting cross-legged on the sand as their dog, Montana, rooted around in the surf, only her head and shoulders visible above the water.

Months ago, Marina had asked Annie if she'd mind taking in

a dog for a few weeks until she could find it a good home. Because it was a big dog, she didn't have enough room for it at the pet shelter. "She's a Newfoundland," Marina explained. "They're used as therapy dogs and water-rescue dogs. Her name's Montana and she weighs a hundred and sixty pounds, but she's unbelievably gentle." Annie protested, but Marina pushed harder, promising it would only be for a few weeks. "I'll give you dog food and she comes with her own doghouse. Harrison said he'd bring it over. You won't even know she's there."

"Fine," Annie said, hoping she wouldn't regret it. "I'll take her for two weeks, but not a day more, and she's *not* allowed in my house."

Hours later, Harrison delivered Montana, who looked like a genetically altered black bear, and a massive doghouse, which she refused to use. After Annie and the boys went to bed that first night, Montana sat on the back steps, staring at the door. She didn't bark or howl or whine, she just sat there, and when they got up in the morning, she was still there. She did the same thing the second night, and again the third, even though it poured rain for hours. In the middle of the fourth night, Annie grabbed a towel and let her in. After she'd dried the dog off, she said, "Stay," and Montana lay down on the scuff rug next to the door. Satisfied, Annie went back to bed, telling herself it was just for one night because it was raining so hard.

The next morning, when Annie got up, Montana wasn't there. Frustrated, she went through the house, determined to drag her outside, pouring rain or not. A massive dog like this one was the last thing she needed to add to her list of problems.

She found the dog asleep next to Luke on his bed. When Luke came up on an elbow and smiled for what seemed like the first time in months, Annie's throat tightened and her intentions went out the window. It was the kind of smile that made Luke look six again, when he'd blow through the door after school each day, saying, "Guess what. I made *another* friend today." The way he used to smile before Eric got sick and Luke's world shriveled to half the size it had been when she was always there for him.

"Thanks for letting her in," Luke said, burying his face in Montana's neck.

Unable to speak, Annie had just nodded.

And now, months after she'd agreed to keep Montana for two weeks and not a day more, just the thought of taking her away from Luke made Annie shudder. As she watched him sitting on the sand looking dejected, she was torn between being mad at him and wanting to join him. More than anything, though, she wished he'd talk to her. It had been months since she and Luke had had a real conversation and she was at her wit's end. Weeks ago, he'd been caught stealing money from an emergency stash Jack kept hidden in his apartment. They'd asked Harrison to talk to him, since he was a state trooper and could scare the crap out of Luke about what he'd be facing if he kept down this path. Apparently their conversation went well, and Harrison assured Annie and Jack that Luke wasn't as screwed up as his recent behavior might suggest. "Give him a few months," he'd said. "I'm sure it'll pass."

Taking her time, Annie got out of the car and crossed the street. She walked past Luke out onto a dock that stretched over the water, and at the end, she stopped and squinted up at the sun. When she heard him walk up behind her, she said, "I thought we had a deal," keeping her voice calm and matter-of-fact.

"What deal?"

When it came to talking back, Luke and Eric had completely different styles. Eric almost never did, making him easy to deal with, whereas Luke liked to manipulate their discussions, seamlessly twisting everything she said until they were arguing about a completely different subject. *But not today,* Annie thought, turning to face him. *Enough is enough.*

"We talked about this last week and you said you wouldn't skip again."

He looked at his shoes. "That was on Wednesday, right?"

She blinked at him in confusion. "What?"

"We talked about it last Wednesday."

"I don't remember what day it was," she said, irritated. "Who cares?"

He tossed a baseball into the air and caught it in his glove. "Because if we talked on Wednesday, and we did, then it doesn't count and there was no deal."

Annie wanted a cigarette in the worst possible way. She considered asking him to wait while she ran back to the car to get one. Instead, she took a deep breath and closed her eyes for patience. "What are you talking about?"

"Wednesday is my carefree day."

"Your carefree day?" she repeated.

"Uh-huh."

"I see," she said. "Exactly how does that work, and what's it got to do with you skipping today, which happens to be a Monday?"

Luke leaned against the railing. "Because on Wednesday, which is my carefree day, nothing that happens bothers me and nothing counts. Not at school, not at home. Nothing. So because you made this deal with me about not skipping any more on a Wednesday, it doesn't count, because—"

"It's your carefree day," she finished for him.

He dropped his eyes and nodded, suddenly looking more vulnerable and apologetic than smart-assed, although she had the distinct feeling he was trying hard for the latter.

"So when did you come up with this idea?" she asked.

"About a month ago, when I was at Dad's for the weekend."

"I see," Annie said again, nodding as she stared out across the water. "And did you talk to him, your dad, I mean, about this carefree day?"

Luke ducked his head. "Actually, it was Dad's idea. He said he thought I should pick one day each week, the same day, where I wake up and have fun and enjoy my life without worrying about all the things I'm always worrying about."

Without warning, tears pricked the back of Annie's eyes. Her son had just told her that he worried about things, which made sense given everything that had happened over the last few years. He was thirteen and on the verge of full-blown puberty. His brother had spent seven years in and out of the hospital (twice on the verge of death), and although Eric seemed okay now, they had all been lulled into a false sense of security about his health one time too many. Beyond that, she and Jack were getting divorced, and they'd recently moved an hour away from the only home Luke had ever known. A wave of sadness hit her as Annie cleared her throat.

"So how's it been working for you, this carefree day?"

"Good," he said.

She took his shoulders and kissed him on the forehead—hard. "I love you, Luke. I just don't tell you often enough. And I'm sorry. I didn't realize you worried so much." He shrugged like it was no big deal. "But even so, there won't be any more skipping, because the next time you pull this stunt, I'm taking a week off work and I'm going to school with you every day, and I'm sitting next to you in every class until it stops."

"Whatever," he said, kicking a rock into the water with brooding indifference.

This who-cares kid with dull and lifeless eyes was making Annie nervous. "Is it so bad living here?" she asked, sliding an arm around him.

"It sucks," he said, shaking her off.

"But you haven't even tried making friends."

"Why bother? They're all losers."

She looked out over the water, listening to it lap against the dock. "We've only been here five months and I'm doing all I can to get us settled as a family—"

A tightening came to his face and he glared at her. "Family? What family? Dad doesn't live here. At least in Seattle we were in the same city."

"You can see your dad whenever you want—"

"Can I live with him?"

Annie crossed her arms. "No, you can't. He works shifts and he can't always be there for you after school or at night."

"I'm thirteen," he argued. "I don't need anyone around after school, and when Dad does work nights, I could go with him."

"It's not that easy."

"And this is?" He took a sharp kick at one of the rail posts. "I hate it here, so why won't you just let me go?"

Annie's eyes glistened with tears. "Because not having you here would break my heart."

"You've got Eric," he said matter-of-factly. "What's the big deal?"

She opened her mouth but nothing came out. What he'd said had hurt, but it didn't surprise her. Eric being sick for so many years had cheated Luke out of moments and days and weeks with her that could never be replaced. Times when she was so busy running in circles, so terrified of losing Eric that she'd alienated Luke without realizing it. Annie shook her head, amazed that she'd managed to give birth to two kids who were so different.

One a thoughtful, naive optimist and the other a smart-ass who believed he could take on the world, owing no one anything in the process. "I'm sure you'll do great," she'd said the day before when Eric told her he'd signed up for a five-mile walkathon with the school. "I'm sure he'll tank," Luke had snorted, getting up from the table.

Shooting him a sideways look, Annie crammed her hands into her pockets. She told herself this was just his way of testing her, of telling her that he needed more attention than she'd been giving him. When a long silence loomed up between them, she slapped her hands against her legs and said, "Okay," with a fake brightness she didn't feel.

"Okay, what?" he said suspiciously.

She answered in a casual, offhand manner, as if it were normal for her to agree with him on such a serious issue. "You're thirteen, so I guess you can make up your own mind. If living with your dad in Seattle is what you really want to do, I won't stop you . . . as long as he agrees that it's okay." She talked without looking at him, keeping her gaze on the water, knowing that if she saw even a flicker of relief on his face, she'd crumple. "I think it's wrong for you and Eric to be split up like that, but it's your decision."

"Okay," he said, brushing sand off his cargo pants. "Good."

Annie heard a flash of unexpected gratitude in his voice, which suddenly made her feel less sure of herself. "Of course, you know you can't take Montana, right?" she said.

Luke gave her an uneasy look that told her he hadn't considered it.

She nodded to where Montana was rolling in the sand. "Keep in mind your dad's apartment doesn't allow pets, and this one wouldn't exactly be easy to hide."

———

Annie kept her face expressionless as she coaxed Montana into the backseat, not allowing herself to feel as if she'd been broken in half until after she'd dropped Luke off at school. And yet, as they drove across town, her resolve began to slip. She wanted to lay a hand on his arm and tell him that she didn't want to lose him, that she was sorry for making such a mess of things. Before she could do either, Luke changed the radio to WSMB in Seattle, where Jack worked as a deejay.

"Did Dad tell you the station's gonna lend him their boat one of these weekends?"

"Yes, he mentioned it," she said, trying to act impressed. "Sounds like fun."

"It has a bedroom and a bathroom and a fridge—"

Jack's voice cut in, interrupting them. "That was Phil Collins with 'Don't Let Him Steal Your Heart Away.' It's currently seventy-four degrees in downtown Seattle, and this is Jack Hillman bringing you another hour of uninterrupted light rock."

Annie pulled up to the school, dragging her teeth back and forth across her bottom lip. "Luke? Keep in mind if you skip again there won't be a boat weekend, okay?"

"Yeah, okay," he said, getting out of the car.

"See you later, pal."

As she watched him walk into the school, Annie tucked her hands under her thighs, trying to figure out how everything had gone so wrong between them. How all of her ups and downs and uncertainties about being a mother over the years had brought her to this moment. Her son had just told her that he didn't want to live with her anymore, and as he did, she'd felt a piece of her heart irreparably tear. She reached out and fingered a clear plastic ball hanging from her rearview mirror. Inside was a tiny blue dinosaur, no more than an inch tall, a reminder of a time long ago when she'd questioned her decision to stay home with the boys for a few years instead of working—especially one day in particular when Luke was three, Eric had just turned one, and they were renting an old house on the outskirts of Seattle.

Jack was away on business and Luke had lost his favorite blue dinosaur, so Annie was in the middle of a house-wide search. The phone rang when she was on her stomach, one arm stretched as far as she could reach under the couch. She knew she shouldn't answer it, but she scrambled to her feet and snatched the receiver from its cradle anyhow. "Hello."

It was Jack, letting her know he was on his way home.

"Good," Annie said. Coming home was good.

Tucking the portable under one ear, she neatly kicked a cupboard door shut just as Eric reached for it, then turned and saw Luke glaring at her for giving up the search for his dinosaur. To keep the situation from escalating, she covered the phone and promised him that she'd just be two minutes. Although he looked skeptical, he wandered off to continue searching on his own.

Jack said he'd be home by midnight, then began telling her about his trip.

"Great," Annie said, lifting Eric down from the glass coffee table and planting his feet on the carpet. He'd picked up an intestinal bug, and she was keeping a close eye on him. Then she held the phone against her chest and yelled out a reminder to Luke that he'd left the baby gate open at the top of the stairs. "Sorry," she muttered, readjusting the phone and tuning back in to what Jack was saying.

Grabbing a baby bottle from the fridge, she asked if the weather had been good.

Jack said it had.

"That's nice," she said, mustering as much enthusiasm as possible while functioning on four hours' sleep from the night before.

Clearly excited, Jack started to describe an account the station had won.

Annie set the baby bottle in the microwave, pressed START, and headed for the bathroom, where she'd seen Eric disappear. When she stuck her head around the corner, he was standing next to his discarded diaper, in the middle of a fresh pile of diarrhea. Seeing her, he grimaced and pointed to the floor as if he too was disgusted with this mess.

"Everything okay?" Jack asked.

"Uh . . . fine. Everything's fine," Annie said.

She grabbed Eric and propped him against her hip in a horizontal hold, then reached for a wet face cloth. She was about to ask Jack to call back when their cat ran into the bathroom chasing a paper ball. His paws hit the diarrhea and he skidded sideways, then floundered in panic before jumping for higher ground. But the toilet seat was up, so he neatly landed *in* the bowl, then, like a rocket, shot straight back out and raced down the hallway, dripping wet.

"You *sure* everything's okay?" Jack asked.

Annie had the phone wedged between her ear and her shoulder, and her neck was starting to ache. No, things weren't okay, but before she could tell him this, the doorbell rang, and within seconds, she heard the front door open, and then Luke's small voice rang out.

"Mommy, dat man's here."

Eric was doing everything he could to wriggle out of her grasp as she hurried to the front door. Suddenly she remembered she was wearing a pajama top with zebras on it and no bra. As she shifted Eric up higher on her hip, the phone slid out from underneath her chin, dropped to the floor, and skidded across the room.

Blue dinosaur temporarily forgotten, Luke stood at the door wearing a Batman cape, grinning at the electrician, who was there to fix their ceiling fan.

Annie snatched the phone back up and Jack's voice cut through the calamity. "What the hell's going on?"

The electrician didn't have kids of his own. Annie could tell by the stiff, awkward responses he gave Luke when he asked if he could see the man's tools.

"Obviously this isn't a good time," Jack said, sounding frustrated.

When is? Annie thought.

The electrician took off his shoes and pointed to the ceiling fan in the living room. She nodded that he could go in. He grabbed his ladder and Luke trailed after him, bare feet slapping against the hardwood floor. Annie sat down to finish cleaning Eric's bum and it hit her that the electrician was smelling the same rank air she was.

"What you doin'?" Luke asked the electrician, getting an unintelligible response even Annie didn't understand.

"I'm gonna let you go," Jack said, clearly annoyed.

At that moment, the electrician saw the Great Dane they were dog-sitting for a friend lope around the corner into the living room, evident to Annie by how quickly the color drained from his face. Phone forgotten, she set Eric down and ran to grab Hannibal's collar. However, holding back such a big dog wasn't easy. He wriggled free and reached the electrician before she could.

Eyes wide, the electrician folded his ladder and hurried to the front door. Hannibal followed, sniffing at his legs as he made a grab for his shoes. Not bothering to put them on, he yanked the door open and left, muttering that he'd forgotten a part and would call her later.

"Sure," Annie said, "you do that."

She closed the door, leaned her forehead against it, and started to cry, thinking, *I did not sign up for this.*

Seconds later, a tiny hand slid into hers, jolting her back to reality.

Annie turned and there was Luke, mouth quivering. "What's wrong, Mommy?" Then Eric began crying too, waddling over on unsteady legs and still in need of a fresh diaper.

Sinking down to the floor, she hauled them both into her lap. "I'm sorry, guys," she said, sniffing. "Mom's having a bad day, that's all."

Luke tilted his head and looked at her for a long time. Then he reached into his pocket and asked her to close her eyes. Humoring him, Annie took a ragged breath and squeezed them tight. Taking her hand, he turned it over and gently laid something on it. When she opened her eyes, a tiny blue dinosaur was balanced perfectly in her palm.

"I love you," Luke said, looking shy. "So you kin have my dine-sore forever."

Annie's chest tightened, and in that moment, she knew she wouldn't trade this for anything. Not only would she sign up for it, she'd be first in line. The electrician could take a hike and her career was going to have to wait a few years. The sun was up on a new day, her kids loved her, and she was the proud owner of a blue dinosaur.

EIGHT

nnie walked into Kozak's Funeral Home to a peachy odor instead of the antiseptic smell she had only recently gotten used to. She froze when she saw Rudy's burgundy velvet drapes heaped in a pile next to her desk and her mom rounded the corner with a stack of magazines from his office. Annie's purse dropped to the floor.

"Mom! What are you doing?"

Erna waved her off. "Relax, for heaven's sake."

"Relax? When Rudy sees this, he's gonna flip out."

"Oh, everything's fine. Rudy came back half an hour ago to pick up some paperwork he'd forgotten and we had a nice chat. I asked him to buy ammonia and a few other things when he finishes up with that accountant of his."

"You did *what*?"

Erna grabbed Annie by the arm and pulled her down the hallway into the kitchen, where she'd rearranged everything. "What do you think? Do you like it?" she asked, but Annie just stared in amazement. "No?" Erna patted her on the arm. "Well, I do. It's much cozier this way." The kitchen wall phone rang and she grabbed the receiver before Annie could react.

"Kozak's Funeral Home . . . Oh, Marina. Yes, she's here." Erna lowered her voice. "I'm helping with the phones. . . . Today's paper? No, she hasn't said anything—"

Annie yanked the receiver away. "I'll call you back in ten minutes," she said, hanging up.

Before she could explain to her mother, the front door opened, and Erna hurried back to reception. Annie stuck her head around the corner and watched as Rudy set a cardboard box of cleaning supplies on her desk.

"Here you go," he said to Erna, eyes twinkling. "Everything you asked for."

Her mom did something then that Annie had never seen her do before. Blushing, she dropped her gaze and brushed an imaginary spot off her blouse. Using the palm of one hand, Rudy smoothed down his comb-over, shuffling from one foot to the other as he waited for her to check what he'd bought. Annie, watching them, touched upon a truth so foreign to her that she almost missed it—her mom and Rudy were flirting.

Rudy glanced up and saw her. "You're back."

Annie managed a nod.

Looking embarassed, he flipped a thumb in Erna's direction. "I didn't know your mom lived in town." He made a big production of carrying the box into the kitchen as Erna trailed behind, asking him if he'd ever considered painting the place something other than this horrible, depressing gray.

When the phone rang at her desk, Annie hurried over and fumbled for it. "Kozak's Funeral Home."

"Stop hanging up on me!" Marina complained.

"Sorry."

"Is Luke okay?"

"Uh-huh," Annie said, sliding into her chair. "Luke's fine."

"I can't believe Mom was answering the phones. That's hilarious."

"That's not all she was doing," Annie said under her breath.

"What?"

"I'll tell you later. Did you call the number in that ad?"

"Yes, but an electronic recording kicked in asking me to leave a message."

"What did you do?" Annie asked.

"I left a message."

"No," she groaned. "Why would you do that?"

"You want to know who it is, don't you?"

"Of course, but I don't want whoever it is tracking me down before I know who he is. This guy could be a nut or something."

"Relax," Marina said, sounding pleased with herself. "I left my name and number, said I was your sister, and that if anyone wanted to contact you they should call me. Then I phoned the *Peninsula Post* and asked who placed the ad."

"Did you find out?" Annie asked, hopefully.

"No. They said they'd signed some kind of agreement and couldn't release the name of the person, which seems odd, don't you think? When I got pushy, they passed me over to some woman in advertising, who got herself all tied up in knots, and then she put me through to an assistant managing editor."

Annie slapped the desk, laughing. "That's great!"

"Not really. He took my name and number, and told me he couldn't make that decision, that he'd have someone else get back to me."

"This is crazy," Annie complained.

"Depends on who ran the ad. It could be romantic if it's the right person."

Annie closed her eyes. "Marina? On the front page of the local paper, there's an ancient picture of me wearing horn-rimmed glasses. That's not romantic."

"Right. Sorry."

Bafflement hung in the air between them. Annie twisted the phone cord around her arm, wishing the unhappy task of trying to guess who'd placed the ad would disappear, not because she was deeply resistant to the idea of having romance in her life, but because she believed someone was probably playing a joke on her, and it wasn't funny.

"Wait a minute," Marina said, snapping her fingers.

Annie perked up. "What?"

"I'll bet it's Chris Carby. He used to have a thing for you, and now that you're both living in Eagan's Point, unattached and available . . ."

"That was twenty years ago," Annie pointed out.

"Right, but the ad said you were the *first* woman he ever loved and that alone takes the possibilities back a few years."

"I guess," Annie said, sounding skeptical. She pulled the newspaper out of her purse and laid it on her desk, smoothing out the creases so she could read the ad again. And as she did, the muscles in her back loosened even though she hadn't realized she was tense. "Maybe it's Julie," she said.

"Julie Coyne?"

"Right," Annie said, trying to remember something.

"Why would Julie do something like this?" Marina asked.

"Because of an argument we had a few weeks ago."

"About what?"

"I accused her of being too gullible when it came to men, and she told me there's nothing more appealing to a woman than a man who's in love with her. I laughed and told her hell would freeze over before any man ever got under my skin by flattering me or falling all over himself to get my attention."

"What's that got to do with this?" Marina asked, sounding confused.

Annie shrugged. "Maybe she's hoping I'll phone her and swoon about how romantic the ad is. Then she'll confess. You know, one of those 'gotcha' jokes."

"She'd do that?"

"Wouldn't she?" Annie tried, clinging to her theory.

Silence.

"I'm gonna call her," Annie said. "I'll talk to you later, okay?"

For as long as Annie could remember, Julie Coyne had been obsessed with getting married. In high school, Julie would doodle in her notebooks *Mrs. Julie Block*, *Julie Yvonne Block*, or *Julie and Brent Block*. Then, if Brent Block didn't work out, she'd start all over again, writing *Mrs. Julie Norden*, or *Mr. and Mrs. Norden*. The summer they turned fifteen, she and Annie spent most of their Saturdays sitting outside St. Mary's Catholic church in Eagan's Point, waiting for brides and grooms to emerge. And as handfuls of confetti and rice rained down on newlyweds they didn't know, Julie would say, "He'd look better in a traditional tux" or "She should have worn something off the shoulder." Today, she was more socially active than anyone Annie had ever known, and yet she still wasn't married.

After Annie and Jack had split up a year and a half ago, Julie had stopped by one night, determined to drag Annie out of her funk. "Come on," she'd pressed. "Get someone to watch the boys for a few hours and come out with me." She had joined an organization called Meet Market Adventures, a pay-as-you-go Web-based group that posted monthly activities in various cities, and she wanted Annie to go with her to a few events. You could participate in anything imaginable, from llama trekking, a day on a dude ranch, kickboxing, ballroom dancing, white-water rafting, bungee jumping, archery . . . even a night at a circus and trapeze school.

Annie had flipped through the brochure Julie handed her and laughed. "Who could I meet llama trekking who'd be even remotely interesting?"

"Keep in mind, I met Gary hang gliding."

"You broke up three months later," Annie reminded her.

Julie pointed a hey-you're-quick finger at her. "Right, but if I hadn't met Gary, I never would've met Jonah."

Annie stared at her. "Jonah?"

Julie nodded conspiratorially. "He's Gary's landlord. He has a mail-order business on the side, and we've been seeing each other for two months now."

Annie made a face. "That is such a non-grown-up thing to do."

But it was a Julie thing to do, and one of the reasons Annie loved her so much: for her eternal optimism when it came to searching for the perfect man. Julie didn't judge men based on what they did for a living or on how much money they made, and sometimes she dated guys you couldn't have paid Annie to eat a meal with, but she never gave up. Over the years, she'd dated so many guys that Annie often had to interrupt her, saying, "Wait a minute. Are we talking about the stand-up comedian or the guy who sells water beds?"

"I want three Saturdays of your time," Julie insisted, crossing her arms.

Annie gave her a long look and shook her head.

"Why not?"

"Think about it, Jules. I haven't been on a date in years."

"No problem. I'll give you pointers."

Annie didn't have the heart to mention the obvious: that no matter how stone-cold gorgeous Julie was, with chocolate-colored hair that fell to her waist, her dating strategy wasn't getting her anywhere.

"You pick the first event," Julie said. "Then I'll pick the next one and so on. We'll start this weekend. After work on Wednesday, I'll watch the boys while you go get your hair done—I've already made an appointment for you. Then, on Thursday, I'll pick you up at lunch and we'll go get manicures. My treat. Friday night I'll come over around eight. . . ."

Halfway through Julie's speech, Annie tuned her out and decided to go, because she suddenly realized she was sick of the silence after the boys went to bed each night, the size and the shape of it pressing her down like wet cement. The potential permanence of it tying her up in knots.

Julie tapped her hand. "How's that sound?"

"Fine. But I want it on record that I was forced into this."

For the next six months, she and Julie attended enough Meet Market Adventure events around the Seattle area to fill a scrapbook. The first one was a tour of a tattoo parlor, and Annie was nervous, until she realized that there were no men in the group who even remotely interested her. With that pressure off, she gamely volunteered to have a seahorse tattooed on her ankle, thinking, *Why not? I need to do something different.*

When she came to, she was lying on the floor with a dozen people staring down at her. Not three minutes into getting her seahorse, she had passed out and fallen off the tattoo parlor's table onto the floor. "Maybe you'll meet someone next weekend," Julie said when she'd dropped her off at home later, but Annie just waved her off, trying not to bump her ankle as she got out of the car.

For a few months, they attended events on a regular basis until Julie got engaged to Jonah and then their social lives came to a screeching halt. Planning the wedding consumed every minute of Julie's time. She picked the dresses, the cake, the band, and the flowers (yellow lady slippers mixed with bone white roses). She also designed the wedding invitation, which had the bride's and groom's handprints embossed inside, covered with a translucent fabric spritzed with perfume moments before each invitation was mailed. Annie went home three nights in a row reeking of Giorgio, thinking, *Thank God, this is almost over!*

Then the unthinkable happened.

Two weeks before the wedding, Julie phoned, crying. Every Sunday, the *Seattle Times* ran a Smooch Cam photograph taken at that week's Sonics basketball game with a caption above it that read: *We Caught You Smooching! If this is you at yesterday's game, call us to claim your prize.* Unfortunately, that week's photo showed Jonah locking lips with a blonde in a miniskirt.

"Can you believe this?" Julie wailed. "Two weeks before our wedding!"

"I know," Annie said, commiserating with her. "But two weeks before the wedding is better than two weeks after, right?"

Before long, they started attending Meet Market Adventure events again, and Annie tried dating, although the men she saw were either easily forgettable or sadly memorable. One took her to an all-you-can-eat buffet and then talked about his ex-wife for two hours as he filled and refilled his plate. Another took her to a WWF wrestling match and got thrown out when he tried to jump into the ring after the wrestler he'd been rooting for was knocked unconscious. Following that, she had dinner with a quiet, balding guy who seemed polite and thoughtful, but behind the wheel of a car, he was a madman, recklessly passing on the shoulder when traffic got backed up at a red light, shaking his fist at other drivers, and narrowly missing a collision in his haste to land the *perfect* parking spot.

Discouraged, Annie told Julie she was swearing off dating for life. Then, days later, someone she'd met through work asked her out for coffee, and she went. His name was Greg Atwood. He was divorced, had a daughter who lived with his ex-wife, and seemed blissfully normal. Annie cautiously enjoyed his company over coffee and a few lunches. Then he asked her out to dinner, and she agreed, but an hour before he was supposed to pick her up, her babysitter got sick, and it looked like she was going to have to cancel. When Jack and the boys walked in from an afternoon Sonics game, she was pacing in her kitchen, trying to decide what to do. Jack took one look at her dressy outfit and asked if she had a hot date.

"Not anymore," she said, flushing. "My babysitter's sick."

An uncomfortable silence fell. "Go ahead," Jack finally said, slipping off his jacket. "I'll stay with the boys."

Annie blinked in surprise. "Are you sure?"

"Go," he said, waving her off. "We'll order pizza and watch a movie."

The stylish restaurant was crowded when Annie and Greg arrived. Elegant background music was playing and almost every table was filled with well-dressed couples. Annie, who'd never been there before, found the place small, expensive, and airless.

The maître d' appeared. "Ah, Mr. Atwood. We've been expecting you. This way, please."

Annie followed him to their table with Greg behind her. When the maître d' pulled out her chair with a flourish, she sat, feeling like a fish out of water, wishing they'd gone for pizza and a walk on the beach.

"Anything to drink, madam?" the waiter asked.

"Yes, white wine please. Anything dry."

He nodded with an air of distant approval, then turned to Greg.

"Scotch and water, extra ice."

"Very good, sir."

Annie looked around the room, wishing she'd worn something dressier. Her hair was pulled back and she had on fake pearl earrings the boys had given her for Christmas, a bottle green blouse, and a black skirt that hugged her all the way to her knees. When she looked up, Greg was staring at her.

"Am I underdressed?" she asked.

"Not at all," he said enigmatically. "You look fantastic."

Annie reddened.

He reached across the table and covered her hand. "Tell me, how are things going with your separation?"

"Okay," she admitted, although she didn't feel like talking about it.

When the waiter returned, Greg ordered for both of them without asking what she would like. Annie frowned. Did she look incapable of ordering her own food? While they waited for their meals, he talked nonstop and she played with her earrings. He said he'd made a fantastic trade on some stock the day before, so he'd splurged and got an hour-long massage. In the next breath, he complained that he rarely got any time to himself, although he did manage to jog ten miles a week and almost never missed the two hundred daily sit-ups he felt were necessary to stay in such excellent physical shape.

Embarrassed, Annie looked at her plate. She couldn't remember the last time she'd done one sit-up. "How's your daughter doing?" she asked, hoping to change the subject.

"Fine. She's going to a music camp this summer."

"What kind of music is she interested in?" she asked, taking a sip of her wine.

"I'm not sure," he said, frowning. "Piano, I think."

By the time their meals arrived, Annie was sick of listening to Greg talk about the "wonder of me." Topping that off, as soon as they'd finished dinner, he ordered her a dessert she hated. When he finally signaled the waiter for the bill, she pushed back from the table, relieved to be leaving. She slid her feet back into her pumps and made her way across the room, wishing she'd worn more comfortable shoes.

Greg pushed the door open and stood to one side to let her pass. Outside, he took her elbow and steered her toward his Mercedes. "Why don't we go back to my place?"

Annie gently shook him off and slipped off her shoes again. "I've got a better idea. Why don't we walk along the beach instead?"

Arching his eyebrows, he agreed, although she could sense walking along the beach wasn't what he'd had in mind. Moments later, they were on the boardwalk with the lights from the harbor bouncing off the water. Greg stopped, took her face in his hands, and kissed her. It was a wonderful kiss, and as his mouth brushed against her neck, Annie was sure it had been years since anyone had kissed her like that. Eyes half closed, she opened her mouth to say something, but he held a finger to her lips and said, "Let's talk later," then pulled her into the dark shadows behind a row of trees that ran the length of the boardwalk.

Confused, Annie glanced back at the well-lit section of beach they'd been heading toward when suddenly one of Greg's hands was trailing down her back as the other began unbuttoning her blouse.

Startled, she tried to laugh it off. "Greg, I really don't think—"

"Good," he whispered, cutting her off. "Don't think. Just relax and leave it to me."

Ignoring her murmurs of protest, he reached down and ran a hand up her thigh.

Annie tried to pull away. "Don't."

Greg acted as if he hadn't heard her. Within seconds, he was tugging at her skirt, inching it up her hips, and then he was kissing her harder than before, his hands tightening on her arms. Annie wriggled out of his grasp, slammed both palms against his chest, and pushed away. Hard. "I said don't, damn it!"

He stepped back and ran both hands through his hair, breathing heavily. "Jesus, what kind of game are you playing, Annie? You know you want it as much as I do."

She stared at him, shaking her head. "No, Greg. I don't."

Giving her a disbelieving snort, he swiveled and walked toward the water.

She pulled down her skirt and rebuttoned her blouse, amazed that she'd misread him and hurt that he hadn't gone slower instead of pawing at her like a sixteen-year-old. By the time she was finished, her adrenaline had leveled off and she felt a little more composed. She picked up her shoes and stared at Greg's back, then turned and slowly began making her way up the beach toward the boardwalk.

"Where are you going?" he called after her.

"Home."

"I'll give you a ride," he said, sounding impatient.

Annie shook her head and kept going, not bothering to turn around.

She had to walk ten city blocks to get home, which wasn't bad until it started raining. Blinking back tears, she hurried along the darkened tree-lined streets, wondering at each glowing window she passed who lived there and whether their lives were as screwed up as hers seemed to be. Halfway home, her panty hose began giving way to gravity, sliding down her hips and pulling her panties along with them. Stopping at a Starbucks to use the bathroom, she yanked them off and threw them in the garbage before adjusting her skirt and buying a coffee to go.

By the time she trudged up the alley behind her house, she was exhausted. When she closed the gate, she was startled by a sudden burst of laughter coming from her open kitchen window.

Grabbing a plastic lawn chair, she set it against the house and climbed up to look inside, and what she saw stayed with her long after she climbed down. At the kitchen table, through a grainy window damp with rain, she watched her boys playing cards with their dad: Eric laughing so hard that his back shook and Luke looking thrilled as he laid down his cards.

Later that night, as Annie peeled off her wet clothes and threw them in the tub, she couldn't help thinking how much their lives had changed, how much she and Jack had changed. When they first got married, they used to sit across from each other at their tiny drop-leaf kitchen table, his knees touching hers as they shared sections of the morning paper. They were broke, but they were happy. The winter Luke was born, they couldn't even afford a movie, so Jack would turn up the stereo and they'd dance together outside on their cement patio, wearing parkas and mittens, the neighbors staring at them like they were crazy. One Christmas, she bought him a plaque that read: *After silence that which comes nearest to expressing the inexpressible is music—Aldous Huxley.* For years, their life had been like that. Friends. Lovers. Partners on a remarkable journey.

Then Eric got sick and everything started to change.

NINE

*A*nnie had just finished leaving a message on Julie's voice mail at work when Erna and Rudy wandered back into reception discussing the benefits of redecorating. "The minute I walked in here, I thought to myself 'autumn colors,'" Erna said. "Something warm and soothing. And what you need in reception," she said, opening her arms wide, "is a few comfortable couches instead of these awful plastic chairs."

Rudy nodded, rubbing his eyes. "There's not enough room for couches."

"Why?" Erna asked.

"Why?" he echoed, looking around.

She snapped her fingers. "You know what would be perfect? A sectional. There's a sale at Lipton's Furniture this week. Maybe you should see if they have any, but don't pick anything brown or gray. Look for something brighter, something in an orange or red tone."

Rudy belted his hands together over his stomach. "Would you help me pick one out?"

Erna gave him a coy smile. "Tell you what. I'll do that if you take me to the clinic for my flu shot when we're done."

Rudy agreed and they went back into his office to get his car keys. When they returned, Erna's purse dangled from the crook of her arm and Rudy was rubbing his eyes again.

"Are you serious?" he said, looking worried.

"Absolutely," Erna said. "Trust me, itchy eyes can be a sign of a minor infection like conjunctivitis but it's also one of the first symptoms of Reiter's syndrome, a condition that can lead to urinary problems or crippling arthritis."

Frowning, Rudy called to Annie, "Would you call my doctor and set up an appointment?"

"Give the boys a hug for me," Erna said, waving on her way out the door.

Annie stared after them, shaking her head in disbelief. Her mom's behavior didn't surprise her, but Rudy's did. A small smile played at her lips as she realized that they might be a good fit. After all, her mom was sixty-five, had been widowed for years, and was infinitely fascinated with the preventive maintenance of the human body, whereas Rudy was fifty-nine and single, and he made his living mastering the art of postmortem repair after all preventive maintenance had failed. Annie was still smiling when the phone rang.

"Kozak's Funeral Home."

"Did you call Julie yet?" Marina demanded.

"I left her a message."

After updating Marina on everything she'd witnessed between Rudy and their mom, Annie phoned her landlord to let him know that her dryer wasn't working. Then she wedged the phone between her ear and shoulder and called Jack, leaving a message on his voice mail, telling him that they needed to talk about Luke.

When a delivery from Imperial Caskets arrived, Annie unlocked the receiving door and snuck a cigarette as they unloaded, reading the ad once more, looking for clues: *Do you recognize this woman? . . . How did I lose the only woman I ever loved?. . . . The*

answer isn't straight, or simple. . . . We knew each other years ago . . .
She was the first woman I ever loved. . . .

Maybe it is Chris, she thought, remembering the night before.

After they'd sat down to eat, Chris did most of the talking while she took small bites of food, caught between a boozy haze and a confused emotional state about their friendship.

"I've learned a lot about myself over the last few years," he said. "Odd things I've never thought about before, like how I hate big cities, but love small towns, that I can be a little reclusive, that I've got a soft spot for animals."

"You and half my family," Annie quipped.

Chris sat back, laughing. "Isn't it strange how things worked out, though? Both of us with marriages that didn't last and now both of us living here in Eagan's Point again? Not that I'm complaining," he said quickly. "I'm pretty content with my life. I might not be sharing it with anyone right now, but I still like to believe there's someone special out there for me."

Annie nodded agreeably. *Of course there is,* she wanted to say, but she'd just finished her third glass of wine and fear of slurring kept her from opening her mouth.

"Life's too short not to be happy," he said, "so I think we owe it to ourselves to be honest about our feelings." He silently offered her more salad, but she waved him off. "And you know what? Now that I'm older, I realize we all have to take a few emotional risks to find the happiness we're looking for."

As he said this, he was looking right at her, making sure she was listening to him.

Annie smiled. She was.

She nodded as she poured yet *another* glass of wine, opting for more alcohol instead of food.

Dropping his gaze, Chris carried on. "One of the hardest

things I've ever had to do was end my marriage," he admitted. "But the worst part was realizing that I didn't love Deanna. My dad died a month after I told her the truth, so moving back to Eagan's Point was an easy decision to make. To this day, I honestly think burying myself with work at the shop saved me from sliding into some serious depression over it all."

Annie tilted her head, considering him with newfound respect for doing something to build a future for himself instead of moving through his days in a state of weary acceptance, the way she had over the last few years. Taking a halfhearted stab at her salad, she opened up and told him all about Eric getting sick years ago, about the fear she had lived with every day since, how she'd never admitted to anyone (until now) that Jack's leaving had knocked her flat. And how she often caught herself thinking about everything that had happened between them, wondering where they'd gone wrong. When she finished, she sighed. Her feelings were complicated and exhausting, and no pill was ever going to make anything right again.

"Well, if it's any consolation, I wasn't the best husband," Chris admitted.

Annie shook her head as if to say that couldn't be true.

He stopped eating and smiled at her. "God, it's nice to see you, Annie."

As a warm, melting sensation filled her, she put her fingers together and raised them to her lips, trying not to cry. It was so good to be home in Eagan's Point, and such a bonus to be able to spend time with Chris after so many years away.

"You know what?" he said. "I honestly think there's only one person who ever really understood me."

She lifted a brow.

He nodded, as if to say, *Yes, you.*

Annie stiffened in anticipation. Was he hinting that he felt something for her beyond their old friendship? Nervous, she shifted in her chair. She didn't want to talk about this right now. She needed time to think. Then something Marina often said came to mind.

Don't you ever do anything spontaneous?

Annie closed her eyes. It felt as if the room was spinning. When she looked again, she caught herself staring at Chris. There really was something steady and indestructible about him. Something safe. And he had such a great smile, with all that hair hanging so adorably in his eyes.

Don't you ever do anything spontaneous?

Dropping her napkin on the table, she pushed back her chair and stood on legs that felt like sticks of Jell-O. Straightening her shoulders, she leaned on the table for balance, trying to focus. It was crucial to get this right, to look sexy and sure of herself, even if that wasn't how she felt inside. *I need to find out if there's something more lurking underneath this friendship of ours. I need to check in on the physical attraction factor and see if there are any sparks.*

Frowning, Chris set down his fork. "Annie? You okay?"

She nodded, giving him what she hoped was a coy look. Then, before she could change her mind, she walked around the table and slid into his lap, accidentally on purpose leaning in close enough that her lips brushed his—trying hard to be whatever he wanted her to be. When she thought about it later, she would remember kissing him with gusto. She'd slid an arm around his neck and smiled, trying to look mysterious, half expecting him to kiss her back, wondering how she would feel when he did.

He didn't. Instead, a faint twitch of a smile came over his face as he gently cupped her chin. "Oh, Annie. You're wasted."

For a moment, time stood still, and she felt stupid, but that was quickly replaced by humiliation. She looked everywhere but at his face, finally settling on the tips of her shoes, dangling a few inches off the floor, more embarrassed than she'd been in years.

Chris slid an arm around her waist, pulling her close. "Look, Annie, this isn't the best time to talk," he said. "But I think we should, later, after you've had some sleep, okay?"

Annie looked out the window at the blackness that suddenly seemed so inviting. What kind of loser got drunk and hit on a friend she hadn't seen in years? She slid off his lap and brushed back her hair. "Sounds good," she managed, clearing her throat. "Let's talk tomorrow. Or next week. Better yet, maybe next year . . ." Her head hurt and her humiliation was rapidly beginning to overpower the mind-numbing effects of way too much wine. She walked to the door, hugging herself.

"Annie?" He waited until she turned around. "We will talk," he said, speaking slowly and precisely. "Just not right now."

Making every effort to leave with some semblance of dignity, she produced a lopsided smile, thankful that she lived only three blocks away.

As though reading her mind, he said, "You're not walking home alone." He held up a finger, asking her to wait, and grabbed a jacket. Giving her no room to argue, he followed her outside, taking her elbow to help her down the steps.

They walked side by side in silence, he with his hands in his pockets, and she with her chin tucked against her chest as she tried to navigate what suddenly seemed like an impossibly narrow sidewalk.

"I almost never drink," she said, hoping this would explain her behavior.

"I didn't think so."

Her eyes flickered to him. "I must've had half a bottle, huh?"

"At least, but who's counting?"

She looked down, playing with the frayed edges of her scarf. "Chris, things haven't been easy the last few years—"

He stopped, took both of her hands, and gently rested his forehead against hers. "Forget it," he said. "You're allowed. To get drunk. To have fun. It's been years since we've seen each other and I've missed you, too."

She ducked her head, too embarrassed to say more.

At her house, he helped her up the steps and she waved him away when he asked if she'd be okay. *This isn't so bad,* she'd rationalized after he left. *Because when I wake up tomorrow my head will feel like it's going to lift off and my eyes will be burning, but at least now I'm far better equipped to tell Marina where she can shove all her spontaneity.*

TEN

Chris Carby folded the *Peninsula Post* and tucked it into his recycling bin. He and Annie had known each other since they were kids. She had flattened him countless times playing floor hockey in third grade, taught him how to use a slingshot in fifth grade, and talked his parents into buying him contact lenses so he could throw out his Coke-bottle glasses in ninth. It was Annie who'd come to his defense when he was frog-marched out of high school after a bottle of vodka was found in the yearbook office. She later admitted that she and Julie Coyne had snuck it up there. He'd watched her grow from a pigtailed tetherball wizard into a young woman who left guys gaping as she shimmied across the dance floor at graduation, doing low, long hip circles to Tina Turner's "Private Dancer." They'd grown up fighting as kids, learned to like each other by eight, and become conspirators the year she turned twelve and learned she was adopted.

Annie ran away from home several times that year, begging him to lie if anyone came looking for her. He didn't feel good about it, but he couldn't say no, so when her dad called one night, he told him he didn't know where she was, even though he'd just finished making a thermos of Lipton Noodle Soup to take to her.

He found her huddled on a cot they had set up at the back of the corrugated tin storage shed behind Carby's Bait & Tackle. For a while, he covered for her, but when the police starting talking about organizing an official search, he threatened to turn her in if she didn't go home. She disappeared that night and he spent the next day pacing until she finally phoned her parents from a gas station on the outskirts of Seattle.

He had seen Annie outgrow sloppy overalls and move on to cropped tops with tight jeans, had watched her macramé a plant hanger for her mom's birthday, and had gone with her when she bought her dad a K-Tel Patty Stacker for Father's Day. They had skipped class together, gotten drunk on the beach, and painted an egg on the ceiling of his bedroom—something Annie said she'd always wanted to do. It was a huge sunny-side-up egg and he'd never had the heart to paint over it. In inch-high letters, in the middle of the yolk, she'd written something her dad had once told her: *Who we are begins with where we came from, but grows along-side those we share the journey with.* Chris's old bedroom was now his office, and whenever he stretched out on the couch in there, he'd stare up at Annie's egg and laugh, thinking she was still the most interesting woman he'd ever known.

When they were sixteen, their relationship ran into a small snag. Even now, Chris could remember all the details. Annie was wearing blue jean overalls with a red T-shirt, her blond hair piled up on her head. The yearbook office was hot because it had orig-inally been a storage closet with no ventilation, yet she insisted on keeping the door shut.

"Why have an office if it doesn't give you privacy?" she often said.

When he couldn't find her at lunch hour, he went up there looking for her, but the door was locked, so he knocked and waited. It finally opened a few inches and Annie peeked out, whispering, "I'm on the phone."

"You're always on the phone," he said, pushing against the door. "Open up."

"It's a private call," she said, blocking it with her foot.

"I'll wait."

She scowled. "Can't you come back later?"

He shook his head and checked a scab on his hand. "Nope."

The door closed. Then it opened and she pulled him in, putting a finger to her lips. He dropped into an old wing chair the janitor had given them and stared at the wall, waiting for her. She was sitting on a broken desk they'd been given, pushed up against the far wall, waving her hands in the air as she whispered into the phone. When she glanced over at him, he made a pistol with his finger, pointed at her, and pretended to shoot.

"You're dead for skipping class this morning," he whispered.

She mouthed, *Screw it*, and got tugged back into the phone conversation.

The reason they had a phone in the yearbook office at all was Annie's doing. Witnessing some mind-blowing manipulation, he'd watched her talk the janitor into letting them use a phone jack no one else ever used in the music room next door. It was hidden behind a filing cabinet, so Annie had drilled a hole through the baseboard and run the line through it, then brought in an old phone from home.

She hung up and sighed. "I need to ask you something, okay?"

"Ask away."

"Do you know how to kiss?"

He blinked a few times before giving a small, tentative nod. "Sure."

"Good, because I need some help."

She handed him a poster announcing Friday's school dance. "Here's the thing. Rob Simmons asked me to the dance, and, of course, I said yes—I told you I liked him, right? But this morning Julie told me she heard he's an amazing kisser, so if I don't get good at it by Friday, he's never going to ask me out again. . . ."

Her voice trailed off and Chris stared, holding his breath as he waited for what might follow. Looking embarrassed, Annie pressed her hands together between her knees. "So could you help me practice?"

He swallowed, then found taking a breath useful. "Sure."

"Thank you," she said, jumping up and almost hugging him off his feet.

Acting as nonchalant as possible, he shrugged. How tough could it be? After all, he'd seen it done in the movies. But because Annie had caught him off guard, he didn't have time to think or plan, and he didn't consider that this might make things awkward between them later. He was just nervous about getting it right.

In the end, it happened fast. Too fast for him to worry about faking it.

Annie shook out her arms. "You ready?"

Another nod.

"Okay, I'm gonna kiss you on the mouth, but just a little bit."

She did, but he didn't, missing the mark on how fast these things seemed to happen.

Annie frowned. "Okay. Good. Uh . . . now this time you kiss me back, okay?"

Looking as serious as possible, he tried again, and this time they both hit the mark. He kissed her and she kissed back, and when they pulled away, she didn't frown or smile, but he was sure he saw her face fall with disappointment. Chris gazed at her, worried. Then he took her by the arm, pulled her to him, and kissed her again, only slower this time, and when they finished, Annie raised her hands in the air between them like she wasn't sure where they should go. She stuck them in the front pockets of her overalls, looking at her feet.

"What's wrong?" he asked.

She took a while to answer. "Nothing. I just think maybe I shouldn't be so worried about it, you know? I mean, if Rob wants an expert kisser, he'll have to find someone who has *time* to practice, 'cause who has that kind of time?"

The way she said it told him that it hadn't occurred to her until then that kissing each other might change things between them. His emotions were all mixed up too, and it worried him that this might damage their friendship.

After that, Annie acted awkward around him for a while, and a black emptiness came over him that he worked hard to hide. Annie wasn't like other girls he knew; she didn't spend hours in front of a mirror every morning, and she didn't giggle or shake her behind when she walked past a group of guys. As his mother often said, they were like two peas in a pod. They shared matching slingshots, a love of kayaking, and a fascination with every gadget ever advertised on TV. They also worked together on the school yearbook (she as editor, he as photographer), and because of her, school was actually bearable. More than anything, he didn't want to lose what they had.

During dinner a few weeks later, his dad asked if everything was okay, and he shrugged and said yes. Then, when his mom got up to clear the table, his dad leaned over and whispered, "Timing is everything," obviously thinking he was having girl trouble.

After the kissing incident, Annie began to spend more time with Julie Coyne, and Chris's mom started getting on his back. "I'm worried about you, Chris. You spend too much time alone," she complained. "Why aren't you dating? You should be going out instead of always hanging around at your father's shop." And as she pushed, he silently suffered, unable to quell the growing realization that he was disappointing her.

Two months before they graduated from high school, after

weeks of incessant pestering from his mom about his lack of a social life, Chris finally worked up enough courage to ask Annie on
a date, hoping to kill his illogical paranoia about girls.

The worst thing she can do is say no, he reminded himself as he
climbed out of his dad's car that fateful night. He was just outside
town at a beach party at an inlet, reserved by unspoken consent
for teenagers who wanted a bonfire and somewhere to party.
Within minutes, he saw Annie on the far side of the fire, and as he
worked his way over to her, he took a few chugs of beer to build
up his nerve.

She grinned when she saw him. "Hey, nice to see you!"

"I needed to get out," he said, shrugging.

Julie walked by and gleefully hip-checked him, sloshing half
of her drink onto the ground. "This is a first. Chris Carby at the
inlet. What'd you bring to drink?" As usual, she was working every
corner of the party, and when he flushed but didn't answer, she lost
interest and left, jiving to the music blaring in the background.

Chris stared into the fire, wondering how he was supposed to
do this without making a fool of himself. The odds weren't in his
favor. After all, he wasn't the kind of guy girls typically dated. He
was the kind who drove everyone home when they'd had too
much to drink. He heard the hiss of a beer can pull tab somewhere behind him and then a burst of laughter from two girls sitting on the hood of someone's car.

Annie gave him a nudge. "You okay?"

"I'm fine," he managed. "It's just . . ."

"Just what?"

He took another swig of beer. Then, trying to sound casual,
he said, "I was, uh . . . I was wondering if I could take you to a
movie next weekend?"

It suddenly seemed stone quiet standing there watching Annie
bring her hands together and blow through them. He couldn't

speak, he couldn't swallow, and he was sure if she didn't say something fast, he'd recant and tell her he was only joking. After what seemed like an eternity, her expression softened and she said, "Only if I get to pick the movie." His relief was so huge that he didn't know what to do with it, so he took another swig of beer, trying to act nonchalant. Then Julie came back, interrupting them, so he excused himself and slipped away to sit on a rock in the dark, wondering what he was supposed to do next.

Their first official date was quickly followed by three more; they went roller-skating and bowling and took in another movie. But weeks later, when Annie gently suggested that they just be friends, he assured her this was fine. Within days, they had slipped back into the same easy routine they'd known before, where she would borrow one of his sweatshirts and he'd pretend to be mad, when really he was secretly pleased, relieved things were back to normal.

Heaving a sigh, Chris stared at his hands. When Annie had left his house the night before, she'd looked defeated. Gone was the confident, I-can-do-it-myself Annie he'd always known, replaced by someone who'd come home to lick her wounds, someone beaten down by life. He wanted to discuss what had happened between them, but now that he was leaving Thursday to guide a three-week salmon-fishing charter up the Canadian coast, it looked as though it would have to wait until he returned.

ELEVEN

Annie was marveling at the lunch Sawyer had packed for her when Jack returned her call.

"I got your message," he said. "Is this a bad time?"

"No, it's fine," she said, pleased he'd called back while she was at work because she didn't want the boys to overhear them. "I need to talk to you about a conversation Luke and I had earlier today."

"Okay, but first, have you seen the *Peninsula Post*? You're on the front page—"

"I know," she said, flushing. "I've seen it."

Pause. "So who's the guy?"

"I don't know. Marina called the number, but all she got was electronic voice mail. It's probably someone's idea of a joke."

"Pretty ballsy joke. Have the boys seen it?"

"Not yet," she said, reaching for her coffee. "They were too busy circling each other this morning after their weekend of hand-to-hand combat."

That got Jack's attention. "What happened?"

"Luke took a pair of hair clippers and shaved Eric's head."

"What?"

"He shaved Eric bald."

"And Eric agreed?"

"Only because Luke said he'd shave his too, but then he changed his mind."

"Unbelievable," Jack said.

Sighing, Annie tucked her hair behind her ears. "Anyhow, that's not why I called. Luke skipped school again today and I had to get my mom to cover for me at work so I could go out and track him down. I finally found him down at the Docks with Montana. He told me he hates it here. He said he wants to live with you."

Jack cleared his throat. "With me?"

Annie heard hope in his voice and sensed a softening that worried her. "Uh-huh," she said. "I told him it was his choice but that you'd have to agree, knowing, of course, that you wouldn't. So . . . I wanted to ask if you'd talk to him and explain how crappy that would be, him and Eric living in different homes." She knew Jack well enough to know this would bother him, the idea of the boys being split up. She waited for him to say, *Absolutely*, but he didn't say anything.

"Jack?"

"Yeah, I'm here."

"I'm worried about Luke. He seems mad at the world these days."

"He's thirteen, Annie."

"He's good at it."

More silence.

"Could you talk to him about this, Jack? He's so withdrawn these days I don't know what's going on with him anymore, and he almost never talks—"

"He talks to me."

Annie closed her eyes. This was no surprise but that didn't mean it didn't hurt. "Great, then share with me. What's going on in his life? Does he have a girlfriend? Is he having sex already? Drinking? Trying drugs?"

"Christ, Annie," Jack said.

Pushing out of her chair, she began pacing. "Well, how would you feel in my shoes? My son just told me he'd rather live with you, and I'm now threatening him with public humiliation in front of his peers just to keep him in school."

Jack was quiet for a long time. Annie heard him shift the receiver to his other hand, and when he started talking, his voice was softer than before. "Lately, whenever he's here, he seems fine. He's curious about the work I do at the station. He's been asking me about certain artists, how they write their song lyrics, stuff like that. And I know he might be skipping a lot these days, but he's keen about a project his class is working on, asking me tons of questions about family, our relatives, his heritage, things like that."

Annie listened, wanting to know, not wanting to know, torn between resentment and envy when it came to how different Luke was with his dad.

"That's good," she finally said.

"And just so you know," Jack added, "Harrison's been great with him since that stealing incident. He's called Luke a few times to see how he's doing."

"I know. Marina mentioned it the other day. Luke thinks he walks on water." Annie hesitated. "Anyhow, when you get the chance . . ."

"Sure," Jack said. "I'll talk to him."

Annie's life could easily be summed up in three stages: Life Before Jack, Life with Jack, and Life After Jack. Before she met him, she knew exactly where she was going, how she was getting there, and approximately how long it would take. During the week, she brought a bagged lunch to university each day, ate Chinese take-out with Julie on Fridays, did her laundry every Sunday morning, and had a moderately busy social life. Then Jack came along and turned everything upside down.

How they met was a story that had been told and retold at weddings, funerals, and reunions when they were still together. Jack would run his hands through his hair as he described how he'd spent countless, eye-popping hours teaching Annie how to drive long after everyone else had given up on her, and she would explain how they fell in love without ever intending to.

"Trust me," he'd say. "Romancing Annie was the last thing on my mind when she was behind the wheel of a car."

"Because I was more challenging than his average student," she'd add.

"More challenging than *any* student."

"I took a few more lessons than the average person does."

"Loads more," he agreed.

Although Annie had always been a tireless perfectionist—restless, unable to relax, and expecting more from herself than she ever seemed able to deliver—by the time she was twenty-two, her inability to pass a simple driver's exam had become the bane of her existence. As a passenger, she would often slam her foot down on an invisible brake, cringe if the car rolled through a stop sign, or lean against the passenger door if she felt the car was too close to the center line. She knew every sign, signal, and safe-driving practice in the book, often blurting them out before she could catch herself. "Hidden intersection ahead," she'd say, flapping a hand in the air, or "Watch out! This lane's for buses only." Statistically, she knew left turns were more dangerous than right because of oncoming traffic, how to approach traffic circles, and who had the right-of-way. She could tell you how to handle a skid if you lost a tire, what to do if your engine flooded, and how to drive in dangerous conditions such as ice, sleet, snow, or rain. But when it came to the practical part, the actual driving of a car, she had issues.

The first time Annie failed a road test she was sixteen. Ten minutes into it, the examiner asked her to pull over, hugged his clipboard to his chest, and told her to come back when she could control her hyperventilating. A year later she tried again and almost made it through the test before swerving to miss a pop can, bouncing onto the sidewalk, and crashing into a wrought-iron fence. The summer she turned eighteen, she finished the road test, but when the examiner asked her to parallel park, she backed into the side of another car, ripping off a side mirror. She didn't try again until she was twenty-two and only then because her boyfriend, Peter, had paid for the lessons as a birthday gift.

Peter was tall, with long legs, a quiet disposition and a penchant for wearing black turtleneck sweaters. Although he almost always had a drink in his hand—a beer after class, a martini before dinner, a vodka and tonic in the evening—he was forever a gentleman. Just seeing him waiting for her at the end of each day brought a smile to Annie's lips.

"A bit quiet, isn't he?" Julie whispered one night when they were out.

But Annie shrugged and said, "I prefer brains over brawn."

Peter almost always agreed to do whatever she wanted. If she felt like bowling, they went bowling. If she wanted to go to a movie, she also picked which one they saw. "What should we do tonight?" she'd ask, and he'd say, "Doesn't matter to me" or "I'm easy." He told her he was happy being with her no matter what they did, so their social schedule (or lack of one if Annie was feeling antisocial) fell directly into her lap. Peter was dependable and laid-back, and Annie felt safe with him.

They were at a friend's wedding one weekend when she

asked him if he could get her a vodka and orange juice. When he brought back vodka and 7-Up by mistake, she pushed it to one side. "I *said* vodka and orange."

"Sorry. I'll go back."

"Skip it. I have a headache anyhow and I'm freezing cold. Why don't you just get the car and we'll go?"

Peter shrugged into his coat. "Okay. Give me a few minutes and I'll warm it up first."

"Great," she said, distracted.

As soon as he left, Julie slid into the chair next to Annie, almost spilling her drink. "Why do you talk down to him like that?"

Annie considered for a moment. "I don't."

"Yes, you do, and you haven't the slightest idea how bitchy you sound when you do."

"I'm tired, that's all."

Julie leaned in close, slurring against her ear, "We've known each other for years, so let's be honest, okay? First, I love you, but if you talked to me like that, I'd have to paste you. And second, doesn't it make you nuts that he's got no backbone?"

Annie took the drink Julie was waving around and set it on the table. "You're drunk."

"Uh-huh, but if you told him to shave his head, he'd do it. How much fun izzat?"

"He's dependable," Annie said.

"So's my Volvo. Doesn't mean I'll ever stop shopping for a Corvette."

"You just don't know him," Annie said, building a pyramid with empty drink cups.

"Who wants to?" Julie said, hiccupping.

Annie lifted her chin a notch. "We're so close, you can't imagine."

"Sure you are." Julie smiled at some joke Annie didn't get.

Then she got up and weaved her way out onto the dance floor, waving at someone.

Annie guzzled the drink Peter had brought her earlier, and when he came back, she pulled him down into the chair next to her before she could change her mind.

"There's something I need to tell you," she said.

"What's that?"

She looked at her shoes. "I'm terrified of driving, so that's why I don't have my license."

"Really?" he said, looking surprised.

"Really. Whenever I get behind the wheel of a car, I feel sick to my stomach and before I know it, my foot hits the gas pedal instead of the brake, and then I get this ticlike twitch behind one of my eyes. My brain knows what to do, but my arms start moving in slow motion or else they jerk around like they're spastic."

She stopped and waited for him to say how crazy this sounded, but his eyes just softened and he said, "We'll have to get you fixed up then."

"There's no need," she assured him. "You're a good driver and I'm a happy passenger, so why bother?" Then she'd kissed him just a tad longer than was polite in front of all those people, believing the issue was settled.

A month later, Peter gave her a gift certificate for driving lessons with Deluca's Driver Training in Chicago. Amazed he hadn't discussed it with her first, Annie flipped through the brochure, murmuring her thanks even though she was secretly annoyed.

Deluca's Driver Training—Using a new approach to an old practice, our students learn how to drive using simulators and skid-controlled test cars before ever getting behind the wheel of a regular car. We guarantee your success. After ten weeks in our program, if you don't pass your driver's exam, we'll repeat your training at no cost. Try us. You won't be disappointed.

Feeling obligated, she made an appointment the next day and Peter dropped her off for her first lesson the following Saturday. She was fidgeting in the waiting room at Deluca's when an older woman called her name.

"I'm Carol," she said, ushering Annie into an office. "Good to have you here." She handed Annie some paperwork to fill out and asked her to sit down.

Annie cleared her throat. "I was wondering, could I get a patient instructor? Not that all of your instructors aren't patient. It's just that I've taken lessons before, but they were a bust, and I think they would've gone much better if I'd had someone with a little more patience, someone who actually *talked* to me, maybe someone with a personality, or a sense of humor, because I get so nervous."

Carol pulled a folder out of her desk and flipped it open. "No problem. We'll set you up with one of our senior instructors."

Relieved, Annie slid back into her chair. *I don't care if I get an old geezer in a wheelchair with a pocket protector, just as long as he doesn't yell at me or heave those long, slow sighs that tell me I'm not doing it right.*

Three weeks later, she was back in Carol's office, feeling as disillusioned as the two instructors who'd taken turns teaching her how to drive.

Carol squeezed her shoulder on the way into the office. "I hear we've been having some trouble," she said, perching on the side of her desk.

Annie nodded but didn't say anything.

"Don't worry. This time I have the perfect instructor for you."

"I hope so, because if this one doesn't work, I'm buying a life-long bus pass."

Carol explained that Mr. Hillman was an unorthodox instructor, but that he'd been working for Deluca's part-time for two years and had helped some of their most frustrated customers get their licenses.

Annie's first session was set up for the next day and she arrived five minutes late. She was expecting someone older, some-one with a handlebar mustache or sweat stains under his arms, not the man she saw outside, backlit by the open doors of Deluca's. He was in his late twenties, filled out his jeans like a Calvin Klein poster boy, and had a George Clooney smile to go with it. She tried hard not to stare and failed miserably. There were two other people outside with him: a short, balding man and a middle-aged woman with a bad perm. Annie squinted at them as they walked in small, tight circles on wooden stilts. Clearly this wasn't where she was supposed to be. She swiveled to leave.

"Excuse me? Can I help you?"

"Sorry," she said, glancing back over her shoulder. "I think I'm in the wrong place."

He looked at his clipboard. "Are you . . . Annie Fischer?"

"Uh . . . yes."

"Then you're exactly where you should be," he said. "I'm Jack. Nice to meet you."

"You too," she managed.

He tilted his head and gave her a crooked, boyish smile that hit her right behind the knees. "So I hear you've put everyone else through the ringer and now it's my turn?"

Annie's shoulders fell. "You're my instructor?"

"Jack Hillman, at your service."

"And you're going to teach me how to drive."

Jack grinned. "That's what driving instructors do."

She pointed outside to the man and woman who were taking turns stepping up onto a long wooden box with their stilts and then back down again. "If you're a driving instructor, what are they doing?"

"We'll get to that." He gently took her elbow and guided her out into the warm morning sun. "Annie, I'd like you to meet Della Clark and Sol McNabb."

"Hello," Della said.

"Nice to meet you," echoed Sol.

Annie gave them a nervous smile. "Hi."

Jack glanced at his watch. "How about if you two spend another five minutes on those stairs and then we'll move you over into the simulators?"

Sol's eyes lit up. "Sounds great."

Jack turned to her. "Annie, you can come with me and we'll go over some questions and get you set up too."

Ann blinked at him. "For what?"

"For everything you'll need to learn to drive."

Skeptical, she followed him to a small table outside and slid into the chair across from him, prepared to explain her way out of this, only to look up and find herself face-to-face with that smile again—the same one she would tell Julie about later that night. "When he looks at me like that, I have trouble putting one foot in front of the other."

"Let's get started," Jack said. "Do you play tennis, squash, or racquetball?"

Annie frowned. "What's that got to do with driving?"

"Just yes or no, please."

"No. I don't play tennis, squash, or racquetball."

"Ever play video games?"

"Never."

He made three quick check marks on his clipboard. "Do you dance?"

"Pardon me?"

"You know, ballet, tap, jazz. Do you dance, and if so, are you any good at it?"

Annie pushed away from the table, looking slightly put out. "Are you *hitting* on me?"

"No, I'm not," he said matter-of-factly. "Think we can move along here?"

Embarrassed, she dropped her eyes. "Sure."

"Are you a perfectionist or easygoing?"

"I can be *a bit* of a perfectionist," she said, shrugging.

"Either you are or you aren't."

She glared at him. "Okay. Let's see. . . . I'm anal about my panties being folded before they go in the drawer. I hate it when someone leaves a newspaper lying in pieces on the floor, and I sleep nude, even on the coldest winter nights, because it lets your skin breathe. You decide."

Jack wrote this down, murmuring, "Anal at times . . . Has folding issues . . . Likes to sleep uninhibited. Great. Do you skate or Rollerblade?"

"Neither."

"Play an instrument?"

She gave him a curt no, telling herself that as soon as they were done, she was marching straight into Carol's office and demanding her money back. This guy was beyond unorthodox. He was borderline offensive.

"Fears or phobias?"

Annie gave him a tight stare, and when she answered, he did too, saying, "Driving," at the same time, with a grin on his face.

"Okay. Let's get you set up," he said, pushing back from the table.

Realizing, too late, exactly what he meant, Annie's eyes widened as he picked out a pair of stilts from a pile lying on the ground, each with footrests set a little higher up off the ground than the last pair.

"One more thing," Jack said. "Are you competitive?"

She gave him a baleful stare. "I can be. Why?"

"Good. Then here's the deal. Follow my instructions for the next ten weeks, give everything I suggest a good, solid try, and if you don't pass your road test at the end of it all, I'll buy you dinner for two at the restaurant of your choice in Chicago."

Annie smiled, the idea of beating him suddenly so appealing she forgot she really did want her license. He held up a pair of stilts and she climbed on, committing herself to at least one lesson, hands clenched around each stilt with a look of fierce determination on her face.

Her first lesson quickly led to a second, which took her to a third, and as each one progressed, she noticed an undercurrent of tension between them that wasn't her imagination. There was a constant tug and pull when she and Jack sparred that was impossible to ignore, and although his boyish charm seemed to work overtime with everyone, she couldn't help but notice the way his eyes lit up whenever she came through the door. In each session, her emotions would swing from heart-pounding elation when he smiled at her to raging frustration if he corrected her. She would finish her lesson flushed or distracted, complaining to Peter all the way home. How Jack was flaky, that he had no idea how hard this was for her, how she hated it when he used something she'd done as an example for the others.

"Do you want to quit?" Peter asked one day, and she rolled her eyes and said of course not—she was no quitter.

Then, during one of her rants halfway through the ten-week program, Peter said something that pulled her up short. "Just think. Only five more lessons and you won't have to deal with him again."

It was then, as she sat absolutely still in the passenger seat next to Peter, that it hit her. She was unavoidably and unbelievably attracted to Jack.

Peter put a hand on her arm. "Are you okay?"

"Yes," Annie said, "I'm fine."

But she was thinking about Jack. How she flushed with pleasure whenever he teased her, and how much she looked forward to seeing him each week. "It's hard acting normal when Peter picks me up," Annie complained to Julie later that night.

"My heart bleeds for you," Julie said.

"What am I going to do?"

"About what?"

"About Peter."

"Upgrade," Julie said, shrugging. "You're attracted to a drop-dead-gorgeous George Clooney look-alike you see twice a week, and the last time I checked, you weren't married. Where's the dilemma?"

After the next lesson, with Annie finishing her turn in the skid-controlled test car without knocking down any pylons, she ran over to Jack, grinning. "Hey, hotshot, did you see that? I didn't knock down one pylon. I missed the cardboard guy on the bench *and* the fake kid at the crosswalk!"

Jack was sitting on a chair with his muscled arms resting on his thighs. "Not bad," he agreed. "Too bad you clipped the woman with the stroller, though."

Near the end of her lessons, Annie asked Jack to explain the list of questions he'd asked her at the beginning. Although he'd never done any formal research and his theory was homegrown from intuition, his logic was impressive.

"Have you ever watched someone trying to dance when they haven't got an ounce of rhythm? It's painful to watch but it doesn't mean they can't learn. I was working at a country bar one night with the radio station I'm doing my internship with when I saw this couple struggling out on the dance floor. The woman obviously couldn't dance if her life depended on it, so the guy had her stand on his feet like grandparents do with grandkids at weddings, right? Then he got some duct tape from behind the bar and taped her hands and feet to his.

"It was amazing," Jack said, shaking his head. "They spent half an hour dancing like that, and before long, she became an extension of his limbs. He was sweating like crazy as he went through the paces over and over again—encouraging her every step of the way—and as he did, I watched her confidence lift inch by inch. When he finally took off the tape . . ."

"She knew how to drive?" Annie asked.

Jack gave her a slow smile. "No," he said. "They danced an almost perfect two-step like partners in crime, like they *belonged* together. And as she danced, her face lit up, and before I knew it, I was smiling too, because what he'd done made sense. Then I got thinking about this part-time job I'd taken with Deluca's, how maybe I could use some of his logic. You see, to some people, dancing or playing tennis or walking on stilts or driving a car are no-brainers. Performing the task is a simple extension of their limbs. But to others, it's a form of physical dyslexia that can be almost debilitating."

Annie gave him a slightly amazed smile, but she wasn't really paying attention. Instead, her eyes were fixed on his mouth and her mind had wandered off to some imaginary place where Jack was slow dancing with her duct-taped to his feet.

Jack cleared his throat. "All this guy did was get her to try something new, something outside of her normal comfort zones."

"And she liked it?" Annie asked, propping her chin on one hand.

"She loved it," Jack assured her.

TWELVE

*I*t was almost five before Annie finished cataloging the shipment of caskets and urns that had arrived that afternoon. She would've been done earlier, but her mom phoned when she got home and saw the front page of the *Peninsula Post*.

"Why didn't you tell me about this when I saw you earlier today?" Erna said. "Did you think it'd upset me or were you worried I'd call the phone number myself?"

"Both," Annie lied.

"Well, I did call, and I got one of those computer voices asking me to leave a message, but I didn't because I thought I'd talk to you first."

Annie begged off, asking if they could talk about it when she got home, and Erna agreed, although she said she was sure Rudy wouldn't mind if they talked now.

Later, when Annie finally pulled into her driveway, she was relieved to put this day behind her. As usual, her mom had picked the boys up after school and driven them home, giving them an hour alone without supervision, something Annie had reluctantly agreed to when she took the job at Kozak's. Today, Eric was practicing jump shots against the basketball hoop on their garage. She watched him sink a shot, catch the ball on its way down, and dribble a few figure eights low between his legs without looking up.

"How were tryouts?" she asked, getting out of the car.

"Won't know for two weeks," he said.

"Well, make sure you call me at work when you do," she said, emptying the mailbox on her way inside. She kicked off her shoes at the back door. Luke was stretched out on the couch in the living room, watching TV. "Hey, pal, how was the rest of your day?"

He shrugged, murmuring something unintelligible.

Flipping through the mail, Annie found the usual bills, along with a monthly statement from an outpatient clinic in Seattle listing all the invoices from Eric's treatments over the last few years, less the paltry payment she and Jack were able to make each month. As usual, just looking at it depressed her, so she dropped everything on top of the microwave and went to change.

It was ten thirty before she locked the house and went upstairs for the night. Eric was asleep, mouth open and arms thrown over his head, and Luke was on his stomach, with one arm draped over Montana, who was stretched out on the bed next to him. When Annie leaned down, Montana's tail thumped against the blankets.

"Night, you old bear," she whispered, patting her head.

She pulled the door half shut behind her, then opened the window at the end of the hallway and stuck her head outside, breathing in the cool night air. She propped open the frame with a wooden spoon she kept on the windowsill and crawled out onto a flat six-foot section of roof wedged between her bedroom window on one side and the boys' on the other. Once she was settled, she reached into her sweater pocket for her cigarettes and something tapped her on the back. Startled, she swiveled around and saw Luke standing at the window.

"Mom? What are you doing?"

At first she hesitated, mouth moving but nothing coming out. Then she slowly smiled and reached for his hand. "Wanna join me?"

He looked at her like she was crazy. "You serious?"

"Sure. Come on out."

Taking her hand, he hoisted himself up onto the windowsill and looked around outside. "What are you doing out here?" he asked again.

"Getting some air."

Annie pulled a granola bar out of her other pocket and offered him half. He took it, but he seemed a little nervous, probably because he was trying to act like the conversation they'd had earlier was no big deal.

The porch light went on in Mr. Kale's yard across the back alley.

Annie pointed and said, "Watch this."

Mr. Kale's back door opened and his basset hound waddled outside. Taking his time, the dog made his way down the steps and slowly circled the yard before doing his business in the middle of the grass. When he was through, he lifted his head and let loose with a low, long howl that made Luke's eyes go wide.

"Now watch this," Annie said, motioning to the house next door to Mr. Kale's.

Seconds later, the door flew open and Libby Johnson stepped out onto her deck wearing a green housecoat with pink curlers in her hair. "Shut that bloody dog up!" she yelled, banging a spoon against a metal pot.

Mr. Kale shook his fist at her. "Go suck an egg, Libby! He's doing his constitutional."

Annie and Luke could see Libby's indignant glare from under the porch light. Dropping the pot, she pulled her shoulders back and yanked open her housecoat. "How's this for a constitutional then, you old fool? Not any more pleasant than me listening to that thing howl every night, is it?"

Looking disgusted, Mr. Kale picked up his basset hound, marched inside, and slammed the door, with Libby following suit seconds later.

"They do this almost every night," Annie said, laughing.

Luke's eyebrows shot up. "And you come out here to watch them?"

"No. I come out here to take stock. They just happen to be part of the scenery."

He thought about this. "What's 'taking stock'?"

"Let me see," she said, looking up at the sky. "I guess it means . . . taking a look at where you're at with your life, weighing if you're happy or if there's something you'd like to change."

"And you come out here every night?"

"No, just now and then, when I have a bad day."

He shot her a sideways look. "Like today?"

Thinking about their talk on the beach earlier, she said, "Yes, like today."

He wrapped his arms around his knees and they sat in silence for a while, Annie too pleased that he was out there with her to break the mood, and Luke lost in his thoughts. When they finally did climb back through the open window, Montana was waiting for them, looking as confused as Luke had earlier.

"Hey, girl, it's okay," Luke said, nudging her back into his room.

Annie closed the window and followed them. "I'm going out for a paddle early tomorrow morning," she whispered, leaning against the door, "so if you wake up and I'm not back yet, keep an eye on Eric, okay?"

"Yeah, whatever," Luke said, rolling over on his side.

"And no locking him in a closet," she said, turning to leave. "Or duct-taping him to a kitchen chair. Or talking him into eating Montana's Milk-Bones . . ."

Not bothering to turn over, Luke said, "Okay. Okay. I get it."

Annie was out on the water earlier than usual the next morning, pushing hard to work the tension out of her shoulders from the day before. Five minutes after she left shore, she turned the kayak around and pointed it out into the bay. Then she closed her eyes and began paddling again, only slower this time, with a gentle rhythm. Some people meditated or did yoga before they started their days. Others jogged. She paddled with her eyes closed. Her dad had taught her years ago how to breathe in the calm silence of the water as a fresh day rose up around you, letting it seep into your mind and soothe you. There was no traffic out here. No stop signs or one-way streets or parking issues. No worrying about Eric or Luke or what the future might have in store. For a few minutes each morning, it was just her and the wonder of the water.

"Why do you do this?" Annie had asked her dad years ago.

"It helps me prepare for whatever the day might bring."

"Does it make you tougher?"

"No. It makes me more tolerant."

She was about to ask what he meant, but he closed his eyes and looked like he was in such a good place she didn't want to interrupt him. Not understanding bothered her, though, enough that she looked it up in the dictionary later, a habit when something confused her. *Tolerant: to have patience with or put up with.*

I get it, Annie thought. *He's talking about Mom.*

This was twelve-year-old logic formed from observations and selective eavesdropping. Like how they always went for a Sunday drive after church, she and Marina in the backseat, trying to get comfortable in their dress clothes, and her parents in the front. Most Sundays they followed the shoreline, and Annie would lean her face against the window and become lulled into a dreamlike state as cars and houses and trees whizzed by in a steady blur. But some Sundays this wasn't possible. Some Sundays tension filled the air like thick smog and she wanted to crank open her window and take in some fresh air.

On these Sundays her dad looked sick, with dark circles under his eyes and day-old stubble on his face that made him look older than usual. Her mom would lift her back against the seat, unapproachable and unsympathetic, and if he gently suggested that they cut the drive short and head home, Erna would stare out the window with a determined jut to her chin, saying, "No, this can be your penance" or "Just because you went carousing last night, don't expect the girls and me to change our plans today."

Marina was usually busy practicing her autoharp (a zitherlike electronic harp that drove Annie crazy with its off-key screeching), so Annie would slump down in the backseat and search the dictionary for a higher understanding of the words that worried her. *Penance: an act of punishment for doing wrong.* Frowning, she moved on, looking for *carousing* even though she wasn't sure how to spell it, and then, when she did, certain she must have heard wrong after she read what it meant. *Carouse: to participate in a lively, noisy, drinking party.*

She wanted to inch forward, tap her mom on the shoulder, and say, *He was working late. What's so bad about that?* And yet she could sense from what wasn't being said in the front seat that her input wouldn't be appreciated. In fact, she somehow knew if she said anything at all, she'd be in trouble for listening to their conversation when she should've been drowning in Marina's autoharp music.

Annie turned her kayak around and headed back to shore, thinking about her parents' marriage and how it had managed to survive when hers hadn't. Over the years, she had seen them fight, but she had also seen their love for each other win out in the end every time. They could be arguing one minute and swaying to the music with their arms around each other the next. One night her dad was working late and her mom was chopping pecans with pie plates spread out all over the kitchen counter.

Annie flipped her textbook shut, got up from the table, and said good night.

There was an angry tilt to her mom's head and her face was flushed as the knife bounced up and down on the cutting board. "Good night," Erna said, a piece of dark hair falling from behind her ear across her face.

Her dad came home minutes later. Annie heard his car pull into the driveway. Then the back door opened and there was a loud thump when he dropped his briefcase on the floor. She heard their voices raised in anger, muffled but distinguishable, followed by long pauses and soft murmuring. Slipping out of her bedroom, she peeked around the corner and saw her mom point a rolling pin at him, demanding to know why he was so late.

Ignoring her, Annie's dad placed a finger on her mom's lips, whispering with great sincerity, "How can you look this beautiful with flour all over your face?" Her mom looked like she was trying hard not to soften, keeping her eyes fixed on the fridge, but when he gently pulled her close, she gave up. They leaned into each other and soon they were dancing with their eyes closed, him humming along to Frank Sinatra's "Day by Day" on the radio, and her pressing her cheek against his.

That was her parents. Arguing one minute and slow dancing the next. Today, whenever Annie talked about him, her mom would shake her head and say, "Yes, your dad could walk into any room and fill it up without ever saying a word. He made friends with every waitress, cashier and businessman within a hundred miles of here. He was a charmer, no doubt about it. I don't think I ever met anyone who didn't enjoy spending time with that man." She said it with pride in her voice, something that never failed to amaze Annie, something she'd come to admire. How did you spend thirty years with someone and still feel like that?

THIRTEEN

etermined to get to work on time, Annie dropped the boys off at school five minutes earlier than usual. At Kozak's, she had just put her purse under her desk and changed the radio station when Rudy stuck his head around the corner to tell her Marina was on line one. Her sister sounded excited.

"The editor of the *Peninsula Post* just called me back about yesterday's ad."

Annie's eyebrows shot up. "And?"

"He said the paper can't release the name of who ran it for another month."

Thinking she'd heard her wrong, Annie paused. "Another month?"

"Right. But this is the part you really aren't going to believe," Marina said. "Annie, apparently there are a total of five ads, each one slightly different than the last, and all of them are set to run on the front page of the *Peninsula Post*—just like yesterday's— every Monday for the next month."

"What?"

"I'm not kidding."

Annie reached for a pen. "Give me this guy's name and number."

She knew there was tons of latitude when it came to freedom

of the press, but she was determined to find out who was running these ads. It was a short call. Stan Turner, editor of the *Peninsula Post*, was unavailable to talk to her, but his assistant promised Annie he'd get back to her as soon as possible.

Next, Annie tried phoning Julie at work, but her voice mail was full and Annie couldn't leave a message, so she called the switchboard and asked to have her paged. "I'm sorry," the receptionist said. "Julie's on vacation." Glancing at her calendar, Annie suddenly remembered that Julie had booked a few days off to attend a Meet Market Adventure event in San Francisco, where a group was bungee jumping off some bridge. Thanking the woman, she hung up and called Julie's cell, getting voice mail.

"It's Annie. Call me as soon as you get this."

When Julie finally did return her call late that afternoon, Annie didn't bother to say hello before asking if Julie had run the ad in yesterday's paper. Silence met her on the otherwise static-filled line. "Because if you did, this isn't funny," she added.

"What are you talking about?" Julie said.

"There was a personal ad on the front page of the *Peninsula Post* yesterday that said *Do You Recognize This Woman?* and it included my university graduation picture. It said we knew each other years ago, that I was the first woman this guy had ever loved, and that he's looking for me. There was a phone number, but whenever anyone calls it, we get computerized voice mail. Marina tracked down the editor of the paper, but he refused to tell her who ran the ad. Then he told her there are going to be four more, one running every Monday for the next month."

"Are you serious?" Julie said. "Annie, that's insane!"

Annie's heart sank and she slid down in her chair until her chin was resting on her chest, feeling her last sliver of hope disappear. "Yes, I'm serious." She tipped her head back to stare at the ceiling, wondering if maybe she hadn't heard a touch of nervousness in Chris's voice when he'd called her after seeing the ad yesterday.

"Wait a minute," Julie said. "You thought I took them out?"

Annie smoothed and resmoothed a crease in her skirt. "I guess I was secretly hoping you had. At least then I'd be dealing with the devil I know instead of someone I don't."

Familiar airport sounds broke through the line—a monotone flight announcement followed by the low hum of a plane taking off somewhere. "I wouldn't do something like that," Julie said, sounding offended. "Look, I've gotta catch my flight, but I'll be back in Seattle in a few hours. Can you fax me a copy of yesterday's ad?"

"Sure."

"Annie?"

"Uh-huh?"

"I think I know who it might be."

"Who?"

"Peter Dawson," she offered. "He always thought you walked on water, even after what you did to him with Jack years ago."

It was an obvious guess that immediately made Annie feel uncomfortable. She'd briefly thought of Peter too, but the very idea that it might have been him had left her mind racing for another possibility, any other possibility.

Julie was getting caught up in this. "Hey, maybe it's Jack."

"That'd be a long shot," Annie said. "First of all, he's as broke as I am, and secondly, I can't see him doing something like this. It's not his style. Beyond that, our marriage is limping across the finish line, remember?"

"Right," Julie said.

"Go catch your flight. We'll talk later."

Julie told her that when she got home, she would dig up the

number of her second cousin, an old friend of Peter's from university who might know where to reach him. Annie thanked her and hung up, trying to push aside a ripple of guilt as she remembered how awkwardly her relationship with Peter had ended.

Years ago, in the middle of one of her group driver-training classes with Jack, she'd slipped out early, frustrated by her inability to parallel park a simulator car. She was in the staff kitchen at Deluca's, where someone had drawn a circle on the wall with a message in the middle: *For stress reduction, bang head here. Repeat if necessary or until unconscious.* She had seen a few students use it, in jest of course, but all the same. That was where Jack found her, with her forehead pressed against the stress-reduction circle, looking "so severely cute" that he said he had to smile. They'd known each other for only six weeks, but the attraction was unmistakable. They didn't talk—they sparred. And even their most basic conversations were laced with innuendo on both sides.

That day, when he tapped on the kitchen door and asked if she was okay, Annie looked around for something to throw at him and decided on a wet dishcloth. He stepped to one side as it sailed past, hitting the wall behind him with a splat and sliding to the floor.

"This is ridiculous!" she said. "I can't believe I spend time here with my hands duct-taped to the wheel of a simulator car."

"But look how much better you're getting," he tried.

"I don't see it," she said, rubbing gunk from the tape off her hands.

Raising his hands in the air, palms out, Jack took a step toward her. "Okay. Fair enough. You've still got work to do, but it's been at least two weeks since you've knocked over any pedestrians, and that's big, Annie. That's *huge*."

She crossed her arms and set her jaw, wanting to leave, even though her legs didn't seem to be cooperating.

"And I'm not just saying that so I can spend more time with you," Jack said. After a few seconds of silence, their eyes met and they both smiled, she tentatively and he with a glint of boyish charm. "Although I have to admit, I do enjoy all that cuteness and attitude."

Annie looked at her shoes, listening to a door slam somewhere nearby.

"Want to tell me what's really wrong?" he asked, but she just shook her head, feeling miserable. "Okay," he said. "Let's try a new line of conversation. What are you doing this weekend?"

"Not much."

"Are you still seeing that guy?" he asked, pouring himself a coffee.

The room went quiet and Annie told him that technically she was.

"Either you are or you aren't," he said, smiling again.

She flushed. "I haven't told him it's over yet."

Setting his cup down, Jack crossed his arms. "Why not?"

"Because I don't want to hurt him."

He pushed off the wall and leaned down close to whisper against her ear, "But it's no good dragging it out, is it?"

"No," she said. "It isn't."

Slowly, Jack slid one hand around the back of her neck and kissed her, a kiss that brought all her senses to life. She kissed him back. Then he closed the door and locked it, bracing one hand against the wall above her shoulder before leaning down to kiss her again. His hands moved up her back as he gently worked his way down her neck with his mouth, and then they were touching each other where strangers don't, as a sensation unlike any other flooded through Annie. Her body trembled as he inched her sweater up and over her head, trailing his fingers along the length of her bare arms.

Seconds later, he broke away from her, breathing hard. He ran a thumb over her raw lips. His voice was husky. "Jesus, what am I doing? I've got students waiting."

"Right," Annie said, although it came out like a croak. She raked a hand through her hair, grabbed her sweater off the floor, and pulled it back on over her head.

Tense silence filled the room.

"Look," Jack said, "why don't we—"

Someone tried to open the door, rattling the knob in frustration. Annie smoothed down the front of her jeans and Jack unlocked it. The receptionist came in frowning. A kind, middle-aged woman, she asked Jack if something was wrong, then turned, saw Annie's face, and flushed knowingly.

Jack's eyes met Annie's as she shouldered her purse and slipped past him through the open door, and although she didn't see him again for another week, it took her only a few seconds to figure out how it had felt when they'd kissed. Like they had known each other forever; like two distinct pieces of a puzzle sliding into place.

No, she thought. *Like lightning in a bottle.*

Deciding to take the bus home, she'd hurried outside, and there was Peter, leaning against his car, waiting for her. When he saw her, his face lit up with such an expression of hope and anticipation that her throat tightened. He'd been so supportive about her getting her license that she felt sick when she thought about telling him it was over.

"Good lesson?" he asked.

Unable to meet his eyes, she said, "Uh-huh."

He handed her a bouquet of daisies. "Thanks," she said, burying her face in them. He opened her car door and she slid in, but as he went around to the driver's side, she closed her eyes, recounting everything that had just happened with Jack to convince herself that she hadn't imagined it.

"Feel like celebrating?" Peter asked, pulling into traffic.

Annie blinked. "Celebrating?"

"You know, because of all your progress."

"Actually, I'm not feeling that great. Can you take me home?"

He seemed hurt, shooting her inquiring, sidelong glances as he drove. And as he did, Annie toyed with her purse, miserably trying to figure out how to tell him the truth, how to explain so it wouldn't hurt so much. She'd tried hard not to be attracted to Jack, but it was out of her control. She was drawn to him in a way she'd never been to anyone before, and lately anything Peter did paled in comparison.

"Annie, what's going on?" Peter asked.

"I'm just tired. I'll be fine after I get some sleep."

When she turned to look at him, he squinted at her, and then his jaw tightened and he looked away. Annie shifted uneasily and stared out the window. Five minutes passed and the silence between them suddenly seemed so strange that she cleared her throat and thanked him again for the flowers.

"You're welcome," he said, keeping his eyes on the road.

Annie's street was filled with brain-jarring potholes they usually laughed about, but that day Peter's face was expressionless as he drove up to her apartment building. She leaned over and kissed him on the cheek, surprised when he pulled away slightly.

"Are you all right?" she asked, reaching for the door.

He leveled a devastating gaze at her, but didn't answer.

"Peter?"

"I'm fine," he said, turning away.

There was an awkward pause and then Annie got out, sensing things had somehow altered between them already, but not certain why. Finally she leaned down and asked, "Are we still on for dinner tomorrow night?"

He was silent for so long that she wasn't certain he'd heard her. Then he nodded and said, "Sure, see you tomorrow."

Annie watched him drive away before going inside, feeling an odd combination of freedom mixed with despair. Turning the key in the lock, she opened the door to her apartment and stepped inside, but when she looked up at the mirror on the adjacent wall, she went very still. Closing her eyes, she groaned, stunned at how painfully obvious it was—even from ten feet away—that her sweater was on inside out.

The next night, she walked to Peter's apartment, prepared to tell him the truth and shoulder the blame. The elevator was empty and her shoes rapped against the hardwood floor in the hallway as she made her way to his door, rehearsing what she planned to say. She hesitated before she knocked, and when he didn't answer, she dug out the key he'd given her and let herself in.

His stereo was cranked up louder than usual. Frowning, Annie kicked off her shoes and went around the corner, stopping halfway across the room. Peter stood outside on the balcony, and next to him was an astonishingly beautiful woman. They were standing so close that at first Annie thought they were kissing, and although they weren't, the implied intimacy caught her off guard. The girl had dark hair and a dramatic face, and one of her arms was draped possessively around Peter's neck. Turning, Peter saw Annie and shrugged in mock helplessness, as if this woman hanging off his neck was doing so against his will. Glancing back over his shoulder, he stepped inside, took Annie by the arm, and led her into the kitchen.

"What's going on?" Annie asked.

"She's an old girlfriend," he explained, not meeting her eyes. "I'd persuaded myself I was over her, but when she phoned and came by to see me . . ." His words trailed away, leaving the rest to her imagination.

Annie's heart jumped with relief before sinking just as quickly. Frowning, she studied his face. Peter was many things—thoughtful, sweet, sensitive—but he wasn't—and by his own admission, never had been—all that good with women.

"What's her name?" she asked.

"Leanne," he said, staring at the floor.

"Funny, you've never mentioned her before."

Peter shrugged. "I guess I never felt comfortable telling you about her. I'm sorry."

On her way down the hallway, Annie glanced back at the brunette, noticing that she now looked suspiciously bored. Peter followed Annie to the door and she handed him her key before turning to leave.

"Take care, Peter," she said softly.

"Annie?"

She stood with her back to him. "Yes?"

Pause. "Do you love him?"

It took her a few seconds to answer. "Yes, I think I do."

Today, Annie looked back on what had happened between Peter and her with regret, believing he'd deserved better, wishing she'd sat down with him to explain and apologize. Grabbing her purse, she locked the front door of Kozak's and went back to the receiving entrance, where she pushed the heavy door open and fumbled through her purse for her cigarettes. When she was finished smoking, she crushed the butt and went back to reception to call Marina. Sawyer answered instead, sniffling.

"Sawyer? Do you have a cold?"

"No. Did you want to talk to Mom?"

Annie frowned. "Yes, but are you okay?"

"I'm fine. Just a minute and I'll get her for you." The phone clunked against the counter and Marina picked up.

"What's wrong with Sawyer?" Annie asked.

"Oh, she's upset but she'll get over it."

"Upset about what?"

"Trust me," Marina said. "You don't want to know."

"I'm her godmother and I want to know," Annie said. "Let me talk to her."

Marina sighed. Then she called Sawyer and asked her to pick up the extension. "Don't say I didn't warn you," she whispered, hanging up when Sawyer took the other phone.

"Hey," Annie said. "What's the matter?"

Sawyer paused to blow her nose. "Mom and I had a big fight. You know that sphynx cat I told you about yesterday? The one someone dropped off at the rescue shelter that Mom had the vet look over?"

Annie frowned, vaguely recalled her mentioning it. "Uh-huh."

"Mom won't let me keep him," she said, starting to cry all over again.

"But you guys already have two cats. And anyhow, you only have another year at home and then you can get one of your own when you move out."

"But I don't want another cat," she wailed. "I want this one. He's a sphynx. You know, one of those bald cats like in the Austin Powers movies?" Annie shivered involuntarily, suddenly remembering Mike Myers holding a hairless cat that looked like an overgrown rat. "I've gotta go," Sawyer said, trying to get herself under control. "I had a free study period this morning, but it's over in ten minutes, so I have to get back to school."

Annie had been doodling on an envelope as they talked: a few tiny squares surrounded by larger ones, encircled by one huge square; every corner tight and perfect so that nothing could slip inside. She tapped her pen on her forehead and closed her eyes, wishing now that she'd just kept her mouth shut and stayed out of it.

"Do you still want to talk to Mom?" Sawyer asked.

Crumpling up the envelope she'd been doodling on, Annie decided to make a decision and run with it. "Sawyer, I'll make you a deal. If you watch the boys one night a week for the next year, I'll take this cat and keep it for you until you graduate from high school."

"Really? You mean it?"

"Tell your mom she can bring him over Thursday night, and if he gets along with Montana, he can stay."

"Thank you, Auntie. This really made my day!"

Annie hung up smiling because, until now, hers hadn't been so stellar either.

FOURTEEN

*F*or as long as Annie could remember, Orenda McMillan had lived in the same house on the north side of Eagan's Point. She was part Iroquois and her name meant *magic power*, and although she wasn't a traditional therapist, she entertained more visitors each month than Annie could imagine traipsing through her house in a year. Orenda was effortlessly one of Eagan's Point's favorite people, with the teenagers who slinked through her front door at all hours—it was never locked—and the housewives who arrived with fresh baked goods. At sixty-five, with waist-long gray braids and leather moccasins, Orenda looked lost in the past, yet she had an uncanny ability to burrow into anyone's mind and ferret out truths they couldn't see for themselves. Months ago, she and Annie had struck a private deal. Every Thursday after work, Orenda would listen to Annie talk about her issues, with Orenda interjecting a word of wisdom here and there, and in exchange, Annie would give Orenda a one-hour back massage.

That week, Annie set up her portable massage table as Orenda took off her badly pilled sweater and draped it over a chair. What followed was a one-way rant from Annie about everything that was on her mind, including the unknown man behind the mysterious ads, worry about her boys, her impending divorce, her stalled career, and the ever-present financial pressure that never went away. When she finally ran out of steam, she stopped massaging

Orenda's back to take a drink of water, feeling more overwhelmed than usual.

"You know, Annie," Orenda said softly, "I still can't decide if you're grieving for the past, or if you're just too scared to bring yourself to move on." Staring at her, Annie slowly set down her water bottle, realizing it was both, only she hadn't known it until then.

Annie had just gotten home and climbed into the bathtub when she heard Marina call out from downstairs. The boys made it down before she did, and when she entered the kitchen, they were standing next to Marina and Sawyer, trying to look inside a soft-sided pet carrier.

"You sure you don't mind?" Marina asked.

"I don't," Annie assured her, shoving magazines to one side to make room on the table.

"His name's Lurch," Sawyer said, unzipping the carrier. Reaching in, she gently lifted out what at first glance looked like a hairless, five-pound sewer rat.

Annie inched around behind Eric, who appeared thrilled. He'd always been a kid who took you as you were and clearly this openess extended to the animal kingdom. She couldn't decide if Lurch looked more like ET crossed with a gremlin or a kangaroo that had been bred with a rat. He had overlarge ears for the size of his wrinkled body, a long, tapered tail, and sky blue, lemon-shaped eyes. Even Luke couldn't hide his fascination as Lurch dropped onto the table and uncoiled in a lazy stretch. Oddly graceful, he moved between Luke and Eric with his head lifted in the air as they took turns petting him. Then, with one effortless leap, he was up on Sawyer's shoulder, where he draped himself around her neck and yawned.

"Maybe we should introduce him to Montana," Marina suggested.

Annie fixed a smile on her face. "Sure."

Luke opened the door and Montana loped into the kitchen, massive head swinging from side to side. Marina peeled Lurch off Sawyer's neck and set him on the kitchen table. Curious, he immediately jumped down onto the floor and slowly began wrapping himself around Montana's trunklike legs. Eventually, Montana got bored and lumbered into the living room, where she climbed up onto the couch and dropped in a heap. Seconds later, Lurch followed, curling up into a ball next to her.

Sawyer picked up her hair, made a ponytail high on her head, and let it drop. "Looks like they're going to get along fine," she said, clearly pleased.

Laughing, Marina shouldered her purse. "Okay, Annie, if you're wondering where he should sleep, just empty a dresser drawer and throw in an old blanket. The woman who gave him up said that's what she did."

Feigning enthusiasm, Annie waved her off like this was no problem, although the idea of having a ratlike cat living in her dresser held little appeal. However, after they'd left, she took a deep breath, gathered up Lurch, and carried him upstairs, where she reluctantly emptied a dresser drawer, lined it with an old beach towel, and set him inside.

It was after eleven when she finally locked the house and grabbed her cigarettes. She wanted a few minutes to herself, but halfway up the stairs, she noticed the hallway window was already propped open. She stuck her head outside, and there was Luke, alone and pensive, staring at the stars with his headphones on and his iPod cranked up loud enough that even she could hear Bob Dylan singing "Knockin' on Heaven's Door." She thought about sending him to bed, but then he saw her and lifted his chin at Mr. Kale's house across the alley.

"You missed 'em," he said, pulling off his headphones.

It had been a long day, yet she was secretly pleased that he was there, waiting for her. Clearly this was a crack in his armor, maybe even his way of telling her that he'd changed his mind about wanting to live with his dad. Annie crawled out on the roof next to him.

"So how about an update on our neighbors?" she asked.

"Mr. Kale and his dog came out like last time," Luke said. "Then Libby stomped outside and got her garden hose, dragged it over to the fence, climbed up on a plastic lawn chair, and blasted them with water."

"That's new," Annie said, surprised.

"Mr. Kale kept stepping in front of his dog, blocking his face from the water with his hands and yelling at her to leave 'em alone. Libby finally turned it off and yelled back, telling him to keep his dog quiet or she'd do it again. Then she went inside and slammed the door so hard I thought it was gonna fall off."

Annie shook her head. "Pleasant woman."

For a long time neither of them said more. Annie sat there barely breathing, wanting this moment to last, aware only of the light on Luke's face from the window and the way his hair had grown long, falling over his eyes. Like hers, it tended to frizz. She wanted to brush it away and tell him she loved him, but she knew that would ruin everything. She tried to make conversation, but as usual, only fifty percent of Luke showed up for the conversation. Her questions got longer, his answers became shorter.

Did he want to talk about school? Not really.

What did he want for his birthday this year? A new bike.

For Christmas? Same thing.

Yawning, he finally said, "I'd better get to bed," like he normally made that choice all on his own. He crawled around behind her and dropped inside. She heard his feet hit the floor and then he said, "Mom?"

"Uh-huh?"

"I won't tell anyone you're smoking again."

Annie smiled, pleased to be back on familiar ground. This was the Luke she knew best, the one who liked having the upper hand. "Okay," she said, sort of jokey. "And I won't tell anyone about the Victoria's Secret catalog under your mattress." She turned around, but he was already gone, so she wasn't sure if he'd even heard her. Resting her forehead on her knees, she told herself to be thankful that at least he was still here.

At three in the morning, Annie woke to the sound of running water. Rubbing her eyes, she slipped on her robe and, holding it closed with one hand, hurried to the bathroom, where light was shining from underneath the closed door. She stuck her head into the boys' room and saw that Luke was asleep, but Eric's bed was empty, his blankets, sheets, and mattress pad piled in a heap on the floor. Realizing what had happened, she took out a clean set of sheets and a spare blanket, and turned on the hall light outside their room so she could see better.

When Eric returned, she pulled back the clean covers and told him to crawl in.

"Guess I drank too much," he said, not looking her in the eye, embarrassed and unwilling to talk about the old bed-wetting problem that had cropped up again since they'd moved. Pulling the blankets up, he whispered, "Mom? I was thinking I'd ask Coach if I could hang around for games even if I don't make the team. What do you think?"

Luke rolled over, startling them. "Why embarrass yourself? If you don't make the team, leave it alone, loser."

It took serious self-control for Annie not to swat him. Instead, she winked at Eric. "My dad used to tell me, 'Find a need and fill it,' and I think that's what your brother's working on. Tell you what," she said to Eric. "Wait till you find out if you've made the team or not, and then decide." She kissed him good night, and then Luke too, which was more than he deserved, but she was determined not to lose any ground with him.

"See you guys in the morning."

Exhausted, she crawled back into bed, turned on her side, and burrowed into the pillow. Ten minutes later, frustrated and unable to sleep, she kicked back the blankets, wondering again who'd taken out the ads. Monday would be here soon and she still didn't have a clue who it was. She flipped her pillow over to the cool side, wishing she could stretch out on her bed from corner to corner and sleep until her body decided it was time to wake up again. As she was nodding off, Lurch jumped up next to her, curled nose to tail, and promptly fell asleep. Annie rolled over and gave her pillow a quick punch.

The second stage of Annie's life—Life with Jack—had never been predictable. Although he could be a workaholic, and she'd often played solitaire on the floor of his control booth to keep him company at night, there were other times when he'd wake up at five in the morning, bundle her into his car, and drive down to the lake in Chicago so they could watch the sun rise. Two weeks before she'd graduated from university, he'd talked her into entering a sailboat race on Lake Michigan to raise money for The Diabetes Foundation. He told her their boat was being sponsored by his radio station but he failed to mention these were motorized *model sailboats*, so she arrived expecting a pleasant afternoon sail and ended up waist deep in the lake wearing a pair of rubber overalls, next to fifty other people with handheld remote controls.

They had to maintain their balance in the choppy water as

they maneuvered their sailboat around a few buoys and sailed it over to their partner standing a hundred feet away. Their partner then had to perform the same feat in reverse. First-, second-, and third-place winners would each receive a weekend for two at the Hilton, including dinner and champagne. Unfortunately, they finished last because Annie's rubber overalls filled with water from an undetected hole and she panicked, dropping her remote control in the lake. Jack took her home to change, and then out to dinner, where he asked her to marry him, explaining that he'd hoped to finish at least third so the weekend for two and champagne could've been part of his proposal.

They were married in Eagan's Point on June 5, 1992.

That morning, Annie had risen early and spent an hour on the water lost in thought as she watched the sun rise up over the trees. After she paddled back to shore and hung up her kayak, she double-checked that she had everything she needed and then hiked up to her penny tree. It was the perfect way to begin her wedding day, and as she strode along the trail, she was thrilled to see that it looked like the weather was going to cooperate.

The faster her pace, the more impatient she was to get there, and when she finally did, a crushing sadness came over her. *Today is my wedding day,* she thought, knowing that in a few hours her hair would be pulled back in a sleek knot and her mom would be fawning over her as Marina sorted through makeup bottles. Then, after she'd carefully slid into her dress, her mom would zip her up and tell her she loved her, and when she was ready to leave for the church, she'd take out an old butterfly brooch that no one else would recognize and pin it to the nest of ribbons on her bouquet. Barring any unseen catastrophes, she'd float through the ceremony with a smile, knowing that she and Jack were feeling exactly the same—longing for their life together to begin.

Her mom's backyard had been transformed into an outdoor restaurant with an open-air marquee tent covering enough tables to seat one hundred, and a temporary hardwood dance floor in the middle. She knew this crowd wanted to celebrate, so there would be lots of sloppy kisses and tears mixed with a few bear hugs. People would mill about, drinking and laughing and talking. They would eat, the band would play, and everyone they loved would dance, and when they finally left at the end of the night, Lionel Richie's "Endless Love" would be echoing in her ears.

Annie had pressed the back of one hand against her mouth. It was her wedding day and the only thing that kept it from being perfect was her dad's absence. If he were there, he'd be wearing a crisp suit with a bow tie, and at some point, he'd take her by the hand and ask, *Do you love him?* And without a flutter of hesitation, she would whisper, *Like crazy.*

"I came to tell you I love you, Dad," she said, squinting up at her penny tree. "And to thank you for choosing me all those years ago." Then she stood there and cried, lowering her head and letting the tears fall until she was so cried out she was sure there would be no tears left for the rest of the day.

An hour later, she was in the bathtub when her mom knocked on the door and stuck her head inside. Erna's eyes were red and it was obvious that she too had been crying. "Someone sent flowers," she said, squeezing through the door with a box.

Annie sat up. "What's wrong?"

"Nothing," she said, but her jaw quivered as she perched on the edge of the tub and set the box across her knees.

"Don't lie to me," Annie said. "You've been crying."

Erna took off her glasses and cleaned the lenses with her shirttail as Annie waited for her to say something. When she didn't, Annie gently poked her in the leg with a finger. "Mom?"

Erna put her glasses back on, and when their eyes met, hers lingered on Annie's a little longer than usual. "I need you to make me a promise," she finally said.

"What?"

"After you open this—" She stopped and looked away, took a breath, and started again. "After you open this, I want you to promise me you won't tell Marina."

"That's it?" Annie said.

"That's it."

Annie was about to ask why when her mom stood and handed her the box. She took it from her, sending waves of bubbles slopping over onto the floor. Erna stretched out a hand to move a lock of wet hair off Annie's face. Then, on her way out the door, she paused and said, "I love you, Annie." When the door closed behind her, Annie untied the ribbon on the box and carefully lifted the lid. Inside were a dozen red roses and an envelope with her name on it. Seconds later, she set the box down, crying all over again. The roses were from her dad and so was the letter.

Dear Annie,

> *As I write this, you are sixteen and asleep in your room twenty feet away. Tomorrow you're going to your first beach party with Julie and you're excited, so excited I didn't have the heart to say anything when I noticed you'd snuck a few beers to take with you. If you're reading this, then congratulations are in order. My little girl getting married. The very thought makes me shiver with worry, which is why I decided to write you and Marina each a letter. If I don't live to do it myself, your mom will deliver a dozen roses to each of you on your wedding day, along with this note.*

> *Ten minutes ago, I pushed my wheelchair in to kiss you good night, but you were already asleep, your hair fanned out on*

the pillow, and when I leaned down to kiss you, I almost got punched because, as always, just the slightest touch against your cheek sent both arms flailing. (Don't forget to tell your future husband about this little flaw of yours, Annie girl. After all, he's in for a lifetime of bruises he'll have to explain after marrying you.)

Because I can't be there to offer you advice, I feel it's my place to say a few things here. No matter who you marry, Annie, he never would've measured up to all that I'd want him to be, although there are a few things I can't help but hope for. I hope he's a hard worker. I hope he knows how to laugh and when to cry. I hope he's the kind of man who won't lie or cheat or steal to provide for his family, and I hope he loves you to distraction. There are so many things I want for you, and so much I hope you'll have the chance to experience in your life, but mostly I hope life is kind to you and I hope you love to the tips of your toes. Everything else will follow. . . .

Love, Dad

It was a day packed with emotion, a day filled with memories. Annie was twenty-three then, naive enough to think that she and Jack were invincible, and in love enough to believe they'd make it through anything life threw at them. She knew there would be highs and lows, but she was ready. *We can handle it,* she thought with confidence as she slid into her dress that day. *We'll show everyone how it's done, this loving each other until death do us part.*

For the next few years, life was good. Luke was born eleven months after they were married, she loved her job as a physical therapist, and Jack developed an on-air following of dedicated fans. Thankfully, her pregnancy with Eric was also uneventful and he was born two years after his brother. Then Jack got offered his dream job with WSMB in Seattle and they rented a U-Haul and moved out to the West Coast. That first night in Seattle, they toasted each other with paper cups of wine, surrounded by un-packed boxes and wrapped in the contented silence of two people who were excited about their future. Of course, what they didn't know then was that years later it would all be torn apart, wrapped in a different kind of silence, deafening proof that no relationship is invincible.

FIFTEEN

Annie groped for the blaring alarm clock and pressed SNOOZE, then pulled the blankets over her head. It was Monday and the second ad would be waiting for her on the front page of the *Peninsula Post*. Maybe she would stay in bed all day. Maybe she'd call Marina and get her to drive the boys to school. Then, after they were gone, she'd grab an armful of snacks and make her way back upstairs, where she'd tip everything out onto the bed and channel surf until she felt it was safe to face the world again.

"Morning," Eric said, coming into her room.

"He's right here," she said, nodding to where Lurch was curled up next to her. It had been several days since Marina and Sawyer had dropped him off, and contrary to what Marina had said, he hadn't spent one night in his dresser drawer.

Stretching out on the bed, Eric began petting him.

Annie threw off the covers, bracing for the day ahead. Staying in bed sounded great in principle, but in practice it would send the wrong signal to the boys, so it looked like guilt would once again win out over how she really wanted to spend the day. *Three cheers for guilt and parental responsibility.*

"Nice picture," Luke said from the doorway. "My bald brother, our new bald cat, and my age-advanced mom."

Annie froze. "What do you mean?"

"The paper just got here," he said, dropping it on the bed next to her before heading back out the door.

Annie's ears were ringing and her neck had started to itch. Taking a deep breath, she picked up the newspaper. The ad was in the same spot as the week before, but today her university graduation picture was next to another one, an age-advanced photo of what she "might look like today." Gone were the glasses and the twenty-something freshness, replaced with a shorter hairstyle and a tilt of her head that implied subtle maturity.

HAVE YOU SEEN THIS WOMAN?

THIS AGE-ADVANCED PHOTO MIGHT BE WHAT SHE LOOKS LIKE TODAY. YEARS AGO, SHE LIVED IN EAGAN'S POINT, WASHINGTON. TODAY, SHE MAY BE MARRIED, COULD HAVE A DIFFERENT LAST NAME, AND MIGHT LIVE IN ANOTHER STATE. STILL, SHE WAS THE FIRST WOMAN I EVER LOVED AND I CAN'T FORGET HER. HER NAME IS ANNIE FISCHER. IF YOU KNOW WHERE I CAN FIND HER, PLEASE CALL (212) 555-1963.

Feeling self-conscious, Annie reached up to smooth down her hair, which always looked like a hornet's nest until she washed it each morning. The phone rang and she fumbled for it. "Hello."

"Hi, Annie," Jack said. "Have you seen today's paper?"

"The one with two pictures of me looking like a fool?"

"Actually, I think you look kinda cute," he said, laughing.

Annie felt herself flush. "Obviously we aren't looking at the same pictures."

"I was calling to talk to Eric before I go on the air, but since you answered, I may as well tell you I talked with Luke this week-end about him wanting to come live with me."

Annie sat up straighter. "How'd it go?" she asked.

Jack sighed. "He really wants this, Annie, and he's stubborn as hell about it too. He's agreed to wait until school is done at the end of June, but then he made me promise we'd sit down and talk about it again."

"Right," Annie said.

It was a full ten seconds before Jack cleared his throat and changed the subject. "Hey, this guy with the ads seems pretty serious. Has he called you back?"

"No," she said, glad to talk about something else. "And I've tried everything over the last week, including harassing the editor of the newspaper with phone calls, but I keep getting the same explanation every time. Apparently the paper signed some kind of confidentiality agreement with this guy, and under that agreement, they aren't allowed to release his name until the last ad has run."

"The last ad?" Jack said, confused. "What do you mean?"

"There are five ads," Annie explained. "One every Monday for five weeks."

"Really?" he said, sounding distracted. "Well . . . let me know who it is when you find out."

"Sure," she said. Then she covered the receiver and told Eric his dad was on the phone.

"Man, they're up early today," Eric said, pointing out her bedroom window.

Annie handed him the phone and leaned over to see Libby Johnson and Rose Dixon huddled at the community picnic table on the grassy island of their cul-de-sac out front, reading the morning paper. Rose was sixty and one of the biggest gossips in town. Not long after they'd moved in, Annie had made the mistake of going out to the picnic table one morning to read the paper, and within minutes, Rose had joined her, peppering her with questions and digging around for dirt on her life. As she watched, Rose pointed at something in the paper, leaning over to show Libby. Then she nodded with conviction, and jabbed a gnarled finger into the air toward their house.

"Unbelievable," Annie said, half to herself.

Eric hung up and swiveled the paper around to where he could get a better look at it. "This really is sorta weird, isn't it?" he said, frowning. "Your hair looks good, though."

Annie smoothed down the knit cap on his head, turned him around to face the door, and gave his butt a bump with one knee. "Go get dressed."

Sitting on the bed, she read the ad again, skeptical that Chris would have placed them. Yet the idea of it being Peter made her uncomfortable and she didn't believe Jack would put himself out there for the world to see. Sighing, she closed her eyes, thinking about something Marina had said last week, wondering if maybe she hadn't been right, that Annie didn't know any of them the way she thought she did. "Let's face it," Marina had said. "Men get stupid when they're in love."

Annie was standing at the kitchen window eating a bowl of cereal when Eric came downstairs a few minutes later. He grabbed a banana from the fruit bowl and waved it at the fish tank. "By the way, you're wrong about the fish, Mom. They aren't doing so good. There's not much air floating up from that thing."

Frowning, she went over to the tank and tapped a finger against the glass. "I'll have to remember to buy a new air stone."

The phone rang and she grabbed it. "Hello?"

"What do you think?" Marina asked.

"That this is getting ridiculous."

"I think it's kind of romantic myself," she said. "Although the age-advanced photo did throw me off a little." Pause. "Annie? There's more you don't know yet. The *Seattle Examiner* picked it up too. They printed it on the front page of their people section this morning. Harrison called me from work when he saw it."

Annie closed her eyes tight. She suddenly wished she was a drinker so she could slide back into that boozy haze she was in a week ago at Chris Carby's house, because right now the thought of drifting through the next month in a don't-worry-be-happy mode looked infinitely better than going through it sober.

"Can you read it to me?"

"There's not much to read. It's just the ad followed by two paragraphs saying how someone is looking for this woman."

Annie glanced at the clock. If she hurried, she still had time for a quick paddle (something she desperately needed even though it was starting to rain) and then at work she'd make two calls: one to Julie to see if she had managed to track down a phone number for Peter Dawson, and another to Stan Turner, the managing editor of the *Peninsula Post*. Enough was enough.

On the drive to school that morning, as rain sluiced down the windshield making it almost impossible for Annie to drive, Eric asked if he could get her opinion on a homework assignment. His teacher had asked students to describe in a hundred words or less one of their "best days" in a real or imagined scenario.

"Here's mine," Eric said, reciting out loud. "I get up early and walk to the ocean, where the shore is rocky in both directions as far as I can see and seagulls fly up into the air screeching like they're mad at me when I run toward them. Then I go for breakfast at Bianca's Café with my mom and my brother and my grandma, and when we get home, I play basketball for the rest of the day, until the sun goes down."

He looked up to catch Annie's eye in the rearview mirror. "How's that sound?"

Before she could answer, Luke said, "Sounds lame."

"I wasn't asking *you*."

Annie glanced from Luke to Eric in the rearview mirror, then back at the road again, trying to focus on driving. "Come on, guys. Cut it out."

"I could do better than that," Luke said, taunting him.

"Fine, then," Eric said. "Go ahead."

Annie's eyes narrowed, waiting.

"Okay. Here's one of my best days," Luke said in a mocking voice. "I wake up late after sleeping until noon. The sky is blue, with no rain in sight for, like, a year, and there's a U-Haul in the driveway. Dad's sitting behind the wheel waving at me and Montana's already loaded in the back. And, oh, wait. He's telling me to jump in so I can morph out of this bad dream I'm living and won't have to listen to you or anyone else in this stupid town again."

Annie pulled up to the school and parked, letting the car idle. She stared at Luke in the rearview mirror, keeping both hands on the wheel.

Behind her, Eric said, "You're such a jerk," and Luke had the decency to drop his gaze.

She almost said something, then didn't.

When had this bitterness started? When had Luke become such a sarcastic ball of resentment, and exactly what had triggered it? Was it Eric getting sick years ago, she and Jack splitting up, the move to Eagan's Point, or . . . all of it? And if so, how could she say, *That's life, Luke* without sounding sarcastic herself? How could she explain that no matter what the future had in store for any of them, no one had the option to go back?

For a fraction of a second, she considered telling him about one of her best days. It would actually be night and wintertime in Canada, and she would step outside at her uncle Max's and make her way across his backyard to a roaring fire pit surrounded by people wearing eiderdown jackets and drinking Kahlúa and milk. Eric would be propped against her hip in a snowsuit, not quite a year old yet, and Jack and Luke would be walking ahead of them, necks craned back as the northern lights danced across the sky and fresh snow crunched under their boots. She and Jack would look at each other across the fire and crack up when Luke asked Uncle Max why all of his friends were so crazy. They would climb into bed, hours later, cradling their sons between them, and even though Jack would be asleep already, she would whisper, "I can't imagine being anywhere else in the world right now."

Annie swallowed hard, willing herself to push aside a memory she hadn't thought about in years. "Have a good day, guys," she said as casually as possible, waiting for them to get out.

After they did, Eric stuck his head back inside. "You okay, Mom?"

Annie closed her eyes. Nodded.

She forced herself to wait until they were inside the school before driving away, and as she did, it occurred to her that she could use a trip to her penny tree. *Only this time, maybe I'll take the boys with me. Maybe it would do us all some good.*

SIXTEEN

The last stretch of trail always grabbed Annie by the throat. She knew every tree, every rock, and every dip well enough that she was certain she could find them in the dark. Each time she went, the sensation was the same: an overwhelming recognition that wherever she was in her life, and wherever she might be in the future, nothing short of a forest fire would change this place for her. Her penny tree helped her to know who she was, but it also reminded her of who she had been. She hadn't known it when her dad gave the tree to her, but it had anchored her as much as it had set her free.

Veering off the path and into a throng of waist-deep ferns, she turned to make sure Eric and Luke were still behind her. They were, although both of them were alternately glowering at each other and shooting her surly looks.

"Not a word until we get there," she warned them.

"Where are we going?" Eric asked.

"You'll see in a few minutes."

When Luke opened his mouth, presumably to protest, she lifted a hand and added, "Not one more word or your Xbox gets packed away for a month and every basketball in the house gets deflated. Got it?"

Her determination to come here had taken shape early that morning, when she was still in bed. After a long week of prying phone calls from friends, neighbors, and reporters asking about the second ad in the *Peninsula Post*, she'd been hoping to sleep in. But what began as a mild disagreement between the boys quickly escalated to shoving, followed by Luke throwing a basketball at Eric, missing, and breaking a lamp. That was all it took—a broken lamp—for Annie to break her silence and take them to her penny tree, which she'd never shared with anyone.

A casual observer might have wondered why this woman was dragging her boys off into the forest instead of staying on a perfectly good hiking trail, and it was this thought that made Annie smile in secret anticipation. She stopped to let them catch up. They were walking beside each other with their heads down. Luke was gesturing with his hands, saying something, and Eric was nodding. As they got closer, she heard Luke say, "If you want, I'll sell it to you for twenty bucks."

"Sell what?" Annie asked.

Eric looked up. "His old bike helmet."

"He's not *selling* you his old bike helmet. You're his brother! He can give it to you." And then to Luke: "What are you doing?"

"I could use the extra money," he said, shrugging.

"Can't we all, but that doesn't mean you scam your brother." Shaking her head, she turned and resumed walking. "Come on. We're almost there."

Her dad's outcrop rock was a big hit. More than once the boys inched toward the edge to look down at the rocks below as Annie sat cross-legged in the middle, drinking coffee. "This isn't where we're going," she told them. "But I wanted to show you this too because it was my dad's favorite spot."

"You never talk about Grandpa," Eric said, turning around. "What was he like?"

Annie shrugged. "He was my dad, so to me, he could move mountains."

She felt Luke staring at her, studying her face. "Of course, he wasn't *perfect*," she added, shifting to get comfortable. "When I was six or seven, he loved watching hockey games on TV, but ours was so old that he was always wrestling with the rabbit ears on top to fix the snow on the screen. He'd get mad and start swearing, and then, when your grandma wasn't looking, he'd set down his drink, pull a stool over next to it, and get me to stand there and hold the ears in one spot until the game was over."

"That's the worst thing he ever did?" Luke asked.

Sorrow rose up in her, fresh and tender. "Yes," she whispered. "I guess it was."

"Was he good at anything?" Eric asked.

Annie looked away, thinking. "He was. He had a natural ability to tell stories, an ability that can't be taught. But there were other things too, things you take for granted when you're a kid. All I know is when he was here, I didn't appreciate him, and after he was gone, I just wanted him back."

Again, Luke looked like he wanted to say something, but he didn't. Instead, he walked to the edge of the outcrop rock and looked down, jamming his hands into his pockets. Hoping to send their thoughts in a new direction, Annie stood and brushed herself off.

"Just seventy more paces and we're there. Are you ready?"

Eric linked an arm through hers and counted off each pace from the edge of the outcrop rock, but Luke trailed behind, acting uninterested. When they reached the base of the tree, Annie stopped and turned to look at them. She tried repeating the same words her dad had spoken years ago, saying them exactly as she'd heard them from his lips, as he would have heard them from his father, and yet they didn't seem to have the same effect on the boys as they'd had on her.

"Wait a minute," Luke said. "You're giving us a tree?"

"No," she said, clearing her throat. "I'm *sharing* it with you."

He took a swig from his water bottle. "Can we build a tree house in it?"

"No, but you can come here if you want."

Squinting, he tilted his head and looked up at the tree, then wiped his mouth with the back of his hand. "Why would we do that?"

Annie shrugged. "To be alone. To think things through . . . To daydream."

Lowering his voice, he leaned toward her. "Can't I just go up on the roof at home?"

She closed her eyes for patience. "Where was I?"

"The tree," Eric offered.

"The tree," she said, nodding. "That's right. My dad gave it to me almost twenty-five years ago and now—"

"And now you have something earth-shattering to say about it?" Luke interrupted.

Silence stretched between them, tense and awkward. Annie waited for a moment to get herself under control. "Why do you do this?" she finally asked.

Luke stared at her. "Do what?"

"Ruin everything."

"Oh, I think you do a pretty good job of that all by yourself, Mom," he said, hoisting his water bottle in a cheery toast. "You just don't want to admit it. Like how after Dad left, you tried to act like nothing was *wrong*, like nothing had *changed*. But everything had changed. Everything."

Annie had been anticipating this outburst for a while now. Bracing for it, actually. She touched her fingers to her eyes and shook her head, remembering the first moment she ever saw Luke. How she had loved him like a shot when they'd handed him to her in the delivery room. How she still did, even at times like this when he pushed and pushed until she wanted to slap him, and then, seconds later, wanted to cry for having wanted to slap him.

Eric slid down the tree with his knees drawn up. "God, I'm so tired of this."

"Of what?" Luke demanded.

"Of all the fighting."

There was a long, heavy pause. Then Luke said, "I'm out of here," and strode off. "See you at home."

Watching him leave, Annie was torn between calling out to him and letting him go. When he got like this, he was at turns a boy, full of a boy's bravado, and then a visibly angry teenager: moody, irrational, ready for confrontation.

Annie wrapped her arms around herself, hugging her elbows. "I don't know what to do anymore," she whispered. And then, to Eric: "He's having such a hard time with your dad and me splitting up."

Eric got to his feet. "Mom?" he said, his voice coming out as a squawk.

"Yes?" she said.

He examined a tear in his jacket with unusual interest. "I'm having a pretty hard time with it myself."

Annie blinked at him.

"I'm sorry," he said softly.

"For what?" she said, alarmed to see his mouth trembling.

"For everything." His voice was unsteady. "For how much you worry, for how bad things were between you and Dad when I was sick, for how you and Luke fight so much, for being so much . . . trouble." He was crying now, and Annie was so astonished that she found it hard to take in what he was saying.

"Eric, none of that's your fault."

"Maybe it's not *my fault*," he said, sniveling, "but it's *because* of me."

"No," Annie said. "It's not."

"Yes, it is," he said, sounding frustrated. Fierce, even. "I've known for years, Mom. Everything that's happened is because of me."

"Oh, Jesus," Annie said, closing her eyes tight.

She had suspected that Luke blamed her for everything, and she had come to accept that Jack had stopped talking to her about it long ago, but now Eric felt responsible? After all this time, how had she failed to recognize that he felt this way? Annie stared into his face. She pulled him close and rested her chin on top of his head, trying to make sense of it all. When she said, "No, sweetheart," whispering it into his hair, "none of it was because of you," he cried even harder.

It wasn't until later, when she was in a more rational frame of mind, that it occurred to her how hard it must have been for Eric to say what he did, and yet she was glad he had. Thinking back, Annie tried to remember if there'd been any signs she'd somehow missed, but nothing came to mind. Forever an optimist, Eric was always reassuring her that everything would be okay—after she and Jack split up, when she lost her job, even when she told him they were moving to Eagan's Point. All he'd said was "For how long?" And when she'd hesitated, gently replying, "Maybe a few years. We'll see," there had been nothing, not even a flicker of disappointment, just a nod and a reassuring smile.

As she twisted and turned in bed that night, unable to sleep, her secret admirer and his ads in the *Peninsula Post* were the farthest things from Annie's mind. Divorce in principle she knew about—divorce in practice, no. But she understood something more clearly now than she had before. When one of you said it was over, it never was if you had kids, and when Orenda McMillan finally got to the core of her, no matter how much they talked about the past or the present or the future, Annie knew she would find Jack and the boys there too.

SEVENTEEN

At work the following Monday, Annie read the third ad for the second time, shaking her head in amazement that two weeks had gone by and she still had no idea who'd placed them.

DO YOU KNOW THIS WOMAN?

I READ SOMEWHERE THAT AT LEAST ONCE IN HIS LIFE A MAN WILL MAKE A FOOL OF HIMSELF OVER A WOMAN. WITH THESE ADS, I'VE DECIDED TO TAKE THAT RISK. ANNIE FISCHER IS TERRIFIED OF SPIDERS, BELIEVES CELEBRATING ISN'T CELEBRATING WITHOUT BALLOONS, AND WOULD RATHER GO KAYAKING THAN SHOPPING. SHE HAS A STRAWBERRY-SHAPED BIRTHMARK ON HER RIGHT SHOULDER AND INCREDIBLE EYES (ONE BLUE, ONE GREEN). I KNEW HER YEARS AGO AND I CAN'T FORGET HER. IF YOU KNOW WHERE I CAN FIND HER, PLEASE CALL (212) 555-1963.

"Your mom says you still don't know who put these ads in?"

The voice startled her and Annie turned to find Rudy standing behind her as he read the morning paper. Stunned, she gave him a steady, unblinking gaze. He might as well have asked her if she was happy with her life, so unusual was his sudden interest. "No," she finally managed. "I don't."

"Well, he sure seems set on finding you, doesn't he?"

"Looks that way," she said, feeling a blush start.

He glanced up at her, then quickly back to the paper. "If it ends up he's some kind of oddball, and there's anything I can do, let me know."

Eyes wide, Annie watched him go back into his office. Other than his love of golf and the funeral home, Rudy usually treated everyone else around him with disinterest, so this was new. The phone rang and she grabbed it.

"Is Ms. Hillman there please?"

"Speaking."

"It's Joan Marsh with Robertson Middle School calling—"

"Great," Annie said, pushing back from her desk. "Luke's skipping again?"

"No, Ms. Hillman. I'm calling about Eric."

Annie picked up her coffee and put it back down again. "Eric?"

"Yes. The principal asked if you could come talk to him. We've been having some trouble this morning. . . ."

What was she talking about? Eric was never any trouble. Luke was the one who tested everyone's patience and pushed them to their limits—not Eric.

". . . and then the basketball coach met with him, but now he's sitting alone in the gym, and he won't talk, Ms. Hillman. Not to anyone."

A sick feeling came over her as Annie realized what was wrong. "Do you know if he made the basketball team?"

"No, ma'am, he didn't."

Annie nodded, then cleared her throat. "I'll be there in fifteen minutes."

Glancing up at the clock, she saw that it was only nine thirty and yet here she was needing to leave work for personal reasons again. Determined not to jeopardize her job, she grabbed the phone and called her mom.

When it came to her boys, Annie liked to think she was prepared for almost anything. What if the power went out? (She stocked up on candles.) What if a button popped off one of their shirts? (She kept miniature sewing kits in the car and in her purse.) What if one of their fillings fell out and she couldn't get them to a dentist? (Temporary filling kits could be purchased at any drugstore and lasted a few years, if kept dry.) At home, in a box marked *emergencies*, she had her own miniature pharmacy, just in case. But today when she parked in front of the school, she pushed her car door open and sat with her feet touching the pavement, feeling helpless.

What are you supposed to do when your kid's heart gets broken? Because I don't have any Band-Aids for this one.

For Annie, losing Eric was never an option, not even when his doctors outlined the odds against him after their initial diagnosis. While he was hospitalized the second time, a five-year-old girl with the same disease died, and their doctor gently warned Annie and Jack that they should brace for the worst.

"Don't even go there," Annie had said, cutting him off.

When the chemotherapy left Eric so weak he could barely lift his head off the pillow, she'd stayed with him, massaging his legs and telling him stories. And on those rare nights she didn't spend at the hospital, she slept at home with his favorite blanket wrapped around her pillow, the scent of him enough to carry her through the night.

Now, as she climbed the stairs to the school, Annie rummaged through her purse. Eric had never been any trouble, even as a baby. He'd always adjusted to any environment they put him in, making the best of it. It used to worry her that he was too forgiving and accommodating, too easygoing for his own good. His second-grade teacher had called her and Jack once to tell them he'd been giving his lunch away. Annie instantly pictured a five-foot bully backing him up against a wall, but the teacher assured her this wasn't the case. Eric had been giving his lunch to another boy who never brought more than an apple. Instead of telling him not to share his food, Annie packed him a bigger lunch. "I agree, what he's doing won't fix the problem," she told the teacher. "But if he believes he's making a difference, then that's all that matters, isn't it?"

She stopped at the office to meet with the basketball coach. He sat in a chair adjacent to hers, looking uncomfortable.

"Ms. Hillman," he said, folding his hands in his lap, "there's a notation in Eric's student file that says he has a medical condition."

Annie nodded. "Yes."

"It's called . . . hystiocytosis?"

"Right," Annie said, shifting in her chair.

"And it's rare?"

"Yes, but it's not contagious."

"I know," he said gently. "But basketball is a very physical game and he could get hurt."

She stared at him, waiting.

The coach sighed. "Robertson Middle School doesn't want a lawsuit on our hands, so we can't take on the responsibility of letting him play."

"But he's good?"

"Pardon me?"

"Does he have talent?" she pressed.

"Oh, yes. He's real quick with the ball and . . ." His voice trailed off and he shook his head. "Ms. Hillman, Eric's hystiocy-tosis hasn't been in remission for long, and from what I understand, any sharp jarring or impact on his bones could retrigger the disease—isn't that correct?"

"Anything's possible," she conceded.

A long silence loomed up until the coach finally said, "This isn't easy for me. I'm sorry."

Annie rose to leave. "Where is he?"

The coach stood. "Ms. Hillman, please understand. The roster was tight and I had to take Eric's medical condition into consideration when I made my decision."

No longer caring, she waved him off. "Just tell me where he is."

The doors to the gym were open, and as Annie walked across the polished hardwood floor, her footsteps echoed against the walls. She climbed the stairs that led to the stage, and saw Eric slouched against the back wall with one leg extended and the other bent at the knee. His favorite knapsack lay beside him, covered with stickers from the Sonics and the Lakers and probably every other NBA basketball team that had ever existed. She bent and kissed the black knit cap he had crammed on his head, then slid down the wall next to him.

"I've got something for you," she said, pulling her purse into her lap. She unzipped it, reached inside, and held out a closed fist. When he put out his hand, she dropped something into it. Looking confused, he squinted at an amber nugget in the middle of his palm, no more than an inch long, with a crystallized ant trapped inside.

"What is it?" he asked.

"An amber fossil that's at least twenty million years old. The resin from what are now extinct trees used to weep down onto the ground, trapping all kinds of plants and bugs, crystallizing them into amber fossils."

"Where'd you get it?"

Annie smiled. "From my dad. He gave it to me after the first night of my sixth-grade play. It ran for five nights straight and I had the part of a talking broomstick. My costume was too tight, my lines were embarrassing, and the audience laughed every time I waddled onstage. After the first night, I went home crying and said I wanted to quit."

"How'd this help?" he asked, turning it over on his palm.

"He told me to carry it in my pocket to give me courage to go out there and face everyone, so I did. And for the next four nights I ad-libbed new lines instead of the ones I'd been given, dumbing them down so everyone laughed harder." She looped an arm through his and gave him a squeeze. "And now it's yours. Two ounces of frozen amber with an ancient ant trapped inside to give you courage to face whatever you need to face."

"Thanks, Mom," he said, curling his hand around it.

Annie stood and brushed herself off, watching him closely. "There was one other thing your grandpa made me promise I'd always do when life knocked me down."

He looked up at her expectantly. "What?"

"Get up," she said, reaching for his hand.

When Annie got back to work, several vehicles were parked in front of Kozak's, including a white van with a CBS logo on it. Two men were talking outside on the sidewalk. Annie recognized one of them from the Seattle nightly news. Feeling her face redden, she got out of the car and watched as he walked toward her. Then someone tapped her on the shoulder, startling her. Turning, she came face-to-face with a balding, heavyset man.

"Afternoon, Ms. Hillman," he said. "I'm George Mercer and I work for the *Seattle Examiner*. Your neighbor called me after recognizing you in the paper."

Flustered, Annie took a few steps back, almost bumping into still another reporter, who gave her a dazzling smile and got straight to the point. "I'm Noreen Redden with CBS, Ms. Hillman. Nice to meet you. Do you have any idea who placed these ads?"

"How do you feel about them?" George Mercer asked, stepping closer.

Annie continued backing away as they began firing questions, trying to outdo each other.

"Do you have any comments?" asked the CBS reporter.

George held up the newspaper. "Have you called the number in the ad yet?"

"I'm not sure . . . I don't know . . ." she stammered.

Feeling like a bug under a microscope, she hurried inside. Rudy stopped the reporters at the door, asking them to leave in a tone that left no room for argument.

Later that afternoon, Annie got home from work seconds before Mr. Tucker pulled into her driveway. Shooting him an exasperated look, she waited for him at the back door. For two weeks now, she'd been using the dryer at the local Laundromat, leaving increasingly frustrated messages on his machine. His wife had finally called her back the day before, apologizing. He'd been away on another fishing trip, but she'd send him over as soon as he got home.

"What's wrong with your dryer?" Mr. Tucker asked.

"It won't run." Annie held the door open to let him in. "See for yourself."

Carrying his toolbox, he went down the hall, calling out over his shoulder, "By the way, you didn't tell me you had a dog when you signed the lease."

"Probably 'cause we didn't have one then," she countered.

He pulled the dryer out from the wall and leaned behind it to check the plug. "Dogs ain't allowed in the house."

"Neither are people who don't take off their boots," she said, staring pointedly at his feet.

He raised an eyebrow, but didn't say anything.

A few minutes later, he went down the hallway and out the door, swearing under his breath. When he came back, he was carrying an appliance dolly, and this time, he wiped his feet on the scuff rug at the door when he entered.

"Motor's gone," he said.

"Which means . . . ?" Annie asked.

His eyes were rheumy and he looked tired. "That I'll have to buy a new one. This one's fifteen years old, so replacing the motor don't make sense."

She gave him her best smile. "But you've got a backup for me, right?"

"Nope. You'll have to line dry your clothes or take 'em to the Laundromat until I can get you one. Might take a week or so, but that's all I can do."

Closing her eyes for patience, Annie told herself it wasn't Mr. Tucker's fault. Then she held the screen door open so he could maneuver the dryer outside. Luke gave him a hand getting it down the steps, and after he drove away, she went down to the basement and rummaged around until she found the clothespins she'd seen when they moved in. Using the Laundromat was more of a headache than it was worth, especially because people kept recognizing her from the ads and wanted to talk about them.

Upstairs, she grabbed a basket of wet clothes and stepped

outside. She couldn't remember the last time she'd seen anyone use an outdoor clothesline and had actually laughed when she first saw this one hooked up between the house and the garage. When she was looking for a house to rent, she'd found two close to the ocean, and although this one was older, she'd taken it because it had an oversize claw-foot bathtub, a cherry red enamel kitchen sink that made her smile, and this old clothesline. Setting the basket down, she grabbed a T-shirt, shook it out, and clamped it on the line with two clothespins.

Eric stopped dribbling and balanced his basketball against one hip. "So that's what people used to do, huh, before they had dryers?"

Annie nodded. "You bet. Years ago, everyone hung all their clothes out for the neighbors to gawk at and then they prayed it wouldn't rain."

"Probably worked good if you lived in a desert."

"Probably," she agreed.

The phone rang, and she slipped inside to grab it. "Hello."

"Annie Hillman?"

"Speaking."

"Daniel Frost from the *Seattle Times*, Ms. Hillman. I was wondering—"

"No comment," she said, hanging up.

Before going back outside, she decided to take out spaghetti and fill a pot with water. She'd already called Jack from work to tell him Eric hadn't made the team and he'd promised to phone tonight before he went on the air.

When the phone rang again, Luke grabbed it. "Hello?" Pause. "Uh . . . no, I can't."

He hung up and Annie asked who it was.

"A reporter."

"What did he ask you?"

Luke shrugged. "If I could tell him a little bit about you."

Annie marched over to the answering machine and turned off the phone ringer. Heading upstairs to her bedroom, she did the same thing there, stuffing the portable underneath her pillow. When she came back downstairs, Eric was setting her empty clothes basket on the table.

"I finished hanging everything up for you," he said.

Luke appeared in the doorway from the living room. "Man, you're a suck-up," he said.

Annie swiveled to face him. "That's enough! If you talk to him like that again, Xbox is off limits for the rest of the week." After he went back into the living room, she thanked Eric. "That's the nicest thing that's happened to me all day." Then she glanced out the window and noticed with dismay that he'd taken her literally, hanging all of their jeans and T-shirts out on the line, along with their underwear—including four pairs of her cotton panties, which were now flapping in the wind for the entire neighborhood to see.

Annie took a few minutes to change and when she came back downstairs, Luke was slouched on the couch watching MTV, a plate with what looked like the remnants of a sandwich under a napkin on the coffee table.

"You ate?" she asked.

"Uh-huh."

Sighing, she trudged upstairs and knocked on the boys' bedroom door. "Eric?"

When there was no answer, she knocked again.

Silence.

She turned the doorknob, stuck her head inside, and frowned. Torn pieces of his favorite Steve Nash posters were lying on the floor and his binder of collector cards was upside down in a corner. Obviously not making the team was still bothering him.

Frowning, she crouched down to look under the beds. She noticed a narrow slice of light coming from under the closet door and remembered the bare bulb inside with a pull chain.

"Eric? You in there?"

There was a long pause and then his voice, small and forlorn, came through the door. "Not now, Mom, okay? I wanna be alone."

Annie sat down on the edge of his bed. At times like this, she wished both her boys were still little, with rounded bellies hanging over Batman underwear, thirst or hunger the only things that slowed them down. She missed them crawling into bed with her in the middle of the night. She missed them telling her secrets and giving her wet, toothy kisses. She missed Eric sucking his thumb, and how, if Luke got hurt, she could never get away with applying just one Band-Aid. Times when they were so busy being little boys she couldn't open their bedroom door without sending LEGOs flying everywhere.

"Did you want something to eat?" she asked Eric.

"Maybe later."

Straightening, she set her hands on her hips.

As a little guy, Eric had been crazy about LEGOs. When he was in the hospital, he would sit up in bed with one dinner cart covered in LEGOs and a second one for his meals. On his first day of school, when asked what he wanted to be when he grew up, he had stood in front of the class with his shoulders pulled back and said he was going to move to Denmark and work for a company named LEGO. He'd said it with conviction, certain this would be the case, refusing to entertain failure as a possibility. Annie went to her bedroom closet, thinking, *The same way he approaches everything he does today*.

After rummaging around for the Rubbermaid container, she tiptoed back to his room and set it on the floor. Quietly, she removed the lid and grabbed a handful of LEGOs. Setting one piece on the hardwood floor, she took aim and flicked it with her thumb and index finger, sending the LEGO skidding across the room and under the closet door.

A muffled "W-wha . . . ?" was followed by silence.

She stretched out on her stomach and lined up a dozen pieces, then began flicking them one by one under the closet door. A red piece, then a blue one, followed by a yellow one.

"Mom, what are you doing?" Eric asked, working hard not to sound pleased.

She set her chin in her hands. "How'd you know it was me?"

The door creaked open and he stuck his head out. "Because you never give up. Even when it's annoying, I know it's you."

She sat up and held out an arm for him to snuggle into. At first he hesitated, but then he did, and for the next half hour, they sat side by side on the floor, building something with LEGOs that resembled nothing in particular.

"Uh, Mom?" Luke said, sticking his head into the doorway.

"What?"

"I think you might want to come downstairs and see this. . . ." His voice trailed away.

Hurrying downstairs, Annie glanced at the TV in the living room and felt her face go slack. One of the reporters she'd seen earlier was standing in front of her house on TV. Stunned, she went to the window and peeked out from behind the curtains. The reporter from the *Seattle Examiner* was talking to Rose and Libby at the picnic table, and another one was walking backward up her driveway, his cameraman filming him.

"I don't believe this," she said, dropping onto the couch.

On TV, she heard, "I'm here in Eagan's Point, Washington, at the home of Annie Hillman, a woman who has inadvertently sparked media attention with a series of personal ads that were placed in the *Peninsula Post* by someone who's anonymously searching for her. We have learned that Annie works as a receptionist at a local funeral home, is in the midst of a divorce, has two sons, and graduated from the high school here in Eagan's Point before attending the University of Chicago." Turning, he gestured to the house. "But who is Annie Hillman? Everything we see here indicates a single mother working hard to make ends meet. Nothing more, nothing less . . ."

Annie winced as the camera moved left, noticing that TV made the house look shabbier than usual. The railing on her front steps was broken on one side and missing on the other, her kitchen window was cracked, and the siding was falling off in spots. The camera took in a jumble of weeds poking through cracks in the driveway, then her ancient Yugo, including a crushed box of Kleenex in the back window, a row of bicycle-reflector stickers across the bumper, and two deer whistles poking out from under each of the side mirrors.

"At least we don't have a tarp stapled to our roof," Luke said.

Frozen, Annie watched the camera pan up the driveway, zooming in on Eric's rusty basketball hoop before taking in their backyard. "Oh my God," she said, covering her mouth with both hands. The camera hovered on Montana's doghouse before following the length of the clothesline, slowly taking in all of the boys' sweatshirts, jeans, and socks, along with her cotton panties, swinging in the wind.

When Annie checked the answering machine two hours later, there was a message from Chris Carby telling her that he'd be home next Thursday, that his fishing charter was going well, and when he got back, he'd love to take her out for dinner. There was also a message from Julie, telling Annie that she'd tracked down her cousin, but he was on sabbatical somewhere in Europe, so she'd e-mailed him about Peter Dawson and was hoping to hear back soon. Her mom had also left one: "Annie, after you went home today, a man called Kozak's looking for you. I gave him your home phone number and that cellular number you gave me the other day. Did he call yet?" And last of all, there was a message from Jack: "Eric, it's Dad. When you get this message, give me a call at work. I'll be on the air until midnight."

EIGHTEEN

*A*fter leaving a message for Eric, Jack hung up and turned off the TV in the station's staff lounge. Earlier, he'd been watching the news when he flipped to channel six and saw a reporter standing in Annie's driveway. His first instinct was protective: to step in, take over, and demand a stop to all this. Instead he'd watched in frustration, knowing that unless he was invited—unless it upset the boys or Annie asked for his help—this was a line he couldn't cross. But staying out of it wasn't easy for him, especially since he knew firsthand what it was like not to have a father to turn to for help.

He had never wanted kids, but then he'd met Annie and something shifted inside, something so scarcely measurable that at first he thought he'd imagined it. That was when all his plans went soft. Like how he had always said he would hitchhike through Europe when he finished his broadcasting course, and then didn't, or how he had saved for years to buy a 1965 Corvette, only to spend it all on an engagement ring for Annie. He told himself there was no way a woman could derail his plans or get under his skin, yet that was what Annie did, with a mixture of vulnerability and stinging independence that mesmerized him. Now, fifteen years later, including thirteen raising their boys and almost two since they had split up, here he was, unable to stop thinking about Annie, mostly because of a conversation he'd had with his sister, Elaine, at lunch today.

After their mom died in January, Elaine began going out of her way to make sure they saw each other more often. They used to have lunch every six months, but now they got together every few weeks whether Jack wanted to or not. Elaine had seen the ads about Annie, so when she phoned him that morning, it was all she could talk about. What was going on? Had he talked to Annie about it yet? Did he have any idea who this guy could be? Jack had agreed to meet her for lunch, hoping she'd be a little less fascinated by the time they got together.

Unfortunately, Elaine had showed him no mercy.

When he arrived at the restaurant, she was already there, copies of the ads on the table in full view. At first, Jack didn't mention them and neither did she. They ordered sandwiches and coffee and talked about her latest trip to the Bahamas (Elaine was a flight attendant). Finally, she leaned forward with an air of heady expectation.

"Okay, spit it out," she said. "How's it going?"

"Today?" he said. "Or with life in general?"

"Honestly, Jack," she said, picking up the ads. "How do you feel about these?"

"I don't know," he said, shrugging. "How should I feel?"

"Concerned. Curious. Anxious. Pick an emotion, any emotion," she said, a little sourly. "I'm sure this whole situation has been weighing on your mind a lot."

"Not really," he said. "I haven't thought about them that much."

"Don't lie to me," she said, crossing her arms. "You're my brother, and I think I know you well enough to know this must be bothering you. It can't be easy watching another man go to these lengths to get Annie's attention. You were married for years, Jack."

"Thanks for pointing that out," he said, taking a bite of his roast beef on rye.

"Do you have any idea who it could be?"

"No, I don't."

"Have you talked to Annie about it?"

"Not really."

"Why not?" she pressed.

"Because it's none of my business," he said, a little more clipped than he'd intended.

Elaine studied him. Then, after a few minutes, when they were both almost finished eating, she slowly nodded, as though realizing something. "You wish you'd thought of it," she said, half to herself.

Swallowing, Jack looked straight at her. "What?"

She nodded at the ads, smiling. "You wish it were you."

He set his sandwich down and wiped his mouth with a napkin. "Right now, for the boys' sake, and Annie's, I wish someone would get caught streaking through the White House because obviously it's been a slow news week, but no, I don't wish it were me." And yet, even to his own ears, his voice suddenly sounded irritated and slightly nervous. He kept talking as he stood and shrugged into his jacket. "And anyhow, what Annie does with her life isn't my concern anymore, so leave it alone, okay?"

"I can't, Jack. I'm worried about you."

"Don't be. I'm fine."

Elaine grabbed his arm. "Come on. Please talk to me. What do you want? What do you *really* want?"

He searched her face. He was used to the way Elaine was forever prodding and pushing, rooting around through his life to make sure he was okay. He knew if he didn't answer, they would end up talking about it the next time they had lunch, and the next, and the next. His jaw tightened and he put his hands in his pockets.

"What do I want?" he said. "I want to be at a place in my life where I'm happier more often than I'm not. I want to hold my sons for the first time all over again. I want to laugh the way I did years ago when I was teaching Annie how to drive. I want to love my family with that bottomless feeling that made me have to close my eyes and catch my breath because it all seemed so . . . big. That's what I want, okay? All of it."

Looking relieved, Elaine nudged the ads across the table toward him. "You can still have it," she whispered.

Jack shook his head. "The past is the past."

"There's always the future. . . ."

But he was done talking. He raised a hand and turned away, and Elaine got up and hugged him, harder than usual, before they both went back to work.

That conversation had been bothering him all afternoon. Jack laced his hands behind his head. In half an hour he had to go on the air, and he hoped Eric would call back before then. He also wouldn't mind asking Annie how she was doing. Maybe he'd offer to help in an offhand way—one that didn't make it obvious he was sticking his nose where it didn't belong—because no matter how he felt, he knew it wasn't his business.

Nineteen

"Sometimes I pray," Annie said, working on Orenda McMillan's lower back.

"What do you pray for?" Orenda asked.

Pausing, Annie thought about this. "Nothing fancy. For things to be the way they used to be. Eric healthy, Luke happy, Jack and me on speaking terms." She'd already told Orenda about what had happened when she took the boys to her penny tree over the weekend, and how she'd been mentally going over the scene again and again all week since then.

Orenda sat up and took her hand. "Annie, listen. When it comes to Eric's health, you approach each day like you're waiting for the other shoe to fall, but maybe it never will. And when you talk about your relationship with Luke, you make it sound as though it's broken when maybe all it needs is a splint. You and your boys might be bruised and scared, but you have each other. You're not making the most of it, though. You need to spend more time with them. You need to do something *different* with them."

"But I'm in debt up to here," Annie said, slicing a finger across her forehead. "I can't afford to do much of anything with them right now."

Orenda smiled. "You don't need money. You just need a little imagination."

"I thought I'd start when things get better," Annie said, feeling cowed.

"Start now, Annie, or things will never get better. Your boys see you coping, but they don't see you living, and there's a big difference. The way they're feeling right now—Luke blaming you, Eric feeling responsible—is magnified when they watch how you handle things."

"And you think spending more time with them will help?" Annie asked.

Orenda patted her hand. "It's better than doing what you've been doing."

Fair enough, Annie reasoned, but spending time with the boys was easier for Jack. After all, he shared their love of basketball, fishing, sailing—things she couldn't compete with. Minutes later, while Annie was still lost in thought, Orenda asked, "How's Eric been doing since your talk at the penny tree?"

Annie shrugged. "Right now I think he's most upset about not making the basketball team."

"What about Luke?"

"Depends," Annie admitted. "Since the weekend, he's been locking himself away in his room for hours at a time. Last night I got tired of him holing up in there, so I took the hinges off his bedroom door and put it outside in the garage."

Orenda frowned as she considered this.

"How did he react?" she asked.

Annie's face reddened. "He hung a bedsheet over the doorway."

Nodding, Orenda smiled and said, "You can't build a relationship with a hammer, Annie."

"Good point," she conceded in a half whisper.

Driving home, she thought about everything Orenda had

said, and by the time she was halfway across town, she had decided to take the boys to a drive-in movie. She'd read in the local paper that the Starlite Drive-in had recently been retrofitted and reopened after its closure fifteen years ago. It was only twenty miles away and affordable if she skipped paying the phone bill this month. As she tossed the idea around, her own memories of going to the drive-in seemed more wondrous and extraordinary than they had before, and suddenly, it seemed important that she take them. Imperative, in fact.

"Guess what," she said, nudging the entertainment section of the paper across the table at breakfast the next morning. "I'm taking you guys to the Starlite Drive-in this weekend. It'll be fun." Eric and Luke looked at her like she'd lost her mind. "Tonight they're playing *Star Wars III: Revenge of the Sith* and on Saturday it's *War of the Worlds*. You guys pick."

At first, they both said they didn't want to go, but she persisted, telling them they didn't have a choice. Then they argued about which movie to see. Luke wanted *War of the Worlds* and Eric said he preferred *Star Wars*, so she finally had them do rock paper scissors to settle the argument, and Eric won, sending Luke storming up to his room.

They left the house at eight thirty that night and hadn't made it ten miles outside town before a state trooper pulled them over.

"Everything okay, ma'am?" he asked when Annie rolled down her window.

"Fine," she said, turning up the wattage on her smile.

Luke busied himself rubbing a scratch on the dashboard. Frowning, the officer leaned down and glanced into the backseat at Eric, then stepped away a few paces, taking a look at their rusty old Yugo from front to back.

Seeing his confusion, Annie said, "You're wondering why I'm driving so slow, right?"

He lifted an eyebrow. "That question did cross my mind when I clocked you doing thirty in a sixty zone."

"I can be an overly cautious driver," she explained. "But I can speed up a little, if you think that'd be better." He asked to see her license and Annie handed it over. "We're going to the Starlite Drive-in to see a movie," she added, hoping he wouldn't blow the incident out of proportion.

Nodding impartially, he read the back of her license. "Tell you what," he finally said, adjusting his sunglasses as he handed it back. "I'll let you off with a warning if you promise me I'll never see you driving this slow on the highway again."

Hugely relieved, Annie said, "That'd be great."

"And, ma'am?"

"Yes?"

"Turn off your four-way flashers."

Annie flexed her hands on the steering wheel, waiting for him to leave. As soon as he got into his patrol car, she double-checked the highway in both directions, turned on her signal light, and pulled out, accelerating to forty, then fifty, and soon, almost sixty miles per hour.

"Brace yourself!" Luke said, gripping the dash. "She's a speed demon."

Ignoring him, Annie flicked her gaze nervously back and forth from the road to the speedometer. Less than a mile from the drive-in, she failed to slow down at a railroad intersection and went over the tracks at fifty miles per hour. A bump in the road on the other side of the tracks started the car bouncing. Up and down they went. Up and down. Then up higher and down even farther as they ricocheted off the seats so hard that their heads hit the roof.

"What the hell . . . ?" Annie said.

She instinctively slammed her foot on the brake and then let

go. The tires squealed in protest, leaving skid marks on the highway, and sending the car's front end down farther and up even
higher than before. It was relentless. Up and down, u-u-up and
d-d-down. The boys put their hands up against the roof as she
moved over to the side of the highway and let the car slowly buck
to a stop.

"I think it's your shocks," Luke said. "They've probably been
going for a while. You know how we always bounce a little when
we hit that small dip at the end of Grandma's street? Well, when
your shocks go and you're on the highway doing fifty instead of
twenty, it's gonna be a lot worse when you hit a bump."

"Oh," Annie said, glancing in the rearview mirror. "Eric, are
you okay?"

"Fine," he said, looking stunned. "God, though."

When they finally got to the Starlite Drive-in, crawling
through the main gates at ten miles an hour for fear of bouncing
again, Annie parked in the last available spot in the middle of the
front row and they walked over to the concession stand to buy
popcorn and drinks. Like the original drive-in, the concession
was housed in the same building as the bathrooms, but where the
old one had been a utilitarian brick building with almost no character, the new one was a contemporary remake with a corrugated
steel roof, floor-to-ceiling glass, cork floors, and neon lights.

Annie was standing near the exit, waiting for Eric and Luke,
and had just taken a sip of Sprite when Luke walked out of the
men's room and into the sliding glass doors separating it from the
concession stand. After smacking into the glass and stumbling
backward, he quickly righted himself and looked around to see if
anyone else had seen him. Annie burst out laughing, snorting
Sprite out her nose before she could swallow it.

Rubbing his forehead, Luke glared at her.

Seconds later, she was in stitches again, doubled over, hugging her stomach with one arm and pointing at Eric, who had done exactly the same thing. Only he'd come around the corner from the men's bathroom in an even bigger hurry, so when he hit the glass, he actually bounced off, unable to catch himself as he fell backward onto the cork floor. She was laughing so hard she was having trouble breathing, mouth open, but nothing coming out other than a squeaky *ah-ah-ah-ah-ah* sound.

"God, Mom," Luke hissed. "Tone it down, will you?"

"Sorry," she said, walking over to Eric. "Are you okay, pal?"

"Uh . . . I guess," Eric said, looking more disoriented than embarrassed.

Taking his elbow, she helped him up and guided him over to the exit. Biting back a smile, she looked sideways at Luke. "He's okay," she said.

"I can see that," Luke said, trying not to smile.

As she watched him, something fresh and tender lifted up in Annie's chest. Waving them both closer, she leaned forward and whispered, "I did exactly the same thing a few minutes ago."

Eric stepped back. "Are you *serious*?"

"Face-first," Annie admitted, thrusting the palm of one hand out in front of her for effect.

"That's hilarious," he said, laughing.

Luke shook his head, trying to look disgusted, but a smile tugged at the corners of his mouth and Annie could tell he was secretly amused.

"Man," Eric said, "it's hard not to tell we're related."

"And that's a good thing?" Luke said.

Yes, Annie thought. *That's a great thing.*

In that moment, their moods flipped upside down, and on the way back to the car, as the boys gave each other a few playful shoves, Annie felt lighter than she had in months—happy, even. *We're going to be fine,* she thought. *No matter what happens next week or next month or even a year from now, no matter who took out these crazy ads or how awkward this divorce might be, we're going to be just fine.*

Before the movie started, Annie offered to sit in the backseat so the boys could see better, and Eric climbed into the driver's seat. Not even halfway through the movie, in the middle of a spectacular fight scene loaded with special effects, she closed her eyes and leaned her head against the window.

Minutes later, she heard Luke say, "Fire!"

"Bang?" Eric replied, sounding confused.

"No, stupid, there's *a fire.* Look!"

Annie sat up, blinking. The movie screen towering up in front of them like a mini-skyscraper was leaking thick black smoke around its outer edges, and rising up from the bottom was a mesmerizing hue of orange and red and yellow. Paralyzed by what she was seeing, she stared at the brilliant collage of flames that, at first glance, looked like another special effect for the movie. Then cars on either side of them began coming to life, engines revving as they backed up and careened toward the main gate, lights blinking on and off.

"Oh my God!" she said, fumbling to open the back door.

Climbing out, she opened the driver's door and grabbed Eric by the elbow, pulling him out. "Wicked!" he said, jumping into the backseat and unrolling his window to get a better look. Annie rubbed her face to wake herself up and then reached for her car keys, but when she tried starting the old Yugo, there was no sign of life. Nothing. No grinding, no coughing, not even a faint murmur of protest.

"You're kidding," Luke said. "It won't *start?*"

Pandemonium had broken loose all around them, a chaotic mix of cars and trucks and vans honking in panic as they tried to fit through the narrow bottleneck of an exit intended to take them out of the drive-in and onto the main road. A few SUVs went bouncing down a short, rocky incline into a grassy ditch that led through the drive-in's narrow entrance on the other side. It was a vision Annie knew she would never get over: people at their worst, fear pushing them to make stupid, selfish decisions based on their need to escape the fire.

"Get moving!" one man screamed, gunning the engine of his Volkswagen van as he shook his fist out the window at the car in front of him.

"Screw you, buddy," an older woman yelled back. "Where am I supposed to *go*?"

Swallowing, Annie tried to start the car again.

Nothing.

Frustrated, she hit the steering wheel with the flat of her hand, then tried a few more times, furiously cranking the key in a clockwise motion, punctuated by a few expletives when nothing happened. "Here," she said, handing her cell phone to Luke. "Try calling Uncle Harrison." As an afterthought, she grabbed his arm, swiveled to look at Eric, and said, "Sorry about the swearing."

Sirens blared in the distance and someone had turned off the movie. The fire was giving them its own cinematic show as the flames quickly engulfed the screen, licking higher and higher into the sky. Glancing around in panic, Annie saw that theirs was the only car left in the first three rows.

"Come on, guys," she said, shouldering her door open. "Let's get out of here."

"There's no service," Luke said, handing back her cell phone.

The sirens were louder now, bouncing off the ten-foot-high wooden wall of a fence built to keep everyone corralled inside the drive-in. Annie grabbed her purse, yelling at the boys to follow her. As they ran from the wall of fire rising up behind them, her heart was doing flip-flops in her chest. A few people waved flashlights in the air, swinging small puddles of light back and forth along the gravel road as they helped guide everyone out. Unprepared for how far away the exit actually was, Annie ran as fast as she could, sweat beading on her forehead as the boys kept pace beside her.

It started to rain when they were halfway across the lot, and by the time they reached the exit, they were sopping wet. A young man waved them over next to one of the ticket booths, which was already crammed with employees from the concession stand.

"Stand here," he said, pointing to a dry spot under the roof's overhang.

Minutes later, shivering and wet, Annie and Luke and Eric huddled against the wall of the ticket booth as the massive movie screen broke free from its metal moorings and fell forward, folding in on itself before smothering their old Yugo like a huge blanket.

"Unreal," Eric said under his breath.

"I'm taking you to a drive-in," Luke mimicked. *"It'll be fun!"*

Annie's shoulders started to tremble in a strange, uncontrollable way. She was dizzy with relief that no one had gotten hurt and yet mesmerized by the sight of the fire. The rain increased in intensity, pelting down around them in a renewed burst, bouncing off the ground like minuscule rubber balls, creating a series of hisses that could be heard all the way across the field as it put out pockets of fire that had taken hold in the dry grass.

"Mom?" Eric said. "You can let go of my hand now."

"Oh." Annie looked down. "Sorry, pal."

"I don't know what's better," Luke chuckled, "getting rid of our stupid car or not having to watch the end of that movie."

Annie pretended she hadn't heard him. Instead, she stared at a small crowd of people gathered to their right, hooting and yelling as they waved a dozen glowing light sabers in an adrenaline rush of solidarity for the movie they'd come to see.

"That was wild!" one of them said.

"Did you see it land on that old clunker of a car?"

The drive-in just burned down, she thought, shaking her head in disbelief. *And we were right here when it happened.*

Later, after the fire trucks arrived and put out the blaze, the only vehicle left was an old pickup that belonged to the owner of the drive-in. He and his wife graciously offered to drive Annie and the boys home, so they climbed into the back and folded their arms around their knees to keep warm. Halfway there, Luke said, "How much further?" in a way that suggested this couldn't be over soon enough for him, and Eric started to laugh. Once he got going, he couldn't stop, and before long, despite himself, Luke was laughing too.

All the way home, both of them laughed so hard they were almost doubled over. And the simplicity of it overwhelmed Annie. If ever there was a moment she would look back at, point to, and say, "That's when it all became clear to me," that was it. As she listened to the spongy hum of the truck's tires on the highway, her boys laughing on either side of her, she realized how lucky she was. Reaching down, she laced her fingers through each of theirs, and when Luke actually let her, she smiled.

For the first time in ages, life isn't just coming at me, she thought. *I'm coming at life, spending time with my kids, living each moment without letting it flatten me.*

Twenty

*L*ate Sunday night, before the fourth ad ran in the *Peninsula Post*, Marina called Annie offering this advice: "Remember when Austin Carrington was having trouble with that woman who wouldn't stop mailing him cards?"

Annie rubbed her eyes. "Do I know an Austin Carrington?"

"He's the top audiologist on *Days of our Lives*, someone who specializes in evaluating and treating people with hearing loss."

"And your point is . . . ?"

"That Austin had anonymous cards mailed to him at work one entire season, and as the months went by, he almost came unglued over it. He stopped eating and then he started having trouble sleeping and when he was at work he couldn't focus—"

"Okay. I get it," Annie said. "So what happened?"

Marina lowered her voice to a half whisper. "It was his mother."

"His mother?"

"Uh-huh. She was feeling bad for him because he'd been dumped by his wife six months before that—she'd left him for a beekeeper in Virginia—so to perk him up and make him feel better, his mom started mailing him these romantic, anonymous cards, only it backfired and he started losing clumps of hair from all the stress."

Annie rubbed her eyes. "You're saying you think *Mom* took out these ads?"

"No, I'm just saying that maybe we need to open our minds and take a broader look at who we've been considering, that's all. . . ."

Listening to her, Annie smiled, remembering how stubborn Marina used to be when faced with any problem. How obsessed she became as a teenager during her crossword-puzzle phase, stomping off to school each morning with the newspaper in hand, puffs of dust shooting out from her feet as she walked, muttering under her breath as she considered one solution after another.

"Marina, I love you," she said. "But I could never live with you again."

"Why not?" Marina asked, sounding hurt.

"Because I'd never get any sleep."

Monday morning, after her usual half hour paddle, Annie showered and dressed for work, taking longer than normal. She tried on three different outfits, Lurch watching from the bathroom counter with a regal but suspicious air. For a change, Annie applied a different color eye shadow, something bolder and more dramatic. She put on a pair of earrings she hadn't worn in years and pulled her hair up and away from her face, practicing facial expressions in the mirror. She tried smiling wide as if she didn't have a care in the world, then a more pensive look with her gaze down, and finally elegant but in control, lifting one eyebrow slightly, mimicking a reporter she'd seen on TV the day before.

Eric called out from downstairs. "Mom? The paper's here."

Buttoning her blouse, Annie took a deep breath, feeling better than she had in days, ready for anything.

WOULD YOU PLAY POKER WITH THIS WOMAN?

ANNIE FISCHER IS THE ONLY WOMAN I'VE EVER MET WHO KNOWS THAT THE ODDS OF GETTING A FULL HOUSE IN A GAME OF POKER ARE SIX HUNDRED AND NINETY-THREE TO ONE, ALTHOUGH SHE'S NEVER PLAYED AND REFUSES TO FOR THAT REASON ALONE. TO ME, SHE'S ALWAYS BEEN MORE BEAUTIFUL BY ACCIDENT THAN MOST WOMEN ARE ON PURPOSE. WE KNEW EACH OTHER YEARS AGO, BUT SOMEHOW WE LOST TOUCH. IF YOU KNOW WHERE I CAN FIND HER, PLEASE CALL (212) 555-1963.

Unable to help herself, Annie smiled at the "beautiful by accident" comment. The poker comment wasn't any help. Everyone knew how much she hated poker. She'd looked up the odds years ago after someone tried to talk her into a game of strip poker, and since then she'd shared them with too many people to count, having memorized how bad they were. Glancing at the clock, she told the boys, "Grandma's picking us up in ten minutes and I don't want to be late for work, so make sure you're ready."

They were waiting for Erna when Marina phoned to tell Annie that *USA Today* had picked up the story about the ads.

Annie closed her eyes tight. "Of course they did."

"Here, let me read it to you," Marina said, sounding excited. " '*Anonymous Ads Pique National Curiosity* by Lindsey Henderson. Now heading into its fourth week, the *Do You Recognize This Woman?* ad campaign is drawing national media attention from across the country. Opening himself up to public scrutiny by placing a series of personal ads to find the first woman he ever loved, Mr. Anonymous has held firm in his refusal to come forward until next week. The *Peninsula Post* confirmed yesterday that two more ads will run, although Mr. Anonymous was apparently given the option to pull them.'"

Annie sighed at her end of the phone. "Julie said she'd bet money it's Peter Dawson, but she hasn't tracked down a phone number for him yet."

"Come on," Marina pressed. "There must be something in these ads that gives you a hint about who it is. What about your strawberry-shaped birth mark?"

"That's no help. Anyone who's ever seen me in a sleeveless top would have noticed it."

Later, when she'd had time to consider, Annie realized that the reality of what was happening was diminished by her disbelief that the ads were being placed at all. After all, how often did the average person open a newspaper and see her face on the front page? Better yet, how often did you walk out the front door to find your neighbors serving coffee and muffins to reporters parked in front of your house?

Monday morning on *Live with Regis and Kelly*, Kelly said she thought it was romantic that a guy would place ads to find the first woman he ever loved. Tuesday, Matt Lauer brought it up on the *Today* show, and after that, Jay Leno's staff included it in his nightly warm-up when he joked that some poor guy had obviously lost a bet or else his mind. The ads were the number-two pick for David Letterman's Top Ten List called How to Draw Attention to Yourself.

By midweek, the number of reporters had doubled in front of Annie's house. Trying to ignore them, she counted the number of steps from her back door to her driveway, where the boys were waiting for her in her mom's Volkswagen Beetle, on loan until she could afford to buy a new car.

Someone called out, "Annie, any comments on this week's ad?"

"Can you give us five minutes?" someone else asked.

Keenly aware of all the prying eyes, Annie shook her head no. She climbed into the car, shut the door, and buckled her seat belt. Then, flexing her hands on the steering wheel, she backed carefully down the driveway, both boys slouched in the backseat, trying to ignore all of the peering faces, aware that within minutes they would all be parked in front of Kozak's.

Annie glanced up from her desk later that morning to see a lone figure coming into view through the window at the end of the street. It was her mom, all five feet two of her, speed walking up the hill toward the funeral home, arms swinging like an army sergeant's. After lending Annie her car, she'd rented one for herself, but she'd been power walking around town each day to get into better shape. Rudy came out of his office and leaned against Annie's desk, chuckling.

"That woman has more energy than someone half her age," he said.

Annie watched as her mom veered off the sidewalk toward a CBS news van and tapped on the passenger window. The reporter inside lowered the glass and they had a brief conversation that ended with him shaking Erna's hand before she said good-bye and entered Kozak's.

"What are you doing?" Annie demanded, meeting her at the door.

Erna did a few side stretches. "I noticed that reporter rubbing his back yesterday and then he popped a few pills . . ."

Annie's eyes went wide.

". . . so I gave him some advice."

"What kind of advice?"

Straightening, Erna squared her shoulders. "I told him if he hadn't already, he might want to see an orthopedic surgeon because sometimes pain in the lower back can be an early sign of Paget's disease, which affects men twice as often as women."

Annie ran her hands over her face.

"It's a horrible disease," Erna said. "It causes all kinds of abnormal bone growth, and as it advances, it becomes most noticeable in the head and the face. Your skull starts to grow, your facial features become repulsive, and your nerves are squeezed. Sadly, it can even make you deaf."

Annie stared up at the ceiling. "I hate it when you do this, Mom. I really do."

Rudy laughed. "Well, I think it's thoughtful. And if he does have this disease, he'll be thanking her now, won't he? No harm done. Erna, let's go call that woman you mentioned to see if she can give me a quote on a skylight."

By lunch, the reception area was buzzing. A local carpet rep had stopped in with samples for Rudy to look at, some woman was measuring the windows for new blinds, and Erna was on the phone getting a quote for the installation of a skylight. Annie was eating a bowl of soup in the kitchen when her mom stuck her head around the corner.

"Annie? There's a beeping sound out front that's been driving me crazy. I traced it to your purse. It's your cell phone." She handed it to her. "It's vibrating, so the battery must need charging." Giving her daughter a smile, she left to rejoin the crew out front.

Frowning, Annie turned the phone over. She'd charged it the

night before, so the battery couldn't be low. Squinting at the display, she pushed back from the table and dropped her spoon, splattering tomato soup across her blouse. Someone had sent her a text message that read: *Soree mi ads stird evry 1 up. Wasnt the plan. Tlk 2 u l8r.*

Setting the phone on the table, she placed her fingers on her temples and began massaging. Then she grabbed a wet dishcloth and tried to wipe her blouse. After composing her thoughts, she phoned Julie at work.

"I was hoping you'd call," Julie said, computer keys clicking in the background. "My second cousin finally e-mailed me back."

"Great. Does he know where Peter lives?"

"Uh-huh. He gave me his phone number. You aren't going to believe this, though. Peter owns one of the biggest mushroom farms in Idaho."

Annie's eyes widened. "A mushroom farm?"

Julie was laughing now. "Yes. As in shiitake, portobello, oyster. Apparently it's a very sophisticated business. Grab a pen and write down this number. . . ."

Annie did. Then she folded the piece of paper in half, stood, and began pacing with a renewed burst of nervous energy. "This situation is getting stranger by the day," she complained. "Mr. Anonymous sent me a text message a few minutes ago."

"Are you serious?" Julie said. "Read it to me."

Lowering her voice to make sure no one overheard, Annie repeated the message she'd been sent earlier.

"This is great," Julie said.

"Why?" Annie said. "Because it increases my stress level another notch?"

"No, because he's opened the lines of communication and now you've got a phone number to work with."

Annie squinted at the display on her phone. "I don't think that's going to help much. It's the same number that's in the ad."

"Why don't you message him back?"

Embarrassed, Annie admitted that she didn't know how.

Pause. "How is it that someone who's been inexplicably drawn to every gadget that's ever been for sale on TV doesn't know how to text message on her own cell phone?" Before Annie could answer, Julie said, "Never mind. Call Marina and tell her to come over. I'm sure she'll be able to figure out how to use it."

Ten minutes later, Marina pushed through Kozak's front door, looking harried from her drive across town, and Annie pulled her into the kitchen before Erna could interrupt them.

"Okay. Where's your phone?" Marina asked.

Annie pointed to where she'd left it on the table.

Marina picked it up, frowning. As she played with the buttons, looking at the multitude of options available, Annie said, "Julie finally tracked down Peter Dawson's phone number."

"Good," Marina said. "Give him a call and see what he says." She began pressing buttons in earnest. "Okay, here we go."

Annie leaned over to watch. "What are you doing?"

"Messaging him back so we can try to figure out who he is." Annie slid into a chair, nodding. That sounded like a good idea. Marina talked as she keyed it in, " 'Tlk 2 me now, not l8r.' " Then she pressed SEND and sat back, smiling. "Now we wait."

Annie crossed her arms. "Want some tea while we do?"

Marina nodded. "I'll make it. You phone Peter and see if he's the one."

Annie grimaced as she picked up the phone. What was she supposed to say to someone she'd dumped so long ago? Someone she hadn't seen or talked to in sixteen years? Without giving herself time to think, she dialed the number Julie had given her, telling herself he probably wouldn't be there anyhow.

A woman answered after two rings. "Valleydale Mushrooms. May I help you?"

"Uh, yes . . . Is Peter Dawson there?"

"Just a moment. I'll get him."

You will? Annie thought, edging forward on her chair, wishing she hadn't called. This was crazy. What was she thinking?

Words were exchanged, brief and muffled. Then: "Peter speaking."

Although time had robbed her of the ability to picture his face clearly, the moment Annie heard his voice, she felt as if she had been shot back in time. "Peter? It's . . . Annie. Annie Fischer from Chicago?"

There was a pause, and when he answered, she heard a smile in his voice. "Annie? Now there's a voice from the past. How are you doing? Don't tell me you're here in Boise?" She heard the legs of a chair being dragged across the floor.

"No, I live in Eagan's Point now. I was just . . . I thought I'd look you up and see how you were doing, that's all."

There was a brief pause. "Fine. How about you?"

Marina scribbled something on a slip of paper and pushed it across the table. *Ask him if he bought the ads!*

"Good," Annie said, distracted. "I'm good."

"Married?" Peter pressed, teasing her a little.

"Separated."

"Sorry to hear that," he said, sounding like he was. "Any kids?"

"Two," Annie confirmed. "Both boys, both handfuls in their own way. Enough about me, though, what about you? It's been years since we last talked. Tell me what you've been up to. Ever get married? Have kids yourself? Travel the world?"

All she had to do was ask and he opened up and summarized his life. How even though he had traveled extensively, he'd never married or had kids. At least, not yet anyhow. How his business had kept him hopping for years and how he'd only recently begun reassessing where he was in his life: if he was happy, if he'd chased all his dreams, if this was really where he wanted to be.

Marina's hand clamped down on Annie arm. "Ask him!"

Annie slapped it away.

". . . and that's when I decided to invest in mushrooms," he explained. "A decision that's paid off a hundred times over." He barely paused before explaining which mushrooms yielded the best crops, when to pick them, how to package each kind appropriately—all details that were lost on her.

Annie smiled. When it came to mushrooms, Peter was clearly a man in his element. As he talked, describing how his company had a competitive edge over other well-known mushroom growers, her mind flashed back to when she and Julie went to Mexico on spring break during their first year of university. She had been seeing Peter for six months by then but the trip with Julie had been planned for over a year. It was supposed to be a chance to get away and have some fun, just the two of them.

On the fourth day there, they were tanning on the beach when Julie poked Annie in the arm. "Sit up! You aren't gonna believe this."

Annie struggled to her elbows. A man was walking down the beach toward them carrying a suitcase. He was tall and thin, wearing a black turtleneck sweater with jeans and hiking boots, an image so foreign in bikini-clad, ninety-degree Mexican weather that Annie wiped her eyes with her towel, certain she must be seeing things.

She wasn't. Moments later, Peter stopped in front of them, smiling. "Well? Aren't you going to say anything?"

Confused, Annie lifted a hand to shade her eyes from the sun. She looked at Julie, who was busy chewing on her bottom lip, and back to Peter. Then, instead of saying hello, she frowned and gestured to Peter's face. "When did you shave off your mustache?"

Reddening, he ran a hand down his face. "I never had a mustache."

Convulsing with laughter, Julie rolled over onto her stomach.

Annie got to her feet. "God, Peter, I'm so sorry," she said. "I hardly slept last night, and I'm so hungover, but it really is great to see you. You just looked so pale and out of place when I saw you coming down the beach that I was sure something looked different."

Peter raised his eyebrows. "I wanted to surprise you."

"You did," Annie assured him.

"I was trying to be romantic," he added.

"I know," she said, although *romantic* wasn't the first word that sprang to mind.

Now, as his voice cut through her thoughts, bringing her back to reality, Annie flushed with shame for how casually inconsiderate she'd been to him.

". . . and that made starting this business even more stressful. Six months into it, I almost lost everything. Then, two years later, after a ton of cash-flow nightmares, we finally turned a big corner. Today, I own a condo in Maui and a summer home in the Hamptons. What more could a guy want, right?"

"Amazing," she said. "Sounds like you're doing well." She clenched the phone harder. "Uh . . . Peter, I'm at work right now so I can't talk much longer. I got your number from an old friend and . . . well, actually, I wanted to ask—"

"Annie?" he interrupted.

"Yes."

She heard him shift the receiver to his other hand. "Would you like to meet me for dinner tomorrow night?" He was quiet, a hopeful kind of quiet. "If you can arrange it at your end, I'd be happy to fly into Seattle."

His voice trailed off as memories of him from the past ran together in Annie's head, all of them fond and affectionate. She could almost see him, head tilted to one side as he waited for her to answer. *This is so disorienting,* she thought. *And yet there's a peculiar familiarity in talking to him after all these years, a shared history that feels nice.*

Taking a deep breath, she said, "I'd like that." Then, after agreeing on a time and place, she jotted down the address and slowly lowered the receiver into its cradle.

"Okay," Marina said. "I'll bite. Why didn't you ask him?"

"We're having dinner in Seattle tomorrow night," Annie said, playing with a button on her blouse. "So I thought I'd ask him in person."

Her cell phone beeped, signaling a text message.

Marina grabbed it and read out loud, saying, " 'Cant tlk now. Tlk l8tr.' " Setting it down, she shot Annie a pitying look. "You know, your cell phone number isn't exactly common knowledge."

Annie's heart sank. "Maybe not, but then again Mom did give it to some man who called Kozak's looking for me last week."

"It could've been a reporter," Marina pointed out.

"Or Peter," Annie added.

"Jack has it?"

"Of course."

"Chris Carby?"

Another nod.

Sinking lower in her chair, Annie took a sip of coffee. She thought about the ads more often than she wanted to admit and their purpose still wasn't magically clear to her, especially since whoever was placing them could have tracked her down in a much less public way if he'd really wanted to. For days now, she'd gotten out of bed each morning feeling strong, determined not to think about the ads for more than an hour during the day, but her self-discipline clearly needed work because her allotted hour was typically used up long before she ever took her morning coffee break. More than anything, she wished whoever it was would step forward and ask for her forgiveness while this whole thing was still borderline forgivable.

It was an odd sensation, having dinner with Peter after not seeing him for sixteen years. Before he arrived at the restaurant, late and apologizing, every instinct told Annie to leave, that the farther she went down this path the more awkward and difficult it would be to retreat. If he was the one who'd taken out these ads, what was she supposed to say? But before she could leave, there he was, stooping to kiss the top of her head in a world-weary way he'd probably chosen to mask his nervousness.

Other than a few wrinkles, he hadn't changed much. Still all arms and legs, still the same unflappable air that had always made him seem a little British to her. No ups or downs, just flat down the middle, calm and steady, reminding Annie of how he never used to dramatize anything, saying things like "You're breathtaking when you smile" in the same tone as "Pass the salt" or "We've got a flat tire" with the same weight as "I want you to have my children."

The first hour of their visit was enjoyable. They shared stories and got caught up on each other's lives—flirting a little, teasing each other, taking turns giving shots about things that had happened in the past—but somewhere along the way it took a sharp turn, possibly after Peter waved the waiter over and ordered his third drink, popping it back the way a functional drunk does, the kind who needs a handful to make it through each day, but can hide it well.

"Remember that time we went fishing?"

Annie closed her eyes and thought hard. "Fishing?" she said.

She remembered flying to Canada with him for a few days one winter, wet snow pinching their faces as they'd ice fished on the Athabasca River with her uncle Max—Peter drinking brandy from a flask, complaining bitterly about the inhumanity of knocking a helpless fish over the head with a billy club, and she too embarrassed to look Uncle Max in the eye.

Peter sighed. "It was one of the hottest nights that summer and you woke me at two in the morning to go fishing in Lake Michigan. You sat at the end of that dock in the dark, casting for hours while we talked. Remember?"

"I do," Annie lied.

He looked away. "Did you know that even now, after all these years, that's still one of my favorite memories?"

Reaching over, he took her hand, his eyes looking huge and hopeful. There was a pause, and Annie knew she should say something to fill it, but she didn't know what. Instead, she excused herself to go to the bathroom.

When she returned, he was standing next to the dance floor, a circle of gleaming hardwood set in the middle of two dozen dinner tables. Music was playing in the background as he moved in place, snapping his fingers by his side, looking awkward and out of place—trying to be now what he'd never been before.

Annie cringed, remembering how he'd danced years ago, easily comparable to the contorted mass of tics and twitches Elaine on *Seinfeld* had become known for. When it came to their relationship, he had always let her decide how they would spend their time, and yet on this one small issue, in his own passive-aggressive way, he'd remained unbendable. If they went out and there was a dance floor, Peter danced, and she felt obligated to join him, even though she was mortified doing so. In a flash that seemed to come from nowhere, she suddenly missed Jack: his hand resting against the small of her back, strong and sure as he effortlessly guided her across a dance floor; his deep, grainy laugh anchoring her when things weren't going well; him looking at her the way her mom used to look at her dad.

She thought about walking past and pretending she didn't know him, but then Peter turned and said, "Want to dance?"

She considered saying, "I'd rather have a tooth pulled without anesthetic," but before she could, he looked away.

A tiny sigh escaped him and then he looked back, trying to make a joke of it. "I took lessons years ago," he said. "It's not like it used to be."

Determined to save him from himself, Annie said, "Could we just have coffee?"

"Of course," he said.

Over dessert, they stayed clear of her failed marriage to Jack, talking about the boys instead. "Raising two kids can't be easy," Peter said at one point.

"It's not," Annie agreed. "But I can't imagine my life without them."

Peter nodded, suddenly looking shy. "I still hope to have kids myself someday," he admitted. "Five years ago, I thought that would've been the case by now. I was in love with a woman I'd met in Calcutta, and for a while, all we talked about was the future. How we'd travel the world together, build our dream home, and have a few kids."

"What happened?"

"Her parents interfered," he explained. "And instead of marrying me, she married a man twenty years older, an arranged marriage her father had set up years earlier. Can you believe that?" he said, signaling the waiter for another drink. "In this day and age?"

"I'm sorry, Peter."

"Don't be," he said, waving her off.

When the feeling came, it took Annie a few seconds to recognize that it was intensely familiar; an abject wave of sadness so strong and self-realizing that she had to put her fork down. Peter was a good man, with good intentions, but there was no heat between them. Not then and not now. He was ethical and handsome and kind, but there was no magic, no tug and pull, no chemistry. Not even a drop. And when she had been with him years ago, until she met Jack, she'd really only been pretending to feel something for him.

Peter was staring at her. "You were wondering if it was me, right? Running these ads everyone's been talking about?"

She gave him a small smile. "I was."

In a voice that sounded as sad as he looked, he said, "It's not."

"I know," she whispered.

He double sighed, swirling what was left of his drink in small circles in the glass. "There's never been anything right about us, has there, Annie?"

She paused for a moment. He was trying to be honest with her, and she appreciated that in theory. *But you're missing the point, Peter,* she thought. *This isn't about pass or fail. We are who we are and shame shouldn't be part of it.* Making her voice as kind as she could, she said, "No, but that doesn't mean we can't enjoy our evening."

He lifted his glass in a mock toast. "Fair enough."

Annie stared at his drink. She stared at it long and hard, wondering if he realized he was already on his fifth, sensing that the drinking he'd done years ago had grown into a much bigger problem. She took the glass from him and slowly set it on the table. "Don't do this anymore, Peter," she said with authority and sadness. "Please."

He gave her a long blink, nodding with what seemed like conviction.

"I'm sorry if I hurt you years ago," she said before she could change her mind.

He held up a hand. He didn't want her apology.

It was a small moment, but an intense one, and she knew if she didn't say it now, she would always be sorry that she hadn't. "Peter, I need to ask you something," she said, in a leap of maturity that had been lacking years ago.

"What?"

Pause. "Would you like to dance?"

He looked down, trying not to smile. "Like you wouldn't believe."

What followed was an image that would stay with her forever: Peter caught in a cone of light on that beautiful little dance floor, pleasure flooding his face as he danced, arms and legs akimbo in a way no choreographed dance lesson could ever match. Instead of hugging the edge of the dance floor self-consciously, Annie gave herself up to the music too, oblivious of those who might be watching as she tried out the power of not giving a damn that anyone was. And by the time they finished, dancing to everything from a two-step to an odd hip-hop song neither of them had ever heard, they were both exhausted. Peter's tie was askew and her hair had come unpinned, and as they walked off the dance floor, an elderly couple clapped.

When Peter hugged Annie good-bye, he did so with the kind of awkwardness they call dignity, gathering her gently against his chest. "Good luck, Annie. I hope everything works out for you," he said. "And thanks."

"For what?"

"For coming."

"I'm the one who should be thanking you," she said, giving him a peck on the cheek.

Nodding, he opened his wallet and pretended to look for something.

As he walked her to where she'd parked her mom's car, he began fast talking about opening another mushroom farm somewhere in England, going on and on in a way that seemed to lift him up even as it brought Annie down, making her sad that he had no one in his life.

Driving home, she realized something about herself she hadn't known until then. That emotionally, she'd always been a little inaccessible, keeping her bags packed when it came to the people who loved her, poised to run long before they could ever hurt her. And because of this new realization, she felt changed, knowing herself as she hadn't before.

TWENTY-ONE

*D*ropping the newspaper on his desk, Jack stood and walked to the window. If you asked him to pinpoint when everything started falling apart between him and Annie, he would say it happened gradually, like a string of dominoes falling in slow motion. At first, they had worked as a team, budgeting, planning, putting money away. They didn't aspire to be millionaires. They simply wanted to buy a nice home in a safe neighborhood, somewhere for their kids to grow up. They were careful and it didn't take long before they could afford an older home in need of repair. Then, the summer Eric turned three, they upgraded and bought a bigger house, everything they'd always dreamed about, right down to a tree house in the backyard.

They moved in at the end of August, and Eric was diagnosed with hystiocytosis in December, two weeks before Christmas. The bills started piling up, and within a year, their savings were already wiped out because half of Eric's medical procedures weren't covered by insurance. Six months later, they both realized they had no option but to sell their house. The money they received from the sale helped pay off the bulk of their debt at the time, including almost a hundred thousand owed for Eric's medical treatments.

Eric was in the hospital the day they moved out of their house into a subsidized rental unit with two bedrooms, paper-thin walls, broken closet doors, and rotting floorboards. After a quick tour through their new home, Luke went back outside and got into the car. When Jack tried talking to him, Luke said, "Eric's gonna hate it here," as though that would change their minds about moving, as though they had a choice.

"No, he won't," Jack said. "He'll make the best of it, just like the rest of us."

Later that night, Annie sat down beside Jack on the couch and laid her head against his arm. "Things will get better," she said, trying to reassure him.

"I know," he replied, believing they would, not knowing that Eric was about to get even sicker, unaware that another six months would pass before his son made it out of the hospital again.

Over the next two years, Jack and Annie drifted farther apart as they struggled to make ends meet, juggling here, borrowing there, whatever it took to pay for Eric's medical needs. At one point, Annie's mom came into the city to help out, and eventually Annie had to quit her job and stay home with Eric. He was in and out of the hospital so often that she couldn't find a job that would give her the kind of flexibility they needed. After all, no one wanted to hire a physical therapist who could work one week but not the next.

They traded their SUV for an old clunker with over sixty thousand miles on it. To save money, Jack started taking the bus to work. To make more, he took on extra shifts. Even so, neither seemed to make a dent, and the bills kept coming, relentless in their predictability. Jack would never forget finding Annie crying next to their broken furnace one morning with a toolbox at her feet; a problem they couldn't afford to fix for a month. He remembered their phone getting cut off and Marina paying the bill so it could be hooked up again. He remembered months going by in a blur during which he'd buried himself in work, spending less and less time at home, feeling powerless and humiliated and small.

Mostly, though, he remembered this: Eric getting sicker by the day, and Annie taking charge, in that order.

One afternoon, shortly after Marina had paid off their long-overdue phone bill, Jack arrived at work to find a handful of people in the staff lounge watching a local talk show on TV. Some author was promoting her book, which had recently hit the *New York Times* bestseller list. She was a small woman with a birdlike face, and the talk show host, Rachel Tice, seemed completely captivated with her story.

Jack grabbed a coffee and sat down to watch.

As the author put it, the book was based on "a drastic experiment." She and her husband had spent one year purchasing only the essentials. Anything that could be considered a luxury was given up. They stopped buying daily lattes, using cell phones, and watching TV. "We were absolutely brutal about our commitment to this experiment," she said, explaining how they gave up high-speed Internet access, junk food, fast food, CDs, DVDs, magazines, books, hair appointments, even going to the movies. Instead of dining out, they hosted dinner parties at home. Instead of driving to work, they took the train.

"For twelve months," she said, lowering her voice conspiratorially, "we didn't buy a single piece of clothing, not even a new pair of socks."

"That's incredible," Rachel Tice said, shaking her head with admiration.

"It really was fascinating," the author said. "Because it helped us clearly define the difference between *want* and *need*. It helped us to reassess the numerous personal indulgences we'd become used to."

"Sounds like it must have been a difficult year," Rachel commiserated.

The author turned her face away, all dramatic and suffering.

"Mostly, it was sad. To see how entrenched our habits were. But we went through many conflicting emotions. It was irritating, exhilarating, thought-provoking, and, at times"—she paused for effect—"even deeply humiliating."

Jack shook his head, marveling that anyone would write a book like this, let alone buy it.

"Has it changed the way you live today?" Rachel asked.

The author hesitated, considering the question. "Well, I can't say that we've completely revised our habits. However, we're far more conscious of our motivations when we do make purchases that aren't necessary, far more *present* in the decision-making process."

Rachel Tice nodded. "Who do you think should buy this book?" she asked, sending the interview in a new direction.

"Everyone," the author said, thumping the arm of her chair. "We all overindulge and we all spend too much money. We are a nation of robotic consumers. I'm sure half of this country would go into shock living the way my husband and I did for the last year."

No, lady, Jack thought, *because half of this country lives like that every day.*

On his way home after work that night, he'd stopped at the hospital, and when he walked into Eric's room, he'd found him coloring with his fat-tipped markers, looking unusually pale and drawn. It had the strangest pull on him, seeing his son like that, and for a few seconds, Eric's fragility made Jack feel equally weak and helpless.

A nurse was busy changing Eric's IV, and when she saw Jack in the doorway, she smiled. "This son of yours is quite the artist."

"He sure is," Jack agreed.

Eric looked up and smiled. "Dad," he said.

His eyes were bloodshot, and what was left of his hair looked like small tufts of down on a rare and exquisite bird. After giving him a hug, Jack sat on the edge of the bed and turned on the wall-mounted TV.

"I thought I'd swing by and watch the Sonics game with you," he said.

For the first quarter, Eric tucked himself under Jack's arm like a broken bird. Then, with no warning, he suddenly pushed away, leaned over the side of the bed, and threw up all over the floor. Waiting for the worst to pass, Jack gently held him as his narrow back lifted and dropped with uncontrollable heaves. More than anything, Jack wanted to tell him that everything would work out, that he would fix it, but he knew he couldn't.

After a few moments, Eric stopped and said, "It'll be okay, Dad," tilting his head sideways to reassure him. "It never lasts long." Then his hand snuck into Jack's as he leaned over and patiently waited to hurl again. And as he did, Jack marveled that his son seemed made of tougher stuff than he was, tougher than anyone he knew, in fact.

As his relationship with Annie continued to suffer, Jack's own slow, downward spiral sent him into some of the saddest and loneliest months of his life. In the end, when he and Annie were more strangers than husband and wife, he realized he couldn't live like that anymore. After he'd moved out, his only solace lay in the simple repetition of successfully making it through each day; up by six, out the door by seven, working back-to-back shifts as often as possible, and sleeping with his head on his desk too many nights to count.

For almost six months, Jack's boss let him live rent-free in a small apartment WSMB leased in downtown Seattle for out-of-town guests. Then, when a friend of Jack's got offered a contract job in New York, he sublet his apartment at a reduced monthly rate. He had a fridge with nothing in it, a microwave he never touched, and a dishwasher that had never been filled. It was somewhere to go, but it wasn't home.

At first, he missed entire days of the week, immersing himself in his job and asking himself how he and Annie had managed to lose something that had once been so amazing. Not long after they were married, he'd told her what they had was incredible. She'd studied him for a few seconds, not saying anything, but when he got up the next morning, there was a note taped to the bathroom mirror: *I've got a better word. Extraordinary: highly exceptional; remarkable . . . You use yours. I'll use mine.*

Eventually, he got good at being by himself, and then he had started seeing someone. Her name was Linda and they worked together at WSMB. Several times while he and Annie were having problems, he and Linda came close to sleeping together—a simple nod from one or the other might have done it—but they never did. Linda was great company and she wanted a serious relationship, but after a few months, she told Jack she thought he wasn't ready to have someone new in his life. Which meant, of course, that she had her own life and was moving on. The saddest part was that Jack hardly noticed her absence.

TWENTY-TWO

When Annie arrived at work Thursday morning, Kozak's reception area was buzzing. Two women she'd never met before were delivering plants, and an effeminate-looking man dressed in khaki shorts and a pink dress shirt was flipping through paint-chip samples.

"Hi, I'm Kenneth," he said, waving. "I won't be in your way long." He set his paint chips down and scratched frantically at one of his calves.

"Are you okay?" Annie asked.

"I think I ran into some poison ivy this morning," he said, flushing.

"Morning, Annie," Rudy said, coming out of his office. "Your mom will be by later to take care of all this." He waved toward Kenneth and the women, who were now busy positioning plants. "I've hired her to help me fix up the place."

"Great," Annie said, offering him a tight smile.

"I'm on my way to the golf tournament," he said, putting on his sunglasses. "So if there's an emergency this afternoon, call my cell phone. I'll leave it on, but I won't be returning regular calls until tomorrow."

Minutes later, Annie was on the phone when her mom arrived. Erna reached over and chucked her lightly under the chin, shaking her head the way she did when she was worried about one of her girls. Then she made a beeline for Kenneth, who was sitting on the new sectional that had been delivered the day before. Her mom was still talking to him when Annie hung up and caught the tail end of their conversation.

Erna pointed to a spot just above her wrist bone. "See this?" she said, bringing her arm so close that Kenneth had to lean back. "That's leftover scarring from poison ivy, but I don't think that's what you have."

Kenneth looked worried. "You don't think so?"

Erna leaned down for another look at his legs.

"I tried cortisone cream this morning," he offered. "But it didn't help."

Straightening, she said, "You should go to a walk-in clinic right away. I don't want to scare you, because it could be a case of poison ivy, but itching like this anywhere in the lower half of the body can also be a first sign of Hodgkin's disease. . . ."

Annie watched the color drain from Kenneth's face.

"It's also a symptom of something called Hanot's cirrhosis," Erna added. "But that's a liver disease that typically only affects middle-aged women, so I wouldn't worry about that one."

"I'll be back later," he said, bolting toward the door.

"We'll be here," Erna assured him. "And good luck, dear."

Annie closed her eyes and made a bargain with God. *No more, okay? I'll hand out blankets to the homeless every winter for the rest of my life, just no more.* She slowly counted to ten. "Mom, I want you to stop doing this."

"Doing what?" Erna asked, digging in her purse.

"Diagnosing everyone you meet."

Erna dumped a handful of vitamins onto the coffee table, carefully selecting a few. "What are you saying? You don't want me here?"

"No, that's not it. Rudy hired you to revamp the place, and you're a master at delegation, so frankly I can't think of anyone better equipped to do the job, but while you're here, please refrain from offering everyone medical advice, okay?"

Erna lifted her chin a notch. "I'll do my best, Annie," she said, sounding hurt. "But I won't make any promises."

By two that afternoon, Annie had taken one call from a woman looking for the best discount on a prepaid funeral, another from a guy who wanted to use Visa to pay for his stepdad's coffin so he could collect airline points, and one from an elderly man who asked if his Australian coin collection could be buried with him. After her mom promised to watch the phone for a few minutes, Annie went into Kozak's storage room to verify the receipt of a coffin for which Merv Singer had lost the shipping records.

As she climbed the ladder, her eyes drifted to the window. The last time she'd checked, everyone out front had appeared in the throes of boredom. The reporter from the *Seattle Examiner* had pulled out a lawn chair and was reading. A CBS reporter was dozing in the front seat of his van as his cameraman and makeup assistant played cards in the back. Another reporter from NBC had abandoned his SUV, walking up and down the sidewalk as he talked on his cell phone.

Reaching over, Annie pushed the window open, relishing the fresh air that poured into the dusty room. For a change, the sky outside was clear and blue, with few clouds in sight. From the street out front, she heard a car door slam, a succession of quick honks, and then someone whistling. She sighed, imagining the reporters taking notes and speculating about what was going to happen with this story—the same way she was. Minutes later, she was double-checking shipping waybills on a row of coffins when Erna opened the door.

"Annie?"

"Uh-huh."

"Line two's for you."

"I'm busy, Mom. Could you take a message?"

Pause. "It's Rachel Tice."

Annie double sighed. "You know what? That's not funny."

"I'm not kidding," Erna said, crossing her arms. "She told me she wanted to speak to you, and she said she didn't mind holding, either."

Annie stared down at her mom, thinking how crazy the situation was. For years, Rachel Tice had been elbowing her way up the ranks, first as a pit bullish reporter known for her crisp jackets and short skirts, next as the cohost of a Seattle-based physical fitness show (think willowy blonde in a skimpy leotard, wearing weights Velcroed around her ankles) and recently with her own regional talk show. Rachel Tice didn't have Ellen DeGeneres's sense of humor or the instant likability of Oprah, but she had honed her ability to get people to tell her things before it occurred to them that they could say no. On the few shows Annie had watched, Rachel had leaned forward when her guests talked, nodding with sincerity and understanding. Suddenly, Annie felt like laughing, like climbing down the ladder, sitting in the middle of the floor, and laughing until she couldn't laugh anymore.

"Are you going to take the call?" Erna pressed.

"No, Mom. Take a message, okay?"

There had never been waterfalls of emotion between Annie and her mom. Affection, yes. Respect, of course. And they were great at small talk. But when it came to sharing what Annie worried about, dreamed about, or believed in, she couldn't remember ever completely laying herself bare with her mom. At least, not the way she had with her dad. Annie had never met her real mother, although years ago she'd briefly opened that door and then walked away. It was one of the most important decisions she'd ever made, one she'd had no time to prepare for. If the most amazing gift she'd ever been given was her penny tree, then Jack deserved credit for what she considered a close second.

The weekend before her twenty-third birthday, she was working at a health clinic in Evanston, trying to log enough hours to complete her degree, and Jack was almost finished with a yearlong radio-host internship at Chicago's WJKL. They'd been arguing about which movie to see Saturday night. He'd picked *Terminator 2, Judgment Day*, but she had her heart set on *Fried Green Tomatoes*, so they tossed a coin and Annie won, grinning until her face hurt as Jack graciously agreed to accept his fate.

He was late picking her up the next day and Annie was sure they'd never make the theater on time. Her shoulders fell when from her basement window she saw a limousine round the corner and park at her curb. Someone must have been celebrating something special, but it wasn't her.

When her buzzer rang, she jumped.

Opening her door, she yelled up the stairs, "Wrong apartment. Try again."

Another buzz, longer and more insistent.

Muttering, Annie grabbed her purse and decided to wait outside after helping the address-challenged limo driver. She locked her basement apartment, hurried up the stairs, and stepped outside. "What apartment are you looking for?"

"One oh four," he said, smiling.

"Then someone gave you the wrong number. I live in one oh four and I didn't call for a limo. Who are you supposed to be picking up?"

Another polite smile. "Annie Fischer."

She stared at him.

"Ma'am?"

She blinked, confused. "Uh-huh."

"Are you Annie Fischer?"

"Uh . . . yes, I am."

He extended an arm toward the limousine, smiling wider. "Jack Hillman made arrangements to have you picked up."

"He did?"

"Yes, and he also asked that I give you this." The driver handed her an envelope. Baffled, Annie ripped it open. Inside was a note from Jack.

> *I'm waiting for you, so get in and let the nice man drive you across town. Don't ask any questions. He knows nothing. Just get in, buckle up, and leave everything to me. P.S. No, it doesn't matter what you're wearing, and no, I'm not trying to get out of seeing* Fried Green Tomatoes. *This is your birthday present a little early. We'll see your movie next weekend.*

Laughing, Annie followed the limo driver and climbed in as he held the door for her. What was Jack up to? And where did he get the money to rent a limo? They'd both been saving to go skiing in Vermont this winter and she knew he didn't have any extra cash lying around, especially for something like this. The driver pulled into traffic. Annie changed seats and tapped on the window separating them. The window lowered. "Yes, ma'am?"

"Where are we going?"

His eyes twinkled in the rearview mirror. "Sorry, ma'am. Mr. Hillman said you'd ask, but I was given instructions not to tell you."

She flashed her best smile and tried again. "Oh, come on. He'll never know."

Her driver chuckled and raised the window.

Annie's soft, little sigh said she gave up, but her mind was racing. What was Jack up to? The limo went north along Jartie

Drive, then up Witting Park Road and left onto Kensington, leaving her more confused. It was eight at night and the hot, humid day had quickly settled into a hot, humid evening. As the car turned another corner, Annie suddenly recognized where they were, and as she did, her throat tightened.

She would remember no image from that night more clearly than what she saw as the limo pulled up in front of an old three-story building. She stared at the stone steps that led up to a wrap-around porch overlooking the street. Jack was waiting at the bottom, and behind him, on one end of the porch, was a small table with a candle flickering in the semidarkness.

She had been here before. More than once, although never inside. She knew every tree and shrub out front, had seen the oak entrance doors being replaced with new glass ones, and had marveled at the churchlike window installed above them. Tilting her head back, she looked up at the sign hanging from the roof by two chains: *St. Joseph's Home for Boys and Girls.* Then, under it, in smaller letters: *Giving hope to orphaned and abandoned children since 1944.*

The first time she came here, she was eighteen, after she moved to Chicago from Eagan's Point to attend university. She'd taken a bus across town and sat on the curb across the street staring at it, thinking all kinds of thoughts. Like how, on August 26, 1969, a seventeen-year-old girl had climbed those stone steps carrying her newborn daughter, knowing even as she did that she would be leaving without her.

It was cold and raining and well below the normal temperature for that time of the year. Annie knew this because she had traced Chicago's weather back to that exact date in an effort to physically re-create what had happened after she was born. Her parents had given her copies of her adoption paperwork, but the information was sparse. She was born in Mercy Hospital and her mom had spent seven days there before being released. Then, five days later, she'd signed Annie into the care of St. Joseph's Home For Boys and Girls. Her name was Dorota Shroeder. Annie had studied her signature, making photocopies of it, then slowly tracing each letter over and over, looking for some connection with this stranger, this woman who'd given birth to her and would always be part of who she was, even though they were strangers.

Annie had come here a half dozen times, and each time she'd gotten a little closer, progressing from the curb on the other side of the street to walking up and down the sidewalk out front, and then finally sitting on the bottom step with her arms wrapped around her knees. More than once, she'd heard music blaring through open windows and hoots of laughter coming from the fenced-in backyard. On one visit, a woman came out the main doors, walked past her on the steps, and stopped to ask if she could help, but Annie said no, she was fine. She was just resting until her bus came.

It had been more than a year since her last visit, and the vines that had been slowly twisting up each of the porch pillars now hung in rich abundance from the rain gutters. To Annie, they seemed as unstoppable as the spirit of this place, and the thought of someone cutting them down saddened her.

The limo driver opened her door and she climbed out, the reality of what Jack had done suspended by her disbelief. Normally he was awful at keeping secrets and this was one she suddenly wished he hadn't been able to.

"Surprise," he said, strolling up to meet her.

"What's going on?"

She'd told him about it, of course. That she came here and why. When he'd received his internship, he'd told her about an organization the station was working with called Children in Need or CIN. They hosted a handful of events each year with local radio stations to raise charitable contributions for organizations that catered to abused, neglected, or homeless children, and St. Joseph's was on their list.

Jack took her elbow and guided her up the old stone steps before she could argue. Her eyes must have conveyed her panic because he lifted his hands in the air and said, "Relax. You don't have to go inside. I decided to do this tonight because everyone's at the annual barbecue at the lake. This way it'll be quiet out here on the porch."

"But—"

"I wanted to do something special for your birthday, so I came up with this idea. . . ." He explained how the limo driver was a friend who had taken the same course he had at the Illinois Center for Broadcasting, and who now worked part-time driving limos. "I set it up with him weeks ago and he agreed to do it for nothing." He motioned to the table, looking nervous. "Then I phoned Alice Muldoon, the executive director at St. Joseph's, and asked her if I could borrow a table and two chairs. Takeout was all I could afford, but I didn't think you'd mind."

Annie looked at the table on the porch, set with paper plates, plastic cutlery, wineglasses, and an array of Chinese take-out boxes. "Quite the surprise," she said, gingerly crossing the porch and lowering herself into one of the chairs. "So, what? You thought you'd help me make it up off the steps and onto the porch?"

"Something like that."

He poured the wine and started opening take-out boxes as Annie regulated her breathing and looked around. Jack offered her a glass as he told her what he knew about St. Joseph's. Alice had been the director for almost thirty years, which made Annie stop with a spoonful of rice midair. Doing the math wasn't hard. She was twenty-two, so that meant Alice had probably met her real mom, had maybe even held Annie when she was a baby.

She set her glass down. "I'm not going inside."

"You don't have to."

"And I don't want to meet this Alice person, either."

"Good, because she's not here."

Jack took a sip of wine and continued to tell her about St. Joseph's. One of the few orphanages left in Chicago, it had a working kitchen with a dining room, where they had two sittings for dinner every night. There were twelve bedrooms on the top two floors—eight equipped with bunk beds and four set up with cribs for infants. Children who were removed from abused families came here as a stopgap on their way into the foster-care system. Homeless and abandoned kids usually stayed longer, sometimes a year or more before they were either adopted or placed in a foster home.

When they were finished eating, Jack reached under his chair and pulled out a parcel wrapped in brown paper. "Happy birthday," he said, handing it to her. When he bestowed on her that crooked smile she loved so much, she silently forgave him for tricking her. She was about to open the package when he lifted a hand and said, "Wait." He leaned away and fumbled under the table. There was a quick flash and the smell of sulfur, and then he set down before her a tiny white cake with one blazing candle.

Looking pleased, Jack leaned back in his chair. "Before you open the present, you should know it's only on loan. You have to give it back to St. Joseph's next week."

Frowning, Annie unwrapped it.

"It's your file," Jack said.

Dazed, she fingered a lumpy folder. "What's in it?" she asked.

"Don't know," he said, shrugging. "I haven't read it. Alice wrapped it up for me. Then she conveniently lost it for a week."

"Which is when I have to give it back?"

He nodded.

Drunk with anticipation, she stared at that folder. Jack stood and looked at his watch. "There's a coffee shop two blocks away. I'll go get some." Before she could answer, he was down the steps and gone. She ran a trembling finger up one side of the folder and down the other before flipping it open.

Her gaze landed on a picture of a young woman that was clipped to legal documents. Her heart started to pound. She was looking at herself, only this woman was thinner, almost gaunt, with dark circles under her eyes and higher cheekbones. They shared the same tousled blond hair and the same nose. Hands trembling, Annie turned the picture over. On the back, it read *Dorota Shroeder. August 26, 1969.* There was an envelope too, addressed to *Annie,* sealed with tape that was lifting at the edges and yellowed from time. Peeling the tape off, she opened it and removed a letter and an old butterfly brooch. Tiny emeralds encrusted its edges, but the stones had gone cloudy with age. Her eyes welled with tears as she unfolded the paper and read what her seventeen-year-old mother had written years ago, in delicate cursive letters:

> Annie, I don't want to leave you at St. Joseph's. I know this even before I get there. But I've been told they will find you a home with people who can take care of you, and I can't. I don't know where to begin, even though each time I hold you, I know in my heart that you are the most magnificent mistake I've ever made. My mother gave me this brooch. It was hers, then mine,

and now it will be yours. From this day on, and in all things, I wish for you a wonderful life. . . .

Later, Jack offered to help Annie look for her mother, and although it had seemed like the right thing to do, she kept coming back to the childlike handwriting of that seventeen-year-old girl: how young she had been when she gave birth to her, how scared and uncertain, how unprepared to be a mother. The woman who'd abandoned her had really been a terrified young girl who'd made the only choice she felt she could. At first, Annie felt guilty and confused by her lack of desire to search for her, but finally, after a lot of thought, she decided not to, because the brooch and her mother's note had already answered the most important question: that her mother had loved her.

TWENTY-THREE

*A*nnie was beyond frustrated by the *Peninsula Post*'s refusal to release the name of who was running the ads, but even so, she decided to phone Stan Turner once more to vent about it. Surprised when she was put through to him right away, she straightened her shoulders and demanded that he tell her who it was, making him sigh at his end of the phone.

"I've told you the paper's position several times now, Ms. Hillman. I'm sorry, but the man who bought them signed a contract, and under that contract, he requires anonymity until the last ad has been run. I'm sure this is unnerving for you—"

"Unnerving?" she said, pushing out of her desk chair at Kozak's. "Half a dozen reporters are camped in front of my house, Mr. Turner. They follow me to work every morning. They're asking my kids for comments. For God's sake, they're interviewing my neighbors. And I've now got a talk show calling me."

"I wish we could help," he said, "but the paper isn't responsible for the ads. We're simply the vehicle this guy used to get your attention. However, after he does come forward, taking legal action against him is always an option for you."

Annie suddenly realized that she was grasping at straws, that she wouldn't be free until the last ad was printed. She dropped back into her chair, hit with overwhelming emotional exhaustion.

The other line rang as a courier approached her desk with a new microwave balanced on his hip. She pointed him toward the kitchen, thanked Mr. Turner for his time, and took the other call. The moment she heard Eric's voice, she froze.

"Are you okay?"

"I'm great," he said. "Coach Hogan told me I could call you from his office. Guess what. It looks like I made the team after all. Coach said I can play backup the first few games, and we'll go from there 'cause Dad phoned him and agreed to sign some kinda waiver that makes it okay for me to play."

Annie blinked. "He did?"

"Uh-huh. Isn't that great?"

"Yes, that's . . . great."

Eric rattled on, excited. "We have a practice next Wednesday at five and then the first game of the season is on Friday night against Clallam Bay. Anyhow, I gotta get back to class. Talk to you later."

"Sure," Annie said. "Talk to you later."

Hearing Eric so happy made her day, although she was surprised Jack had stepped in without talking to her first. And yet as she hung up, she was secretly pleased that he had.

On her way home from work, Annie heard the ambulance's siren long before it pulled out from the alley behind her house and raced off down the street. *Oh my God, did it come from my house?* Slamming on the brakes, she clenched the wheel and had to work hard to keep her breathing regular as she turned onto Ranier Crescent. Nothing *looked* wrong. Rose and Libby were sitting outside at the community picnic table, playing cards with two reporters. Another neighbor was watering his lawn.

Hands shaking, Annie parked and ran inside.

"Eric! Luke!" She dropped her purse on the floor and hurried into the kitchen. Eric was kneeling in front of the fish tank with Lurch draped over one shoulder, and Luke was in the living room watching MTV.

"I saw the ambulance," she said, trying to keep her voice steady.

"Mr. Kale had a heart attack," Luke explained, flipping to another channel. "Rose said he's gonna be okay, but he has to spend at least a week in the hospital."

Relieved, Annie slid into a chair.

Eric shifted Lurch onto his other shoulder. "Mom, if we don't get a new air stone for this tank, our fish aren't gonna make it."

Before she could respond, Luke interrupted. "Uh, guys? You might wanna look at this."

Annie joined him in the living room as he turned up the volume. He had flipped channels to the local news, and the TV screen was framing her landlord's pickup truck as it backed slowly up her driveway with what looked like a new dryer strapped in the back. She watched Mr. Tucker park, get out, and then promptly confront a reporter. Mr. Tucker smoothed his hair and straightened his collar, grinning stupidly into the camera.

"Do you know Annie Hillman?" the reporter asked.

Mr. Tucker explained that he *owned* this house, that Annie *rented* from him, that he was just stopping by to drop off a new dryer and do some maintenance. "Name's Tucker," he added. "Simon Tucker."

"What a loser," Luke said, watching Mr. Tucker wheel the dryer up the driveway.

Erna called when Annie was making dinner and she assured her mom that they were fine. Yes, the reporters out front were annoying, and no, she hadn't called Rachel Tice back. She'd just hung up and was reaching to turn the answering machine on when the phone rang again.

"Hello," she said, tucking it under her ear.

"Annie Hillman please."

"Speaking."

"This is Rachel Tice. I hope I'm not bothering you. I called you at work earlier today, but you were tied up, so your mom was kind enough to talk to me for a few minutes instead." The hair on Annie's arms lifted. Her mom hadn't mentioned this. "Anyhow, the whole idea that someone would run these ads is so captivating that I had to call and ask if you'd consider doing a show with me."

"I don't think so," Annie said.

"Just so you know," Rachel pressed on, "I called the *Peninsula Post* this afternoon and they agreed to act as an intermediary between me and Mr. Anonymous." She paused for effect. "He's agreed to do the show with you if it's something you'd like to do."

Annie froze, staring at the fruit bowl. "He did?"

"If that's okay with you."

"And he'd be there, too?"

"That's right," Rachel said. "Filmed in our studio in Seattle next Friday."

Annie frowned. Why would he agree to make this into a bigger public spectacle than it already was? After a slightly uncomfortable pause, she said, "No, I don't think—"

"Ms. Hillman, if you could just please hear me out. I honestly don't want to talk you into doing something you're not comfortable doing, but your mom and I had a nice talk earlier today and she told me that one of your sons has been sick for a long time, and how hard the last few years have been on you and your family. When I heard that, I decided to approach the network to ask if they'd be willing to pay for your appearance on the show."

That was when Annie first realized this conversation wasn't going to turn out the way she thought. She slid into a chair and then stood up again, pacing the length of the kitchen, uncertain what to do. Her first reaction was to hang up, phone her mom, and blast her for sharing private information with a talk show host she'd never met.

Ignoring the silence, Rachel Tice pushed on. "Annie, I got approval this afternoon. The network's willing to pay you fifty-six thousand dollars to do the show, which I believe is the full amount owing on your son's outstanding medical bills, right?"

If Rachel Tice had seen the slack-jawed disbelief scribbled on Annie's face, she might have pressed harder and moved in for the kill. But she didn't, so she waited for a few seconds before gently explaining that if Annie did agree to do her show next Friday—which would take less than an hour of her time—then, of course, Mr. Anonymous wouldn't come forward to reveal himself on Monday after the last ad ran in the *Peninsula Post*. Instead, he would wait a few more days and reveal himself on *The Rachel Tice Show*.

"I know this is a lot to take in," Rachel said, sounding apologetic. "So why don't you think about it and call me back?"

"Yes," Annie said, feeling dazed. "Thanks for calling. I'll . . . get back to you."

After Annie hung up, she went upstairs, locked herself in the bathroom, and snuck a cigarette. As she sat there contemplating Rachel's proposal, she realized that the ads had always seemed a little surreal to her, but the idea of actually going on television to meet Mr. Anonymous left her shaking her head in astonishment. When she was done, she flushed the butt and called Marina on the portable.

"What do you mean you don't know what to do? This is a no-brainer, Annie. Call her back and tell her you'll do the show."

"But what if I make a fool of myself on TV?"

"You won't," Marina assured her. "Ignore the camera and do the show."

When Annie hesitated, Marina pushed harder. "Keep in mind, we're talking about an hour of your life here, Annie, and then all of Eric's bills get paid off. What's to think about? Pick up the phone and call her back."

Annie would never forget the first time she heard the word *hystio-cytosis*. Eric had had a biopsy three days earlier and he was in a drug-induced sleep in the hospital. All of his limbs had gone limp, and she was watching his tiny chest rise and fall under the hospital blanket—her three-year-old son, looking much too small to be in such a seriously large bed. Jack was throwing a paper ball in the air, up and down, up and down, but when the doctor walked in, he stopped and came over next to Annie.

The doctor was carrying a clipboard and after he introduced himself, he said, "I'm sorry. There's no easy way to say this."

He told them about the disease and everything went still and quiet.

Jack stared at a spot on the far wall, his back ramrod straight. Annie said the word out loud a few times, as if doing so would make it easier to understand, growing frustrated when she couldn't pronounce it properly, then angry when the doctor repeated it for her.

He gently explained all the symptoms, along with Eric's "difficult-to-predict prognosis," and as he did, Annie's mind raced to find a way out of it. As she listened to him, this doctor, she rationalized that he would've heard about this disease from someone else, yet another specialist who'd learned what it was from the governing body of some research group that had completed extensive studies involving hundreds and hundreds of obscure experiments. . . . *And somewhere along the way, as information passed from one group to another,* she thought, *they got it wrong.*

"Hystiocytosis is an orphan disease," he explained.

"Which means . . . ?" Jack asked.

"That it's rare. Orphan diseases affect fewer than two hundred thousand people, and sadly, there are thousands of rare disorders out there just like this one. Unfortunately, what makes things even more difficult is that orphan diseases haven't been 'adopted' by the pharmaceutical industry because they provide little financial incentive for the private sector to make and market new medications to treat or prevent them."

Annie held up a finger, indicating that he should stop. "We want a second opinion."

Looking weary, as if this were the kind of news he delivered more often than anyone should have to, he loosened his tie and nodded. "Of course. That can be arranged, Mrs. Hillman. But the diagnosis is clear."

Annie's stomach hitched and she pushed past Jack and stumbled into the bathroom to splash water on her face. As she did, she listened to them talk, Jack asking questions that quickly changed her anger to fear.

"So it's not cancer?"

"No, but it's treated like cancer."

"With radiation?" Jack asked.

"With chemotherapy."

Annie closed the door and threw up in the sink, continuing until she broke blood vessels around her eyes from the force of it. When she was done, she rinsed her face and came out, but the doctor was gone. Jack opened his arms wide and she walked into them. She leaned against his chest and told him that just because they could give it a name didn't mean Eric had it.

But she was wrong.

It took forever for her to register the truth. Weeks later, she still found herself asking for clarification. What did they mean by this? Had that happened to others who'd had this disease? Outwardly, Eric seemed fine. No cuts. No bruises. No swelling. No blood. Nothing that indicated the horror of what was going on inside his body, other than how pale he was, or how quickly he seemed to be losing weight. Annie wanted to absorb it into her own body, take it all on herself and leave him weak but free from it. A few times when they weren't sure that he'd live, during two huge swaths of time separated by a year when things had looked promising, she rarely ate or slept. Instead, she paced the floor of his room, whispering, "If you take him, you may as well take me." Soft threats she knew meant nothing, fear talking as loud as it could.

During such times, an overwhelming sense of helplessness took over. To compensate for not being able to fix Eric, she decided to do everything she could to make his days more bearable, breaking almost every hospital rule in the process. If she wanted to sleep next to him, she did. If he wanted to be held, she'd lift him off his bed and cradle him until her arms ached. When he told her he missed watching Elmo, she rented every Elmo video she could find, borrowed a VCR, and played them for him day and night. LEGOs littered the end of his bed; Spider-Man dangled from the ceiling; ice cream was a staple—all Band-Aids at best, his comfort all that mattered.

None of it strong enough to beat this thing, she thought.

To keep herself sane, she wrote everything down. His weight, how he responded to his hormone-treatment program, the number of days he'd been sick, the number of birthdays he'd celebrated in a hospital room. All of it was meticulously recorded so on their way back up the other side of this deep hole, she'd be able to say, *Oh, right. That was six months after his last chemotherapy session. . . .* Often, days went by during which she wouldn't leave the hospital, until Jack told her that it had to stop, that she needed to step back a little. And during all of those hours and days and weeks that she spent with Eric, her thoughts were laced with guilt when it came to Luke and Jack. But even though she knew that she was failing them, that she should balance things better, she couldn't stop putting all of her energy into Eric. Annie promised herself that when he beat this, she'd go back and fix everything else that had been damaged along the way, thinking she'd have the option, that it could wait until then.

Again, she was wrong.

At the end of each day, Annie had nothing left to give to any-one else. Every night, after getting the basics out of the way—How was your day? Everything okay at work? Did you pay the phone bill?—she and Jack took turns fussing over Luke: she bor-dering on mechanical, Jack overdoing it to compensate. Then they would get ready for the next day as she alternately ignored or denied that she had a few other problems growing right under her nose, like how Luke had stopped hugging her back when she said good-bye each morning, or how Jack no longer waited up for her when she stayed late at the hospital.

In bed each night, she was conscious of Jack's breathing, of his arm draped around her stomach, of his chest pressed up against her back. But the thought of making love held no appeal. Jack would move his hands up her back, kissing her neck, and she'd try not to cry, wanting to tell him that his heartbroken acceptance of Eric's illness angered her, yet knowing there was no right way to cope. Of course, there were also good days, and yet Annie still felt as though she were on a roller coaster, unable to level off the highs and lows into something more livable for all of them.

Looking back on it now, she could pinpoint the beginning of the end. She had stopped at a Walgreen's one day, and the simple act of buying shampoo made her realize how much she'd changed. She went down the cosmetics isle, one side filled with rows and rows of shampoo bottles. You name it, they had it:

Strawberry Essence, Mango Extract, Orange Delight, Kiwi Escape. Distracted, she picked up one bottle after another, turning them over to read the backs, where, of course, they all said the same thing: *Lather. Rinse. Repeat.* Then a woman walked past pushing a cart with a fussing toddler in it, a *healthy* fussing toddler. Trying to soothe the child, the woman rolled her cart back and forth as she picked up first one bottle and then another, comparing them.

Annie glanced at her hair, streaked in that trendy way with two shades of blond, at her black leather boots, at her raspberry-colored fingernails, as she carelessly tossed a few bottles into the cart. Sneaking a look, Annie saw that it was filled with items meant to pamper, to round off the edges, buff up the skin, plump up the hair. All normal, self-indulgent products that the average woman would buy.

But none of it necessary, she thought. *None of it needed to survive.*

The toddler was wriggling to get out of the cart. Impatient, the woman grabbed her and yanked her back down. "Just a minute, Jess! I'm almost done."

Annie's hands were trembling as she put the shampoo she was holding back on the shelf. Although it made no sense that she should feel guilty for buying a few things for herself, that it should be okay to indulge herself now and then, she knew she couldn't. For a while now, she had subconsciously been telling herself that until Eric was better, she would turn away from self-indulgence. She would pull back, shut down, and give up anything that wasn't necessary, sacrificing what she could to ease her sense of helplessness.

"I miss you, Annie," Jack had whispered one night against the back of her neck.

"I'm right here," she said.

"No, you're not."

A few nights later, she woke and Jack was gone.

Getting out of bed, she saw light coming from the bathroom and heard water running. The door was cracked open wide enough for her to see him hunched over in the bathtub, his shoulders shaking as he wept. It left her weak to see him so crushed. It scared her enough that she pushed the door open and dropped to her knees on the floor next to the tub. Taking his hand, she promised him that when all of this was over, she'd go back to being who she'd been before. But even as she said the words, she sensed that their marriage no longer had a few hairline cracks. There were holes all over it.

Thinking back now, Annie could see all the warning signs that she had failed to notice. Then it had been like forgetting to water your favorite plant, a plant that was right in front of you every day. At first, it starts to wilt, and the leaves slowly begin to dry up, and then one day you look over at it and you know it's beyond saving, that no amount of water, fertilizer, sunshine, or soft music is going to nurture this thing back to life.

It was eleven before Annie thought to check the answering machine for messages. After deleting a half dozen from reporters and one from a collection agency, she listened to a message from Julie, wondering how she was holding up, followed by one from Chris Carby.

"Hi, Annie, it's me," he said, sounding amused. "I got back from my fishing charter a few hours ago and wasn't in the door ten minutes before I heard how you've got the whole town stirred up. I saw the first ad before I left, but what's going on with the rest of them?" She heard a bell in the background on the recording, indicating that someone had walked into the shop, followed by a burst of laughter. "Anyhow, I've gotta go. Give me a call tomorrow, okay? I'm working on the weekend but I'd like to take you for dinner next week." There was a pause and then Chris said, "By the way, is that your Yugo parked beside the fire hall?"

Locking the house, Annie made her way slowly upstairs. Eric was asleep but Luke's bed was empty. Smiling, she went to the hallway window and crawled out onto the roof. She was exhausted, but sharing a few minutes with him like this now and then was the best connection they'd had in ages, so no way was she going to discourage him.

"Got anything to eat?" she asked, sitting cross-legged next to him.

He nodded at a box of Ritz crackers beside him.

Seconds later, they watched as Libby stepped outside and stood with her arms crossed, staring over into Mr. Kale's yard.

"She's late tonight," Luke whispered.

Libby slipped through the gate and approached a dozen clay pots lined up in a row along the back of Mr. Kale's house, each filled with flowers. Squatting, she lifted one and then another until she found the key she was looking for. Then she straightened, brushed off her hands, and unlocked Mr. Kale's back door.

"Here, boy," she said, leaning inside. "Come on."

Annie and Luke shared a confused look, watching as she disappeared inside the house. When she returned a few minutes later, she had Mr. Kale's basset hound squirming under one arm. She set him down on the grass, snapped on a leash, and made her way back to her own yard. The dog followed, but as soon as they climbed the steps to her deck, he sat down and refused to budge. Setting her hands on her hips, Libby frowned as she considered the problem. Then she took a few odd, mincing steps toward the back door in an effort to have him chase her.

"Come on! Let's go."

The dog lay down and began to shake.

Libby went inside and returned with a bowl and an apple. She sat and began peeling it. The dog perked up, lifting his head as she cut the apple into slices and placed them in the bowl on her lap. Staring into the distance, she took a piece and popped it into her mouth. The dog inched closer. She took another piece and nibbled on it, which made him jump up and put his feet against her leg, sniffing at the bowl. Annie smiled as she watched, certain that she could hear Libby cooing as she tilted the bowl toward him and let him devour the rest of the apple.

Luke shook his head. "Who knew, hey?"

Annie agreed, wishing she could trade places with Libby, thinking how enjoyable—no, how relaxing—it would be to take care of Mr. Kale's basset hound while he was in the hospital instead of going on *The Rachel Tice Show*, which she had decided to do an hour ago.

Twenty-four

At six o'clock Friday morning, Annie turned off her alarm clock and rolled out of bed, almost flattening Lurch in the process. Throwing on her clothes, she went downstairs and peeked out the living room window. The last ad wouldn't run until Monday and that meant today was a slow day. So far, only one reporter was stationed at the community picnic table, and he looked half asleep as he nursed a cup of coffee. Grabbing a banana, she went back upstairs to the boys' bedroom and gave Luke a gentle shake.

He rolled over, squinting up at her.

"I'm sneaking out for a paddle," she whispered. "You guys probably won't be up before I get back, but I've got my cell phone with me just in case."

"Sure," he said, yanking the blanket over his face. "Whatever."

Slowly inching the back door open so it wouldn't squeak, she slipped outside and hurried across the grass to the alley, feeling like a thief leaving a crime scene. Keeping her shoulders hunched and her head down, she jogged to the Docks, grabbed her kayak, and took it down to the water. She had skipped her morning paddle yesterday, so now she couldn't wait to get out on the bay.

Climbing into her kayak, she sighed. When she got to work this morning, she'd phone Chris and see what night he wanted to go for dinner. She had listened to his message again this morning, but nothing about his tone of voice or what he'd said raised her alarm. Right now, though, she was trying to wrap her brain around the idea of going on *The Rachel Tice Show*, and she needed to figure out how she was going to feel if Chris was the one running these ads. He was a whip when it came to business, and over the years, he'd also become as physically buff as a firefighter, but she was having trouble making the leap from the guy she'd always known to someone she might actually desire.

Thinking about the memories they shared made Annie smile. Chris had never been great at small talk and he lacked a certain intuitiveness, but he'd always been great with kids. Years ago, when Eric was six, Chris had stopped by the hospital one day to say hello and entertained Eric with a truckload of facts meant to mesmerize. Like did he know that six eight-stud LEGO pieces could be combined 102,981,500 ways? Or that a standard-size Slinky was made up of eighty feet of wire? Something he proved right there in the hospital hallway, using a measuring tape he just happened to have with him. Annie couldn't think of a single reason not to be attracted to Chris, yet she suddenly knew that she wasn't. She loved him the way she loved Julie and that was where it ended.

Turning the kayak, she pointed it out into the bay, closed her eyes and began paddling again, more slowly now, with the gentle rhythm that always relaxed her. She planned to call Rachel Tice this morning and tell her she'd do her show. Then she would try to think up the perfect reaction if it was Chris who'd bought the ads, rehearsing what she'd say in a way that didn't humiliate or make him feel small for doing it—in a way that showed the world how special he was to her, even if she wasn't in love with him.

The street in front of Annie's house had come alive with reporters by the time she snuck back down the alley. Three were huddled around the picnic table with Rose and Libby, who were busy handing out muffins. When Annie slipped in the back door, Luke glanced over at her from where he stood at the front window eating a bowl of cornflakes.

"Rose and Libby are a buncha head cases."

"Maybe," she conceded. "But they're also a great distraction."

She craned her neck to make sure no one was waiting to pounce, then opened the front door and grabbed a copy of *USA Today* that someone had been kind enough to drop off for her each morning since the paper had begun covering the story. Undetected, she closed the door, slid the dead bolt home, and went back into the kitchen.

Now Eric was up too. "Morning."

"Morning," she said, sliding into a chair.

Scratching his head, he adjusted his knit cap and hung over her shoulder, reading a sidebar article on the front page.

Anticipation Better Than The Real Thing?
by Ian Holt

In a news climate overwhelmed with high alert terrorist warnings, suicide bombings, tsunami disasters, increasingly destructive hurricanes, and growing global distrust, it's easy to see why the homegrown *Have You Seen This Woman?* ad campaign has captivated so many people for the last few weeks. In the midst of the now all-too-familiar out-for-number-one mentality found on today's numerous reality shows, people across the country feel these ads are refreshing and the man behind them

inventive in his attempts to charm ex-love Annie Fischer.

"What's more compelling than a man who's
willing to share with the world his adoration
for the first woman he ever loved?" asks Jana
Felt, a producer at CBS. "It's refreshing,
plain, and simple."

Sally Weingartner, V.P. and Creative Director at DDB, an advertising agency in Chicago,
agrees. "People are drawn to these ads because
they exploit human emotions that we all share,
blatantly ignoring what anyone else thinks in
the process. These ads are about loss, regret,
and the tender reaching out by someone who's
willing to lay himself open to public scrutiny
as he tries to do what at one point or another
in their lives everyone wishes they could do—
have one more shot at a relationship that went
off the rails."

Naysayers point out the obvious. In the
end, what if Annie doesn't feel the same way
about Mr. Anonymous? What if anticipation is
better than the real thing when this guy finally
does come forward? Rhonda Guay, a reporter
with NBC, was quick to respond: "Even if it is
too late for a relationship between these people, who cares? On some level, the attention
has to be flattering for Annie. And let's face
it. This guy's not motivated by some paid reality show that leaves people feeling cheated
in the end. This is obviously coming from his
heart."

Annie stirred sugar into her coffee, amazed at how interest in her predicament had mushroomed.

"I wonder who this guy is?" Eric said, leaning over her shoulder.

Luke came downstairs, tossing his Hacky Sack in the air. "You and the rest of the world, cue ball."

Annie's immediate reaction was to snip at him for being so insensitive, but she didn't want any arguments this morning, so instead she gave Luke a tight stare, communicating what she thought without saying a word.

Hoping to surprise the boys, she'd decided to take them geyser gazing in Yellowstone National Park the upcoming weekend. They didn't know it yet, but they would be leaving early the next morning, and she was excited about it, thinking it would help the three of them reconnect. Equally important, she wanted to get her mind off the last ad that was running in Monday's *Peninsula Post*.

The idea had first come to her when Harrison mentioned in passing that he'd been subpoenaed as a witness in a court case in Billings, Montana, and had to drive down there for a few days. First, Annie asked if she could borrow some camping gear, knowing Harrison was equipped with everything she might ever need. Then she asked if he wanted company on the drive, explaining what she wanted to do. Would he mind dropping her and the boys off at a campsite and picking them up on his way home?

Some of her favorite memories of growing up were of hiking through Yellowstone's Upper Geyser Basin, watching mud pots burping like they were getting ready to boil, steam hissing from fissures and vents in the earth below, and pools of water gleaming like glass beads. "Now *this* is Mother Nature at her best," her dad used to say.

Yellowstone was a virtual country of its own, with a weekly

newspaper, more than three hundred fifty staff, army-size camp-sites, and sprawling visitor complexes. Surrounded by endless boardwalks and interpretive trails, its attractions were linked by a figure-eight highway called the Grand Loop, and in the summer, a passing bear or moose often provoked mile-long traffic jams. But it was the geysers Annie loved best—the collective quiet of people waiting for them to erupt, and the sense of wonder in watching one when it did.

As a kid, she would go-go dance around her bedroom the night before they left on their annual trip, getting herself psyched up. They always started at the visitor center, where she and her dad would buy a boardwalk guide and jot down all of the erup-tion predictions posted for visitors. Their trek varied a little each year, but it always started with Old Faithful. An arc of wooden benches surrounded the geyser, and when it erupted, it shot water higher and higher into the air until it reached a height of one hundred fifty feet. After about three minutes, and much frantic photography, it would suddenly be over, but when everyone else stood to leave, Annie always lingered, closing her eyes and tilting her head back, hoping for the spiderlike touch of geyser mist to land on her face.

"Legend has it," her dad used to whisper, "that geyser mist is pure magic, the kind that makes right all that's gone wrong in our lives."

Unable to hold back her surprise any longer, Annie decided to tell the boys now. "Hey, you guys, guess what we're doing this weekend."

"Helping rebuild the drive-in?" Luke said, rooting through the fridge.

"Taking in a Sonics game?" Eric said hopefully.

"No. We're going to Yellowstone National Park."

That got their attention. Luke pulled his head out of the fridge, frowning, and Eric's face scrunched up in confusion.

"We're going camping," she said, as if this was something they did every day, "and then I'm taking you geyser gazing."

"Camping?" Luke said, as if he'd heard wrong.

"Uh-huh."

"And *geyser gazing*?"

"That's right," she said, sensing enough wiggle room, enough curiosity, to carry on. "Uncle Harrison has a court case in Billings, Montana, early Monday morning so I took the day off and we're driving with him to Yellowstone National Park. We're leaving at six tomorrow morning. He's going to help us set up a tent at a campsite and then pick us up on his way home. We'll be staying within walking distance of the Upper Geyser Basin, and while we're there, you're going to see Old Faithful, the world's most famous geyser."

Eric was squinting at her, trying to take it all in.

"Of course, that's not the only geyser we'll see," she assured them. "We'll spend Sunday hiking around the basin, and we'll stop at a dozen others and watch them blow too. It's an almost cultlike thing, geyser gazing, and—"

Glaring at her, Luke slammed the fridge door shut. "What's *with* you?"

"Excuse me?" she said, trying to keep her voice even.

"Are you sick or dying or something?"

"No," Annie said, staring at him in astonishment. "Why would you ask that?"

His voice was tight and irritated as he lifted a hand in the air, ticking off one finger at a time. "Geez, I don't know. Let me think here. First, you get fired from your job. Then you have some kind of breakdown and start popping pills every day before moving us to this dinky little town. Then it was the tree thing and the drive-in movie from hell, and now you want to take us camping and geyser gazing? What's going on, Mom? You know as much about camping as the average Seattle taxi driver. We've never been camping, not even when Dad lived with us, and we don't have a tent or sleeping bags or even a lantern. And maybe we haven't seen a geyser blow, either, but why start now?"

Annie felt her confidence wobble, but both of them were looking at her, waiting, so she said, "Because it's important to me and I'd like to share some new experiences with you." Her voice started to rise and she set her hands on her hips. "I know things are different than they used to be for you guys, a lot different, but if I go out of my way to set something up that I'd like to share with you, then at the very least I expect you to humor me."

An uncomfortable silence fell.

Luke gave her a long blink, followed by a blank expression. "Sorry."

Annie held up her hand to stop him. She didn't want an apology. "Here's the deal," she said, more forcefully than she intended. "We're going camping and geyser gazing, and I think you should open your minds a little because there's always the slim chance that you might actually enjoy it." As she said this, her eyes teared up and she was immediately embarrassed. She hadn't meant to cry. "Please," she added as an afterthought, and then she went upstairs to take a shower.

As she climbed into the shower, she couldn't help but think about a conversation she'd overheard between Eric and Luke before they'd moved to Eagan's Point. The boys were packing boxes in the living room when she came down the hallway and slowed to a stop.

Eric cleared his throat and said, "I'm worried about Mom."

After a pause, Luke said, "Why?"

"Because she seems so . . . *sad.*"

The pain in Eric's voice made Annie's stomach hurt, but when Luke scoffed and said, "Quit being a dip and pass me the packing tape," she realized he was trying to make Eric think everything would be okay, and it worried her that it wasn't.

Annie shifted in the front seat so she could watch Luke and Harrison in the rearview mirror. They were putting the tent up and they were laughing—she didn't know at what—but Harrison had a hand on Luke's shoulder, and their hilarity gave her a stab of envy. Eric was asleep in the backseat, arms folded across his chest, head against the window, so she climbed out of the car, zipped up her jacket, and went to help them.

"Looks like you could use an extra hand," she said.

"That's not a bad idea," Harrison agreed.

Minutes later, as all three of them struggled to set up the tent, Annie asked Harrison when it had last been used. He straightened and thought for a few seconds, trying to remember.

"Great," Luke said under his breath. "Family dies from suffocation in collapsed tent."

An hour later, the tent was up, Harrison was gone, and a fire was roaring.

"Who wants a bowl of tomato soup?" Annie asked, getting a yes from Eric and a grunt from Luke, who was busy hanging a clothesline between two trees. But before she could find a pot, the air went unusually still. Five minutes later, lightning tore across the sky to the west and thunder crashed above them. The rain came first, slamming down in sheets, pushed by pockets of wind that seemed to come from nowhere. Thankful that Harrison had hung a tarp over their tent for extra protection, Annie and the boys grabbed what they could and ran inside. Tying back the tent flaps, they watched as golf ball–size hail slammed down all around them, bouncing off the picnic table and cast-iron camp stove.

"Great idea, tenting," Luke said, giving her a sarcastic thumbs-up.

When the hail finally stopped, Annie told the boys she needed help getting more wood and a pail of water. It was growing dark, so she wanted to finish their chores now. Heading off down the road, they found a pump and a woodpile, and within minutes, they were on their way back, Annie carrying the water and the boys weighed down with firewood. Walking along the road to their campsite, they heard the people next to them fighting, and they stared, unable to look away. A short, doughy man with a glum expression was sitting on a stump as his daughter stormed back and forth in front of him.

"Honey, it'll be fine," he assured her.

"No, Dad, it won't. I told you to pitch it here," she said, pointing to a spot in the grass behind her. "But no, you had to pitch it next to the picnic table, and now my portable DVD player is wrecked and *that's not fine!*"

The man's glasses were crooked and his face was flushed, and as Annie watched him, she wondered which was worse: being ignored, the way Luke often ignored her, or being screamed at, the way this man's daughter was screaming at him.

At least they were communicating.

Surprising her, Luke said to the couple, "Would you like some help?" He set his wood down and walked over to them. Annie frowned, but a closer look revealed that their neighbor's tent had been flattened, very possibly because of the huge tree that was balanced half on and half off the end of the picnic table next to it.

The man stood, looking sheepish. "Thanks. That'd be great."

Annie was surprised to see Luke blush and realized that sometimes the most obvious details went right over your head when you were a mom. The tantrum-throwing young girl was close to Luke's age, and as soon as he walked over, she busied herself fixing her hair and straightening her tube top.

Annie introduced herself and the boys to the man (Bill Evans) and his daughter (Sadie), before offering to help too. The Evanses were from Oregon, driving across country to Rhode Island for a family reunion. "We have to be there next week," Bill explained. "My wife thought it'd be a great chance for Sadie and me to spend some time together and see the country. She suffers from MS, so she flew out ahead of us." Half an hour later, what was left of their tent had been salvaged and set up in a new spot. "Thanks again," Bill called out as Annie and the boys returned to their campsite next door.

A noise woke Annie at two in the morning. Rolling over, she noticed that the tent flap was open. Pushing it to one side, she poked her head outside and was surprised to see Luke and Sadie sitting side by side at the fire. She opened her mouth to say something, then hesitated, and decided not to. Sadie was strikingly attractive, with blond hair cut short at the back of her neck, falling with razorlike precision at an angle across her face. Intrigued, Annie inched back into the tent, listening with her chin resting on the back of her hands, scarcely daring to breathe for fear of being caught eavesdropping.

She heard Luke say, "I'm not a big talker," and then Sadie replied, "That's okay. I'll talk, you listen, and then we'll both be doing what we're good at." But whereas Luke was usually as remote as the moon, that night Annie listened to him tell Sadie all about his family: how his parents were getting divorced; how his dad was on the quiet side, but a really good guy; how Eric was a dreamer; how his mom was . . . emotional.

Emotional? Annie thought, frowning. *I'm emotional?*

Sadie told Luke about an argument she'd overheard between her parents a few months ago, before her mom was diagnosed with MS. ". . . then divorce came up and they started fighting about who would get custody of me. For weeks after that, I couldn't eat, waiting for them to tell me, but nothing happened. And then Mom got sick and now here we are." She paused. "What about your parents? Do they still talk to each other?"

"Not a lot," Luke said.

"Do you see your dad often?"

"Not as much as I plan to."

He sounded defiant and determined, and it saddened Annie beyond description knowing that when he made up his mind about something, nothing could sway him. Like how she'd tried to reason with him about first grade, telling him he was a little young, that holding him back for a year wouldn't be a big deal. But when it came time to say good-bye that first morning, Luke had gently disengaged her fingers, whispering, "I'm okay, Mom." And she'd said, "I'm not," in a shaky voice after the classroom door had closed behind him.

By ten thirty the next morning, Annie, Eric, and Luke were all sitting on the arc of wooden benches surrounding Old Faithful. Luke immediately lost himself in his handheld Tetris game. It wasn't even close to noon, but the air was already glassy with the promise of a hot day, and within half an hour, a crowd of at least fifty had gathered.

A middle-aged woman wearing a T-shirt that read, *Just Do It*, stared at the empty spot next to Luke for a ridiculously long time. She was on the small side, leaning toward skinny with muscles that were corded and stringy instead of bulging. She was talking to herself, but it was the feather duster she was holding that caught

Annie's eye. After leaning down to inspect the bench, she dusted it, and as she did, Annie heard her say, "Filthy, bloody filthy,"

Luke looked up from his game.

Tucking the feather duster into her back pocket, the woman gingerly sat down next to him and took out her camera.

Pulling away from her, Luke shot Annie a look that said, *What the hell?*

Ignore her, Annie mouthed, hoping he would.

Staring at Old Faithful's massive cone, the woman with the duster started talking, half to herself, half to anyone else who cared to listen. "There are roughly one thousand active geysers in the world and five hundred of them are located in Yellowstone . . ."

Luke stared at her, one eyebrow lifted.

"With this one," she continued, pointing to Old Faithful, "the longer the eruption lasts, the longer the interval until the next eruption. For instance, a two-minute eruption results in an interval of about fifty minutes whereas . . ."

Frowning, Luke leaned over toward Annie. "Is this part of the show?"

"I don't know," she whispered. "Just be patient."

Thankfully, they didn't have long to wait. After some preliminary gurgling and spurting that sent a stir of murmured anticipation through the crowd, a large burst of water suddenly rose up from the cone, and seconds later, Old Faithful was in full eruption, a flume of water shooting one hundred sixty feet into the air and then fanning out at the insistence of a mild breeze. There was a collective gasp followed by exclamations in several foreign languages, the feather duster woman's loud and enthusiastic "Woohoo!" drowning out everyone else. Not more than three minutes later, Mother Nature's brilliant demonstration was finished, and all they could see from where they were sitting three hundred feet away was Old Faithful's cone-shaped crater surrounded by puddles of water.

It was over in seconds, the way most accidents are. One second Annie and the boys were strolling along the boardwalk on their way to see the Beehive geyser, watching a few burping craters in the distance, and the next she was flat on her back, wondering what had happened. Later, the boys told her she'd slipped on a Popsicle someone had dropped.

At first, Eric stood above her, perfectly still, as did Luke. Annie tried to sit up, and in an avalanche of understanding, she realized that she was hurt. Her right ankle was throbbing, and when she tried to put pressure on it, shooting pain stopped her in her tracks.

"Mom?" Eric said, kneeling next to her. "Are you okay?"

Before she could answer, the feather-duster woman darted past him and took over. "Okay. What have we got here?" In what seemed like less than a blink, she pulled a pair of yellow dishwashing gloves out of her knapsack and snapped them on. Then, gently, and with great care, she helped Annie to her feet, holding her by one arm while Luke took the other.

"Can you put any weight on it?" she asked, frowning at Annie's foot.

"A little," Annie said, trying again.

Pulling her feather duster out of her back pocket, the woman dusted a small section of the boardwalk before kneeling to examine Annie's ankle. She turned it first one way and then the other, saying, "Patient has restricted range of motion. Looks like the talofibular ligament could be sprained. Then again, it might be a hairline fracture." With a grim look on her face, she stood and pulled off her gloves. "No weight bearing," she said to Annie in a stern voice. "At least, not until we can get this x-rayed."

"I'm sure she'll be fine," Luke put in.

Tucking the feather duster in her back pocket, the woman pointed in the direction they'd just come from. "Follow me, folks."

"Wait a minute," Luke said, frowning. "Do you work here?"

Ignoring him, she strode off ahead of them, creating chaos where there was none, waving her arms in the air as she yelled at small clusters of oncoming tourists, "Someone's hurt here. Make way please!"

Watching her, Luke groaned.

"I said someone's hurt here," the woman's voice rang out. "Clear a *path*, people!"

"Come on," Eric said, shaking Luke out of his reverie. "Grab Mom's other arm."

Eric draped Annie's arm over his shoulder and wrapped his arm around her waist. Luke did the same thing on her other side, and then they set out, helping her hobble back toward the visitor center. As they did, the feather-duster woman ran ahead of them, stopping occasionally to glare at tourists who seemed genuinely confused by all the yelling. "What's the matter? Are you deaf?" she'd say, shaking her duster at them. "This is an emergency. I said clear a path. Someone's hurt here!"

Mortified, Annie kept her eyes glued to the boardwalk.

When they were halfway there, the absurdity of the situation hit her, and she started to giggle, which slowed them down considerably. Before long, all three of them were laughing, great snorts of laughter escaping through their mouths and noses, until finally tears were running down their cheeks. After losing sight of the woman around a bend ahead of them, Eric stopped and wrapped both arms around his middle. "God, Mom," he sputtered, laughing so hard he could hardly catch his breath. "She's nuts."

The woman circled back to find them, jogging around the corner. "Okay, here's the plan. You boys help your mom over there," she said, pointing to the benches near Old Faithful. "And I'll call an ambulance and round up some paramedics."

An ambulance? Annie thought, alarmed. *Paramedics?*

"This is nothing to laugh about," the woman said, pointing her feather duster at Eric.

Barely containing a fresh outburst, Eric clamped a hand over his mouth and tried to pull himself together. Surprising Annie, Luke stepped forward and took over, handling the woman deftly, agreeing with everything she said to appease her and then ignoring her completely as soon as she'd turned away. "Come on," he whispered, laughing as he tugged on Annie's arm. "We'll take a shortcut through the bush and lose her."

Annie looked to see if he was joking and was amazed at how a smile could transform his face.

"Wait," Eric said. "Look."

Annie and Luke turned to see two park officials making their way along the boardwalk toward the woman. When one of them asked what her name was, she slipped the duster into her back pocket and said, "Maaarrrrry," so slowly and uncertainly you could tell it was a lie. Nodding, the park officials each took an arm and gently guided her over to the visitor center, where a bus was parked out front, its four-way flashers on and LONGVIEW STATE MENTAL HOSPITAL painted on its side.

"Do you see that?" Eric said, eyes wide.

"A total fruitcake," Luke added.

Annie considered the rest of the day a bust because she couldn't show the boys any more geysers. Later that afternoon, as she hobbled around their campsite on what seemed to be a sprained ankle, she found herself wishing they hadn't come at all, convinced the weekend was a complete flop. That idea seemed to be confirmed six hours later when she woke in the middle of the night and had to pee. Instead of trying to make it to the women's bathroom in the dark, she limped into the bush behind their tent. After squatting down, balancing most of her weight on her good foot, clutching tufts of grass with one hand and flapping the other one behind her to keep the mosquitoes away, she was about to declare mission accomplished when she stood up and realized she'd mistakenly peed on Luke's favorite sweatshirt, which had fallen from the clothesline.

Early the next morning, before Harrison arrived to pick them up, Annie heard the boys talking outside the tent as they tried to start the fire—about the crazy woman and her feather duster ("Man, what a head case!"); how Old Faithful was "beyond wicked" when it finally erupted ("Did you see how high it shot?"); and how they "couldn't wait to tell Dad" ("Maybe we can talk him into bringing us back next summer.").

Crawling to the entrance of the tent, Annie opened the flap and looked out. When she was old and gray and often accused of dramatizing, she would swear she didn't imagine it. In the pale light of dawn, as the world gradually lightened all around them, she watched her boys share a few moments of camaraderie, and for an instant as she tilted her head back and closed her eyes, against all logic, she was sure she felt the featherlight dusting of geyser mist touch her face.

TWENTY-FIVE

When Harrison dropped Annie off at home late that night, and she limped through the front door, the last ad in that day's *Peninsula Post* was the first thing on her mind. During the drive back from Yellowstone, she'd called Marina and had her read the ad over the phone, then asked her to leave a copy on the kitchen table. Marina had been feeding Montana and Lurch while they were away, so that would be no problem. Since Jack planned to take Tuesday off work, Annie and Harrison had swung through Seattle and left the boys at their dad's apartment. It meant that Eric and Luke would miss two days of school, but spending time with their dad seemed more important right now.

Dumping her gear, Annie slid into a kitchen chair and grabbed the newspaper. This ad still showed her graduation picture from fifteen years ago and the age-advanced head shot she'd been looking at for weeks, but now another photo had been added—a further age-advanced photo that made her look at least sixty, but an incredible sixty. Annie let out her breath, realizing only then that she'd been holding it. Growing old had never scared her, although she'd wondered what she'd look like. In this picture, she liked what she saw.

Her hair was longer and shot with gray, pulled up and away from her face, with a few wispy strands falling out, caressing the back of her neck. There were wrinkles too, but she looked strong and proud, and her chin was lifted a notch higher than in the previous pictures—a small thing, but something she noticed right away. *I look like a woman with a lifetime of wisdom etched on her face. Like a woman who's made all kinds of choices, some good, some bad, but someone who is now richly content with her life.*

COULD YOU GROW OLD WITH THIS WOMAN?

ANNIE FISCHER LIKES INFOMERCIALS BUT HATES TV, CAN MANEUVER A KAYAK BUT HAS TROUBLE WITH A CAR, LOVES THANKSGIVING BUT HATES TURKEY. THIS AGE-ADVANCED PHOTO MIGHT BE WHAT SHE LOOKS LIKE TODAY AND THE ONE NEXT TO IT IS HOW I IMAGINE SHE WILL LOOK THIRTY YEARS FROM NOW—THE KIND OF WOMAN WHO COULD TAKE AN OLD MAN'S BREATH AWAY. IF YOU KNOW WHERE I CAN FIND HER, PLEASE CALL (212) 555-1963.

Fighting back tears, Annie stared with amazement at the woman she might one day become, wondering about the man who seemed to get her as no one else did. Who are you? she wondered, and for one giddy moment, she felt better than she had in months. In fact, who it was no longer mattered because he'd lifted her spirits and self-esteem more than ten bottles of Zoloft ever could. Maybe this was every woman's secret wish, to have a man feel this way about her. Because having someone this bold and sure and determined tell the world how he felt about you was impossible to ignore—it was close to intoxicating.

An hour later, she was in the bathtub, soaking her foot and enjoying a cigarette, when she heard a key in the lock downstairs.

The door opened and Marina called out, "Annie?"

"I'm up here!" she yelled back.

Montana, lying outside the open bathroom door, cocked her head but didn't get up. Annie heard cupboard doors slam, and glasses tinkling against each other, followed by the hollow pop of a cork. When Marina came upstairs, Montana's tail thumped against the floor. Squatting to give the dog a pat, Marina stepped over her into the bathroom holding a bottle of Wolf Blass wine, two glasses, and a small plastic bag.

"How's your foot?" she asked, leaning against the door.

Annie lifted it out of the tub, turning it one way and then the other. "A little swollen, but better today than it was yesterday."

"Good. I brought enough Chinese food to feed an army, wine, and a pint of double-chocolate ice cream."

"I hate ice cream," Annie reminded her, taking a drag on her cigarette.

"It's not for you, and if you don't put that out, neither is the Chinese food." Stepping farther into the room, Marina set the plastic bag on the toilet lid. "I got you something."

"What is it?"

"A new dress for you to wear when you go on *The Rachel Tice Show*. After you get out, try it on and come downstairs."

"Marina! You didn't have to do that."

"Just try it on." She stepped over Montana on her way out. "I'll see you downstairs."

Annie climbed out of the tub and dried off. Opening the bag, she found a simple black dress that looked like nothing much at all, but once she wriggled into it, she ran her hands over the clingy barely there fabric in amazement. It really was a great dress. By the time she combed her hair out and hobbled downstairs to the kitchen, Marina had dinner on the table.

Annie cleared her throat, feeling self-conscious as she stood at the bottom of the stairs.

Marina looked up and stared at her in amazement. "Wow," she said, her voice catching. "You look gorgeous."

"Please."

"I'm serious. You look . . . Michelle Pfeifferish."

"Oh, right! A mousy version, but thanks all the same."

Jumping up, Marina took her by the arm and turned her around, looking the dress over from top to bottom. "Are you blind? It looks incredible, Annie."

"I do like it," she admitted. "But what kind of underwear are you supposed to wear with a dress like this? It'll show everything."

"Trust me," Marina said, pointing to another bag on the table. "After seeing the state of your underwear on TV last week, I added panties to my shopping list."

"At least I won't feel like a frump," Annie said, turning sideways to look at her reflection in the window. "I still can't believe I'm doing this, though. Do you think I made a mistake?"

"No. I think it's great, and I think you should have some fun with it. Keep in mind, this isn't a reality show where you have to smile, fake it, and marry the guy at the end of the show. You get to meet Rachel Tice, talk to some man who's crazy about you, and walk off the stage with no harm done. What could possibly go wrong?"

Annie sat down and speared a piece of limp broccoli, inspected it, then put it on the side of her plate. "I guess you're right."

Marina slid into the chair across from her. "Was it nice getting away from all those reporters for a few days?"

"Yes," Annie said, "not to mention away from Mom."

Marina paused and set her fork down. "I hate it when you do that," she said.

"Do what? Get impatient with Mom and her search for the perfect, disease-free life?"

Marina snapped her fingers. "That. Right there. The way you just said that about her."

"Oh, come on," Annie said, laughing. "Give me a break, Marina. You'd feel the same way if she were at the rescue shelter every day going off on impromptu medical rants and diagnosing everyone who walks through the door with obscure disorders. I know you're more tolerant than I am, but you've got to admit it makes you crazy. Dad had more patience with her than either of us, but I'm sure it frustrated him some too."

"Given everything he put her through over the years," Marina said dryly, "Dad had good reason to be patient with her."

"What do you mean?"

Pause. "Nothing. Never mind."

"No, I do mind. Stop insinuating things and then not saying what's on your mind."

"Look, I don't want to hurt you, okay, Annie?"

She held up a hand. "Hurt me? What are you talking about? What could you say about Dad that would ever hurt me?"

Marina gave her an irritated look. "Annie, how old do you have to be before you pull him down from that pedestal you've got him on? Dad was a drinker, a big drinker, not to mention a shameless flirt. Everyone in town knew it."

Annie suddenly lost her appetite. A peculiar fluttering took over her chest as all the tenderness she had ever felt for her dad came rushing back. For years she had operated with an unspoken pledge of loyalty for him: avoid talking about his drinking or how often he worked late, that much she'd always been sure about.

"There was talk years ago that he'd been having an affair with his secretary before that big accident of his," Marina said, playing with her spoon. "I've never asked Mom about it, but I heard it almost killed her when she found out."

Annie closed her eyes. She didn't want to hear this. One of her favorite memories was the day her dad gave her the penny tree. How they'd walked home together late that afternoon, her feet working double time to keep up, believing he was as close to perfect as God had made any man. And yet, even then, she had known intuitively that she was wrong.

Marina leaned forward, resting her elbows on the table. "Come on, Annie," she said, squeezing her hand. "Be honest. Do you ever remember him coming to your tetherball play-offs? A school concert? A parent-teacher meeting? I loved him too, but he was never really there for us. Not the way Mom was."

Annie took a moment to gather her thoughts, thinking, *He was there for me.* And yet, somewhere inside, she knew her memories of him had been colored by her own set of crayons. *Funny what our minds keep from us,* she thought. *What we refuse to accept and what we will twist around to look like something that's easier to accept.*

"I'm sorry," Marina said. "I didn't mean to bring this up now. Are you okay?"

Annie nodded. There wasn't much else she could do, because sometimes the simplest questions were the hardest to answer. For years, she had believed her dad could do anything, that he was the kind of man who could conjure up a penny tree to solve all her problems as easily as he could whip up an omelet. Every summer, when he used to take her and Marina to watch the Fourth of July fireworks at the Docks, the sky would light up like a rainbow exploding under fire, and Marina would throw her head back and watch, joining in as a huge roar went out from the crowd. But not Annie. Instead, she'd stand next to her dad, taking his hand in case something went wrong, looking up at all that magic from the safety of his side. In moments like that, fleeting, memorable moments, she imagined he was what she'd needed him to be, even though he often shot her worried looks that said he wasn't comfortable with her blind adoration—looks that told her he realized he had a long way to fall.

Marina reached across the table and covered Annie's hands with her own. "Annie, there's something else I need to tell you."

"What?" Annie sniffed, blowing her nose.

Marina's gaze slid off her face. "Do you remember the day I found our adoption papers?"

"How can I forget?"

Choosing her words carefully, Marina stared at her lap. "Breaking into that tin box bothered me for years. I knew whatever was in there was private, but I did it anyhow, and after I got it open, I locked myself in the bathroom, laid everything out on the floor, and went through it all. What I found is something I've tried to ignore ever since, something I've never told anyone, not even Harrison."

"What was in there?" Annie asked, genuinely confused.

After a long pause, Marina said, "A few things," pulling her knees up to her chest and resting her chin on them. "An old cork from a wine bottle, a few postcards from Germany and England, some letters, a picture of us when we were little. But there was also something else, something that didn't make sense. And then I found those legal documents about our adoption, and I got so caught up reading them that I pushed the rest out of my mind. You know, the way you do when you can only take in so much at once?" Her voice trailed away, and for a moment, she struggled with how to continue. "At first, I didn't fully understand what I'd found. Call it denial if you want, but it seemed unfathomable to me, almost unthinkable."

She looked up, then quickly away. "I put it all back, but a few months later, I worked up the nerve to go looking for it again. It was the day Mom and Dad left me alone after school while they drove into Seattle to get you. Remember? It was that time you ran away for a few days and they picked you up at that gas station just outside the city. You came home with a black eye and Mom had a complete meltdown over it?"

Annie nodded. She remembered.

"Anyhow, her tin box wasn't on the top shelf of their bedroom closet anymore, so first I had to figure out where she'd hidden it. Eventually I found it inside her sewing machine case, and after I got it open, I was careful how I took everything out so I could put it back inside exactly the way it was before."

Annie swallowed. "What was there?"

"A picture . . . of a little boy and a tiny hospital bracelet that said Nicholas Fischer. In the picture, he was two or three. He had blond hair and impish blue eyes. The date on the back of the bracelet was May 28, 1963."

What was she talking about? Annie thought.

"A few weeks later, I went to the town archives and checked the microfilm for the *Peninsula Post* and on June 12, 1963, there was a birth announcement for Nicholas Fischer, born May 28, 1963, to parents Timothy and Erna Fischer of Eagan's Point."

Annie blinked in disbelief.

Marina's voice dropped. "Then I found an obituary from a few years later that said he'd died on August 10, 1966. Only it didn't say how, so I kept looking. I found an article the week before his obituary warning residents that a three-year-old boy from Eagan's Point had died from meningitis. It told parents to watch out for flulike symptoms like a rash, stiff neck, high fever, or excessive vomiting." She glanced up at Annie. "With meningitis, you can have a perfectly healthy child running around the house and days later—"

"I know," Annie interrupted, not wanting to think about it. She stared at Marina for a few seconds, tears welling. "I can't believe you've never told me this before."

"I couldn't, Annie," she said sadly. "You had a harder time adjusting to being adopted than I did. At least I got to meet my grandparents before they died, but you were so mad for so long, and when everything finally started getting back to normal, Dad had his big accident, and we were so busy dealing with it . . ."

"Then that means Mom lied to us," Annie said, half to herself. "Remember? She told us she couldn't have children."

"I know," Marina said, pushing her plate away. "And I've thought about that a lot. But knowing Mom, I think she was probably worried we'd think we were their second choice, you know? She always wanted us to feel special, Annie, especially after we found out how she and Dad hid for so long that we were adopted. I think she probably blamed herself a little too, for not recognizing the symptoms and catching it in time. For not being able to save him."

Annie dropped her face into her hands as memories of her mom came back to her, running together in her head. The way she used to fret excessively whenever Annie or Marina got sick as kids, working herself into such a state that she'd barely sleep until they were well. How she had cradled Luke as a newborn, tears brimming as she rocked him. How often she'd driven into the city to sit beside Eric's hospital bed when he was sick, reading to him when he was at his worst, helping him build with LEGOs, asking Annie if there was anything she could do, "Anything at all." The muffled prayers Annie often heard her mom whispering when Eric was asleep, her shoulders shaking with silent sobs when she thought she was alone.

"Oh my God," Annie whispered, closing her eyes tight.

All that time, all those years, her mom's obsessive fascination with everyone's health wasn't fascination at all. It was fear talking as loud as it could in a woman who'd lost her child—a woman who would, on some level, forever be coping with that loss.

TWENTY-SIX

On Wednesday after school, Annie and Luke were sitting in the bleachers watching a group of eleven-year-olds come into the school gym for basketball practice. Eric was the last kid through the door and Annie almost came to her feet when she saw him. Glancing up into the stands, he shot her a quick smile. He looked pale and gangly, and as usual he was wearing the black knit cap Sawyer had given him weeks ago. Luke nudged her with an elbow, pointing at two of the other kids who were also wearing knit caps, only one was light gray and the other was yellow with blue stripes across the back.

One big kid, a husky boy with huge feet, loped down to the end of the court and effortlessly popped the ball into the air, making a basket. Catching it on its way down, he jogged past Eric and gave him a quick two-handed shove. Unable to stop herself, Annie jumped up to say something, but a hand grabbed her by the elbow and pulled her back down.

"Leave it alone, Annie," Jack said in a calm voice.

He had left a message on their machine earlier telling Eric that he'd be here, so Annie wasn't surprised to see him, although she did protest as she sat down.

"But didn't you see what that kid just did to Eric?"

"He'll be fine," Jack said, inching past her to sit next to Luke.

The boys worked hard, practicing two-handed passes, rebound shots, and offensive plays. Twenty minutes into the practice, they were in the middle of a freeze scrimmage when the coach was called out of the gym for a phone call. Telling half the kids to line up at one end of the gym and the rest at the other, he asked them to do jump shots until he got back.

Eric lined up at Annie and Jack's end and two other kids immediately started harassing him. Annie couldn't hear what they were saying but she could tell by the look on his face that it wasn't complimentary. After he made a basket, thankfully on his first shot, both of them fell to their knees and brought their hands and head to the floor as though bowing down in awe of him. This didn't rattle Eric, though. He just laughed and did the jock thing, wiping his forehead with the back of one hand. Then he stepped over them like they were gnats and went to the back of the line, where everyone else was laughing—not at him, but with him.

"See?" Jack said, leaning past Luke. "He can handle things on his own. It's time to let him go a little, Annie."

When Chris Carby walked into the gym to pick Annie up for dinner, he was surprised to see Jack sitting in the stands. Jack glanced over and gave him a polite nod. Then Annie waved, motioning that she'd be right down, so he leaned back against the wall to wait. He'd only met Jack twice. The first time was when Annie brought Jack home after they got engaged and the second was at their wedding. Both times he had felt uncomfortable. Not that Jack didn't seem like a nice guy, because he did. He seemed like a great guy, someone most people would have trouble finding fault with—if you didn't count that he seemed to have broken Annie's heart.

As Chris watched Annie work her way down the bleachers and across the gym, he realized he was nervous. He still didn't know how he was going to tell her. He just knew he couldn't wait any longer. Unfortunately, he had never been great with words. Years ago, when they were in high school, Annie used to tell him not to be so *honest* about everything. That, for example, when she had asked him what he thought of her new braces, he might have been better off telling her they looked *okay* instead of telling her that they made her look like the front grille of a train. Or when Julie asked him if he thought her nose was big, maybe he could've said, "It's uniquely yours," instead of "It's massive."

Maybe he would warm Annie up first by making her laugh. He could tell her how he had once booked a weekend at a resort on Salt Spring Island for him and a woman he was seeing at the time, and then had to have her airlifted to Vancouver after she had an allergic reaction to buckwheat flour in a dinner roll. How, for days afterward, he had watched her rub calamine lotion on the oozing welts that covered her face, agreeing with her when she said that she'd never looked worse.

No, he thought. *Telling her about my failed relationships isn't what this is about. This is about being honest with her, the way I should have been years ago.*

"Thanks for picking me up here," Annie said, walking up to him. "At least this way I got to watch half of Eric's practice."

"No problem. Where would you like to eat?"

"Why don't we try that new Chinese restaurant downtown?"

He smiled and opened the door for her. "Sounds good," he said, even though he hated Chinese food and would have rather eaten anywhere else in town.

Chris ordered a bowl of wonton soup but ate only half of it, telling Annie he wasn't hungry. They had just finished eating when an older woman stopped by their table to thank Annie for handling the floral arrangements for her husband's funeral. As they talked, Chris found himself wondering what Jack thought about the ads and whether he was concerned about Annie's decision to go on *The Rachel Tice Show.*

"Can I ask you something?" he said after the woman had left. Annie handed him a fortune cookie. "Sure."

"I know it's none of my business, but when I ran into your mom at the bank today, she told me you're doing *The Rachel Tice Show* Friday, and I was just wondering how that's going to work. Do they send a car to pick you up? Is it a live show or does it air a week from now? And did you have to sign some kind of contract?"

"Yes," she said. "I signed a contract. They faxed it to me yesterday. And no, I told them not to bother sending a car. Marina and Mom are driving me into Seattle Friday morning at ten. Then I meet Rachel Tice and her crew, the show will get under way, Mr. Anonymous will reveal himself, we'll have a nice chat, and I should be home by three. As far as I know, it will air Friday in the regular time slot."

Chris was playing with a spoon on the table, acting as if something was bothering him.

"What's wrong?" Annie asked.

"What are you going to do if this guy isn't someone you—"

"Feel the same way about?" Annie said, finishing for him.

"Exactly."

She gave him a tender smile. "It won't matter."

"It won't?" he said.

"No," she said, choosing her words carefully. "Because he's obviously a sensitive, caring guy, and taking into consideration that I must've known him pretty well years ago, I'll probably give him a huge hug, even if I don't believe I could ever be in love with him now."

Chris nodded, keeping his gaze on the table.

"What's your fortune cookie say?" she asked, trying to change the subject.

He cracked it open and read, " 'The future will take care of itself.' "

"Mine says, 'Go out on a limb. That's where the fruit is.' "

Weighing his words, he said, "Remember a few weeks ago when I told you there was something I wanted to talk about?" She nodded. "Well . . . for years I haven't been completely honest with you."

Oh my God, Annie thought, tucking her hands under her thighs. *He's going to tell me he ran the ads. Before we go on* The Rachel Tice Show. *Before viewers can watch my reaction on TV.* Her heart was suddenly pounding in her throat.

Chris looked straight at her. "Annie, I'm tired of pretending. . . ."

She lifted a hand in the air to interrupt. "Wait. I think I know what this is about."

He narrowed his eyes. "You do?"

"Yes," she said. "You're trying to tell me you bought the ads."

Chris frowned, blinking in confusion. "No," he said. "That's not it."

Annie's face fell. "Then what?"

"I'm gay," he said, managing a weak smile.

Annie searched his face for a long time. She was stunned. Shocked. Maybe even a little hurt. But mostly, she felt like an idiot. *Now it all makes sense,* she thought. All those years in high school when he never dated, the catch in his voice when he phoned years ago to tell her that he was getting married, how she hung up thinking that he'd sounded more sad than excited. How she used to think that he spent more time trying to please his parents than he ever did himself. Annie didn't know what to say or where to look, so she gazed down at the table, repeating the words out loud.

"You're gay."

He nodded and an awkward silence took hold of them.

"Admitting it to myself was the hardest part," he finally said. "For years, I wasn't happy, but I tried to make myself believe that I was. After my divorce, I came back here, and at first I didn't plan on staying. I tried to convince myself I just hadn't met the right woman, but after a while, even that excuse got tired. Then, when my dad died and left me the shop, I had to decide who I was going to be and how I wanted to live the rest of my life."

He fixed his eyes on something behind her. "This isn't San Francisco, Annie. Some people here are open-minded but many aren't, and that's why it works best this way—no one knowing, I mean. Because what people suspect and what they know to be true are handled differently when it comes to running a business in a small town. I love my life here and there's nothing I can imagine changing. But I value my privacy too, so because of that, I don't have any plans to parade down Main Street telling the rest of world." He shrugged and ducked his head. "I just thought it was time I told you."

Somewhere in the back of the restaurant, there was a loud hissing sound from something hitting a hot grill, people were laughing, and the tangy smell of sweet-and-sour sauce filled the air. Chris seemed to be waiting for her to say something, but she was overwhelmed.

"Annie? Can I ask what you're thinking?"

Looking straight at him, she dropped her napkin on the table and pushed back her chair. Rarely had she ever felt more like laughing and crying at the same time. Tears welled in her eyes as she stood and went around to his side of the table. Smiling, she slid into his lap and wrapped both arms around his neck. "What am I thinking?" she said. "I'm thinking that I believe this is one of the single greatest moments of our friendship—that's what I'm thinking. And that I love you. Always have, and always will."

Twenty-seven

Annie asked Chris to drop her off in the alley so she could avoid all the reporters out front. When she snuck in the back door, Jack was bent over the fish tank, blowing air into the water with a turkey baster, refusing to give up on the goldfish, which now looked on the brink of death.

"I think they're moving again," Eric said.

"Good. How you doing, kiddo?" Jack asked Sawyer, who was standing at the kitchen table, attaching a tube to a new air stone.

"I need another minute," she said, squinting at the printed directions.

Luke was busy rooting through the fridge for something to eat, so Eric saw Annie first. "Mom! Look what Dad got me for making the team." He held out a new basketball. "It's autographed by every Sonics player."

"Wow," Annie said, taking a look.

Jack turned, stretching to work out a few kinks. "They were floating upside down when we got here an hour ago," he explained, waving at the tank. "So I sent Sawyer out to buy a new air stone and we've been trying to revive them ever since."

Sawyer plugged the tiny motor into the wall and a stream of air bubbles burst forth from the bottom of the tank. They all leaned in to watch and remarkably, within minutes, both fish were revived and circling the pirate ship on the bottom.

Eric gave Sawyer a high five, and Jack grinned, looking pleased.

Rolling his eyes, Luke tossed an apple into the air and caught it. "Hey, Dad? What time are you picking us up on Friday?"

Jack thought about it. "I'll be parked in front of the school by quarter to four, so make sure you're ready and don't forget to bring your bathing suits."

They were spending the upcoming weekend on the radio station's boat and Eric also had his first-ever basketball game Friday night, so they were both excited.

Luke left to take Montana for a walk. Then Eric asked Sawyer if she wanted to play one-on-one and they went outside, leaving Annie and Jack alone. This sharing of their children still felt odd, and as Annie watched Jack slip on his jacket, she wondered if she'd ever get used to it. She and Jack still talked, but it was different now. It was safe talk about the boys and their schedules, the kind of conversation that kept the lines drawn and their emotions in check.

"How are you holding up?" Jack asked.

She shrugged, tilting her head toward the reporters out front. "It's almost over."

"I hear you're going on TV Friday," he said, leaning against the door.

Annie stared at him, letting five seconds pass, waiting to see what he'd say next since she knew she hadn't mentioned the show to him earlier.

Jack frowned. "You are, right? That's what Sawyer told us at the practice."

Annie was amazed once again by the sheer speed with which her family managed to exchange personal and private information about her life. First her mom, now Marina. "Yes, that's right," she said, nudging a dog bone out of the way with her foot. "I'll be there and apparently whoever took out the ads will be too."

An uncomfortable silence rose up between them. Jack cleared his throat. "Can I ask why you'd want to do something like that?"

"Because *The Rachel Tice Show* offered to pay off all Eric's medical bills."

Jack stared at her, face expressionless. "Why would they do that?"

Annie shrugged. "They want to scoop the story of who this guy is."

Pause. "So you're doing it for the money?"

"That's not the only reason," she said, "but I have to admit it did make my decision easier. My face has been on the front page of every major paper for weeks now, and I no longer care what anyone thinks. I'm just curious about who it is, and if doing this show gets our bills paid off in the process, I consider that a bonus."

Nodding, Jack turned to leave. Until then, Annie hadn't noticed how tired he looked, but now she saw the bristle of beard where he hadn't shaved and the dark rings under his eyes. He had his back to her when he said, "Good luck then. I hope it all works out for you." He sounded as though he'd said all he had to say and the rest was up to her. Later, she would forget if she said anything back, but she would always remember the way the screen door bounced shut behind him as he left, how she listened to him leave with the same heavy steps that seemed to carry him wherever he went these days.

Both boys were asleep and Montana was lying on the bed next to Luke when Annie went upstairs later that night. She opened the hallway window and climbed outside onto the roof. Sitting cross-legged, she lit a cigarette and pulled on it hard, telling herself that she'd quit again once *The Rachel Tice Show* was behind her. As she smoked in silence, enjoying the cool night air, Libby's yard light came on and she stepped outside carrying Mr. Kale's basset hound.

"Okay," Libby said, setting him on the grass. "Do your thing."

The dog lay down, put his head on his paws, and stared at her.

Frustrated, Libby set both hands on her hips, then seemed to have an idea. She scooped him up and tucked him under her arm before going through the gate into Mr. Kale's yard, where she set him on the grass. Again, the dog flopped down, staring forlornly at Mr. Kale's house.

Libby squatted in front of him, singsonging, "Come on, buddy. C-o-m-e on. . . ." But he didn't move, his misery so apparent that Libby glanced around at a loss.

Suddenly, with no warning, she dropped onto all fours and tossed her gray hair from side to side. Then, tilting her head back, she mimicked his nightly howl, long and wolflike. The dog cocked his head. Getting up, he rushed to her, howling long and low too, and then he took off across the yard and did his nightly business. When he was done, he trotted back to her, and Libby scooped him up, cooing, "Don't you worry. He'll be home in a few days."

Annie crushed out her cigarette, shaking her head in amazement. Watching tough old Libby Johnson soften up sure wasn't something she thought she'd ever see. Just then she noticed a tiny cardboard box next to her with *Mom* neatly lettered on the lid. Opening it, she reached inside and pulled out the amber nugget she'd given Eric. A Post-it note stuck to it read: *Take it with you for courage when you go on TV.* She laughed as she turned it over in her palm. Her attempts at being discreet about coming out here obviously hadn't worked with either of the boys.

Tucking the nugget back in the box, she remembered how nervous she'd been when she got pregnant with Luke. How scared she was, how hard she'd worked to prepare for her role as a mom. For nine months, she read the way she ate her meals: in abundance and with an appetite. *What to Expect When You're Expecting* gave way to *What to Expect in the First Year*, which in turn took her down roads about early-childhood development and parenting different personality types. She read a slew of books, but none of them prepared her for the moment when her heart stopped beating for that split second when she'd first met each of her boys.

There is no sensation like it, she thought. *You're exhausted, but you don't care. Your back throbs and your body feels like it's been through a meat grinder, but it doesn't matter. You ache in spots you didn't know could ache, and yet none of it diminishes the way you feel when they hand you that baby, whether he's wrinkled and wilted from hours of hard labor, or pink and fresh from a cesarean.* (True to form, she'd had one of each—Luke gave her twenty-eight hours of hard labor and Eric was a C-section.) *The first time you hold them, your emotions are too big and they spill out all over, and in that instant your heart changes forever, shifting a few inches closer to the heart of your child.*

Years ago, when she tried to describe the sensation to Julie, she likened it to when you're walking somewhere in a hurry, slip on a patch of ice, go airborne, and land on your butt. Everything around you slams to a stop. You can't move, you can't breathe, and there's almost always damage—an arthritic ache years later that won't go away or a dull throb that comes on if you go up too many stairs. Like it or not, from that moment on, your tumble on an icy sidewalk, like the arrival of your child, forever becomes part of the fabric of who you are, an extension of your heart and limbs.

She'd gone on to explain how there were a few spots on every child that only a mother knows or cares about. One is the small indentation at the base of their neck where you press your nose when they're babies and you want to wrap yourself in their smell. Another is the tiny crease behind their ear, where you plant whispers like "I love you" or "Sleep tight" as they drift off at night, bum in the air and arms akimbo. These are the spots a mother is immediately drawn to whenever her child is sick, after she presses her face against his to feel for a fever, silently praying it's just a cold.

"It's amazing," she had said, watching her boys playing in the sandbox that day. "In a room filled with babies, you will know yours from his cry. You'll tilt your head to listen, and from the pitch and tone or jagged howl, you'll instinctively know if he has a wet diaper, a lost pacifier, or if he needs food *now*. Before long, you'll know his favorite colors, what he wants for lunch, what he'll refuse to eat for dinner, that spiders fascinate him, but bull-frogs prompt nightmares, and how long it takes him to start complaining on a long car ride. You may even bet on it. And the first time you see him copy your husband, with a hand gesture, or a tilt of his head, your heart will jump into your throat, and for a few seconds, you'll fall in love with the man you married all over again."

As she thought about that now, staring up at the stars, Annie realized she must have told Julie this before Eric got sick because she could remember feeling content at the time, even fulfilled. So it had to have been before everything started falling apart between Jack and her, before she got so wrapped up in the possibility of losing Eric that she lost touch with everyone else around her. She could still remember how Julie, who'd always wanted kids, had hugged her with tears in her eyes, telling her how lucky she was.

Pulling her sweater tighter, Annie climbed back through the open window. Many of her and Jack's arguments ran together in her head, but some were so memorable, so infinitely unforgettable that, sadly, she could reiterate them word for word. "Sounds like you weren't very kind to each other," Orenda had said once, and Annie had nodded, embarrassed that this had been the case. She knew now that you couldn't draw a straight line between any one incident and the failure of a marriage. Yes, there had been a stretch of time when their relationship wasn't great, and yes, they were drowning in debt from Eric's medical bills, but then something else happened—something that sent their marriage spiraling out of control.

Annie had taken Eric downtown for some follow-up tests. When she was told she'd have an hour wait, she grabbed a sandwich at a deli and went over to the park across the street. She was sitting on a bench eating when she heard Jack's voice. She turned and saw him and his cohost, Linda, walking along a path not far away. Her first reaction was to join them, but something in the way they were talking told her this wasn't just any lunch; this was something more and it rooted her to the spot.

They were walking not far from where she was sitting. Annie watched wordlessly as Linda slid an arm around Jack's waist and gave him a squeeze. She'd met Linda only once, but she knew Linda had been with the station for years. Linda was as tall as Marina, with auburn-colored hair that fell to her shoulders, and that day she looked chic in a pair of jeans with sandals and a stone-colored silk blouse.

Panic spread through Annie's body. Then, as she watched them cross the street to go back to work, she told herself she was overreacting. As disbelief gave way to logic, she reminded herself that she'd laid out their marriage in her mind long ago. She'd imagined it evolving through school plays, Christmas concerts, and summer vacations together. The boys would struggle through their teens like all kids did, growing into men. She and Jack would one day stand in awe at a nursery window, palms pressed to the glass as they tried to wrap their brains around the fact that they were grandparents.

Everyone has the odd hairline crack in their relationship, she told herself, tossing her sandwich into a garbage can. But hadn't Jack and she always said they could make it through anything? Of course, it didn't take a rocket scientist to see they needed to spend more time together. They'd talked about it; they just hadn't taken any steps to fix it. At dinner that night, Annie asked him how his day was, but he just shrugged and said it was okay.

The next day, Jack called to tell her he had to work late and she offered to drive downtown with the boys and bring him pizza, maybe set up on the floor of his control booth and let the kids watch for a while. But he told her it wasn't a good night for that. He would grab a sandwich from one of the vending machines instead.

Fantasies don't need a lot of room to grow, especially when your intuition is on high alert, and that day Annie's kicked into overdrive. Bundling the boys into the car after dinner, she drove downtown past the building where Jack worked, relieved to see his car parked out back. Thankfully, the boys had fallen asleep. She'd just turned around in the alley and was about to pull out onto Pike Street to go home when she saw them. Jack and Linda were walking up the sidewalk toward the station (ambling, really), sharing what looked like a cookie. Jack appeared relaxed, laughing at something Linda had said. Then she grabbed his elbow, reached up, and wiped a smudge of chocolate off his mouth. At that moment he glanced up and saw Annie, and he flushed like a kid who'd been caught breaking the rules.

Without a backward glance, Annie pulled out in front of them and drove home.

Later, Jack tried to explain. "Annie, we're friends. Christ, I need someone to talk to! When was the last time we talked? And I don't mean about paying the water bill or who should pick Luke up from school or whether or not one of Eric's doctors thinks we should try a new treatment. I mean talk like we used to, like we aren't just two people coexisting under the same roof."

She was sitting at the table, staring at her hands. "What are you saying?"

"That Linda and I are friends. That's all."

"Okay. So on one hand you're telling me you've got this special friend because you feel alone, our relationship is lacking, and we don't talk anymore. But on the other hand, you're saying you're *just friends*, inferring a complete lack of intimacy. Which one is it, Jack?"

Pause. "We're friends."

Annie didn't need any help guessing how their friendship had evolved. She knew that Linda would have sensed he was going through a rough time and probably offered her support, saying, "Jack, are you okay?" or "I'm here if you need someone to talk to. . . ." Annie could almost script the way it had happened. How their on-air camaraderie had inched forward from where it used to be to where it was now, leaving them on the cusp of a full-fledged affair, and her too drained and exhausted to care.

The next day, she was standing in a checkout line at the grocery store with Eric, who was sitting in the cart eating doughnuts she hadn't bought yet. On the wall behind the checkout counter was a calendar. Annie looked up and saw it was June sixth. There was an old woman in line behind them, and when Eric stuffed yet another doughnut into his mouth, she made a tutting sound with her tongue. Ignoring her, Annie pressed one palm against her chest. Her heart started to race and her breathing suddenly got short and choppy.

The clerk frowned. "Ma'am? Are you okay?"

Annie nodded, took a quart of milk from the cart and slammed it down on the counter. The clerk jumped at the same time Eric did. She dropped a bag of apples. *Wham!* Then lunch meat and a can of tomato soup. *Thump! Whack!* Eric wiped his hands on his shirt and the old woman rolled her eyes in disgust. Annie grabbed a carton of eggs as the calendar loomed down at her from the wall.

June sixth.

To be fair, she was as surprised as everyone else when the eggs hit the calendar with a dull *thwack!* The clerk spun around, mouth open, as the carton dropped to the floor in an oozing mess, followed by the store's calendar.

After Annie had apologized and offered to pay for the damage, after she left the store with Eric, one wheel on her cart pulling to the right, she knew that she and Jack would never be the same—that this was the beginning of the end. June fifth was their anniversary and not only had they both forgotten, but Jack had spent the evening with Linda. At first, this fact angered Annie until she couldn't look at him. Then it hurt where she'd never hurt before. Finally it made her pull away from him even more, until they were barely speaking to each other.

"I think we need to talk to someone," Jack said weeks later.

Brushing her hair, she didn't answer.

"Annie, don't you want to save this marriage?"

She set down her hair brush and stared at him. "I'm not the one who derailed it," she said, angry that he was asking *her* to work at bringing their marriage back on track when all she'd tried to do was keep it running.

In the end, they did try counseling for a year, but it didn't help. If anything, it seemed to push them even farther apart. Jack made it clear that he felt cut off from her, whereas Annie felt he'd let her down and told him so. "Damn you for not being strong enough to handle all of this with me, Jack. What about being there when I needed you, for however long I needed you, through the good times and the bad? What about that?"

At first, when she realized they weren't going to be able to fix their marriage, Annie's disbelief was so huge she feared it would swallow her whole, but finally she admitted to herself that Jack was right—the boys were all that was holding them together.

"We need to talk," Jack said one night.

Annie could sense it coming, but she was a master at deflecting serious conversations to neutral ones, to avoid what she knew was going to hurt.

"Did I tell you what Eric said this morning?" she said. "I was making toast and—"

"Annie, stop."

She stared at him, waiting to see what would happen next.

"I'm leaving," he said, almost in a whisper.

"Be serious, Jack."

But she'd heard the magnitude of his decision in his voice, the indisputable weight and finality of those two little words. She swallowed and gave him a chance to say more. When he didn't, she crossed her arms and asked, "What about the boys?"

"Annie, don't do this," he said, lifting both palms into the air. Then he nodded as if some disagreement had been settled, and he left.

The next morning, she dropped Luke off at school and drove

from Seattle out to Eagan's Point, motivated by a need to visit her penny tree, even though she hated driving on the highway and couldn't stop shaking, even though she knew she should be traveling the posted speed of sixty instead of forty. When she finally got to town, she left Eric with her mom, telling her that she had the day off, that she needed to go for a paddle in the worst possible way. Erna didn't question her; she just stood on the sidewalk holding Eric's hand, looking concerned as Annie drove away.

TWENTY-EIGHT

*E*arly Friday morning, long before the sun had come up, Jack sat down at his desk and stared at his hands, thinking. They were big and clumsy when it came to handling anything that required careful attention, exactly like his dad's had been, and yet that was where he liked to think any similarities between them ended. Whenever his dad had watched baseball, he would yell at the TV, throwing his hands in the air and swinging them around, not caring if he hit someone walking by. Now and then, he would uncurl his index finger from around the bottle of beer he was holding, point at Jack, and say, "You don't look nothin' like my side of the family." He said it to be cruel—to hurt and humiliate—but Jack considered it a gift.

Years ago, on the wall above the kitchen table, his dad had hung a sign that read, *My House, My Rules*, and for as long as Jack could remember, it had remained there. After his dad died, Jack took the sign down, and asked his mom why she had stayed in the marriage when she was so unhappy. Unable to meet his eyes, she said that it had never occurred to her to leave.

The day Jack asked Annie to marry him, he'd felt tall enough to touch the clouds. Being with her used to do that for him. He loved how she talked a mile a minute when she was excited about something, or the way she tilted her head to one side when she was making a decision, how she laughed until no sound came out, and how content he was spending time with her, how certain he was about where he was going with his life.

How did we get from there to here? Jack wondered.

A week before he told Annie he was leaving, he'd called her at two in the morning from a wedding he'd been hired to host in downtown Seattle. He was drunk (a rarity) and no buses were running that late. Could she come pick him up?

They had been attending counseling for a while by then, but things hadn't been improving. On the drive home, he lay across the backseat, looking up at the roof of their banged-up boat of a car. Trying to be funny, he made a few remarks about her driving, but any attempts at conversation were met with monosyllabic replies. Giving up, he closed his eyes, listening as she pulled into the driveway and parked. He heard the distinctive *ding-ding-ding* signaling an open door, and then she was tugging at his feet.

"Come on, Jack," she said. "We're home."

He sat up and grabbed the door to steady himself, then slowly climbed out. Straightening, he gave her a lopsided grin. "Wanna sit outside for a while?" he suggested.

"No," she said, taking his elbow. "Let's go in."

He gently shook her off. "What's wrong?"

"Nothing," she said, heaving a sigh. "It's just that it's late and I'd like to go to bed, and tomorrow I'd like to see things get back to normal."

With a drunk's wounded dignity, Jack said, "I'm pretty keen on that myself, but we're a long way off from normal these days, aren't we, Annie?"

She stuck her hands in her pockets. "I'm trying, Jack," she said.

"Not hard enough," he replied.

"Right," she said. "And yet I'm the one who's sober, and you're the one too drunk to walk a straight line."

"I almost never drink and you know it."

"Why start now then?"

"Maybe because I need a break from you," he shot back. "Christ, Annie, even *you* don't want to spend time with you."

She set both hands on her hips, and within seconds, they were in a full-blown yelling match, using each other as verbal punching bags. For a while, Jack felt like he was looking down at himself, and his stomach did a quick nosedive. His voice didn't sound like his own, his face was twisted with anger, and before he could stop himself, he was slamming his fist against the roof of their car to make her *listen* to him—exactly the way his father would have years ago.

"Damn it, Annie, I feel like I don't even know you anymore!"

She looked at him for a full ten seconds. "What do you want from me, Jack?"

Like a boxer greeting his fans, he turned in a full circle with both arms in the air. "No, what the hell do *you* want from *me*?"

"I want you to be there for us more than you are," she yelled.

"Why?" he said, crossing his arms.

Momentarily flustered, she said, "Because we need you."

Swaying slightly, he planted himself in front of her. "You know what, Annie?" he said, lowering his voice. "I bring home a paycheck every two weeks, but otherwise, you don't *need* me for anything. If I didn't come home for a week, would it matter? Be honest with me. When I didn't show up for dinner tonight, how'd you feel?"

She shot him a look that reminded him of a caged animal, but that she hesitated was what he noticed most. "Tell me the truth, Annie," he pressed, stepping so close that her face was right in front of his. "How did you *feel*?"

Backing away, she crumpled into a lawn chair. "Relieved," she said, holding her head in her hands, crying. "I felt . . . relieved."

Jack stared at her.

"Why?" he prompted, and in the long pause that followed, he felt what was left of his marriage crumble.

After a few seconds, Annie lifted her head, wiping away tears with the back of one hand. "Because lately it's easier when you're not here."

Nodding, Jack took a long look around him. The lid had fallen off one of their aluminum garbage cans and a lawn chair was lying on its side in the middle of the grass. Swaying a little, he crossed the yard to fix these things, mostly because he knew that he could, that it would be easy to do so—mostly because nothing else seemed fixable. When he was finished, he thought he heard a scraping sound somewhere behind them. Turning, he squinted into the dark, trying to see past the overgrown shrubs that were swallowing their back porch.

And there was Luke, tucked into the far corner, fists buried in his armpits.

Jack's mouth went dry. *Oh my God.*

Annie pushed to her feet, advancing across the grass. "Luke? Honey, listen to me," she said, rushing up the steps.

"Go away," he said.

She touched his arm. "Please, Luke—"

"Leave me alone," he yelled, shaking her off.

The moment would be burned in Jack's memory forever. Luke turning around, face pale and strained as he nailed Annie with his eyes, and Annie lifting both palms into the air as she backed away.

A lump shot up inside Jack's throat, and he searched for something to say, but suddenly it seemed too big a task to take on something so broken, and he felt emptied out and ill-equipped to deal with any of it. Although there had been a growing rift between him and Annie for a while now, he'd just seen it widen into a chasm. Crossing it was impossible. He knew he had to leave.

Almost a year after he had moved out, when the boys were staying with him one weekend, Luke suddenly materialized in the kitchen, hands gripping his elbows. He gave Jack a brief, apologetic smile. "I can't sleep."

Jack smiled. *You're like your mother,* he wanted to say. *More than you know.*

A few minutes later, as one of Jack's favorite songs finished playing on the radio, Luke set both elbows on the kitchen table.

"So you and Mom are getting a divorce?" he said.

Jack nodded. "Looks that way."

"How come?"

It was a simple question with no easy answer. Jack swallowed, feeling like a failure, knowing that he'd let his boys down as much as Annie had. Using a pea pod as a visual aid, he opened it with the edge of his thumbnail and unleashed a row of peas onto the table, watching them roll off in different directions.

"Somehow," he said, "everything just fell apart."

TWENTY-NINE

nnie returned from her paddle earlier than usual, peeked over the fence on her way down the alley, and saw the usual reporters gathered out front. When she snuck through the gate, Luke was working outside on his bike, turned upside down on the grass. He squatted next to it with a toolbox at his feet. She was about to say, "Morning," when he stood up and kicked the bike over, swearing under his breath.

"Hey," Annie said. "What's the problem?"

"This thing's a piece of crap!"

"Still having trouble with the chain?"

He nodded, dropping a wrench into the toolbox.

"Maybe you need to oil it," she suggested.

"I need a new bike. That's what I need."

"This one's only two years old."

"Well, it's a piece of crap, so why can't I get a new one?"

Right now, he reminded her of the dogs and cats she saw in the flyers Marina sometimes made up for her shelter that said: *Has been through hell. Needs lots of Love.* Part of her wanted to smooth down the cowlick on his forehead and tell him that she'd skip paying a few bills this month and buy him a new bike. But of course she didn't.

"Luke, throwing things out and replacing them isn't always the answer. And even if I could afford to buy you a new bike, six months from now the chain would need tightening, the tires would need air, and it'd have dents all over it, just like this one. You're better off working with what you've got."

He kicked the toolbox shut and reached down to latch it.

"Tell you what," she said, trying to appease him. "Why don't we take it down to the shop next week and find out how much it'll cost to get it tuned up?"

"Whatever."

"Fine, then," she said, giving him a hard look. "Ask your dad to look it over this weekend. I'm going in for a shower. I'll drive you guys to school in ten minutes."

"Thanks, but I'll walk."

Annie shook her head. Allowing him to walk to school was out of the question, and he knew it, especially because of all the skipping he'd done since they'd moved. "No, Luke, you won't. You know the rules."

"Mom, I'm thirteen," he said, squaring his shoulders. "When are you going to start treating me like it?"

"When you show me you're mature enough to be treated differently."

"And that would take . . . ?"

"Not going back on your word for starters."

"What do you mean?"

She looked past him, doing her best to stay calm, though frustration bubbled up inside her. "You know exactly what I mean. You keep promising me you won't skip school, but then you do. You give me your word you'll lay off your brother, but you don't. He found half a box of oatmeal sprinkled on his bedsheets last week. You superglued his shoes to the back steps two days ago. And even though I can't prove it, I think you probably did tell him you'd shave your head last month and then backed out at the last minute so you could make him look stupid."

Luke took a swig from his water bottle, staring at his bike.

Annie took a few steps toward him. "You know what? Nothing bugs me more than someone who goes back on his word. So if you say you're going to do something, do it, damn it! The choices you make say a lot about the kind of person you are and what you're mature enough to handle. And at thirteen, with all of the problems I've been having with you, you are *not* walking a mile across town to school."

They both stood there in angry silence as Luke's chest rose and fell, but he didn't respond.

Annie turned and went up the back steps. She opened the door, working hard to keep her voice steady. "Did you hear what I just said?"

"Yeah," he said. "I heard you."

The screen door slammed shut behind her, and Annie walked through the kitchen to the front door, where a copy of *USA Today* was waiting on the steps. Outside, Rose and Libby were playing groupies with the reporters, as usual, the drama of the day putting a little more glide in their stride. When Annie opened the door, everyone acted excited to see her.

"There she is!" someone yelled.

"Annie, can you confirm that you're doing *The Rachel Tice Show* today?"

"Are you nervous about meeting Mr. Anonymous?"

For weeks, she'd been polite with the media and her meddling neighbors, but now Annie was tired and dazed, and she no longer cared what anyone thought. Frowning, she leaned a little farther outside. "Yes, I agreed to do *The Rachel Tice Show*, but unfortunately, Mr. Anonymous canceled on us late last night, and without him, there is no show."

For a beat, everyone stared at her, cell phones poised for action, small-town-affiliate reporters watching their big break disappear before their eyes. Trying not to smile, Annie turned to go inside.

"What now?" someone called out.

"When will you find out who he is?"

"I don't know," she said, sighing as she looked back over her shoulder. "But it doesn't look like it'll be today."

Closing the door, she went into the kitchen, hoping her fabrication would throw them off long enough for her to sneak out of town later this morning without anyone following her. Dropping the paper on the table, she reached for the thermos of coffee she'd made earlier.

"Morning, Mom," Eric said, coming down the stairs. "Nervous?"

"A little," she admitted, grabbing him for a hug on his way by. "But I've got an amber nugget that'll get me through the day no matter what."

He grinned. "Sawyer said when you go on TV you gain ten pounds. Is that true?"

Annie pulled a face. "Let's hope not."

Already moving on to more exciting topics, such as his first-ever basketball game at the school tonight, Eric opened the cupboard and grabbed a box of cereal. "By the way, since Dad's picking us up after school today, Luke and I are supposed to bring our duffel bags with us this morning, okay?"

"Sounds like a good idea," she said.

The rest of the morning went by in a blur. Sticking to her routine, Annie dropped the boys off at school, only today she left later than usual, timing it so she'd arrive in the middle of "the five-minute window from hell," when most parents dropped their kids off. In their stress-filled haste to get to work, people honked their horns, cut you off, screamed at their kids, and occasionally waved a raised fist when someone wouldn't *get moving*. Annie hated "the five-minute window from hell" and knew the reporters following her would too. In the end, because they'd gotten used to her morning routine, only a few tried to wait for her in front of the school, most choosing to go on to Kozak's instead. That was when she turned down an alley and drove across town to Marina's, where her sister and mom were waiting to drive her to Seattle.

By noon, Annie and Marina were sitting with one of Rachel Tice's production assistants going over the lights, the cameras, and how everything was going to work. A producer had kindly taken Erna downstairs for coffee, and when they came back a few minutes later, they were talking about some kind of medical condition. Erna's little problem, always exacerbated by stress or worry, was in full bloom, but as Annie listened, she felt an unexpected rush of tenderness for her mom instead of the usual irritation.

"Here, let me show you," Erna said, digging in her purse and handing the producer a quarter. "Put this in your pocket."

The woman did.

"Now feel both sides with your fingertips," Erna instructed.

Frowning, the woman did this too.

"Can you tell which side is heads and which is tails?"

The woman's face scrunched in concentration as she carefully fingered the coin.

"This test checks how the parietal lobes of your brain are functioning," Erna explained. "And if you can't tell heads from tails, it sometimes signals the presence of a parietal-lobe tumor or an oncoming stroke."

Looking alarmed, the producer widened her eyes slightly; then she pulled the coin from her pocket with a triumphant smile on her face. "This side," she said, pointing to her forefinger, "is heads. The other is tails."

"Excellent!" Erna said, lifting her finger off the coin. "You're right."

The producer grinned, pleased with herself.

Somewhere in the background, the persistent ringing of a phone broke through Annie's thoughts. Marina walked across the room holding out her cell phone. "It was ringing in your purse, so I grabbed it."

"Who is it?" Annie asked.

Marina shrugged.

"Hello?" Annie said, kicking off one shoe because her ankle was slightly swollen.

"Ms. Hillman, this is Joan Marsh with Robertson Middle School calling. . . ."

Annie almost started laughing. This wasn't happening. Couldn't be. Not when she was fifteen minutes away from going on television.

"I thought you should know that Luke isn't in school today."

Annie slid her foot back into her shoe and the heel of her nylons tore up the back of her leg in a zipperlike burst. *Of course he's not,* she thought, touching her fingers to her eyes. *He's probably out robbing a bank somewhere. Or maybe he decided to move his carefree day from the middle of the week to Fridays. Yes, that's probably it.*

"Excuse me? Are you there?"

"Yes," Annie said. "I'm here."

Joan Marsh cleared her throat. "Is there anything we can do to help?"

"No," she said. "But thanks for asking. I'll get back to you."

Annie ended the call, thinking, *I'm in Seattle for the day and Luke knows it. He also knows this is the perfect day to skip, because not only is there no way I can go hunt him down until I get back to Eagan's Point, but by the time I do, he'll be with his dad for the weekend out on a boat somewhere, which makes dealing with him close to impossible until he comes home again on Sunday night.*

Marina sat down next to her, blowing on a cup of tea. "Everything okay?"

Not really, Annie thought. *Right now I need Extra-Strength Tylenol, or maybe Xanax. Better yet, a big glass of wine.* She tugged at her new dress, inhaling the perfume Marina had spritzed on her earlier, feeling guilty because she was here instead of home, where she could do something about Luke.

"That was the school calling," she said. "Luke's skipping again."

"Today?" Marina said, setting her tea down.

Annie nodded.

"When you're going through *this*?"

Another nod.

"Unbelievable." Marina frowned as she looked past Annie out the window. Then she snapped her fingers. "Wait a minute. Let me phone Harrison. I'm sure he said he was working around Eagan's Point today. He'll go look for him."

"Thanks, Marina." Harrison was probably the best person to go looking for Luke right now, because if it was Jack or she, the conversation wouldn't go well.

"Don't worry. Everything will be okay." Marina hurried off to phone her husband.

Glancing at the clock, Annie wondered if she should call Jack at work or on his cell to give him a heads-up. Noticing it was lunchtime, she opted for his cell. As it rang, she tried to remember what he'd said last night when Luke had asked what time he was picking them up. Hadn't he said he'd be in front of the school by three forty-five? Jack's voice mail kicked in, so she left a message. "Hi, Jack, it's me. I just got a phone call from the school. Luke's skipping again. It's twelve thirty and I'm in Seattle doing *The Rachel Tice Show*, so Marina's phoning Harrison to see if he can go find him."

When a production assistant walked Annie and Marina to the elevator ten minutes later, Annie was feeling more relaxed. After all, Harrison would probably find Luke sitting on the beach in his favorite spot, and he'd hand him over to Jack at the end of the day so she wouldn't have to worry about it until Monday.

It'll be okay, she told herself. *And this show won't be so bad, either. I'll chat with Rachel Tice, find out who ran the ads, then go home and get drunk for the second time in years.*

The elevator doors opened on the main floor and they stepped off.

Rachel Tice was standing ten feet away, the producer Erna had been talking to earlier next to her, along with two assistants and a short cameraman with a goatee. All of them held their arms straight up in the air. Together, they resembled hostages in a bank robbery, although in reality nothing that sinister was taking place.

"Okay. Looks good," Erna said, slowly circling them with her brow furrowed and her purse tucked into the crook of her arm. "But make sure the sides of your arms are touching your ears or this won't work."

Marina and Annie exchanged a quick, knowing glance.

Annie slid one foot out of her shoe, twisting her ankle first one way and then the next as she watched what was happening.

"How much longer?" Rachel asked, a trace of amusement in her voice.

"Another thirty seconds," Erna instructed. "You need to stay like that for exactly three minutes, and as long as you don't feel any kind of stuffiness or nasal congestion, and you don't get dizzy, then you should be okay."

"What if we do?" the producer asked.

Erna considered this. "Well, nothing is conclusive, but it could mean that you have thyroid disease or else a blockage in the veins that lead to your heart, like a large blood clot or maybe even a tumor."

A somber silence came over the group as they waited.

Erna finally smiled and gave them a brisk nod. "Okay, time's up."

Five pairs of arms flopped back down.

"I feel fine," Rachel declared, shaking her wrists out.

"Me too," said the producer, arching her eyebrows at the two assistants, who nodded their agreement.

Annie noticed that the cameraman didn't seem amused.

He looked Erna up and down skeptically. "You gotta be joking, right?"

"Excuse me?" Erna said.

"You're playing with our heads, right?" he said. "Man, you must think we're a bunch of suckers." He pushed his glasses up the bridge of his nose. "Nobody can tell if they have thyroid disease by doing something this stupid." Laughing, he glanced around at everyone else, hoping for a collective agreement.

An embarrassed flush spread up Erna's neck.

Annie felt a wave of tenderness, quickly followed by an unexpected desire to protect her. Sliding her foot back into her shoe, she moved closer to her mom, as if to say with the position of her body that this was a package deal—they went together.

"You know what?" she said to the cameraman. "First and foremost, this is my mom and you have no right to talk to her like that." She wanted to be firm on this point. "Secondly, she's not joking, and you should feel fortunate to be given this kind of advice free of charge. There are people who would gladly pay for it."

After a slightly uncomfortable pause during which he looked cowed, the cameraman turned to Erna and said, "Sorry, lady. No disrespect intended."

Rachel Tice stepped forward. "Annie Hillman, right?" She took both of Annie's hands. "It's wonderful to meet you."

Annie could smell coffee on her breath and the faint odor of hairspray. "Nice to meet you too," she managed.

"Why don't we head into the studio and talk about the show?" Rachel suggested, linking an arm through Annie's and tugging her down the hallway. "First of all, I want you to relax. We've got lots of time and everything is taped, so we can edit out anything we don't want to include before the show airs this afternoon."

THIRTY

"Thank you for joining us today," Rachel Tice said, smiling at the camera. "I'm excited about today's show. For those of you who've been following the news, a human-interest story surfaced a few weeks ago that has captivated a lot of people. It began with a small personal ad on the front page of the *Peninsula Post* that asked a simple question: *Do you recognize this woman?* Below it was a fifteen-year-old picture of the woman and a brief message explaining that someone was searching for her, although it didn't say who.

"The ad ran again a week later, but this time it included an age-advanced photo of what she might look like today. Then, a week after that, another ad ran including a few touching reflections about the woman that charmed readers across the state. This little ad campaign continued with a fourth ad and then a fifth, stirring up debates about Annie's privacy, the freedom of the press, and this man's right to remain anonymous until the last ad ran, as had been prearranged. Pushing aside critics, these ads have captivated people everywhere, leaving some women envious and I'm sure a few men wishing they'd thought of it themselves. Well, today, we have Annie Hillman joining us on the show along with Mr. Anonymous, who has agreed to come forward and explain why he did what he did."

Rachel tucked her hair behind her ears and gave the camera a big smile. "Now, just so everyone understands, this won't be one of those shows where bouncers rush onstage and hold back some crazed stalker Annie jilted years ago, because we all know I don't do shows like that, right?"

Annie stood behind the partition, fiddling with her necklace, shifting from one foot to the other. She closed her eyes, fighting a sudden burst of nerves, knowing it was too late to turn back now. Marina and her mom stood behind her, murmuring to the production assistant assigned to Annie before the show. Marina was still almost apoplectic with excitement over meeting Rachel Tice and her mom wasn't much better. Annie watched Marina slapping at her pockets before pulling out her cell phone. Thankfully it was on vibrate mode, so the noise it made was minimal.

"Hello?" Marina whispered, taking a few steps back.

Ignoring her, Annie tuned back in to what Rachel Tice was saying as she walked over to the middle of the stage.

"Annie Hillman is separated and the mother of two boys. Like many mothers today, she juggles a job with raising her kids, but she and her husband have also had to deal with something else for years, something more stressful than whether or not the gas bill will get paid this month. Their youngest, Eric, was diagnosed with a disease called hystiocytosis the year he turned three. The pronunciation alone is a good indicator of its rarity and deadliness. Hystiocytosis typically only affects children and unfortunately a lot of them don't survive, but Eric was one of the lucky ones. Today, he's eleven and his hystio is in remission. . . ."

"That was Jack," Marina whispered, tugging on Annie's arm. "He tried to call your cell, but you must have turned it off. Harrison phoned to tell him he's got Luke. . . ."

"Good," Annie whispered back. Thank God Harrison had found him.

"You're on in thirty seconds," the production assistant told Annie.

"Annie, listen," Marina said impatiently. "Jack said he's on his way to meet with Harrison and Luke so the three of them can talk about this."

Annie nodded. That sounded good too.

"Fifteen seconds," the production assistant said.

Marina grabbed her arm. "Annie—"

"Not now," Annie said, shaking her sister off.

Onstage, Rachel kept talking. "With help from the *Peninsula Post*, we contacted Mr. Anonymous last week. At first he flatly refused to do our show until we explained that Annie had agreed to do it, and then he finally said he would. I think you'll be as moved as we were by the background behind this story. So, without further delay, won't you all join me in welcoming Annie Hillman?"

Rachel began clapping. Annie felt the production assistant's hand on her back, easing her forward. Glancing over her shoulder, she saw her mom holding up a fist as a sign of strength. Taking a deep breath, she walked out from behind the partition, making her way across the stage to where three armchairs were arranged against a backdrop of white linen with *The Rachel Tice Show* on it. There were at least a hundred people in the audience and everyone was clapping. Annie's knees went weak, but somehow she managed to get across the stage and into a chair.

"Thanks for coming," Rachel said, squeezing her hand. "I've already told everyone about you and your family, but let's talk a little more, okay?"

Annie nodded, keeping her eyes on Rachel, realizing it was hard not to relax when she was giving you that I'm-in-control-and-we-can-do-this-together smile.

"You have two sons?"

Annie nodded. "Yes. Eric's eleven and Luke's thirteen."

Rachel sat back in her chair. "They live with you in Eagan's Point?"

"Yes, and they see their dad every second weekend."

"And he lives in Seattle?"

"Right."

Rachel smiled. "That'd be Jack Hillman?"

Annie gave her another nod, feeling much better. So far, things were going well. She liked the rhythm. Question. Answer. Question. Answer. Now, as long as Rachel didn't ask her anything hard—

"Are you and Jack on good terms?"

"Of course," Annie said, straightening her back. "Jack's a great guy. He's a good father and he's always there for the boys. I can't imagine not being on good terms with him." But even to her own ears, she sounded defensive, maybe even a little protective. At first she couldn't figure out why and then she suddenly realized that the last thing she wanted was to have Jack painted in a bad light.

Rachel changed the subject, throwing her off a bit. "Tell me, Annie, what do your kids think of these ads?"

She shrugged. "They're curious, but they haven't said much. They have lots going on in their own lives. Typical kids, you know."

"And how does Jack feel about them?"

Annie flushed. "He's asked about them, but he hasn't told me how he *feels* about them. That's not something Jack would do."

"What about you? How have these past five weeks been for you, opening the newspaper every Monday, wondering what will be there, who is searching for you?"

"At first I thought it was someone's idea of a joke," Annie admitted. "But then, when I realized it wasn't, it became . . . a puzzle."

"Any idea who ran the ads?" Rachel asked, searching her face.

Annie took a while to answer. "I've had my suspicions over the last few weeks, but no, I don't know who it is."

Sliding into talk-show mode, Rachel patted Annie's hand. "Well, before we find out, I have a little surprise for you that I hope makes today more memorable." Appearing from nowhere, a crisp-looking woman crossed the stage and handed Annie a small box.

"You lost your car a few weeks ago, didn't you?" Rachel asked.

Annie gave her a small, tentative head shake. "Yes, in a fire."

Rachel's forehead puckered with concern. "How have you been getting around since then?"

"I borrowed my mom's car," Annie said.

Rachel leaned forward and tapped the box conspiratorially, as though there was no one else in the room but them. "Annie, inside this box are keys to a new car that has been leased for you for twelve months to help out until you can get another one."

Annie felt her face go slack.

Rachel motioned to the box, indicating that she should open it. Annie lifted the lid, trying to hold back tears, determined not to make a fool of herself on television. *A new car,* she thought, taking out a set of BMW keys. *Free for twelve months.*

Rachel was clearly enjoying this. "Would you like to see it?" Before Annie could answer, Rachel was up and out of her chair, throwing a smile over her shoulder as she made her way over to a curtain on the far side of the stage.

Giddy from this unexpected turn of good luck, Annie leaned forward, feeling as if she were on *The Price Is Right* and behind curtain number one was a new car for her. A BMW, no less. She watched and waited, wanting to pinch herself.

Basking in the moment, Rachel pulled back her shoulders and smiled wide for the camera. Then she made a Vanna White hand gesture and the curtain slowly opened to reveal an eyeball-shattering lime green Mini, revolving on a raised platform with *The Rachel Tice Show* painted in red on both sides.

Annie's mouth fell open. She glanced around, wondering if this was some kind of joke.

It wasn't. Beaming at the camera, Rachel expanded on her explanation, telling everyone watching that *The Rachel Tice Show* was donating the use of this "leased promotional vehicle" to Annie and her boys for one year, at no charge.

Annie stared at it, thinking, *It should be illegal to drive a car like that.*

"I . . . I don't know what to say," she finally managed.

As an afterthought, Rachel grabbed her by the arm in a jokey way as she slid back into her chair. "You do drive a standard, don't you?"

Squinting at the car, Annie hesitated. *A new car, free for twelve months.*

Then she heard someone say, "A standard's not a problem," and realized it was her. She could almost hear her boys laughing when they saw the show later and called her on it, knowing she'd vowed never to drive anything other than an automatic.

"Okay. Enough of that," Rachel said. "Let's get back to the real reason we're all here today." She turned to Annie and her voice took on a faint, teasing edge. "So are you ready? Do you want to find out who's responsible for stirring up your life with all these ads?"

"That'd be good," Annie said, wishing they would shut the curtain on that headache-inducing car. That or give her a pair of sunglasses.

Rachel gave someone in the background a nod and music began to play.

Not two seconds later, the car was forgotten.

Annie's heart jumped as the lyrics of "I Miss My Friend" by Darryl Worley filled the studio. He was singing about missing his friend, obviously someone he loved, and as he did, she was vaguely aware of a slice of light as a door opened somewhere to her left. She closed her eyes, and in that moment between closing them and opening them again, she suddenly thought she knew who Mr. Anonymous was.

And then there he was, walking toward her, backlit by the light from an open door.

Inside Annie, everything stopped. She couldn't speak. She couldn't even swallow. Looking back on it later, she would remember clapping a hand over her mouth, and even though his entrance couldn't have taken more than a few seconds, it seemed to last forever.

It wasn't who she thought it would be, but of course she knew him. She knew the tilt of his head and the set of his shoulders. She knew the way his hands were forever in his pockets, and how he ducked his chin, like he was doing now, whenever he got nervous. He was wearing a pair of navy chinos with a mustard-colored shirt and his hair was slicked back in a style she'd never seen on him before. His black dress shoes looked too big and he was wearing a mauve tie that clashed horribly with his shirt, and yet just seeing him in that tie brought tears to her eyes—because she had never seen him wear one before and because it had always been one of her favorites. He looked pale and nervous and she had to stop herself from getting up to meet him halfway.

Rachel squeezed her hand. "Surprised?"

Annie managed a nod. *Surprised* didn't even come close.

Doing everything she could to hold herself still, Annie watched as Rachel slid off her chair to give him a hug and thank him for coming. "Everyone, please welcome Luke Hillman," she said, linking an arm through his.

Annie's eyes were glued to Luke as he and Rachel Tice walked across the stage to sit down. He was dragging his teeth across his bottom lip, not looking in her direction. The producer lifted a finger in the air, signaling that they were heading for a break. Annie swallowed, telling herself to breathe. Then, over the crown of Luke's head, she saw Harrison and Jack standing next to the door, and some of her shock moved over to make room for the confusion that quickly followed. Harrison was in his uniform, holding his state trooper hat, all six foot six of him looking triumphant. But Jack was rubbing the back of his neck, the way he did when he felt out of his element. Catching Annie's gaze, he raised a brow, lifting his hands in the air as though asking her what was going on.

Looking from him to Luke, she shook her head. She didn't know any more than he did. But she could not believe she was sitting here, with Luke on one side of her and Rachel Tice on the other. The cameras flicked off and one of the producers waved Rachel over. Giving Annie's hand a squeeze, she said she'd be right back.

Now that they were alone, Luke shot her a nervous look. "Hi," he said.

Annie squinted at him, still trying to process that he was there at all. "Why aren't you in school?" she whispered louder than she'd intended. "What's going on, Luke?"

"Chill, Mom," he said, holding up his hands. "Everything's fine."

"Really?"

"Look, I thought about backing out, okay? A few times. But then this morning, you told me how much you hated it when someone goes back on their word, remember?"

Annie opened her mouth, but nothing came out. Yes, she did remember.

Luke pointed to Rachel Tice, who had one foot on the stage and one off as she handed a clipboard back to her producer. "And you know what, Mom?" he said, leaning closer so she could hear him. "I gave her my word that I'd do this show. It wasn't supposed to turn out like this," he said, waving at the room. "But I'm gonna finish what I started."

He sat back and lifted his chin a notch, pretending to be more certain than Annie knew he was. And as she stared at him, for a splinter of a second, she saw the little boy he used to be—the one who would swoop through the house wearing a Batman cape, ready to take on the world. Then he squared his shoulders, and a hard ache rose in her chest, because that little boy was suddenly gone and she was seeing a flash of the man he would one day become. Strong, determined, ready to take on the world for real this time. No cape required.

Rachel slid into the chair between them. "Okay, are we ready?"

"I am," Luke said.

Annie rubbed her temples. "Sure."

The cameraman lifted one hand in the air, removing one finger at a time as he counted down the seconds until they began filming again.

THIRTY-ONE

Slouching in his chair with his feet thrown forward, Luke ran a thumbnail down the length of the armrest as Rachel Tice welcomed everyone back. Annie instinctively wanted to tell him to sit up and pay attention. Instead, she twisted a Kleenex in her lap, staring at a sweating glass of cold water someone had set on the table next to her.

"Okay," Rachel said, turning to face Luke. "Why don't you start by telling us where you got the idea to run the ads?"

"From a milk carton," Luke said.

"A milk carton?"

Annie bowed her head, folding her Kleenex in half, then in half again.

"Uh-huh," Luke said, nodding. "A few months ago, when I was at my dad's, I heard him talking to my mom on the phone in the other room. They were arguing about something," he said. "And Dad raised his voice, which he almost never does, and then I heard him say, 'Where's the woman I used to know, Annie? The woman I met years ago?'"

Annie felt a deep flush working its way up her neck. She suddenly wished that her hair wasn't pinned up, that it was free so she could lean forward and let it swing down and cover her face, giving her somewhere to hide.

Rachel frowned. "Okay. But what's that got to do with a milk carton?"

"I was having breakfast, eating cereal actually, and the milk carton was on the table. It had one of those ads on it for some kid who'd been missing for, like, you know, years. The kind where there's a picture of the kid next to an age-advanced shot of what they might look like today? Anyhow, I got thinking about what my dad said, and then I started wondering what my mom used to be like too. Back then, I mean. When my dad first met her and they fell in love. Before me and my brother were born. Before they split up."

"I think I see where you're going," Rachel said.

Annie did too. Sort of. But her mind was racing and she wanted to jump in and ask a few questions herself. Like where did he get the money to do it? And how did he get age-advanced pictures of her? Better yet, why would he do it in the first place?

"Sometimes I don't sleep real good at night," Luke admitted. "So I get up and find something to do until I get tired again. And when I get up at my dad's, he's almost always sitting in the dark in his living room, listening to music."

Rachel smiled. "Does your mom do that too?"

"No. She climbs out onto the roof."

Annie's shoulders sagged. She closed her eyes, considered sliding down in her chair, then thought, *Eyes forward, chin up.*

A twitchy smile crossed Rachel's face. "She climbs out onto the roof?"

"Yeah," he said, reddening. "To take stock."

Rachel rubbed her forehead.

"Never mind." He waved a hand as if to erase what he'd said. "You know that song I asked you to play a few minutes ago? It's called 'I Miss My Friend' and I wanted you to play it because my dad listens to it a lot. Anyhow, he was listening to it one night when I got up 'cause I couldn't sleep. I sat with him and listened to all the lyrics. Then, when it was finished, I asked him if there was anything he missed about Mom."

Annie shot Jack a look. He had one hand on his hip and he was massaging the bridge of his nose with the other, shaking his head like he couldn't believe this any more than she could. Lowering her eyes, she took what was left of her Kleenex and began rolling chunks between her thumb and forefinger, watching tiny white balls accumulate on her new dress.

"What did he say?" Rachel prompted gently.

There was an uncomfortable silence as Luke shifted in his chair, and when he answered, he seemed embarrassed. "He said he missed the way she scrunched up her face when she cut her fingernails and how she'd stubbornly use his power tools, even though she didn't have a hot clue what she was doing."

Rachel smiled. "Anything else?"

"Uh-huh. He said he missed how he always knew he could find her in the card section of a store if he lost her when they went shopping. And the way she always puts a few extra stamps on letters before she mails them, just in case. Or how she's never been able to parallel park a car without swearing. And how they always bought metal garbage cans because the plastic ones didn't last from her backing over them . . ."

Annie went very still. It suddenly felt as if everyone's eyes were on her, as if the room had taken on a whole new level of quiet. If she were wearing a baseball cap, she would have happily pulled down the bill to disappear.

Luke leaned forward, resting his elbows on his knees, the same way Jack did whenever he was about to say something important. "That's when I came up with the idea," he said. "But it wasn't supposed to turn into something so big. It was only supposed to be a small ad that ran in the life section of our little paper. But then the *Peninsula Post* made it bigger and put it on the front page. . . ."

"Wait a second," Rachel said, raising a hand. "Let's talk about that before you go any further, because even in the life section of a regional newspaper, five ads like these would've cost you some money."

"They did," Luke admitted, raising his eyebrows. "The first ones I wrote were gonna cost fifty bucks each because they only had one picture of my mom and that's what the *Peninsula Post* charges, but I didn't have that kinda money, so I decided to apply for a paper route."

"And that's how you paid for them?" Rachel interrupted.

"No. Eagan's Point only has two paper routes and they were already taken."

"So what did you do?"

"At first, I tried to steal the money," he said, looking at his feet.

"You tried to *steal it*?" Rachel said, sounding incredulous.

Luke nodded, turning red again. "I took it from this box at my dad's apartment, where I know he always has a few hundred tucked away for emergencies. But I got caught, so I had to give it back, and then my parents were so mad that they asked my uncle Harrison to talk to me about stealing and stuff."

Rachel frowned as if he'd lost her. "Your uncle Harrison?"

"He's a state trooper," Luke explained, sounding impressed. "And when he asked why I stole the money and what I'd been planning to do with it, I told him. We get along real good, so when he asked me why I wanted to do it, I told him that too."

"Why did you want to do it?" Rachel asked.

He shifted in his chair. "I wanted my mom to think it was my dad," he said softly.

"Because you think he still loves her?"

"No," he said, lifting one shoulder. "Because I think they still love each other."

Annie's chin trembled and tears welled in her eyes as emotions she'd buried long ago suddenly swirled inside her.

"But aren't they getting a divorce?"

"Uh-huh. But I think they're wrong."

"Wrong?"

"To get a divorce," he said.

Rachel held up a hand. "Wait. Let's back up again. What happened with your uncle after you told him why you wanted to do this?"

Luke smiled. "He called me a few days later and offered to help."

"He did?" Rachel said.

Annie's eyes went wide. Putting two and two together, she turned and stared at Harrison, who didn't look quite so official now. His gaze darted between her and Jack, who stood next to him in stunned silence.

Luke nodded. "But he made me promise I'd pay him back. He said I could work it off at my aunt's pet shelter this summer."

Glancing over the crown of Luke's head, Annie saw the surprise on Marina's face, then watched her mom slide an arm around Jack's waist, giving him a hug. Rachel lifted a hand to the audience, nodding at Luke, his signal to speak.

"Anyhow, I showed my uncle the ads I wrote and all the information I'd put together. Like I said, he's a state trooper and he knows a lotta people, so he took the picture I had of my mom and he asked a friend of his to do up two age-advanced pictures. One that made her look her age today. . . ."

Don't say it, Annie thought. *Please don't say my age on television.*

". . . and another one that made her look like an old lady. No offense intended to anyone who's old," he added.

Rachel was smiling now. "So he helped you get age-advanced pictures of your mom, and then he paid for the ads?"

"Uh-huh. And he also let me use a private cell phone number he only uses for work, which was good because then we had a number to put in the ad. After all those reporters came to our house and started following Mom to work every day, he also let me use it to send her a text message and tell her I was sorry."

"Who wrote the final ads then?" Rachel asked, looking completely captivated. "You or your uncle?"

"I did," Luke admitted. "But I didn't say anything my dad hadn't already said."

Frowning, Annie glanced at Jack, who now had both hands on his hips. Then something seemed to dawn on him and she saw the color drain slowly from his face.

"For a month," Luke confessed, "every time I went to my dad's, I asked if he could help me with a project I was working on for school about our family. We'd sit down and I'd ask him questions, lots of questions. But to get the answers I needed, I had to throw him off a little, so first I asked him about our relatives, our heritage, things like that. Then I got personal, asking how he and mom met, that sort of thing. I told him I needed to know for the project so he wouldn't get all suspicious and clam up on me."

Rachel nodded as if she appreciated his cleverness.

"Anyhow, my dad said my mom was the first woman he'd ever really loved, that no matter what, he'd never forget her. Then, when I asked why they were getting a divorce, he got real quiet and he told me that somehow they'd lost touch."

Rachel leaned forward, elbows on her knees.

"Uncle Harrison helped me polish the ads, but like I said before, I didn't say anything that my dad didn't." Luke sat back and reached into his pocket. "Here, I'll show you. . . ."

Jack dropped his face into his hands.

Annie watched in amazement as Luke pulled a handheld tape recorder out of his pocket, set it on the table in front of them, and pressed PLAY. Within seconds, Jack's voice filled the room and Luke adjusted the volume.

THIRTY-TWO

When the tape finally finished, Luke turned it off and a production assistant lifted a finger in the air, indicating that they were heading for a break. "We'll be right back," Rachel Tice said in a soft, respectful voice.

The cameras stopped and Annie gave Rachel a smile.

"Excuse me," Annie managed. Then she stood and made her way off the stage and out the door, keeping her eyes straight ahead. And as she did, all she could think about was that there had to be some extra air lurking around outside that she could use.

In the hallway, she found a bathroom, locked a stall door, and sat on the toilet to regroup. *Did all that really just happen?* The bathroom door opened and the tips of her mom's shoes appeared under the stall door.

"Annie? You all right?"

"I'm fine. I just need a few minutes alone."

Erna sighed. Her shoes disappeared and Annie heard water running, then the towel dispenser when her mom pulled down towels to dry her hands. "If you want to talk—"

"No, Mom, I don't. Not right now."

"Right."

A purse zipper opened and Annie could picture her mom digging inside for a bottle of oxygenated water or chewable calcium tablets. Seconds later, her hand appeared under the stall door waving a travel package of Kleenex. "Just in case," she said.

After a brief silence, she tried again. "Annie? You know what I was thinking a few minutes ago? How proud I am of Luke. That he thought this up all by himself. That he took the time and effort to do up such nice ads. But especially because his intentions were so good."

Annie massaged her temples.

"You know what else?" Erna said. "Your dad was a wonderful man, but I don't think he ever would've opened up and said things like Jack did about you on that tape. . . ."

"Dad never would've left you either," Annie shot back.

Pause. "Maybe not, but then I wouldn't have let him go."

Annie blinked twice. "Wouldn't have *let him go*? Pardon me, Mom, but Jack's a big boy, and when he left, there was nothing I could've said to stop him."

"I guess not . . . not at that point, anyhow."

A hot wave passed through Annie's body. "What's that supposed to mean?"

"Never mind. I never should've compared your dad to Jack in the first place. I'm sorry."

A tense and uncomfortable silence took over the room. Annie's mouth opened, then closed. She couldn't believe they were having this conversation through a bathroom stall, the closest thing to a serious talk she and her mom had ever had, and for some morbidly strange reason, she didn't want it to end.

"Dad loved us like crazy," she finally said, shredding a Kleenex.

Erna cleared her throat. "Of course he did, but there are things you didn't know about him too. Things that didn't always make him the easiest man to live with."

"Like what?"

Erna sighed, sounding tired. "Let's see. I loved the man for twenty years. . . ."

"Twenty-four," Annie corrected.

"No," Erna said softly. "Twenty. There were a few in between when I didn't and that's the whole point."

Annie's heart began to race and she balled up the Kleenex. She and her mom had never talked about their lack of closeness, in the same way they'd never discussed Annie's unwavering adoration of her dad, although it was always there, blatant in its disregard for anyone else's opinion.

Erna's voice thickened with emotion. "Your dad was an incredible man. I loved him the day I married him and I loved him the day he died. He was kind and giving and thoughtful, but he wasn't a saint, Annie. No one is."

"Dad was amazing," Annie whispered, but she sounded less than convincing.

"I'm not trying to tear him down. I'm trying to tell you that life is messy, that there's no way around it for any of us. When it comes to marriage, we all have our troubles and sometimes . . . we lose our way. It's not tidy or predictable, and it's never how we think it's going to be. But, Annie, the years fly by at the same speed whether we're in a marriage with the man we love or locked away from the world where we think we're safer from getting hurt."

It had taken both of them too many years to get here and her mom a boatload of courage to take this first step, so Annie folded her bottom lip over her teeth, torn between not wanting to hear her mom out and yet reluctant to stop her from saying whatever she needed to say.

Erna continued. "Your dad used to say that our problems disappear when we laugh and I think he was right. They do, even if only for those few minutes while we are laughing. Rudy made me laugh like that today," she confessed, sounding shy. "And you know what, Annie? I felt ten years younger. And on the drive into Seattle today with you and your sister, I couldn't stop thinking about how much I love you, and how much I miss hearing you laugh . . . and how very much I wish you would again."

Annie covered her mouth with one hand as tears filled her eyes. A toilet flushed in the men's room next door. Then a door slammed and she heard people laughing outside.

Erna tapped a finger gently against the stall door. "I'll leave you alone, but if you need me, I'll be outside."

Never had Annie felt so wrapped in sadness and regret. "Mom?"

Pause. "Yes?"

"Do you miss him?" she asked, trying to keep her voice steady.

"Beyond reason," Erna said, and the door shut behind her like a whisper.

Annie's dad used to share bite-size philosophies with her, and now, as she sat alone in that bathroom stall, she remembered something he'd said the day he gave her the penny tree. After hammering the penny in place, he'd stared up at the tree, smiling.

"It's huge," Annie said softly.

"And majestic," he added.

She frowned. "Why do people say trees are majestic?"

He lowered himself to the ground and tugged her down next to him. "Because they've earned it. After a sapling's roots take hold, they spread out to give it strength. Then, unstoppable, those roots continue to grow, and after years of withstanding rain, hail, snow and every other environmental disaster you can imagine, it has a root system stretching as wide as the tree is tall in every direction. Take this one," he said, tilting his head back and gazing up at her penny tree. "If you could dig up all the roots, they'd probably fill our town's swimming pool. These trees are humbling because we're so much weaker as human beings, so flawed in comparison."

"How are we flawed?" she asked.

"I'll give you an example," he said, touching the tip of her nose. "A tree's roots will grow *around* a boulder they can't go through, but when we run into an obstacle like that in our lives, we often wear ourselves out trying to go through it or else we give up altogether."

At twelve, Annie hadn't understood what he was trying to say, but she still remembered wanting to crawl into his lap as he talked, even though she knew she was too big and her legs would spill over onto the ground.

Now, taking a deep breath, she stood and opened the stall door. Straightening her dress, she walked to the sink and splashed cold water on her face. Then she looked into the mirror. The woman staring back looked like she was brimming with good intentions, because even though all those years ago, she hadn't grasped what her dad had meant, she thought she did now.

THIRTY-THREE

After *The Rachel Tice Show* finished taping, at least a half dozen flash bulbs went off as Annie walked outside to her mom's car. She winced when she imagined her picture in papers across the country, one hand shielding her face from the cameras as she climbed into the backseat, her barely there dress inching up her thighs as if it too wished it could be anywhere else but there. On the bright side, though, she knew it would probably be a small article with an even smaller picture, the charm of the story shrinking in proportion to the media's fascination now that everything was out in the open.

Annie slouched down as Erna pulled into traffic. Marina swiveled in the front seat, eyes flashing with barely contained excitement. "Honestly, I thought it was Chris Carby and I *cannot* believe my own husband was involved!"

"Leave her be," Erna interrupted.

Annie stared out the window, numb with everything that had happened.

Marina dangled a hand over the backseat and nudged Annie's knee. "Come on, fess up. What are you going to do now?"

"I don't know."

Marina stared at her. "You can't leave it hanging like this."

Annie chewed on her lip, ignoring her.

"Leave her alone," Erna said. "She'll talk when she's ready."

The drive home was filled with awkward silence, and when

Erna dropped her off, more than anything, Annie wanted to be alone. The phone was ringing as she fumbled for her keys at the door. She stepped inside, turned on the answering machine, and went upstairs. Wriggling out of her dress, she washed off her makeup, pulled on a sweatshirt and jeans, and padded barefoot down to the kitchen, where she grabbed her cigarettes and a bottle of wine. After letting Montana inside, she went back to her bedroom, curled up on the bed with Lurch, and turned on the TV.

The Rachel Tice Show would be on in five minutes. She took a swig of wine straight from the bottle and flipped through the channels until she found a Dr. Phil wannabe show called *Ask Armand*. A thin, anxious-looking man was listening to his wife explain why their relationship was headed for divorce after less than two years.

"On the first of each month, he meets his ex-wife for dinner," the woman told Armand. "He *says* it's so they can talk about their kids and discuss any 'child-sharing issues' they might have, but I don't believe him."

Armand looked confused. "But when you married him, you knew he had two kids from his first marriage?"

"Of course," the woman said, annoyed.

"And didn't you just say you thought he was a good father?"

"Yes."

Armand turned to the husband. "Okay. How do you feel about this?" The husband looked like he was about to say something, but he suddenly deflated and changed his mind. "Come on," Armand urged. "Spit it out."

Straightening in his chair, the husband licked his lips and glanced at the camera, then began a summation that reeked of such clarity he had to be reading from a teleprompter. "I think my wife needs to accept that I came into our relationship with baggage that's not going away anytime soon. I have two kids who need me and I plan to be involved in their lives."

Armand slapped his armrest. "Good for you."

The husband continued. "I also think her lack of respect for my responsibility as a father tells me we aren't ready to have kids of our own . . . that maybe we should stop trying."

The wife's bottom lip began to tremble.

Empowered, the husband leaned forward. "And you know what? I'm sick and tired of your mom sticking her nose into our business. If our relationship is so shaky you need to talk to your mom about it every time I turn around, and I can't stay in touch with my ex-wife for the sake of my kids, maybe we shouldn't be married at all."

"You figure?" Annie said, and took another sip of wine.

The wife pushed out of her chair, swinging both fists at her husband like she was in a boxing ring. Armand jumped in, holding her back while darting frantic looks at the camera. Then an older woman wearing skintight jeans and four-inch stilettos stormed onto the stage screaming at the husband that he didn't deserve to be married to her daughter.

Annie shook her head. Clearly this wasn't the result Armand had been hoping for, nor did his show have the budget for an on-air bouncer to separate highly dysfunctional families in the throes of a crisis. Annie propped a pillow up behind herself, suddenly feeling better. After all, there was nothing she or Luke had said or done on *The Rachel Tice Show* that came close to this mess.

Flipping through the channels, she found *The Rachel Tice Show* and turned up the volume, cringing when Rachel introduced her, thinking that she looked all wrong—too dressed up and expectant, too hopeful. As she watched, she took another swig of wine, amazed that her voice sounded normal, especially when the camera zoomed in on the lime green car from hell. And then there was Luke wearing his dad's favorite tie, looking every inch like Jack had in all the pictures she'd seen of him when he was that age. There was a heartbeat of silence where she looked shocked, but Rachel's cameraman obviously hadn't gone to the same school as Armand's, because on Rachel's show, there was no edgy, in-your-face shot of Annie as this life-altering moment unfolded, just a subtle one that took in her surprise as Rachel linked an arm through Luke's and walked him over to a chair.

Annie had already heard it, and yet she couldn't take her eyes off Luke as he explained how he'd gotten the idea for the ads. She marveled at how mature he sounded, how intuitive. After a commercial, Rachel came back and there he was again, doing his best to look comfortable although Annie knew better. The last time she'd seen him dressed up was at his grandmother's funeral, and that time he'd complained for hours. When he finished explaining how his uncle Harrison had helped him, she inched forward on the bed, waiting for the taped recording she'd already heard hours ago.

Jack's voice was first, talking about their relatives. He and Luke must have been looking at an old photo album because suddenly Luke burst out laughing and said he sure hoped Mom didn't look that bad when she got old.

"Not a chance," Jack said. "Thirty years from now your mom's going to be the kind of woman who can take an old man's breath away."

"You think so?" Luke asked, sounding skeptical.

"Luke, your mom's beautiful," Jack said. "Take a look at her eyes sometime. They're stunning."

Annie sat up in bed and clutched her knees.

"So you think Mom's hot. Okay. But, Dad, she can't *drive*."

"Maybe not, but how many women do you know who can

maneuver a kayak the way your mother does? She has *character*, Luke, and sometimes I worry that you don't appreciate her the way you should."

"You, either," Luke shot back.

There was a pause, then: "Fair enough."

"Dad? Ever wonder if you made a mistake? . . . Leaving, I mean."

Another pause, longer this time, then a thump, maybe as Jack closed the photo album. "Let's get cleaned up here," he said. "It's way past your bedtime."

The tape recording cut to static for a few seconds, and then they were back, probably on a different weekend. This time they talked about physical traits shared by family members. Jack mentioned that Annie had a tiny strawberry-shaped birthmark on her shoulder, the same one Luke had on his lower back. From there, they moved on to allergies and phobias, and Jack shared a story from when he and Annie were first married, living in a grungy basement suite in Chicago. The guy next door had owned a tarantula that often got out of its aquarium, and when Jack came home from work one day, he found Annie standing on top of a roasting pan with the tarantula trapped underneath it.

"You should've seen your mom," he said, laughing. "Standing on top of that roasting pan crying, but looking so severely cute I wanted to take a picture."

There was a pause before Luke said, "Dad? Ever think you and Mom gave up too soon?"

The silence that followed was long enough that even when Annie had heard it the first time, she'd thought the tape was done. Then a chair scraped against the floor, maybe as Jack pushed back from the table to get up. He sighed, and before the tape finished, in a soft voice, she heard him say, "I'm not the one who filed for divorce, Luke."

The show went to its final commercial and Annie suddenly realized that she'd learned something today. Not about what she and Jack had said to each other over the years, but all that they'd left unsaid.

Rachel brought out a divorce-counseling expert for the last few minutes of the show to share the difference between broken marriages that worked and those that didn't when children were involved. They talked about a variety of studies and statistics, the impact of divorce on children who lived in two homes under shared-custody arrangements, and on those who saw one of their parents only sporadically. Annie was only half listening as she counted the number of years she'd known Jack (sixteen), the number of months since they'd separated (nineteen) and the number of times she'd whispered, "It's over," after he'd left (too many to remember). It had been Eric who'd mentioned in passing that his dad was dating a woman named Linda, and Annie who had filed for divorce weeks later.

Annie sighed, unsure what to do next. Dirty dishes were piled in the sink downstairs and the house was a mess. A picture on one wall was lopsided, so she straightened it, then looked outside. The picnic table was empty and the neighborhood was still. Two houses away, she saw a curtain rise, then fall, and imagined Rose making tea, disappointed now that all the drama was over.

Slowly she walked from room to room, running a hand along the custard-colored walls she'd been wanting to paint since they'd moved in. In the silence, she could hear the steady hum of the refrigerator, then Montana's dog tags jingling as she slid off the couch. The house had never felt so empty or so quiet. The boys hadn't been gone twenty-four hours and she already missed them. How they fought over the bathroom in the morning and the way they raced upstairs after breakfast, elbowing each other out of the way when the weekend loomed up ahead of them like it did today. She checked to make sure their goldfish were alive, then went back to the living room and grabbed the phone. Setting it in her lap, she called Marina.

"It's me," Annie said.

Marina tried to humor her. "A few weeks from now, no one will even remember."

I will, Annie wanted to say, twisting the phone cord around her wrist. Instead, she said, "You know, I've been doing a lot of thinking."

"About what?"

Montana lumbered over, her tail wagging. "A lot of things. Like how I always wanted a teacup poodle but ended up with a bald cat and a gorilla-size dog instead. How nothing in my life ever turns out the way I think it will."

Marina cleared her throat and Annie could tell she was trying hard to sound casual when she said, "So have you decided what you're going to do?"

"About the dog?" Annie said, stalling.

"No, about your life."

Distracted, Annie glanced outside. It wouldn't be dark for another hour and for a change it wasn't raining. The late-afternoon sun was slanting through the front window, making heavy gold strokes on the living room rug. She stood and straightened her shoulders, pausing to hold herself still as she waited for the nervous energy she felt bubbling inside to calm down.

"Yes," she said. "I have."

Ten minutes later, Annie shouldered her knapsack and stepped outside. The walk to her penny tree always made her throat ache and today was no exception. At the outcrop rock, she put her hands on her hips and looked out at the view, giving herself permission to remember things about her dad that she'd worked hard to forget over the years. He never did come to any of her school events and she used to feel uncomfortable whenever he flirted with Julie's mom. More than a few times she found him asleep in his car in the driveway, forehead pressed against the steering wheel, reeking of rum. All memories that didn't change how she felt about him today.

"I love you anyhow, Dad," she whispered.

She understood now that knowing when to walk away and when to hunker down and refuse to leave were equally difficult decisions to make in a marriage; that going back didn't have to mean settling; and that the most fulfilling times weren't always before a storm, but sometimes long after the dust had settled, when you were able to lift your chin and see what was left standing so you could wrap yourself around it with all of the wonder it deserved.

She backed up to the edge of the outcrop rock, and although she didn't need to, she began counting off the seventy paces that would take her to her penny tree. When she finally saw it, she stopped and went very still. Dropping her knapsack, she stepped closer, pleased to see that it was exactly as she'd left it the last time she'd been here. Smiling, she ran a hand over the ridges and furrows of the bark, then over all the pennies nailed there, each one with a nail pounded into it as far over on the left-hand side as it could go.

Her 1969 penny was still there.

There was another one an inch below it from the year her dad was injured, and still another from when he had died, pounded in the day after his funeral in the pouring rain. And under it was the penny from the morning she and Jack got married. To the left of that was a penny from when Luke was born, and a few inches to the right, one from the year Eric came into the world. Reaching into her bag, Annie pulled out a hammer. Then she took a penny from her pocket and held it up against the tree where she thought it should go. It was brand-new, and as she nailed it to the tree, she knew with startling clarity what she wanted to do with the rest of her life, putting to use some advice she'd been given years ago, the last time she'd run away from home.

At the age of twelve, balancing on a cracked toilet seat in a gas station bathroom on the outskirts of Seattle, she'd taken a felt-tip pen and written: *Everything in my life just fell apart. Where do I go from here?* Then she'd climbed down, snapped the cap back on, and stared up at the wall. She knew her dad often stopped here to gas up on their way home from trips into Seattle as a family, so as she walked out to where her parents were waiting for her, she told herself if anyone ever bothered to answer, she would take the advice to heart.

Two months later, at the end of a day, when the sun was just grazing the tips of the trees, they stopped and she went inside to find the answer she'd been waiting for. Pulling the bathroom door open, she turned on the lights, and there it was, written under her question in electric blue ink: *There will come a time when you believe everything is finished and that will be the beginning.*

She'd scribbled the words on a slip of paper, grateful for the advice even though she didn't understand it at the time. And after that, whenever her parents stopped at that gas station, she would go in to use the bathroom whether she needed to or not, just to see the words and walk away feeling as hopeful as she had the first time she'd read them. Years later, she stopped once on her own, but her advice had been covered over with a fresh coat of paint, so she'd climbed up onto the toilet, taken out a felt-tip pen, and put it right back where it belonged, in electric blue ink.

Getting dressed for Eric's game, Annie applied more makeup than usual. It was one thing to wander around the house in sweatshirts looking like a before picture, but it was another to walk into her son's first basketball game looking that way. When she was done, she slipped into sandals and stepped back from the mirror. Not bad. A few lines around the eyes and a little too thin, but there was a surprising look of contentment about her too.

Heading downstairs, she made coffee and called her mom.

"Are you ready for Eric's game?" Erna said.

Annie wrapped her hands around her coffee cup. "Actually, why don't I pick you up and we'll go together?" Rachel Tice's lime green Mini hadn't been delivered yet, so Annie was still driving her mom's Volkswagen Beetle.

There was an uneasy silence. "Well, I . . . uh . . . invited Rudy to come along. He's supposed to pick me up any minute."

Annie raised her eyebrows. "Oh."

"But I could tell him to go without me and meet him there if you like."

"No, Mom. Go ahead. I'll see you there."

"Are you sure?" Erna asked.

"I am."

Annie stared out the window. All her life, her mom had taken care of things before Annie even knew anything needed to be taken care of. For years, Erna had delivered chocolate cupcakes to Annie's class on the first of every month. She'd rag curled Annie's hair every Sunday. And no matter what, she was always sitting in the front row of every school event Annie could ever remember.

"Mom? Do you remember—" Annie stopped, cleared her throat, and tried again. "Do you remember when I used to lie on your bed watching you iron? I'd rest my chin on the back of my hands and I'd watch you, but I never said anything. I just watched."

"Yes," Erna said softly. "You used to do that."

Annie nodded, playing with her bottom lip, remembering the

drowsy smell of baked water filling the air. "You used to spray Dad's shirts with a mist of water, and then you'd lay them out on the ironing board and go to work, and that iron would hiss and spit and shoot bursts of hot steam up around your face the whole time. . . . Anyhow, I know this might sound crazy, but I loved watching you iron. I don't think I've ever told you that."

"No," Erna said. "I don't think you have."

Annie shut her eyes, choosing her words carefully. "There was something peaceful about it, you know? Something reassuring and dependable about the repetition of it. The steady thunk and slide of that old iron was something I could count on, and it made me feel . . . safe."

"Safe is good," Erna whispered.

Annie hesitated. When she was growing up, if you ever went looking for her mom, chances were that you would find Marina with her, and if you went looking for their dad, it was Annie who would be at his side. And today, as this truth came to mind, Annie realized how much she had missed out on.

"You know what else, Mom?"

"What?"

"I don't remember Dad ever ironing."

There was a long pause, and when Erna finally answered, she did so in a shaky voice. "No, Annie," she said. "Your dad didn't iron."

"Mom?" Annie tucked a loose strand of hair behind one ear, forgiving herself for not doing this years ago, telling herself that this was a new beginning for both of them. "You've been an incredible mother," she whispered.

Although outwardly Annie looked composed, inside, her stomach was in knots. Driving to the school, she was distracted. At one intersection, she stopped and waited for the light to turn green.

When a truck pulled up behind her and honked, she glared at the driver in her rearview mirror, realizing only after he'd driven around her that she was sitting at a stop sign.

Minutes later, she parked and walked up to the main doors of the school. She was wearing a navy blouse with a jean skirt, and she was carrying a small box wrapped in brown tissue paper. Smoothing her skirt with one hand, she opened the doors and went inside, stopping to take a breath before entering the gym. It was almost nine and Eric was already on the bench with the rest of the team. He looked up and saw her as the coach stuck two fingers in his mouth, whistling for quiet.

Annie gave her son a wink and he smiled.

The bleachers stretched out along the opposite side of the gym, and today they were filled with friends and family from both teams. Annie skimmed the crowd until she found Rudy and her mom sitting at the top on the far side. Erna was squinting, examining a spot on Rudy's hand as he gave her an indulgent smile, as if he knew she was a little eccentric but couldn't care less. Marina, Harrison, and Sawyer were sitting beside them. Sawyer gave Annie the tiniest of waves, rolled her eyes, and pointed to the bullhorn at Marina's feet, giving fair warning of what she could expect during the game. Then Annie noticed Luke sitting beside Sawyer, wearing a navy knit cap. Chewing on a hangnail, he shot her a shy look, something new, then reached up and pulled off the cap.

Annie blanched before quickly looking down to compose herself. After leaving *The Rachel Tice Show* that afternoon, he'd shaved his head bald, and now, as she lifted her gaze to him, she felt a staggering sense of pride. She mouthed, *Looks good*, and he shrugged and pulled his cap back on.

Jack was sitting next to Luke, and when he saw her, he smiled the same crooked smile that had so often melted her heart over the years—the one that never failed to make her nervous whenever he focused it directly on her. For a few seconds, she felt the way she had when she'd first met him: filled with a reckless, unconditional love that rose up in her throat and took away her air, knowing that where he went, she would go, the two of them a package deal.

Annie knew his face better than her own, had spent countless Sundays dozing on the couch with him and just as many mornings arguing over who should shower first. Then she'd fallen in love with him all over again after their boys were born.

She made her way up into the stands, thinking, *What a good man.* And suddenly what had once seemed unbridgeable between them no longer did. She knew now that she didn't want things to be the way they were years ago, because she and Jack were both so profoundly changed. But she also knew that she wanted to be with him as they grew old so they could finish each other's sentences and he would say, "You see what I go through?" when the boys came home to visit with their families and she had to ask him for the third time to come give her a hand in the kitchen.

Jack was doing his best to look casual, but when she sat in the empty space next to him, she saw relief wash over his face, and as she did, she remembered something her mom had said years ago: *Any family can fall apart, Annie. It's those that manage to stay together after surviving what life throws at them that deserve a little extra respect.*

Eric ran out onto the court with the rest of his team and the game got under way. The crowd called out to their favorite players. They cried foul when things didn't go their way. They cheered when a team scored and groaned when shots were missed, and at the end of the first half, Eric scored his first basket. Annie felt Jack's gaze on her. Then he reached over and interlaced his fingers with hers, and she felt a rush of pleasure, followed by one slow motion moment of contentment so perfect it left her weak. And in that moment, she knew she wouldn't trade her life for any other.

She glanced down at the small box on the seat next to her. It was for Jack, and she planned to give it to him after the game. Inside was a family picture taken years ago, before Eric was diagnosed with hystiocytosis and just after Luke had lost his front baby teeth. It was one of her favorites. In it, Jack had his arm around her and she was laughing at something he had just said. Eric was perched on one of her knees and Luke was smirking at the camera the way he still did now and then—like he knew something you didn't. And today, on a card taped to the picture, she'd added a handwritten note that read, *Have you seen this family?*

ABOUT THE AUTHOR

Holly Kennedy currently resides in the foothills of the Rocky Mountains near Calgary, Alberta, with her husband and two sons. Visit her Web site at www.hollykennedy.com.

The Penny Tree

HOLLY KENNEDY

This Conversation Guide is intended to enrich the
individual reading experience, as well as encourage us
to explore these topics together—because books,
and life, are meant for sharing.

A CONVERSATION WITH HOLLY KENNEDY

Q. *When you began writing* The Penny Tree, *did you know how it would end?*

A. Yes. The ending was never an issue. Nor were the ads, or any of the characters in the story. However, deciding who should run the anonymous ads did prove to be a little tricky. Initially, I chose a character and began writing, but as the months went by, I became increasingly unhappy with my choice. Then, almost a year later, I had an epiphany about who it *really* should be, and I literally froze at my computer. It was then, at that moment, that I knew this story could have the emotional impact I'd been aiming for.

Q. *Do you have a penny tree of your own?*

A. No, but I wish I did. And when the time is right, I plan to give one to each of my boys.

Q. *How did you come up with this story?*

A. The idea came to me when I was going through a rough time in my own life. I'm not a patient person, even with myself, and I'm all about "immediate results," so when something does go wrong, I tend to push it aside and start fresh, as I do when I'm writing. And yet I don't believe marriage should work that way. Sadly, so many people divorce these days that it often makes me wonder what brought them together in the first place and exactly what tore them apart. I believe there is a time and place for divorce, and yet, for me, there is something beautiful, almost incorruptible, about a family that manages to survive a storm. And in this story, I wanted to celebrate that.

Q. Did Jack actually have an affair with Linda?

A. I'm not sure, but I'm of the opinion that it doesn't matter whether he did or didn't. In the writing of this story, what seemed most relevant to me was where his heart belonged. Readers can interpret the events however they wish.

Q. Are parts of this story based on real-life events?

A. Yes, there are a few events that were borrowed from my life. For example, at a recent family reunion, one of my nieces walked into a plate-glass window at a restaurant, followed later by my husband, who was followed by his father moments after that. To me, it was hilarious, because they were from the same family, and I knew right then and there that I wanted to use this in this book. There is another scene in the book that I refer to as the "blue dinosaur scene" and it happened *exactly* as it's written. When the electrician left that morning, I really did start to cry, and then my three-year-old son, Thomas, gave me his tiny blue dinosaur, which sits on my desk today as a reminder of all that is right in my life. There are a few more, but any smatterings of fact have been carefully blended into the fictional side of this story so that most people will never know which is which, unless I con-

fess. However, to clarify, I have never seen a drive-in movie theater burn down, I have never met a woman with a feather duster
in her back pocket, and my boys have never shaved their heads.

Q. Are any of the characters based on people you know?

A. No. Each character was created from my imagination, although there are a few coincidences that have been "borrowed" from my life here too. I wasn't adopted. I've never been
fired. And I can say without a shadow of doubt that I'd make a
horrible physical therapist. My husband loves boats (he has
three canoes and a kayak), whereas I couldn't maneuver either
in a straight line if my life depended on it. I'm a good driver,
but I have been told that my driving style often reflects my personality (an all-or-nothing mentality). Sadly, my nephew was
diagnosed with hystiocytosis when he was three, although he
did survive and is now a healthy young man. I have two boys
(seven and nine). My dad was never a drinker and my mom is
one of the sanest people I know, unlike Annie's mom, who is
delightfully off the wall. I have a Newfoundland dog (Sully),
and before him, we had Montana, who died of cancer at seven,
but I don't have a bald cat (only because my husband won't let
me get one). I have always loved tetherball and I did paint an
egg on the ceiling of the yearbook office at Edwin Parr High
School when I was seventeen. My sister and I are eleven
months apart to the day, and although I love her dearly, she has
ruined me when it comes to enjoying any music played on an
autoharp. Like Annie, I bought my boys goldfish that refused to
die—the same goldfish my husband revived with a turkey
baster four years later when our air stone tanked.

Q. Which character would you be most interested in meeting?

A. Erna, because every time she came into a scene, she made me laugh.

Q. Which character do you feel the least connection to?

A. Annie's dad. In many ways, he was a good man, and of course he did give Annie that beautiful penny tree, but I don't like how his charismatic, larger-than-life persona seemed to override any respect he may have had for his wife. I think I could forgive what happened with Jack, but a serial cheater or incessant flirt who constantly disrespects his wife, not a chance.

Q. Annie often lacks confidence in her role as a mother. Was this intentional?

A. Yes, mostly because this reflects how I feel as a mother. No matter how old any of us get, we never stop growing or changing, and being a mother is a delicate balancing act as you're guiding these little minds through life, even though yours often needs guidance as well. So to me, making Annie appear wholly confident in her role as a mother wouldn't make her real.

Q. How did you come up with a character like Erna?

A. My husband often takes me on "book dates," where we go for dinner and then stop in at a book store afterward. On one of these dates, I picked up a hilarious book on hypochondriacs, and as I flipped through it, Erna slowly formed in my mind, and by the time we'd left the store that night, I knew who Annie's mom would be.

Q. *As the author, was there a moment when you knew Annie had turned a corner in her growth?*

A. Yes. When the drive-in theater burned down and she and the boys rode into Eagan's Point in the back of that old pickup truck.

Q. *In the book, it says, "Some people meditated or did yoga before they started their day. Others jogged. Annie paddled with her eyes closed." What do you do to unwind?*

A. I make a double shot of espresso and I write. For me, nothing else comes close.

QUESTIONS FOR DISCUSSION

1. This novel explores the landscape of a failed marriage, including the two people who chose to marry in the first place, as well as their children, who are innocently on the periphery. Were you most frustrated with Annie or Jack as the story unfolded? Have your group share their opinions and impressions.

2. How would you feel if you opened your local newspaper and found an ad like the one Annie does? Would having your past and present collide like that make you rethink who you are today and how you're living your life?

3. To what extent do you feel Annie's life was shaped by her adoption? Discuss.

4. How does Annie change from the beginning of the story to the woman she eventually becomes at the end? Do you like the change?

5. Annie blindly adores her father and Luke clearly thinks that his dad is beyond reproach. Why do children often falsely idolize their parents? Discuss your opinions.

6. Jack's father was both physically abusive and emotionally unavailable. How do you feel this shaped Jack as a husband and a father?

7. When Annie and her mother have a difficult conversation through a bathroom stall door, what is Erna suggesting: that Annie's standards are too high or that marriages, and the families bound by them, are so much bigger than the issue of fidelity? Do you agree with Erna? What are your impressions of her role in Annie's life?

8. Discuss some of the ways in which, as both child and adult, Annie is pulled in opposing directions and wrestles with conflicting emotions.

9. Was it right or wrong for Jack to have such a close friendship with another woman? Should he have told Annie about it? What would you have done in that situation?

10. Were you surprised by who took out the anonymous ads? Was it who you thought it might be? If you were Annie, how would you have reacted at that moment?

11. Fear manifests itself in different ways with different people. For years, Annie was terrified of losing Eric, while Jack viewed her as the stronger parent when it came to Eric's illness. How do you see it?

12. Has this story changed your perception of marriage, divorce, fidelity, or the sanctity of family? Share your opinions.